P9-CEH-589

CEMETERY DANCE

By Douglas Preston and Lincoln Child

The Wheel of Darkness
The Book of the Dead
Dance of Death
Brimstone
Still Life with Crows
The Cabinet of Curiosities
The Ice Limit
Thunderhead
Riptide
Reliquary
Mount Dragon
Relic

By Douglas Preston

The Monster of Florence (with Mario Spezi)
Blasphemy
Tyrannosaur Canyon
The Codex
Ribbons of Time
The Royal Road
Talking to the Ground
Jennie
Cities of Gold
Dinosaurs in the Attic

By Lincoln Child

Terminal Freeze
Deep Storm
Death Match
Utopia
Tales of the Dark 1–3
Dark Banquet
Dark Company

CEMETERY DANCE

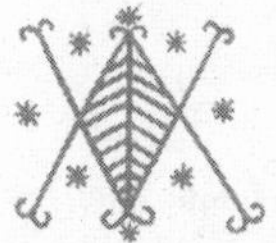

Douglas Preston
and
Lincoln Child

GC
GRAND CENTRAL PUBLISHING
New York Boston

This book is a work of fiction. Names, characters, places, and incidents are the product of the authors' imaginations or are used fictitiously. Any resemblance to actual events, locales, or persons, living or dead, is coincidental.

Grand Central Publishing
Hachette Book Group
237 Park Avenue
New York, NY 10017

Visit our Web site at www.HachetteBookGroup.com.

Printed in the United States of America

First Edition: May 2009
10 9 8 7 6 5 4 3 2

Grand Central Publishing is a division of Hachette Book Group, Inc.
The Grand Central Publishing name and logo is a trademark of Hachette Book Group, Inc.

Library of Congress Cataloging-in-Publication Data

Preston, Douglas J.
Cemetery dance / Douglas Preston & Lincoln Child.—1st ed.
p. cm.
ISBN 978-0-446-58029-8 (regular ed.)—ISBN 978-0-446-51929-8 (large print ed.)
1. Pendergast, Aloysius (Fictitious character)—Fiction. 2. Obeah (Cult)—Fiction. 3. Murder—Investigation—Fiction. 4. Government investigators—Fiction. 5. New York (State)—New York—Fiction. 6. Psychological fiction. I. Child, Lincoln. II. Title.
PS3566.R3982C46 2009
813'.54—dc22

2008048143

Book design and text composition by L&G McRee

Lincoln Child dedicates this book to his daughter, Veronica

Douglas Preston dedicates this book to Karen Copeland

Acknowledgments

For their various and sundry ministrations, we'd like to thank the following: Jaime Levine, Jamie Raab, Kim Hoffman, Kallie Shimek, Mariko Kaga, Jon Couch, Claudia Rülke, Eric Simonoff, Matthew Snyder, and everyone at Grand Central Publishing and beyond who help bring our books to our readers.

We are extremely grateful to those who helped create Corrie Swanson's Pendergast Web site, including Carmen Elliott, Nadine Waddell, Cheryl Deering, Ophelia Julien, Sarah Hanley, Kathleen Munsch, Kerry Opel, Maureen Shockey, and Lew Lashmitt. We raise a glass of Lagavulin 21-year-old to your exceptional talent and literary taste.

And, as always, our endless and abiding gratitude to our families for their love and support.

Readers familiar with upper Manhattan may notice that we have taken certain liberties with Inwood Hill Park.

It goes without saying that all people, places, public and private institutions, corporate and official entities, and religious establishments described in *Cemetery Dance* are either fictitious or used fictitiously. In particular, the ceremonies and beliefs depicted in the novel are completely fictitious and are not meant in any way to resemble, imply, or depict any existing religion or creed.

CEMETERY DANCE

1

Can you believe it, Bill? I still can't. They told me almost twelve hours ago and I still can't believe it."

"Believe it, sweet thing." William Smithback, Jr., unfolded his lanky limbs, stretched out on the living room couch, then draped one arm over his wife's shoulders. "Any more of that port?"

Nora filled his glass. He held it up to the light, admiring its garnet color. Cost him a hundred bucks—and well worth it. He sipped, exhaled. "You're a rising star at the museum. Just wait. In five years, they'll make you dean of science."

"Don't be silly."

"Nora, this is the third straight year of budget cuts—and here they've given your expedition a green light. That new boss of yours is no fool." Smithback nuzzled Nora's hair. After all this time, he still never failed to find its smell—a touch of cinnamon, a hint of juniper—arousing.

"Just think: next summer, we'll be back in Utah on a dig. That is, if you can get the time off."

"I've got four weeks coming to me. They'll miss me desperately at the *Times,* but they'll just have to make do." He took another sip, swirled the liquid around in his mouth. "Nora Kelly: expedition number three. You couldn't have asked for a better anniversary present."

Nora glanced at him sardonically. "I thought tonight's dinner was my anniversary present."

"That's right. It was."

"And it was perfect. Thanks."

Smithback winked back. He'd treated Nora to his favorite restaurant, Café des Artistes on West 67th. It was the perfect place for a romantic meal. The soft, seductive lighting; the cozy banquettes; the titillating artwork of Howard Chandler Christy—and then, on top of everything else, the sublime food.

Smithback realized Nora was looking at him. There was a promise, in those eyes and that sly smile, of another anniversary present to come. He kissed her cheek, pulled her closer.

She sighed. "They gave me every dime I asked for."

Smithback mumbled his response. He was content to snuggle with his wife and perform a mental postmortem on the meal he'd just consumed. He'd sharpened his appetite with a brace of dirty martinis, followed by a charcuterie plate. And for a main course he could never resist the steak béarnaise, rare, accompanied by *pommes frites* and a savory dollop of creamed spinach—and, of course, he'd had a hearty helping of Nora's loin of venison . . .

". . . And you know what that means? I'll be able to complete my analysis of the spread of the Kachina Cult through the Southwest."

"That's fantastic." Dessert had been chocolate fondue for two, accompanied by a plate of delightfully malodorous French cheeses. Smithback let his free hand settle lightly over his stomach.

Nora fell silent and they lay there a moment, satisfied to enjoy each other's company. Smithback stole a glance at his wife. A feeling of contentment settled over him like a blanket. He wasn't a religious man, not exactly; and yet he felt blessed to be here, in a classy apartment in the world's greatest city, holding down the job he'd always dreamed of. And in Nora, he'd found no less than the perfect companion. They'd been through a lot in the years since they'd first met, but the trouble, and the danger, had only served to bring them closer. She was not only beautiful, svelte, gainfully and eagerly employed, immune to nagging, empathetic, intelligent—she'd also proven to be the ideal soul mate. Looking at her, he smiled despite himself. Nora was, quite simply, too good to be true.

Nora roused herself. "Can't let myself get too comfortable. Not yet, anyway."

"Why not?"

She disentangled herself and walked into the kitchen to grab her purse. "There's one more errand I have to run."

Smithback blinked. "At this hour?"

"I'll be back in ten minutes." She returned to the couch and leaned over him, one hand smoothing his cowlick as she kissed him. "Don't go anywhere, big boy," she murmured.

"Are you kidding? I'll be a regular Rock of Gibraltar."

She smiled, stroked his hair again, then headed for the front door.

"Be careful," he called after her. "Don't forget those weird little packages we've been getting."

"Don't worry. I'm a grown-up girl." A moment later, the door closed and the lock turned.

Smithback put his hands behind his head and stretched out on the sofa with a sigh. He heard her footsteps recede down the corridor; heard the chime of the elevator. Then all was quiet save for the low hum of the city outside.

He could guess where she'd gone—to the patisserie around the corner. They made his favorite specialty cakes and were open until midnight. Smithback was particularly partial to their praline génoise with calvados buttercream; with any luck, that was the cake Nora had ordered for tonight's celebration.

He lounged there, in the dimly lit apartment, listening to Manhattan breathe. The cocktails he'd consumed had slowed everything down just a little. He recalled a line from a Thurber short story:

drowsily contented, mistily contented. He had always felt an unreasoning fondness for the writings of fellow journalist James Thurber. Along with those of pulp fictioneer Robert E. Howard. One, he felt, had always tried too hard; the other, not hard enough.

For some reason, he found his thoughts spiraling back to the summer day when he'd first met Nora. All the memories returned: Arizona, Lake Powell, the hot parking lot, the big limo he'd arrived in. He shook his head, chuckling at the memory. Nora Kelly had seemed like a bitch on wheels, a freshly minted PhD with a chip on her shoulder. Then again, he hadn't exactly made a good impression, acted like a perfect ass, that was for sure. That was four years ago, or was it five . . . oh, God, had the time really gone that fast?

There was a shuffling outside the front door, then the rattle of a key in the lock. Nora, back so soon?

He waited for the door to open, but instead the key rattled again, as if Nora was having trouble with the lock. Maybe she was balancing a cake on her arm. He was about to rise to open it for her when the door creaked open and he heard steps cross the entryway.

"As promised, I'm still here," he called out. "Mr. Gibraltar. But hey, you can call me Rock."

There was another step. Somehow, it didn't sound like Nora: it was too slow and heavy, and it seemed to be shambling, as if uncertain.

Smithback sat up on the couch. A figure loomed in the small foyer, framed in the light of the corridor beyond. It was too tall and broad-shouldered to be Nora.

"Who the hell are you?" he said.

Quickly, Smithback reached for the lamp on the adjoining table, snapped it on. He recognized the figure almost immediately. Or he thought he did—there was something wrong with the face. It was ashen, puffy, almost pulpy. It looked sick . . . or worse.

"Colin?" Smithback said. "Is that you? What the hell are you doing in my apartment?"

That was when he saw the butcher knife.

In an instant he was on his feet. The figure shuffled forward, cutting him off. There was a brief, awful moment of stasis. Then the knife darted forward with terrible speed, slashing at air Smithback had occupied less than a second before.

"What the *fuck*?" Smithback yelled.

The knife shot forward again, and Smithback fell over the coffee table in a desperate attempt to avoid the blow, overturning the table as he did so. He scrambled to his feet again and turned to face his assailant, crouching low, hands apart, fingers spread and ready. Quickly, he glanced around for a weapon. Nothing. The figure stood between him and the kitchen—if he could get past, he could grab a knife, even the odds.

He ducked his head slightly, extended an elbow, and charged. The figure fell back under this attack, but at the last moment the knife hand came around, slashing at Smithback's arm and cutting a deep stripe from elbow to shoulder. Smithback wrenched to one side with a cry of surprise and pain—and as he did so he felt the exquisitely cold sensation of steel being driven deep into his lower back.

It seemed to keep sinking forever, plucking at his innermost vitals, piercing him with a pain that had been matched only once before in his life. He gasped, staggered to the floor, trying to get away; he felt the knife slip out, then plunge in again. There was a sudden wetness on his back, as if someone were pouring warm water on him.

Summoning all his strength, he rose to his feet, grabbing desperately at his attacker, pummeling him with his bare hands. The knife slashed again and again at his knuckles but Smithback no longer felt it. The figure fell back under the ferocity of his charge. This was his opportunity, and Smithback wheeled around, ready to retreat to the kitchen. But the floor seemed to be tilting crazily under his feet, and there was now a strange boiling in his chest with every breath he took. He staggered into the kitchen, gasping, fighting for balance, slick fingers scrabbling at the knife drawer. But even as he managed to pull it open, he saw a shadow fall over the counter . . . and then another terrible blow landed deep between his shoulder blades. He tried to twist away, but the knife kept rising and falling, rising and falling, the crimson gleam of its blade dimming as the light began to fail him . . .

All fled, all done, so lift me on the pyre; the feast is over and the lamps expire . . .

The elevator doors slid back, and Nora stepped out into the corridor. She'd made good time, and with any luck Bill would still be on the couch, perhaps reading that Thackeray novel he'd been raving about all week. Carefully, she balanced the cake box in her hands as she reached for her key; he'd no doubt guessed where she'd gone, but it was hard to mount a surprise on somebody's first anniversary . . .

There was something wrong. She'd been so preoccupied with her thoughts that it took her a moment to realize what it was: the door to her apartment was wide open.

As she stared, somebody stepped out. She recognized him. His clothes were smeared and soaked with blood, and he held a large knife in his hand. As he stood looking toward her, the knife dripped copiously onto the floor.

Instinctively, without thought, she dropped the cake and the key and rushed at him. Neighbors were coming out of their apartments now, their voices raised in fear and terror. As she ran toward the figure he raised the knife, but she knocked his hand aside, punching him in the solar plexus as she did so. He lashed out, throwing her against the opposite wall of the corridor, slamming her head against the hard plaster, and she fell to the floor. Spots danced before her eyes as he shambled toward her, knife raised. She threw herself out of the way as it slashed downward; he kicked her viciously in the head, knife rising again. The sound of screaming echoed in the hall. But Nora couldn't hear it; there was no longer any sound, only blurry images. And then those disappeared, as well.

Lieutenant Vincent D'Agosta stood in the crowded hallway outside the door to the two-bedroom apartment. He moved his shoulders inside the brown suit, trying to unstick his damp arms from his polyester shirt. He was very angry, and angry wasn't good. It would affect everything he did, detract from his powers of observation.

He took a long breath and released it, trying to let the anger flow out with the air.

The apartment door opened and a thin, stooped man with a tuft of hair on his pate emerged, lugging a bundle of equipment behind and pushing ahead an aluminum case strapped to a luggage roller. "We're done, Lieutenant." The man took a clipboard from another officer and logged out, followed by his assistant.

D'Agosta glanced at his watch. Three AM. The scene-of-crime team had taken a long time. They were being extra careful. They knew he and Smithback went back a long ways. It irritated him the way they went head-ducking past him, eyeing him sideways, wondering how he was taking it. Wondering if he'd recuse himself from the case. A lot of homicide detectives would—if only because it raised issues at the trial. It didn't look good when the defense put you on the witness stand. "The deceased was a friend of yours? Well now, isn't that a rather *interesting* coincidence?" It was a complication a trial didn't need, and the DA hated when it happened.

But D'Agosta had no intention of letting this one go. Never. Besides, it was an open-and-shut case. The perp was as good as convicted, they had him cold. All that was left was to find the bastard.

The last of the SOC team came out of the apartment and logged out, leaving D'Agosta alone with his thoughts. He stood for a minute in the empty hallway, trying to settle his frayed nerves. Then he snapped on a pair of latex gloves, pulled the hairnet close around his balding pate, and moved toward the open door. He felt faintly sick. The body had been removed, of course, but nothing else had been touched. He could see, where the entryway took a dogleg, just a sliver of the room beyond and a lake of blood on the floor; bloody footprints; a handprint streaked across a cream-colored wall.

He stepped carefully over the blood, pausing before the living room. Leather sofa, pair of chairs, overturned coffee table, more clots of blood on the Persian rug. He slowly walked into the center of the room, rolling his crepe-soled feet down, one after the other, stopped, turned, trying to reconstruct the scene in his mind.

D'Agosta had asked the team to take extensive samples of the bloodstains; there were complex overlapping splatter patterns that he wished to untangle, footsteps tracked through the blood, handprints layered on handprints. Smithback had fought like hell; there was no way the perp escaped without leaving DNA at this scene.

The crime, on the surface, was simple. It was a disorganized, messy killing. The perp had let himself in with a master key. Smithback was in the living room. The killer got in a good blow with his knife, right away putting Smithback at a severe disadvantage, and then they fought. The fight carried them into the kitchen—Smithback had tried to arm himself: the knife drawer was halfway open, bloody handprints on the knob and counter. Didn't get a knife, though; too damn bad. Got stabbed again from behind while at it. They fought a second time. He had been cut pretty bad by then, blood all over the floor, skid marks of bare feet. But D'Agosta was pretty sure the perp was also bleeding by this time. Bleeding, shedding hair and fibers, blowing and snorting with the effort, perhaps scattering saliva and phlegm. It was all there, and he had confidence that the SOC team had found it. They'd even cut out and taken away some floorboards, including several with knife marks; they'd cut pieces of drywall, lifted prints from every surface, collected every fiber they could find, every lint ball and piece of grit.

D'Agosta's eyes continued to roam, his mind continuing an interior film of the crime. Eventually, Smithback lost so much blood that he weakened sufficiently for the killer to deliver the coup de grâce: according to the M.E., a knife through the heart that went half an inch into the floor. The perp had twisted it violently to get it out, splintering the wood. At the thought, D'Agosta felt himself flushing with a fresh mixture of anger and grief. That board had been cut out, too.

Not that all this attention to detail would make much difference—they already knew who the perp was. Still, it was always good to pile on the evidence. You never knew what kind of jury you might draw in this crazy town.

Then there was the bizarre shit the killer left behind. A mashed-up bundle of feathers, tied with green twine. A piece of a garment covered with gaudy sequins. A tiny parchment bag of dust with a weird design on the outside. The killer had floated them in the lake of blood, like offerings. The SOC boys had taken them all away, of course, but they were still fixed in his mind.

Still, there was the one thing the SOC boys couldn't take away: the hurriedly drawn image on the wall, two snakes curled around some strange, spiky, plant-like thing, with stars and arrows and complex lines and a word that looked like DAMBALAH. It had clearly been drawn with Smithback's blood.

D'Agosta walked into the main bedroom, taking in the bed, bureau, mirror, window looking southeast onto West End Avenue, rug, walls, ceiling. There was a second bathroom at the far end of the bedroom and the door was shut. Funny, last time he was in here the door was open.

He heard a sound from the bathroom. The water turned on and off. Somebody from the forensic team was still in the apartment. D'Agosta strode over, grasped the door handle, found it locked.

"Hey, you in there! What the hell you think you're doing?"

"Just a moment," came the muffled voice.

D'Agosta's surprise turned to outrage. The idiot was using the bathroom. In a sealed crime scene. Un-frigging-believable.

"Open the door, pal. *Now.*"

The door popped open—and there stood Special Agent A. X. L. Pendergast, rack of test tubes in one hand, tweezers in the other, a jeweler's loupe on a headband.

"Vincent," came the familiar buttery voice. "I'm so sorry we have to meet again under such unhappy circumstances."

D'Agosta stared. "Pendergast—I had no idea you were back in town."

Pendergast deftly pocketed the tweezers, slid the rack of tubes into a Gladstone doctor's bag, followed by the loupe. "The killer wasn't in here, or the bedroom. A rather obvious deduction, but I wanted to make sure."

"Is this now an FBI matter?" D'Agosta asked, following Pendergast as the agent moved through the bedroom into the living room.

"Not exactly."

"So you're freelancing again?"

"You might say that. I would appreciate it if we kept my involvement to yourself for the moment." He turned. "Your take, Vincent?"

D'Agosta went through his reconstruction of the crime while

Pendergast nodded in approval. "Not that it makes much difference," D'Agosta summed up. "We already know who the dirtbag is. We just have to find him."

Pendergast gave a quizzical rise to his eyebrows.

"He lives in the building. We got two eyewitnesses who saw the killer enter, and two who saw him leave, all covered with blood, clutching the knife. He attacked Nora Kelly on the way out of the apartment—tried to attack, I should say, but the fight had attracted neighbors and he ran away. They got a good look at him, the neighbors I mean. Nora's in the hospital now—minor concussion, but should be all right. Considering."

Another faint incline of the head.

"He's a creep named Fearing. Colin Fearing. Out-of-work British actor. Apartment two fourteen. He'd hassled Nora once or twice in the lobby. Looks to me like a rape gone bad. He probably hoped he'd find Nora home alone, got Smithback instead. Chances are he lifted the key from the super's key locker. I've got a man checking on that."

This time there was no confirming nod. Just the usual inscrutable look in those deep, silvery eyes.

"Anyway, it's an open-and-shut case," D'Agosta said, starting to feel defensive for some unknown reason. "Wasn't just Nora's ID. We got him on the building's security tapes, too, an Oscar performance. Coming in and going out. On the way out we got a full-frontal shot, knife in hand, covered with blood, dragging his sorry ass through the lobby, threatening the doorman before splitting. Gonna look beautiful in front of a jury. This is one bastard who is going *down*."

"Open and shut, you say?"

D'Agosta felt another twinge at the doubtful note in Pendergast's voice. "Yeah," he said firmly. "Open and shut." He checked his watch. "They're holding the doorman downstairs, waiting for me. He's going to be a star witness, a reliable, solid family man—

knew the perp for years. Want to ask him any questions before we send him home?"

"Delighted to. But before we go downstairs . . ." The agent's voice trailed off. A pair of spidery white fingers reached into the breast pocket of his black suit and withdrew a folded document. With a flourish of his wrist, he proffered it to D'Agosta.

"What's this?" D'Agosta took it and unfolded it, taking in the red notary stamp, the Great Seal of New York, the elegant engraving, the signatures.

"It is Colin Fearing's death certificate. Signed and dated ten days ago."

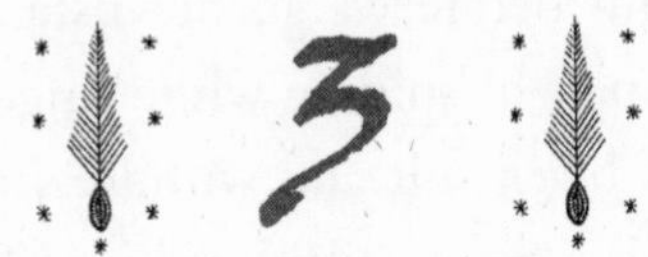

D'Agosta entered the security nook of 666 West End Avenue, followed by the spectral figure of Pendergast. The doorman, a plump gentleman from the Dominican Republic named Enrico Mosquea, sat on a metal stool, hammy legs spread. He sported a pencil mustache and a marcel wave. The man sprang to his feet with surprising nimbleness as they came in.

"You find this son bitch," he said passionately. "You find him. Smithback, he was a good man. I tell you—"

D'Agosta gently laid a hand on the man's neat brown uniform. "This is Special Agent Pendergast of the FBI. He's going to help us out."

His eyes took in Pendergast. "Good. Very good."

D'Agosta took a deep breath. He hadn't quite absorbed the ramifications of the document Pendergast showed him. Maybe they were dealing with a twin. Maybe there were two Colin Fearings. New York was a big city, and half the Brits in town seemed to be named Colin. Or maybe the M.E.'s office had made a hideous mistake.

"I know you've already answered a lot of questions, Mr. Mosquea," D'Agosta went on, "but Agent Pendergast has a few more."

"No trouble. I answer questions ten times over, twenty times, if it help get this son bitch."

D'Agosta pulled out a notebook. What he really wanted was for

Pendergast to hear what the man had to say. He was a very credible witness.

Pendergast spoke softly. "Mr. Mosquea, describe what you saw. From the beginning."

"This man, Fearing, he arrive when I was putting someone in a cab. I saw him come in. He didn't look too good, like he been in a fight. Face swollen, black eye maybe. Skin a funny color, too pale. He's walking kind of funny, too. Slow."

"When was the last time you saw him—before this?"

"Maybe two weeks. I think he been away."

"Go on."

"So he walk past me and into the elevator. A little later, Ms. Kelly come back to the building. Maybe five minutes pass. Then he is coming back out. Unbelievable. He all covered with blood, holding knife, lurching along like he been hurt." Mosquea paused for a moment. "I try to grab him, but he swing at me with knife, then turn and run. I call police."

Pendergast slid an ivory hand across his chin. "I imagine when you were putting the person in the cab—when he came in—you got a fleeting glimpse of him."

"I get good, *long* look. Not fleeting. Like I said, he was walking slow."

"You said his face was swollen? Could it have been someone else?"

"Fearing live here six years. I open door for that son bitch three, four times a day."

Pendergast paused. "And then, when he came back out, his face was covered with blood, I imagine."

"Not face. No blood on face, or maybe just a little. Blood all over hands, clothes. Knife."

Pendergast was silent for a moment, and then said, "What if I were to tell you that Colin Fearing's body was found in the Harlem River ten days ago?"

Mosquea's eyes narrowed. "Then I say you wrong!"

"I'm afraid not, Mr. Mosquea. Identified, autopsied, everything."

The man drew himself up to his full five foot three inches, his voice assuming a grave dignity. "If you don't believe, I ask you: look at the tape. The man on that tape is Colin Fearing." He stopped, giving Pendergast a challenging stare. "I don't care about any body in river. The murderer is Colin Fearing. I *know*."

"Thank you, Mr. Mosquea," said Pendergast.

D'Agosta cleared his throat. "If we need to speak to you again, I'll let you know."

The man nodded, keeping a suspicious eye on Pendergast. "The killer is Colin Fearing. You find that son bitch."

They stepped out into the street, the crisp October air refreshing after the sickening confines of the apartment. Pendergast gestured toward a '59 Rolls-Royce Silver Wraith idling at the curb, and D'Agosta could see the stolid outline of Proctor, Pendergast's chauffeur, in the driver's seat. "Care to take a ride uptown?"

"Might as well. It's already half past three, I won't be getting any sleep tonight."

D'Agosta climbed into the leather-fragrant confines, Pendergast slipping in beside him. "Let's have a look at the security tape." The agent pressed a button in the armrest, and an LCD screen swung down from the ceiling.

D'Agosta removed a DVD from his briefcase. "Here's a copy. The original already went down to headquarters."

Pendergast slid it into the drive. A moment later, the lobby of 666 West End sprang into wide-angle view on the screen, the fish-eye lens covering the area from the elevator to the front door. A time stamp in the corner ran off the seconds. D'Agosta watched—for perhaps the tenth time—as the doorman went outside with one of the tenants, where he presumably flagged down a cab. As he was outside, a figure came pushing in through the doors. There was something ineffably chilling about the way he walked—strangely shambling, almost rudderless, heavy-footed, with no trace of hurry. He glanced up once at the camera, his eyes glazed, seemingly sightless. He was wearing a bizarre outfit, a gaudy, sequined garment over his shirt, multicolored designs on a field of red, with curlicues, hearts, and rattle-shaped bones. His face was bloated, misshapen.

Pendergast fast-forwarded it until a new person entered the camera's field of view: Nora Kelly, carrying a cake box. She walked to the elevator, disappearing again. Another fast-forward, and then Fearing lurched out of the elevator, suddenly wild. His outfit was now torn and smeared with blood, the right hand clutching a massive, ten-inch scuba knife. The doorman came forward, tried to grab him; Fearing slashed at him instead and shambled through the double doors, disappearing into the night.

"The bastard," D'Agosta said. "I'd like to rip his nuts off and feed them back to him on toast."

He glanced at Pendergast. The agent appeared to be deep in thought.

"You have to admit, the tape is pretty damn clear. You sure the body in the Harlem River was Fearing?"

"His sister identified the corpse. There were a couple of birthmarks, tattoos, that confirmed it. The M.E. who handled the case is reliable, if a bit difficult."

"How'd he die?"

"Suicide."

D'Agosta grunted. "No other family?"

"The mother is non compos mentis, in a nursing home. No one else."

"And the sister?"

"She went back to England after identifying the body." He fell silent, and then D'Agosta heard him murmur, sotto voce: "Curious, very curious."

"What?"

"My dear Vincent, in an already puzzling case, there is one thing about that tape that strikes me as especially baffling. Did you notice what he does when he enters the lobby for the first time, on his way in?"

"Yeah, what?"

"He glances up at the camera."

"He knew it was there. He lived in the building."

"Precisely." And the FBI agent lapsed once more into contemplative silence.

4

Caitlyn Kidd sat in the driver's seat of her RAV4, balancing a breakfast sandwich from Subway in one hand and a large black coffee in the other. Her nose was buried in the issue of *Vanity Fair* that lay propped against the steering wheel. Outside, the morning rush-hour traffic on West 79th Street hooted and blared in an uncomfortable ostinato.

A police radio set into the dashboard crackled to life, and Caitlyn glanced down at it immediately.

"*. . . Headquarters to 2527, respond to a 10-50 at corner of One Eighteenth and Third . . .*"

As quickly as it had flared up, her interest vanished again. She took another bite of her sandwich, flipped the pages of the magazine with a free fingertip.

As a reporter covering Manhattan's crime beat, Caitlyn found herself spending a lot of her time hanging out in her car. Crimes often occurred in out-of-the-way corners of the island, and if you knew your way around, your own car beat the hell out of riding the subway or hailing a cab. It was a business where the scoop was everything, where minutes counted. And the police-band radio helped make sure she stayed on top of the most interesting stories. One big scoop—that's what she was hoping for. One really big scoop.

On the passenger seat, her cell phone blared. She picked it up and snugged it between chin and shoulder, performing a complex three-way juggle involving sandwich, phone, and coffee. "Kidd."

"Caitlyn. Where are you?"

She recognized the voice: Larry Bassington, an obituary writer with the *West Sider*, the daily throwaway tabloid where they both worked. He was always hitting on her. She'd agreed to let him buy her lunch, mostly because money was short and payday wasn't until the end of the week.

"In the field," said Kidd.

"This early?"

"I get my best calls around dawn. That's when they find the stiffs."

"I don't know why you bother—the *West Sider* ain't exactly the *Daily News*. Hey, don't forget—"

"Hold a sec." Once again, Kidd turned her attention to the police radio.

". . . Headquarters to 3133, reports of a 10-53 at 1579 Broadway, please respond."

"3133 to Headquarters, 10-4 . . ."

She tuned it out, went back to the phone. "Sorry. You were saying?"

"I was saying, don't forget about our date."

"It's not a date. It's *lunch*."

"Allow me my dreams, okay? Where do you want to go?"

"You're buying, you tell me."

A pause. "How about that Vietnamese place on Thirty-second?"

"Um, no thanks. Ate there yesterday, regretted it all afternoon."

"Okay, what about Alfredo's?"

But once again, Kidd was listening to the police radio.

". . . Dispatch, dispatch, this is 7477, on that 10-29 homicide,

note that victim Smithback, William, is at present en route M.E.'s office for processing. Supervisor leaving the scene."

"10-4, 7477 . . ."

She almost dropped her coffee. "Holy shit! Did you hear that?"

"Hear what?"

"It just came over the car-to-car channel. There's been a murder. And I know the victim—Bill Smithback. He's that guy who writes for the *Times*—I met him at that journalism conference at Columbia last month."

"How do you know it's the same guy?"

"How many people you know with a name like Smithback? Look, Larry, gotta go."

"Gee, how awful for him. Now about lunch—"

"Screw lunch." She nudged the phone closed with her chin, let it drop to her lap, and fired up the engine. Lettuce, tomato, green peppers, and scrambled egg went flying as she popped the clutch and scooted out into traffic.

It was the work of five minutes to get to West End Avenue and 92nd. Caitlyn was an expert at urban driving, and her Toyota had just enough dings and scrapes to warn off anyone who might think that one more wouldn't matter. She nudged the car into a spot in front of a fire hydrant—with any luck, she'd get her story and be gone before a traffic cop spotted the infraction. And if not, well, screw it, she owed more in tickets on the car than it was worth.

She walked quickly down the block, pulling a digital recorder from her pocket. A bunch of vehicles were double-parked outside 666 West End Avenue: two patrol cars, an unmarked Crown Vic, and an ambulance. A morgue wagon was just pulling away. Two uniformed cops were standing on the top step of the building's entrance, limiting access to residents only, but a knot of people huddled below on the sidewalk, talking in tense whispers. Their faces were uniformly pinched and drawn, almost—Kidd observed wryly—as if they'd all seen a ghost.

With practiced efficiency, she inserted herself into the restless, muttering group, listening to half a dozen conversations at once, deftly filtering out extraneous chatter and homing in on those who seemed to know something. She turned to one, a bald, heavyset man with a face the color of pomegranate skin. Despite the fall chill in the air, he was sweating profusely.

"Pardon me," she said, coming up to him. "Caitlyn Kidd, press. Is it true William Smithback was killed?"

He nodded.

"The reporter?"

The man nodded again. "Tragedy. He was a nice guy, used to bring me free newspapers. You a colleague?"

"I work the crime desk for the *West Sider*. So you knew him well?"

"Lived down the hall. I saw him just yesterday." He shook his head.

This was just what she needed. "What happened, exactly?"

"It was late last night. Guy with a knife cut him up real bad. I heard the whole thing. Awful."

"And the murderer?"

"Saw him, recognized him, guy who lives in the building. Colin Fearing."

"Colin Fearing." Kidd repeated it slowly, for the recorder.

The man's expression changed to something she couldn't readily identify. "See, there's a problem there, though."

Kidd leapt at this. "Yes?"

"It seems Fearing died almost two weeks ago."

"Oh *yeah*? How so?"

"Found his body floating up near Spuyten Duyvil. Identified, autopsied, everything."

"You sure about this?"

"The police told the doorman all about it. Then he told us."

"I don't understand," Kidd said.

The man shook his head. "Neither do I."

"But you're sure the man you saw last night was also Colin Fearing?"

"Not a doubt in my mind. Ask Heidi here, she recognized him as well." And the man gestured at a bookish, frightened-looking woman standing beside him. "The doorman, he saw him, too. Struggled with him. There he is now, coming out of the building." And he gestured toward the door where a short, dapper Hispanic man was emerging.

Quickly, Caitlyn got their names and a few other relevant details. She could only imagine what the headline guy back at the *West Sider* would do with this one.

Other reporters were arriving now, descending like buzzards, arguing with the cops who had roused themselves and were beginning to shoo the residents back into the building. Reaching her car, she found a ticket tucked under one wiper.

She couldn't have cared less. She had her big scoop.

Nora Kelly opened her eyes. It was night and all was quiet. A faint city breeze came through the window of her hospital room and rustled the modesty curtains drawn around the empty bed next to her.

The fog of painkillers was gone, and when she realized sleep would not return she lay very still, trying to hold back the tide of horror and sorrow threatening to overwhelm her. The world was cruel and capricious, and the very act of drawing breath seemed pointless. Even so, she tried to master her grief, to focus on the faint throbbing of her bandaged head, the sounds of the great hospital around her. Slowly, the shaking of her limbs subsided.

Bill—her husband, her lover, her friend—was dead. It wasn't just that she'd seen it; she could *feel* it in her bones. There was an absence, an emptiness. He was gone from the earth.

The shock and horror of the tragedy only seemed to grow with each passing hour, and the clarity of her thoughts was agonizing. How could this have happened? It was a nightmare, the brutal act of a pitiless God. Just last night they had been celebrating the first anniversary of their marriage. And now . . . *now* . . .

Once again she struggled to push back the wave of unbearable pain. Her hand reached for the call button and another dose of morphine, but she stopped herself. That was not the answer. She forced her eyes closed again, hoping for the grateful embrace of sleep but knowing it would not come. Perhaps it would never come.

She heard a noise, and a fleeting sense of déjà vu told her this same noise was what had woken her up. Her eyes flew open. It was the sound of a grunt, and it had come from the next bed in the double room. The sudden stab of panic subsided; someone must have been put into the bed while she was sleeping.

She turned her head toward it, trying to make out the person on the other side of the curtains. There was a faint sound of breathing now, ragged, stertorous. The curtains swayed and she realized it wasn't from the movement of air in the room after all, but rather from the shifting of the person in the bed. A sigh, a rustle of starched sheets. The semi-translucent curtains were backlit by the window, and she could just make out a dark silhouette. As she stared, it slowly rose up with another sigh and a wheezing grunt of effort.

A hand reached out and touched the curtains lightly from within.

Nora could see the faint shadow of a hand stroking and sliding along the gauzy folds, setting the curtains swaying. The hand found an opening, slipped through, and grasped the edge of the curtain.

Nora stared. The hand was dirty. It was mottled with dark, wet streaks—almost like blood. The longer she stared in the faint light, the more certain she became that it *was* blood. Perhaps this was someone just back from the OR, or whose stitches had opened. Someone very ill.

"Are you all right?" she asked, her voice loud and hoarse in the silence.

Another grunt. The hand began drawing back the curtain very slowly. There was something horrible about the deliberation with which the steel loops of the curtain slid back along the runner. They rattled with a cold, palsied cadence. Once again, Nora fumbled along the rail of her bed for the call button.

As the curtain drew back, it revealed a dark figure, draped in ragged clothing and covered with dark splotches. Sticky, matted hair stood up from its head. Nora held her breath. As she stared, the figure slowly turned its head to look at her. The mouth opened and a guttural sound came out, like water being sucked down a drain.

Nora found the button and began pressing it, frantically.

The figure slid its feet to the floor, waited a moment as if to recover, and then stood unsteadily. For a minute, it swayed back and forth in the dim light. Then it took a small, almost experimental step toward her. As it did so, the face came into a shaft of pale light from the door transom, and Nora had the briefest glimpse of muddied, lumpen features, puffy and moist. Something about the features, about the shambling movements, brought a dreadful feeling of familiarity to her. Another unsteady step forward, the shaking arm now reaching up for her . . .

Nora screamed, flailing desperately at the figure, scrambling back to get away from it, her feet tangling in the bedsheets. Crying out, stabbing at the call button, she struggled to free herself from the linens. What was taking the nurses so long? She freed herself with a brutal tug, swung out of bed, knocking over the IV stand with a crash, and tumbled to the floor in a daze of horror and panic . . .

After a long moment of fog and confusion, she heard running feet, voices. The lights came on and a nurse was bending over her, gently raising her from the floor, speaking soothingly into her ear.

"Relax," came the voice. "You've just had a nightmare—"

"It was there!" she cried, struggling. *"Right there!"* She tried to lift her arm to point but the nurse had her arms around her, gently but firmly restraining her.

"Let's get you back into bed," the nurse said. "Nightmares are very common after a concussion."

"No! It was real, I swear!"

"Of course it seemed real. But you're all right now." The nurse eased her back into the bed and drew up the covers.

"Look! Behind the curtain!" Her head was pounding, and she could hardly think.

Another nurse came running in, hypodermic at the ready.

"I know, I know. But you're safe now . . ." The nurse gently dabbed at her forehead with a cool cloth. Nora felt a brief needle sting in her upper arm. A third nurse arrived, righting the IV stand.

". . . Behind the curtain . . . in the bed . . ." Despite her best efforts, Nora could feel her whole body relaxing.

"In here?" the nurse asked, rising. She drew back the curtain with one hand, revealing a neatly made bed, as tight as a drum. "You see? Just a dream."

Nora lay back, her limbs growing heavy. It hadn't been real, after all.

The nurse leaned over her and smoothed down the covers, tucking her in more firmly. Vaguely, Nora could see the second nurse hanging a new bottle of saline and reattaching the line. Everything seemed to be going very far away. Nora felt tired, so tired. Of course it was a dream. She found herself not caring anymore and thinking how wonderful it was not to care . . .

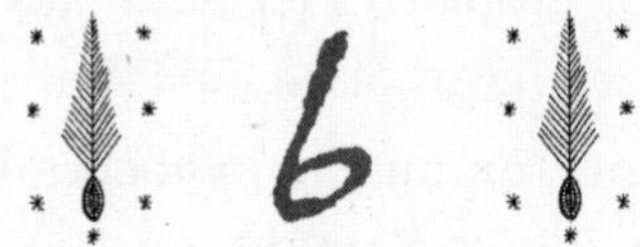

Vincent D'Agosta paused at the open door of the hospital room, giving a timid knock. The morning sun streamed down the hall, gilding the shiny hospital equipment arrayed against the tiled walls.

He didn't expect the strength of voice that answered. "Come in."

He entered, feeling awkward, put his hat down on the only seat, then had to pick it up again to sit down. He was never good at this. He glanced at her a little hesitantly and was surprised by what he saw. Instead of the injured, distraught, grieving widow he expected, he found a woman who looked remarkably composed. Her eyes were red but bright and determined. A bandage covering part of her head and a faint shadow of blackening under the right eye were the only marks of the attack two nights before.

"Nora, I'm so sorry, so *damn* sorry . . ." His voice faltered.

"Bill considered you a good friend," she replied. She chose her words slowly, carefully, as if somehow knowing what needed to be said without really understanding any of it.

A pause. "How are you doing?" he asked, knowing even as he said it how lame it must sound.

Nora's response was simply to shake her head and return the question. "How are *you* doing?"

D'Agosta answered honestly. "Shitty."

"He would be glad you were handling . . . this."

D'Agosta nodded.

"The doctor will see me at noon, and if all is well I'll be out of here soon thereafter."

"Nora, there's something I want you to know right up front. We're going to find the bastard. We're going to find him and lock him up and throw away the key."

Nora gave no response.

D'Agosta rubbed his hand over his bald spot. "To do that, I'm going to have to ask you some more questions."

"Go ahead. Talking . . . talking actually helps."

"Okay." He hesitated. "Are you sure it was Colin Fearing?"

She gazed at him levelly. "As sure as I'm here, right now, in this bed. It was Fearing, all right."

"How well did you know him?"

"He used to leer at me in the lobby. Once asked me for a date—even though he knew I was married." She shuddered. "A real pig."

"Did he give any sign of mental instability?"

"No."

"Tell me about the time he, ah, asked you on a date."

"We happened to get on the elevator together. He turned to me, hands in his pockets, and he asked—with that smarmy British accent of his—if I wanted to come to his digs and see his *etchings.*"

"He really said that? Etchings?"

"I guess he thought he was being ironic."

D'Agosta shook his head. "Had you seen him around in, say, the last two weeks?"

Nora did not reply right away. She seemed to be making an effort to remember, and D'Agosta's heart went out to her. "No. Why do you ask?"

D'Agosta wasn't ready to go there yet. "Did he have a girlfriend?"

"Not that I know of."

"Ever meet his sister?"

"Didn't even know he had a sister."

"Did Fearing have any close friends? Other relatives?"

"I don't know him well enough to say. He seemed a bit of a loner. He kept strange hours—an actor type, you know, worked in theater."

D'Agosta referred to his notepad, where he'd scribbled some routine questions. "Just a few more formalities, for the record. How long have you and Bill been married?" He couldn't bring himself to put the question in the past tense.

"That was our first anniversary."

D'Agosta tried to keep his voice calm, neutral. There seemed to be an obstruction in his throat, and he swallowed. "How long has he been employed at the *Times*?"

"Four years. Before that he was with the *Post*. And before that he was a freelancer, writing books about the museum and the Boston Aquarium. I'll send you a copy of his résumé—" Here her voice went very low. "If you want."

"Thank you, that would be helpful." D'Agosta made a notation. Then he glanced up at her again. "Nora, I'm sorry, but I have to ask. Do you have any idea why Fearing did this?"

Nora shook her head.

"No run-ins? Bad blood?"

"Not that I know of. Fearing was just someone who lived in the building."

"I know these questions are difficult, and I appreciate—"

"What's difficult, Lieutenant, is knowing that Fearing is still free. You ask what you need to know."

"Okay. Do you think his intention was to molest you?"

"It's possible. Although his timing was bad. He came into the apartment right after I left." She hesitated. "Can I ask you a question, Lieutenant?"

"Of course."

"At that time of night, he would have expected us both to be home, right? But all he had was a knife."

"That's right, just a knife."

"You don't break into someone's apartment with a knife if you expect to confront two people. Anyone can get a gun these days."

"Quite right."

"So what do you think?"

D'Agosta had been thinking about that quite a lot. "It's a good question. And you're sure it was him?"

"That's the second time you've asked me that question."

D'Agosta shook his head. "Just making sure, that's all."

"You *are* looking for him, aren't you?"

"Damn right we are." *Yeah, like in his grave.* They had already started the paperwork for an exhumation. "Just a few more questions. Did Bill have any enemies?"

For the first and only time, Nora laughed. But there was no humor in it; just a low, mirthless snort. "A *New York Times* reporter? Of course he did."

"Anyone in particular?"

She thought a moment. "Lucas Kline."

"Who?"

"He runs a software development company here in the city. Likes to shag his secretaries, then intimidate them into keeping their mouths shut. Bill wrote an exposé on him."

"So what makes him stand out?"

"He sent Bill a letter. A threatening letter."

"I'd like to see it, please."

"No problem. Kline isn't the only one, though. There were these animal rights pieces he was working on, for example. I've been making a list in my head. And there were those strange packages . . ."

"What strange packages?"

"He'd gotten two in the last month. Little boxes with strange things in them. Tiny dolls sewed out of flannel. Animal bones, moss, sequins. When I go home . . ." Her voice broke, but she cleared her throat and resumed doggedly. "When I get home, I'll go through his clips and collect all the recent stories that might have angered someone. You should talk to his assignment editor at the *Times* to find out what he was working on."

"That's already on my list."

She went quiet for a minute, looking at him with those red, determined eyes. "Lieutenant, doesn't it strike you that this was a particularly inept crime? Fearing walked in and out without any regard for witnesses, with no attempt to disguise himself or avoid the security camera."

This was another point that D'Agosta had been mulling over: was Fearing really that stupid? Assuming it was him to begin with. "There's still a lot to clear up."

She held his gaze a moment longer. Then her eyes dropped to the bedcovers. "Is the apartment still sealed?"

"No. Not as of ten o'clock this morning."

She hesitated. "I'm being released this afternoon and I . . . I want to get back in as soon as possible."

D'Agosta understood. "I'm already having the—having it prepared for your return. There's a company that does this sort of thing at short notice."

Nora nodded, turning her head away.

This was his cue to leave, and D'Agosta rose. "Thank you, Nora. I'll keep you informed of our progress. If you think of anything more, will you let me know? You'll keep me in the loop?"

She nodded again without looking at him.

"And remember what I said. We're going to find Fearing—you have my word."

7

Special Agent Pendergast glided silently down the long, dimly lit central hallway of his West 72nd Street apartment. As he walked, he passed an elegant library; a room devoted to Renaissance and Baroque oil paintings; a climate-controlled vault stacked floor-to-ceiling with vintage wines in teakwood racks; a salon with leather armchairs, expensive silk carpets, and terminals hardwired to half a dozen law enforcement databases.

These were the public rooms of Pendergast's apartment, although perhaps fewer than a dozen people had ever seen them. He was headed now toward the private rooms, known only to himself and Kyoko Ishimura, the deaf and mute housekeeper who lived in and looked after the apartment.

Over several years, Pendergast had discreetly purchased two additional adjoining apartments as they came on the market and integrated them with his own. Now his residence stretched along much of the Dakota's 72nd Street frontage and even part of the Central Park West frontage as well: an immense, rambling, yet exceedingly private eyrie.

Reaching the end of the corridor, he opened the door of what appeared to be a closet. Instead, the small room beyond was empty save for another door in the far wall. Disengaging its security apparatus, Pendergast opened the door and stepped into the private quarters. He walked quickly through these as well, nodding to Miss Ishimura as she stood in the spacious kitchen, preparing fish intestine soup over a restaurant-grade stove. Like all spaces in the Dakota, the kitchen had an unusually high ceiling. At length he reached the end of another corridor, another innocuous-looking door. Beyond lay his destination: the third apartment, the sanctum sanctorum into which even Miss Ishimura entered only infrequently.

He opened the door into a second closet-size room. This time, there was not another door at the far end, but rather a *shoji,* a sliding partition of wood and rice-paper panels. Pendergast closed the door behind him, then stepped forward and gently drew the *shoji* aside.

Beyond lay a tranquil garden. Sounds of gently trickling water and birdsong freighted air already heavy with the scents of pine and eucalyptus. The light was dim and indirect, suggesting late afternoon or early evening. Somewhere in the green fastness, a dove cooed.

A narrow path of flat stones lay ahead, flanked by stone lanterns and winding sinuously between evergreen plantings. Pulling the *shoji* shut, Pendergast stepped over the pebbled verge and made his way down the path. This was an *uchi-roji,* the inner garden of a teahouse. The intensely private, almost secret spot exuded tranquility, encouraged a contemplative spirit. Pendergast had lived with it so long now that he had almost lost his appreciation for just how unusual it was: a complete and self-sufficient garden, deep within a massive Manhattan apartment building.

Ahead, through the bushes and dwarf trees, a low wooden building came into view, simple and unadorned. Pendergast made his way past the formal washbasin to the teahouse entrance and slowly pulled its *shoji* aside.

Beyond lay the tearoom itself, decorated with elegant spareness. Pendergast stood in the entrance a moment, letting his eyes move over the hanging scroll in its alcove, the formal *chabana* flower arrangements, the shelves holding scrupulously clean whisks, tea scoops, and other equipment. Then, closing the sliding door and seating himself *seiza*-style on the tatami mat, he began performing the exacting rituals of the ceremony itself.

The tea ceremony is at heart a ritual of grace and perfection, the serving of tea to a small group of guests. Though Pendergast was alone, he was nevertheless performing the ceremony for a guest: one who was unable to attend.

Carefully, he filled the caddy, measured in the powdered tea, whisked it to a precise consistency, then poured it into two exquisite seventeenth-century tea bowls. One he placed before himself; the other he set on the opposite side of the mat. He sat a moment, staring at the steam as it rose in gossamer curls from his bowl. Then—slowly, meditatively—he raised the bowl to his lips.

As he sipped, he allowed certain memories to form pictures in his mind, one at a time, lingering over each before moving to the next. The subject of each memory was the same. William Smithback, Jr., assisting him in a race against time to blast open the doors of the Tomb of Senef and rescue the people trapped within. Smithback, lying horrified in the backseat of a purloined taxi as Pendergast careened through traffic, trying to elude his brother, Diogenes. Now, further back in time, Smithback looking on in outrage and dismay as Pendergast burned the recipe for the Arcanum at Mary Greene's grave site. And still further back, Smithback once again, standing at his side during the terrible struggle with the strange denizens of the Devil's Attic, far below the streets of New York City.

By the time the tea bowl was empty, there were no more memories to reflect on. Pendergast placed the bowl back on the mat and closed his eyes a moment. Then, opening them again, he gazed at the other bowl, still full, that sat across from him. He sighed quietly, then spoke.

"Waga tomo yasurakani," he said. *Farewell, my friend.*

Noon. D'Agosta punched the elevator button again with a muttered curse. He checked his watch. "Nine minutes. No shit—nine frigging minutes we been here."

"You must learn to put your spare time to good use, Vincent," murmured Pendergast.

"Yeah? It seems to me that you've been cooling your heels, too."

"On the contrary. Over the last nine minutes, I've reflected—with great pleasure—on Milton's invocation in the third book of *Paradise Lost;* I've reviewed the second-declension Latin nouns—certain Latin declensions can be an almost full-time occupation—and I've mentally composed a choice letter I plan to deliver to the engineers who designed this elevator."

A creaking rumble announced the elevator's arrival. The doors groaned open and the packed interior disgorged its contents of doctors, nurses, and—finally—a corpse on a gurney. They got in and D'Agosta punched the button marked B2.

A long wait and the doors rumbled closed. The elevator began to descend so slowly that there was no perception of movement. After another interminable wait, the doors creaked open to reveal a tiled basement corridor, bathed in greenish fluorescent lighting, the air redolent of formaldehyde and death. A gatekeeper behind a sliding glass partition guarded a pair of locked steel doors.

D'Agosta approached, slipping out his shield. "Lieutenant D'Agosta, NYPD Homicide, Special Agent Pendergast, FBI. We're here to see Dr. Wayne Heffler."

"Documents in the tray," came the laconic voice.

They put their shields in a sliding tray. A moment later, they came back with two passes. The steel doors sprang ajar with a metallic snap. "Down the hall, second corridor, left at the T. Check in with the secretary."

The secretary was busy, and it took another twenty minutes to see the doctor. By the time the door finally opened and they were ushered into the elegant office, D'Agosta was spoiling for a fight. And as soon as he saw the arrogant, annoyed face of the assistant medical examiner, he knew he was going to get his wish.

The M.E. rose from his desk and pointedly did not offer them seats. He was a handsome older man, lean and spare, dressed in a cardigan with a bow tie and starched white shirt. A tweed jacket hung on the back of his chair. His thinning silver hair was combed back from a high forehead. The Mr. Rogers look stopped at the eyes, which were as blue and cold as ice behind horn-rimmed spectacles. There were hunting prints on the wood-paneled walls, along with a collection of yacht racing pennants in a large glass case. *A frigging country gentleman,* D'Agosta thought sourly.

"What can I do for you?" the M.E. asked, unsmiling, hands on the desk.

D'Agosta pointedly took a chair, moving it this way and that before sitting down, taking his time about it. Pendergast slipped smoothly into a seat nearby. D'Agosta peeled a document out of his briefcase and slid it over the half-an-acre of desk.

The man didn't even look at it. "Lieutenant—ah, D'Agosta—fill me in on the details. I don't have time to read reports right now."

"It's about the autopsy of Colin Fearing. You were in charge. Remember?"

"Of course. The body found in the Harlem River. Suicide."

"Yeah," said D'Agosta. "Well, I got five good witnesses swearing he was the killer on that West End Avenue murder last night."

"That's quite impossible."

"Who identified the body?"

"The sister." Heffler shuffled impatiently through a file open on his desk. "Carmela Fearing."

"No other family?"

More impatient shuffling. "Just a mother. Non compos mentis, in a nursing home upstate."

D'Agosta shot a glance toward Pendergast, but the special agent was studying the sporting prints with evident distaste, seemingly oblivious to the line of questioning.

"Identifying marks?" he continued.

"Fearing had a very unusual tattoo of a hobbit on his left deltoid, and a birthmark on his right ankle. We verified the former with the tattoo parlor—it was very recent. The latter was verified by his birth certificate."

"Dental records?"

"We couldn't locate dental records."

"Why not?"

"Colin Fearing grew up in England. Then, before moving to New York City, he lived in San Antonio, Texas. His sister stated he had all his dental work done in Mexico."

"So you didn't call the clinics in Mexico or London? How long does it take to scan and e-mail a set of X-rays?"

The M.E. expelled a long, irritated sigh. "Birthmark, tattoo, sworn and notarized eyewitness identification from reliable next-of-kin—we've more than satisfied the law, Lieutenant. I'd never get my work done if we went after international dental records every time a foreigner killed himself in New York City."

"Did you keep any samples of Fearing's tissue or blood?"

"We only take X-rays and keep tissue and blood if there's a question surrounding the death. This was a open-and-shut case of suicide."

"How do you know?"

"Fearing jumped off the rotating bridge opposite Spuyten Duyvel into the Harlem River. His body was found in the Spuyten Duyvel by a police boat. The jump ruptured his lungs and fractured his skull. And there was a suicide note left on the tracks. But you know all this, Lieutenant."

"I read it in the file. Not the same as *knowing* it."

The doctor had remained standing, and now he pointedly closed the file on his desk. "Thank you, gentlemen, will that be all?" He looked at his watch.

At this, Pendergast at last roused himself. "To whom did you release the body?" His voice was slow, almost sleepy.

"The sister, of course."

"What kind of ID did you check on the sister? A passport?"

"I seem to recall it was a New York State driver's license."

"Did you keep a copy of it?"

"No."

A small sigh rose from Pendergast. "Any witnesses to this suicide?"

"Not that I'm aware of."

"Was a forensic examination done to the note, to ascertain it was indeed in Colin Fearing's handwriting?"

A hesitation. The file opened again. The M.E. scanned it. "It seems not."

D'Agosta picked up the line of questioning. "Who found the note?"

"The police who recovered the body."

"And the sister—did you interview her?"

"No." Heffler turned away from D'Agosta, no doubt in hopes of shutting him up. "Mr. Pendergast, may I ask what the FBI's interest is in the case?"

"You may not, Dr. Heffler."

D'Agosta continued. "Look, Doctor. We've got Bill Smithback's body in your morgue, and if we're to continue our investigation we need it autopsied, fast. We also need DNA tests on the blood and hair samples, equally fast. And a test of Fearing's mother's DNA for comparison, since you *neglected* to keep any samples from the autopsy."

"How fast would that be?"

"Four days, tops."

A small smile of contemptuous triumph twitched across the doctor's lips. "So sorry, Lieutenant, that is impossible. We're quite backed up here, and even if we weren't, four days is out of the question. It'll be at least ten days, perhaps even three weeks, for the autopsy. As for DNA results, that's not even my jurisdiction. You'll have to get a court order to take blood from the mother, which could take months. And with the backups at the DNA lab, you'll be lucky to get final results in less than half a year."

Pendergast spoke again. "How very inconvenient." He turned to D'Agosta. "I suppose we'll just have to wait. Unless Dr. Heffler can manage—how do you term it?—a *rush job* on that autopsy."

"If I did a rush job for every FBI agent or homicide detective who asked for it—and they *all* do—I'd never get anything else done." He slid the document back across the desk. "I'm sorry, gentlemen. Now if you'll excuse me?"

"Of course," said Pendergast. "So sorry to have taken up your valuable time."

D'Agosta looked over with incredulity as the agent rose to leave. They were just going to accept this bullshit brush-off and walk out?

Pendergast turned and strode to the door, then hesitated. "Odd that you managed to work so efficiently with Fearing's corpse. How many days did that take?"

"Four. But that was a straightforward suicide. We have a storage problem here."

"Well, then! Given your storage problem, we would like the autopsy on Smithback completed in four days."

A short laugh. "Mr. Pendergast, you haven't been listening. I'll let you know when we can schedule it. Now if you don't mind—"

"Make it three days, then, Dr. Heffler."

The doctor stared at him. "Excuse me?"

Pendergast turned to face him. "I said, *three days.*"

Heffler narrowed his eyes. "You are insolent, sir."

"And you suffer from an egregious lack of ethics."

"What the devil are you talking about?"

"It would be a shame if it became widely known that your office has been selling the brains of the indigent dead."

There was a long silence. When the M.E. spoke again, his voice was as cold as ice. "Mr. Pendergast, are you threatening me?"

Pendergast smiled. "How clever of you, Doctor."

"What I presume you're referring to is a fully sanctioned and legitimate practice. It is for a worthy cause—medical research. We harvest the unclaimed cadavers for all their organs, not just the brain. Their bodies save lives and are crucial for medical research."

"The operative word here is *selling*. Ten thousand dollars for a brain—isn't that the going price? Who would have thought a brain could be so valuable?"

"For heaven's sake, we don't *sell* them, Mr. Pendergast. We ask for a reimbursement of our expenses. It costs us money to remove and handle organs."

"A distinction that the readers of the *New York Post* might not appreciate."

The man's face whitened. "The *Post*? They aren't writing something?"

"Not yet. But can't you just see the headline?"

The doctor's face darkened, and his bow tie quivered with rage. "You know perfectly well this activity does no harm to anyone. The money is strictly accounted for and supports our work here. My predecessor did the same, as did the M.E. before him. The only reason we keep it quiet is because people would be uncomfortable. Really, Mr. Pendergast, this threat is beyond the pale. *Beyond the pale.*"

"Indeed. Three days, then?"

The M.E. stared at him with hard, glittering eyes. A curt nod. "Two days."

"Thank you, Dr. Heffler. I'm most obliged." And Pendergast turned to D'Agosta. "And now, we really mustn't take up any more of Dr. Heffler's busy, *busy* day."

As they exited the building onto First Avenue and walked toward the idling Rolls, D'Agosta couldn't help but chuckle. "How did you pull *that* rabbit out of your hat?"

"I do not know why it is, Vincent, but there are certain people in positions of power who take pleasure in obstructing others. I'm afraid I take an equally base pleasure in disobliging them. A bad habit, I know, but it is *so* hard at my age to rid oneself of the minor vices."

"He was pretty frigging 'disobliged.'"

"I fear, however, that Dr. Heffler was right about the DNA results. It's beyond his power, or mine for that matter, to hasten that process, especially given the court order required. An alternative approach is thus necessary. And so this afternoon we'll be paying a visit to Willoughby Manor, in Kerhonkson, to offer our condolences to one Gladys Fearing."

"What for? She's non compos mentis."

"And yet, my dear Vincent, I have a feeling Mrs. Fearing might prove surprisingly eloquent."

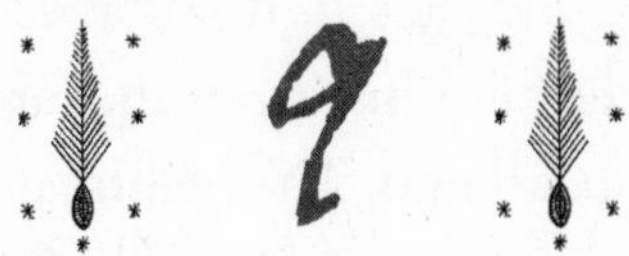

Nora Kelly softly closed the door to her basement anthropology lab and leaned against it, closing her eyes. Her head throbbed steadily, and her throat was rough and dry.

It had been far worse than she imagined, running the gauntlet of her colleagues with their well-meaning condolences, their tragic looks, their offers of help, their suggestions she take a few days off. A few days off? And do what: go back to the apartment where her husband was murdered and sit around with only her thoughts for company? The fact was, she'd come straight to the museum from the hospital. Despite what she'd told D'Agosta, she just couldn't face going back to the apartment—at least, not right away.

She opened her eyes. The lab was as she had left it, two days ago. And yet it looked so different. Everything since the murder seemed different. It was as if the whole world had changed—utterly.

Angrily, she tried to force away the sterile train of thought. She glanced at her watch: two o'clock. The only thing that would save her now was immersion in her work. Complete, total immersion.

She locked the door to the lab, then turned on her Mac. Once it had booted up, she opened the database of her potsherds. Unlocking a drawer of trays, she pulled one open, exposing dozens of plastic bags full of numbered potsherds. She opened the first bag, arranged the potsherds on the felt of the tabletop, and began classifying them by type, date, and location. It was tedious, mindless work—but that's what she needed right now. Mindless work.

After half an hour, she paused. It was as silent as a tomb in the basement lab, with the faint hissing of the forced-air system like a steady whisper in the darkness. The nightmare at the hospital had spooked her—the dream had been so real. Most dreams faded with time, but this one, if anything, seemed to grow in clarity.

She shook her head, annoyed at her mind's tendency to keep circling the same horrifying things. Rapping the computer keys harder than necessary, she finished entering the current batch of data, saved the file, then began packing away the sherds, clearing the table for the next bagful.

A soft knock came at the door.

Not another condolence visit. Nora glanced over at the little glass window set into the door, but the hallway beyond was so dim she could see nothing. After a moment, she stood up, walked to the door, placed her hand on the knob. Then she paused.

"Who is it?"

"Primus Hornby."

With a feeling of dismay, Nora unlocked the door to find the small, tub-like anthropology curator standing before her, morning paper folded under one fat little arm, a plump hand nervously rubbing his bald pate. "I'm glad I found you in. May I?"

Reluctantly, Nora stepped aside to let the curator pass. The disheveled little man swept in and turned. "Nora, I'm so *dreadfully* sorry." His hand continued to nervously rub his bald spot. She didn't respond—couldn't respond. She didn't know what to say or how to say it.

"I'm glad you've come back to work. I find work is the universal healer."

"Thank you for your concern." Perhaps he would leave now. But he had the look of a man with something on his mind.

"I lost my wife some years ago, when I was doing fieldwork in Haiti. She was killed in a car crash in California while I was away. I know what you must be feeling."

"Thank you, Primus."

He moved deeper into the lab. "Potsherds, I see. How beautiful they are. An example of the human urge to make beautiful even the most mundane of objects."

"Yes, it is." *When will he leave?* Nora suddenly felt guilty for the reaction. In his own way, he was trying to be kind. But this just wasn't the way she grieved, all this talk and commiseration and condolence offering.

"Forgive me, Nora . . ." He hesitated. "But I must ask. Do you plan on burying your husband or having him cremated?"

The question was so bizarre that for a moment Nora was taken aback. The question was one she had been deliberately avoiding, and she knew she had to face it soon.

"I don't know," she said, rather more curtly than she intended.

"I see." Hornby looked unaccountably dismayed. Nora wondered what was coming next. "As I said, I did my fieldwork in Haiti."

"Yes."

Hornby seemed to be growing more agitated. "In Dessalines, where I lived, they sometimes use Formalazen as an embalming fluid instead of the usual compound of formalin, ethanol, and methanol."

The conversation seemed to be taking on an unreal cast. "Formalazen," Nora repeated.

"Yes. It's far more poisonous and difficult to handle, but they prefer it for . . . well, for certain reasons. Sometimes they make it even more toxic by dissolving rat poison in it. In certain unusual cases—certain *types* of death—they also ask the mortician to suture the mouth shut." He hesitated again. "And in such cases they bury their dead facedown, mouth to the earth, with a long knife in one hand. Sometimes they fire a bullet or drive a piece of iron into the corpse's heart to . . . well, to *kill it again.*"

Nora stared at the odd little curator. She had always known he was eccentric, that he'd been touched a little too deeply by the strange nature of his studies, but this was something so monstrously out of place she could hardly believe it. "How interesting," she managed to say.

"They can be very careful about how they bury their dead in Dessalines. They follow strict rules at great financial expense. A proper burial can cost two or three years' annual salary."

"I see."

"Once again, I'm so dreadfully sorry." And with that, the curator unfolded the newspaper he'd been carrying under his arm and laid it on the table. It was a copy of that morning's *West Sider.*

Nora stared at the headline:

TIMES REPORTER KILLED BY ZOMBIE?

Hornby tapped the headline with a stubby finger. "My work was in this very area. Voodoo. Obeah. Zombiis—spelled correctly with two *i*'s, of course, not like how they spelled it here. Of course, the *West Sider* gets *everything* wrong." He sniffed.

"What—?" Nora found herself speechless, staring at the headline.

"So if you do decide to bury your husband, I hope you'll keep what I've said in mind. If you have any questions, Nora, I am always here."

And with a final, sad smile, the little curator was gone, leaving the newspaper on the table.

10

The Rolls-Royce purred through the shabby town of Kerhonkson, glided over a cracked asphalt road past a shuttered Borscht Belt hotel, and then wound its way down into a gloomy river valley closed in by damp trees. One last steep bend and a weather-beaten Victorian house came into view, adjoining a low-lying complex of brick buildings surrounded by a chain-link fence. A sign bathed in late-afternoon shadow announced they were entering the Willoughby Manor Extended Care Facility.

"Jesus," said D'Agosta. "Looks like a prison."

"It is one of the more infamous dumping grounds for the infirm and aged in New York State," said Pendergast. "Their HHS file is a foot thick with violations."

They drove through the open gate, past an unmanned pillbox, and crossed a vast and empty visitors' parking lot, weeds sprouting up through a web of cracks. Proctor pulled the vehicle up to the main entrance and D'Agosta heaved himself out, already regretting leaving the cushy seats behind. Pendergast followed. Entering the facility via a pair of dingy Plexiglas doors, they found themselves in a lobby smelling of moldy carpet and aging mashed potatoes. A handwritten sign on a wooden stand in the center of the lobby read:

Visitors MUST Check In!

A scrawled arrow pointed to a corner, where a desk was manned by a woman reading *Cosmopolitan.* She must have weighed at least three hundred pounds.

D'Agosta removed his shield. "Lieutenant D'Agosta, Special Agent—"

"Visiting hours are from ten to two," she said from behind the magazine.

"Excuse me. We're *police* officers." D'Agosta just wasn't going to take any more shit from anyone, not on this case.

The woman finally put down the magazine and stared at them.

D'Agosta let her stare at his badge for a moment, then he returned it to his suit pocket. "We're here to see Mrs. Gladys Fearing."

"All right." The woman pressed an intercom button and bawled into it. "Cops here to see Fearing!" She turned back to them with a face that had gone from slatternly to unexpectedly eager. "What happened? Somebody commit a crime?"

Pendergast leaned forward, adopting a confidential manner. "As a matter of fact, yes."

Her eyes widened.

"Murder," Pendergast whispered.

The woman gasped and placed her hand over her mouth. "Where? Here?"

"New York City."

"Was it Mrs. Fearing's son?"

"You mean Colin Fearing?"

D'Agosta glanced at Pendergast. *Where the hell is he going?*

Pendergast straightened up, adjusted his tie. "You know Colin well?"

"Not really."

"But he visited regularly, did he not? Last week, for example?"

"I don't think so." The woman pulled over a register book, flipped through it. "No."

"It must have been the week before." Pendergast leaned over to look at the book.

She continued flipping through it, Pendergast's silvery eyes on the pages. "Nope. Last time he visited was in . . . February. Eight months ago."

"Really!"

"Look for yourself." She turned the book around so Pendergast could see. He examined the scrawled signature, then began flipping back to the beginning of the book, his eyes taking in every page. He straightened up. "It seems he didn't visit often."

"Nobody visits often."

"And her daughter?"

"I didn't know she even had a daughter. Never visited."

Pendergast laid a kindly hand on her massive shoulder. "In answer to your question, yes, Colin Fearing is dead."

She paused, eyes growing wide. "Murdered?"

"We don't know the cause of *his* death yet. So no one's told his mother?"

"Nobody. I don't think anyone here knew. But . . ." She hesitated. "You're not here to tell her, are you?"

"Not exactly."

"I don't think you should. Why ruin the last few months of her life? I mean, he hardly ever visited, and he never stayed long. She won't miss him."

"What was he like?"

She made a face. "I wouldn't want a son like him."

"Indeed? Please explain."

"Rude. Nasty. He called me Big Bertha." She flushed.

"Outrageous! And what is your name, my dear?"

"Jo-Ann." She hesitated. "You won't tell Mrs. Fearing about his death, will you?"

"Very compassionate of you, Jo-Ann. And now, may we see Mrs. Fearing?"

"Where is that aide?" She was about to press the intercom again, then thought better of it. "I'll take you myself. Follow me. I ought to warn you: Mrs. Fearing's pretty batty."

"Batty," Pendergast repeated. "I see."

The woman struggled up from her chair, most eager to be of help. They followed her down a long, dim linoleum corridor, assaulted by more disagreeable smells: human elimination, boiled food, vomit. Each door they passed presented its own suite of noises: mumbling, groaning, frantic loud talking, snoring.

The woman paused at an open door and knocked. "Mrs. Fearing?"

"Go away," came the feeble answer.

"Some gentlemen to see you, Mrs. Fearing!" Jo-Ann tried to muster a bright, artificial voice.

"I don't want to see anybody," came the voice from within.

"Thank you, Jo-Ann," Pendergast said in his most suave tone. "We can handle it from here. You're a treasure."

They stepped inside. The room was small, with a minimum of furniture and personal possessions. It was dominated by a hospital bed that lay in the center of the linoleum-tiled floor. Pendergast deftly slipped into a chair next to the bed.

"Go away," said the woman again, her voice weak and without conviction. She lay in the bed, her uncombed, snowy hair frizzed about her head in a halo, her once blue eyes now almost white, skin as delicate and transparent as parchment. D'Agosta could see the gleaming curve of her scalp below the straggly hairs. Dirty dishes from lunch, hours old, were parked on a hospital table with wheels.

"Hello, Gladys," Pendergast said, taking her hand. "How are you?"

"Lousy."

"May I ask you a personal question?"

"No."

Pendergast pressed the hand. "Do you remember your first teddy bear?"

The washed-out eyes stared at him, uncomprehending.

"Your first stuffed teddy. Do you remember?"

A slow, wondering nod.

"What was its name?"

A long silence. And then she spoke. "Molly."

"A nice name. What happened to Molly?"

Another long pause. "I don't know."

"Who gave you Molly?"

"Daddy. For Christmas."

D'Agosta could see a flicker of life kindling in those dull eyes. Not for the first time, he wondered where Pendergast could possibly be going with such a bizarre line of questioning.

"What a wonderful present she must have made," Pendergast said. "Tell me about Molly."

"She was made out of socks sewed together and stuffed with rags. She had a bow tie painted on her. I loved that bear. I slept with her every night. When I was with her, I was safe. Nobody could hurt me." A radiant smile broke out on the old lady's face, and a tear welled up in one eye and ran down her cheek.

Pendergast quickly offered her a Kleenex from a packet he slipped out of his pocket. She took it, dabbed her eyes, and blew her nose. "Molly," she repeated, in a faraway voice. "What I wouldn't give to hold that silly old stuffed bear again." For the first time the eyes seemed to focus on Pendergast. "Who are you?"

"A friend," said Pendergast. "Just come to chat." He rose from his chair.

"Do you have to go?"

"I'm afraid so."

"Come back. I like you. You're a fine young man."

"Thank you. I will try."

On the way out, Pendergast handed his card to Jo-Ann. "If

anyone calls on Mrs. Fearing, would you be so kind as to let me know?"

"Of course!" She took the card with something close to reverence.

A moment later they were outside the entrance, in the shabby, empty parking lot, the Rolls gliding up to fetch them. Pendergast held open the door for D'Agosta. Fifteen minutes later they were on Interstate 87, winging their way back to New York City.

"Did you notice the old painting in the hall outside Mrs. Fearing's room?" Pendergast murmured. "I do believe that is an original Bierstadt, badly in need of cleaning."

D'Agosta shook his head. "Are you going to tell me what that was all about, or do you enjoy keeping me in the dark?"

With an amused gleam in his eye, Pendergast slipped a test tube out of his suitcoat. Stuffed inside was a damp tissue.

D'Agosta stared. He hadn't even seen Pendergast retrieve the used tissue. "For DNA?"

"Naturally."

"And that business about the teddy bear?"

"Everyone had a teddy bear. The point of the exercise was to get her to blow her nose."

D'Agosta was shocked. "That was low."

"On the contrary." He slipped the tube back into his pocket. "Those were tears of joy she shed. We brightened up Mrs. Fearing's day, and she in her turn did us a service."

"I hope we can get it analyzed before Steinbrenner sells the Yankees."

"Once again, we shall have to operate not only outside the box, but outside the room containing the box."

"Meaning?"

But Pendergast merely smiled enigmatically.

11

Nora, I am very sorry!” The doorman opened the door with a flourish and took her hand, enveloping her with a smell of hair tonic and aftershave. “Everything is ready in your apartment. Locks change. Everything fix up. I have the new key. I offer my sincere condolence. Sincere.”

Nora felt the cold, flat key pressed into her hand.

“If you need my help, let me know.” He gazed at her with genuine sorrow in his liquid brown eyes.

Nora swallowed. “Thank you, Enrico, for your concern.” The phrase had become almost automatic.

“Anytime. Anything. You call and Enrico come.”

“Thank you.” She headed toward the elevator; hesitated; started forward again. She had to do this without thinking too much about it.

The elevator doors clunked shut and the machine ascended smoothly to the sixth floor. When they opened, Nora didn’t move. Then, just as they began to close again, she stepped quickly out into the hall.

Everything was quiet. A muted Beethoven string quartet issued from behind one door, muffled conversation from behind another. She took a step, then hesitated once again. Ahead, near the turn of the hall, she could see the door to their—to *her*—apartment. Brass numbers screwed onto it read 612.

She walked slowly down the hall until she faced the door. The spyhole was black, the lights off inside. The lock cylinder and plate were brand new. She opened her hand and stared at the key: shiny, freshly cut. It didn't seem real. None of this seemed real. *Jamais vu*—the opposite of déjà vu. It was as if she were seeing everything for the first time.

Slowly, she inserted the key, turned it. The lock clicked, then she felt the door go loose in its frame. She gave it a push, and it eased open on newly oiled hinges. The apartment beyond was dark. She reached inside for the light switch, fumbled for it, couldn't find it. *Where is it?* She stepped into the darkness, still fumbling along the blank wall, her heart suddenly pounding. She was enveloped by a smell—of cleaning fluids, wood polish . . . and something else.

The door began to shut behind her, blocking off the light from the hall. With a muffled cry she reached back, grabbed the doorknob, wrenched the door back open, stepped back into the hall and closed the door. She leaned her head against it, shoulders shaking violently, trying to force down the sobs that engulfed her.

Within a few minutes, she had herself more or less under control. She glanced up and down the hall, grateful nobody had walked by. She was half embarrassed, half afraid of the storm of emotions she'd been keeping bottled up. It had been stupid to think she could just walk back into the apartment where her husband had been murdered only forty-eight hours before. She'd go to Margo Green's apartment, stay with her for a few days—but then she remembered that Margo was on sabbatical leave until January.

She had to get out. She rode the elevator back down to the first floor and walked through the lobby on rubbery legs. The doorman opened the door. "Anything you need, you call Enrico," he said as she almost ran past.

She walked east on 92nd Street to Broadway. It was a cool but still pleasant October evening, and the sidewalks were crowded with people on their way to restaurants, walking their dogs, or just going home. Nora began to walk, briskly; the air would clear her head. She headed downtown, moving fast, dodging people. Out here, on the street, among the crowds, she found herself getting her thoughts under control, finding some perspective on what had just happened. It was stupid to react this way—she had to go back into the apartment sometime, and sooner rather than later. All her books, her work, her computer, *his* stuff—everything was there.

She wished, for a moment, that her father and mother were still alive, that she could flee to their warm embrace. But that was an even more foolish, futile line of thinking.

She slowed. Maybe she should go back, after all. This was just the kind of emotional reaction she had hoped to avoid.

She paused, looking around. Beside her, a line of people were waiting to get into the Waterworks Bar. A couple necked in a doorway. A group of Wall Street types were walking home, all dark suits and briefcases. Her attention was attracted to a homeless man who had been shuffling alongside the building façades, matching her pace; he stopped, too, and turned around abruptly, heading the other way.

Something about the furtiveness of that motion, about the way the man kept his face from view, made her big-city instincts sound an alarm.

She watched the homeless man lurch along, covered in dirty rags, looking precisely as if he was trying to get away. Had he just robbed somebody? As she stared after him, the man reached the corner of 88th Street, paused, then shambled around the corner, looking back once just before vanishing.

Nora's heart stopped. *It was Fearing.* She felt almost sure of it: the same lean face, the same lanky frame, the same thin lips, unruly hair, and leering smirk.

She was gripped by a paralyzing fear—which, just as quickly, gave way to furious anger.

"Hey!" she yelled, breaking into a run. "Hey, you!" She began pushing her way along the crowded sidewalk, halted by the Waterworks crowd. She bullied her way through.

"Whoa, lady!"

"Excuse *me*!"

She broke free and ran; tripped; stood up again; then resumed her chase, spinning around the corner. Eighty-eighth Street stretched eastward, long and dimly lit, lined by ginkgo trees and dark brownstones. It ended in the bright lights of Amsterdam Avenue with its pretentious bars and eateries.

A dark figure was just turning onto Amsterdam and heading back downtown.

She raced down the street, running for all she was worth, cursing her weakness and sluggishness after the concussion and bed rest. She rounded the corner and stared down Amsterdam, similarly crowded with evening-goers.

There he was: moving quickly and with sudden purpose, half a block ahead.

Thrusting aside a young man, she began running again, catching up to the figure. "Hey! You!"

The figure kept going.

She darted between pedestrians, stretching out her arm. "Stop!"

Just before reaching 87th Street, she caught up to him, seizing the dirty material of his shoulder and spinning him around. The man righted himself unsteadily, staring back at her with wide, fearful eyes. Nora released the shirt and took a step back.

"What's your problem?" Definitely not Fearing. Just some junkie.

"Sorry," Nora mumbled. "I thought you were someone else."

"Leave me alone." He turned away with a muttered "bitch" and continued his unsteady way down Amsterdam.

Nora looked around wildly, but the real Fearing—if he'd ever been there to begin with—had vanished. She stood amid the surging crowds, her limbs trembling. With a huge effort, she got her breathing under control.

Her eye settled on the closest bar, the Neptune Room: a loud, ostentatious seafood place she had never been into. Never wanted to go into. Never expected to go into.

She went in, settled on a stool. The bartender came over right away. "What'll it be?"

"Beefeater martini, extra dry, straight up, twist."

"Coming right up."

As she sipped the oversize, ice-cold drink, she upbraided herself for acting like a psycho. The dream was only a dream and the homeless man wasn't Fearing. She was shaken up; she needed to get a grip, calm down, and put her life back together as best she could.

She finished her drink. "How much?"

"On the house. And I hope"—the bartender said with a wink—"that whatever devil you saw before you came in is gone now."

She thanked him and rose, feeling the calming effects of the liquor. Devil, the bartender had said. She had to face her devils, and do it now. She was falling apart, seeing things, and that was unacceptable. That wasn't her.

A few minutes' walk brought her back to her apartment building. She briskly passed through the door, ran the gauntlet of another barrage of well-meaning comments by the doorman, and entered the elevator. In another moment, she was standing at her door. She slid in the key, unlocked it, and felt around the corner for the light switch, which she immediately found.

Double-locking the door and sliding home its newly installed bolt, she glanced around. Everything was perfectly neat, cleaned, polished, repainted. Quickly but methodically, she searched the entire apartment, including the closets and under the bed. Then, opening the curtains of the living room and the bedroom, she turned off the lights again. The glow of the city filtered in, throwing the apartment into shadow, giving a soft, gauzy focus to its surfaces.

She could stay here tonight, she knew now; she could wrestle with her devils.

Just so long as she didn't have to look at anything.

12

The waitress brought their orders: pastrami on rye with Russian dressing for D'Agosta, a BLT for Laura Hayward.

"More coffee?" she asked.

"Please." D'Agosta watched as the harassed-looking waitress refilled his cup. Then he turned back to Hayward. "And that's about where we stand," he concluded.

He'd invited Captain Hayward to lunch to bring her up to speed on the investigation so far. Hayward was no longer a homicide captain—she'd been given a lateral shift and was now working in the police commissioner's office, where she was in line for a plum promotion. If anybody deserved it, he thought ruefully, Laura did.

"So," he said, "you read it?"

She glanced at the newspaper he'd brought. "Yes."

D'Agosta shook his head. "Can you believe they print this stuff? Now we've got all kinds of jackasses calling in sightings, anonymous letters that have to be followed up, phone calls from psychics and tarot card readers . . . You know what this town is like whenever a weird story like this breaks. This is just the sort of shit I don't need right now."

A small smile played about Hawyard's lips. "I understand."

"And people believe this trash." He shoved the paper out of the way and took another sip of coffee. "So . . . what do you make of it?"

"You have four eyewitnesses swearing Fearing is the killer?"

"Five—including the victim's wife."

"Nora Kelly."

"You know her, right?"

"Yes. I knew Bill Smithback, too. A little unorthodox in his methods, but a good reporter. What a tragedy."

D'Agosta took a bite of his sandwich. The pastrami was lean, the dressing warm—just the way he liked it. It always seemed that when a case was pissing him off, he started to overeat.

"Well," she continued, "either it's Fearing or somebody disguised as him. He's dead or he isn't. Simple enough. Got any DNA results?"

"Blood from two people was found at the scene—Smithback's and somebody as yet unidentified. We've obtained samples of DNA from Fearing's mother and we're running them against the unknown blood now." He paused, wondered if he should tell her about the unusual way they were getting the DNA tests done, decided against it. It might not be legal, and he knew what a stickler Hayward was for the proverbial book. "The thing is, if it wasn't Fearing, why would anybody go to the trouble of trying to look like him?"

Hayward took a sip of water. "Good question. What does Pendergast think?"

"Since when does anybody know what that guy thinks? But I'll tell you one thing: he's more interested in that voodoo crap found at the scene than he wants to let on. He's spending an awful lot of time going over it."

"That stuff mentioned in the article?"

"Right. Sequins, a bunch of feathers tied together, a little parchment bag full of dust."

"Gris-gris," Hayward murmured.

"I'm sorry?"

"Voodoo charms used to ward off evil. Or sometimes to inflict it."

"Please. We're dealing with a psychopath. The crime couldn't have been more disorganized and poorly planned. On the security tape the guy looks like he's on drugs."

"You want my opinion, Vinnie?"

"You know I do."

"Exhume Fearing's body."

"In process."

"I'd also see if any of Smithback's news stories have made somebody mad recently."

"Also in process. It seems *all* of Smithback's stories made people mad. I got a list of his recent assignments from his editor at the *Times,* and my men are going through them, following up."

"You're doing well, Vinnie. Let me just add that the crime might not be as 'disorganized' as you think—it might have been very carefully planned and executed."

"I don't think so."

"Hey—no snap judgments."

"Sorry."

"One other thing." Hayward hesitated. "You remember my saying that, before taking the job with the transit police, I worked on the New Orleans PD for eighteen months?"

"Sure."

"Pendergast is from New Orleans."

"So?"

Hayward took another sip of water. "A minute ago, I said that either Fearing's dead or he isn't. Well, there are those on the NOPD who would say otherwise. That there might be a third possibility."

"Laura, don't tell me you buy that zombii crap."

Hayward finished the half of her sandwich, pushed the plate aside. “I’m full. Want some?”

“I’m good, thanks. You didn’t answer my question.”

“I don’t ‘buy’ anything. Just talk to Pendergast about it. He knows a lot more about that . . . particular subject than you or I ever will. All I’m saying is, don’t make up your mind too fast. It’s one of your faults, Vinnie. And you know it.”

D’Agosta sighed; she was right, as usual. He looked around the luncheonette: at the bustling waitresses; at the other diners reading papers, talking on cell phones, or chatting with lunch companions. He was reminded of other meals he’d had with Laura, at other restaurants. In particular, he recalled their first drink together. That had been at a particularly low point in his life—and yet it was also the moment he realized just how much he was attracted to her. They worked well together. She challenged him—in a good way. The irony of the situation was painful: he’d won his disciplinary hearing, kept his job, but it seemed that he’d lost Laura.

He cleared his throat. “So tell me about this promotion you’re getting.”

“I haven’t gotten it yet.”

“Come on, I’ve heard the scuttlebutt. It’s just a question of formalities now.”

She took a sip of water. “It’s a special task force they’re setting up. One-year trial period. A few members of the chief’s staff will be appointed to interface with the mayor on terror response, quality-of-life issues, that kind of thing. Big public concerns.”

“Visibility?”

“Extremely high.”

“Wow. Another feather in your cap. Just wait, you’ll be chief in a couple of years.”

Laura smiled. “Not likely.”

D’Agosta hesitated. “Laura. I really miss you.”

The smile faded. “I miss you, too.”

He looked across the table at her. She was so pretty his heart ached: pale skin, hair so black it was almost blue. "So why don't we try again? Start over?"

She paused, then shook her head. "I'm just not ready."

"Why not?"

"Vinnie, I don't trust many people. But I trusted you. And you hurt me."

"I know that, and I'm sorry. Really sorry. But I've explained all that. I had no choice, surely you see that now."

"Of course you had a choice. You could have told me the truth. You could have trusted me. As I trusted you."

D'Agosta sighed. "Look—I'm sorry."

There was a loud beep as his cell phone started ringing. When it continued, Laura said, "I think you should answer that."

"But—"

"Go ahead. Take it."

D'Agosta reached into his pocket, flipped the phone open. "Yes?"

"Vincent," drawled the mellifluous southern voice. "Did I catch you at a bad time?"

He swallowed. "No, not really."

"Excellent. We have an appointment with a certain Mr. Kline."

"On my way."

"Good. Oh, one other thing—care to take a drive with me tomorrow morning?"

"Where to?"

"Whispering Oaks Mausoleum. The exhumation order came through. We're opening Fearing's crypt tomorrow at noon."

13

Digital Veracity Inc. was located in one of the giant glass office towers that lined Avenue of the Americas in the lower fifties. D'Agosta met Pendergast in the main lobby and, after a brief stop at the security station, they made their way to the thirty-seventh floor.

"Did you bring a copy of the letter?" Pendergast asked.

D'Agosta patted his jacket pocket. "You got anything on Kline's background I should know?"

"Indeed I do. Our Mr. Lucas Kline grew up in a poor family from Avenue J in Brooklyn, childhood unremarkable, grades excellent, always the last chosen for the team, a 'nice boy.' He matriculated from NYU, began work as a journalist—which, by all accounts, was where his heart lay. But it worked out badly: he got scooped on an important story—unfairly, it seems, but when was journalism a fair field?—and was fired as a result. He drifted a bit, ultimately becoming a computer programmer for a Wall Street bank. Apparently he had a talent for it: he started DVI a few years later and seems to have carried it a fair distance." He glanced at D'Agosta. "Are you considering a search warrant?"

"I thought I'd see how the interview goes first."

The elevator doors rolled back on an elegantly furnished lobby. Several sofas clad in black leather sat on antique Serapi rugs. Half a dozen large pieces of African sculpture—warriors with imposing headpieces, large masks with dizzyingly complex traceries—decorated the space.

"It would appear our Mr. Kline has come farther than a 'fair distance,'" D'Agosta said, looking around.

They gave their names to the receptionist and sat down. D'Agosta hunted in vain for a copy of *People* or *Entertainment Weekly* among the stacks of *Computerworld* and *Database Journal.* Five minutes went by, then ten. Just as D'Agosta was about to get up and make a nuisance of himself, a buzzer sounded on the receptionist's desk.

"Mr. Kline will see you now," she said, standing and leading the way through an unmarked door.

They walked down a long, softly lit hallway that terminated in another door. The receptionist ushered them through an outer office where a gorgeous secretary sat typing at a computer. She gave them a furtive look before returning to her work. She had the tense, cowed manner of a beaten dog.

Beyond, yet another pair of doors opened onto a sprawling corner office. Two walls of glass offered dizzying views of Sixth Avenue. A man of about forty stood behind a desk covered with four personal computers. He was standing while speaking into a wireless telephone headset, his back to them, looking out the windows.

D'Agosta examined the office: more black leather sofas, more tribal art on the walls: Mr. Kline, it seemed, was a collector. A polished glass case held several dusty artifacts, clay pipes and buckles and twisted pieces of iron, labeled as coming from the original Dutch settlement of New Amsterdam. A few recessed bookcases contained books on finance and computer programming languages, in sharp contrast with the leering, slightly unsettling masks.

Finishing the phone call, the man hung up and turned to face them. He had a thin, remarkably youthful face that still bore traces of a struggle with adolescent acne. D'Agosta noticed he was relatively short, no taller than five foot five. His hair stuck up in the back, like a kid's. Only his eyes were old—and very cool.

He looked from Pendergast to D'Agosta and back again. "Yes?" he asked in a soft voice.

"I will have a seat, thank you," Pendergast said, taking a chair and throwing one leg over the other. D'Agosta followed suit.

The man smiled slightly but said nothing.

"Mr. Lucas Kline?" D'Agosta said. "I'm Lieutenant D'Agosta of the NYPD."

"I knew you had to be D'Agosta." Kline looked at Pendergast. "And you must be the special agent. You already know who I am. Now, what is it you want? I happen to be busy."

"Is that so?" D'Agosta asked, lounging back in the leather, making it creak in a most satisfying way. "And just what is it you busy yourself with, Mr. Kline?"

"I'm CEO of DVI."

"That doesn't really tell me anything."

"If you want my rags-to-riches story, read that." Kline pointed to half a dozen identical books sitting together on one of the shelves. "How I went from a lowly DBA to head of my own company. It's required reading for all my employees: a volume of brilliance and insight for which they are privileged to pay forty-five dollars." He bestowed a deprecating smile on them. "My secretary will accept your cash or check on the way out."

"DBA?" D'Agosta asked. "What's that?"

"Database administrator. Once upon a time I massaged databases for a living, kept them healthy. And on the side, I wrote a program to automatically normalize large financial databases."

"Normalize?" D'Agosta echoed.

Kline waved his hand dismissively. "Don't even ask. In any case, my program worked very, very well. It turned out there was a large market for normalizing databases. I put a lot of other DBAs out of jobs. And created all this." His chin tilted slightly upward, the self-satisfied smile still lingering at the edges of his pink, girlish lips.

The man's egghead egotism set D'Agosta's teeth on edge. He was going to enjoy this. He leaned back casually in his seat, to more protesting of expensive leather. "Actually, we're more interested in your extracurricular activities."

Kline looked more closely at him. "Such as?"

"Such as your penchant for hiring pretty secretaries, intimidating them into having sex with you, then bullying them or paying them off to keep quiet about it."

The expression on Kline's face did not change. "Ah. So you're here about the Smithback murder."

"You used your position of power to abuse and dominate those women. They were too afraid of you, too afraid of losing their jobs, to say anything. But Smithback wasn't afraid. He exposed you to the world."

"He exposed nothing," Kline said. "Allegations were made, nothing was proven, and any settlements, if they exist, are sealed forever. Alas for you and Smithback, nobody went officially on the record."

D'Agosta shrugged as if to say, *Doesn't matter, the cat's still out of the bag.*

Pendergast stirred in his seat. "How unpleasant it must have been for you that after Smithback's article was published, DVI's stock market capitalization dropped by fifty percent."

Kline's face remained serene. "You know the markets. So fickle. DVI is almost back up to where it was."

Pendergast folded his hands. "You're a CEO now, and nobody's going to kick sand in your face again or take your lunch money. Nobody's going to disrespect you and get away with it these days—am I right, Mr. Kline?" Pendergast smiled mildly and glanced at D'Agosta. "The letter?"

D'Agosta reached into his pocket, slipped out the letter, and began to quote: *"I promise that, no matter how much time it takes or how much it costs, you will regret having written that article. You cannot know how I will act, or when, but rest assured: I will act."* He looked up. "Did you write that, Mr. Kline?"

"Yes," he said, his face remaining utterly under control.

"And did you send that to William Smithback?"

"I did."

"Did you—"

Kline interrupted. "Lieutenant, you are such a bore. Let me ask myself the questions and save us all some time. Was I serious? Absolutely. Was I responsible for his death? It's a possibility. Am I glad he's dead? Delighted, thank you." He winked.

"You—" D'Agosta began.

"The thing is"—Kline rode over him again—"you'll *never* know. I have the finest lawyers in town. I know precisely what I can say and cannot say. You'll never touch me."

"We can take you in," D'Agosta said. "We could do it right now."

"Of course you could. And I will sit silently where you take me until my lawyer arrives, and then I will leave."

"We could book you for probable cause."

"You're bloviating, Lieutenant."

"The letter is a clear threat."

"All my movements at the time of the killing can be accounted for. The finest legal minds in the country vetted that letter. There's nothing in there that is actionable on your part."

D'Agosta grinned. "Why, hell, Kline, we could have a little fun, perp-walking you out the lobby downstairs—after we tip off the press."

"Actually, it would be excellent publicity. I would be back in my office within the hour, you would be embarrassed, and my enemies would see that I am untouchable." Kline smiled again. "Remember, Lieutenant: I was trained as a programmer. It was my job to write long, complicated routines in which faultless logic was of paramount importance. That's the first thing you learn as a programmer, the most vital thing. Think *everything* through, forward and backward. Make sure you've made provisions for any unexpected output. And don't leave any holes. Not a one."

D'Agosta could feel himself doing a slow burn. A silence settled over the large office. Kline sat there, arms folded, looking back at D'Agosta.

"Dysfunctional," D'Agosta said. At least he'd wipe that smug smile off this little bastard's face.

"Excuse me?" Kline asked.

"If I wasn't so disgusted, I could almost feel sorry for you. The only way you can get laid is to brandish money and power, to harass and force. That doesn't sound dysfunctional to you? No? How about another word, then: pathetic. That girl in the outer office—when are you planning to rotate her out for this year's model?"

"Kick your fucking ass" came the response.

D'Agosta rose. "That's a threat of violence, Kline. Made against a police officer." He put his hands on his cuffs. "You think you're so smart, but you just crossed the line."

"Kick your fucking ass, D'Agosta," came the voice again.

D'Agosta realized it wasn't Kline who had spoken. The voice was slightly different. And it hadn't come from behind the desk: it had come from beyond a door set into the opposite wall.

"Who's that?" D'Agosta said. He had grown so angry, so quickly, that he could feel himself shaking.

"That?" Kline replied. "Oh, that's Chauncy."

"Get him out here. Now."

"I can't do that."

"What?" D'Agosta said through clenched teeth.

"He's busy."

"Kick your fucking ass," came the voice of Chauncy.

"Busy?"

"Yes. Eating his lunch."

Without another word, D'Agosta strode to the door, flung it open.

Beyond lay a small room, barely bigger than a closet. It held nothing but a wooden T-bar about chest high—and sitting on it was a huge, salmon-colored parrot. A Brazil nut was in one claw. It regarded him mildly, massive beak coyly hidden by cheek feathers, the crest atop its head raised slightly in inquiry.

"Lieutenant D'Agosta, meet Chauncy," Kline said.

"Kick your fucking ass, D'Agosta," said the parrot.

D'Agosta took a step forward. The parrot gave out an ear-piercing shriek and dropped the nut, flapping its wide wings and showering D'Agosta with feathers and dander, its crest flaring wildly.

"Now look what you've done," said Kline in a tone of mild reproof. "You've disturbed his lunch."

D'Agosta stepped back again, breathing heavily. Abruptly, he realized there was nothing—absolutely nothing—he could do. Kline had broken no law. What was he going to do, cuff a Moluccan cockatoo and haul it downtown? He'd be laughed out of Police Plaza. The little prick really had thought everything through. His hand tightened over the letter, crumpling it. The frustration was agonizing.

"How does it know my name?" he muttered, flicking a feather off his jacket.

"Oh, that," said Kline. "You see, Chauncy and I were, um, discussing you before you came in."

As they stepped into the elevator for the ride back down to the lobby, D'Agosta glanced over at Pendergast. The special agent was shaking with what appeared to be silent mirth. D'Agosta looked away, frowning. At length Pendergast composed himself and cleared his throat.

"I think, my dear Vincent," he said, "you might consider obtaining that search warrant with all possible haste."

14

Caitlyn Kidd nosed her car into a bus-only zone across the street from the New York Museum of Natural History. Before getting out, she draped a copy of yesterday's *West Sider*—with the headline and her byline prominently displayed—on the dash. That, along with her press plates, just might help her avoid a second parking ticket in as many days.

She walked briskly across Museum Drive, inhaling the frosty fall air. It was quarter to five, and as she suspected a number of people were exiting purposefully from an unmarked door set into the ground floor of the vast structure. They carried bags and briefcases—employees, not visitors. She threaded her way through them toward the door.

Beyond the door lay a narrow corridor, leading to a security station. A few people were showing their museum IDs and being waved past the station by a pair of bored-looking guards. Caitlyn rummaged in her bag, plucked out her press ID.

She stepped up and showed the pass to the guard. "Staff only," he said.

"I'm with the *West Sider*," she replied. "I'm doing a story on the museum."

"Got an appointment?"

"I've got an interview set up with . . ." She glanced at the badge of a curator just passing the little guard station. It would be at least a few minutes before he reached his office. "Dr. Prine."

"Moment." The guard checked a phone book, lifted the phone, dialed a number, let it ring a few times. Then he raised his sleepy eyes to her. "He ain't in. You'll have to wait here."

"May I sit down?" She indicated a bench a dozen yards off.

The guard hesitated.

"I'm pregnant. I'm not supposed to be on my feet."

"Go ahead."

She sat down, crossed her legs, opened a book, keeping an eye on the guard station. A knot of employees arrived and began piling up around the entrance—janitors by the look of them, arriving for the night shift. As the guards became fully engrossed in checking IDs and ticking off names, Caitlyn quickly rose and joined the stream of employees already through the security checkpoint.

The room she was looking for was in the basement—a five-minute search on the Internet had secured an employee directory and layout of the museum—but the place was a rabbit warren of intersecting passages and endless, unmarked corridors. Nobody challenged her access or even seemed to notice her, however, and a few well-placed queries finally led her to a long, dimly lit hallway, opposing walls punctuated every twenty feet by doors with frosted windows set into them. Caitlyn made her way slowly down the corridor, glancing at the names on the doors. A smell lingered in the air, faintly unpleasant, that she couldn't identify. Some of the doors were open, and beyond she could see laboratory setups, cluttered offices, and—bizarrely—jars of pickled animals and fierce-looking beasts, stuffed and mounted.

She paused outside a door labeled KELLY, N. The door was ajar, and Caitlyn heard voices within. One voice, she realized: Nora Kelly was on the phone.

She edged forward, listening.

"Skip, I can't," the voice was saying. "I just can't come home now."

There was a pause. "No, it's not that. If I went back to Santa Fe right now, I might never return to New York. Don't you understand? Besides, it's vital for me to find out what really happened, track down Bill's killer. That's the only thing keeping me going right now."

This was too personal. Caitlyn pushed the door wider, clearing her throat as she did so. The lab beyond was cramped yet orderly. Half a dozen pottery fragments lay on a worktable beside a laptop computer. In one corner, a woman on the telephone looked up at her. She was slim, attractive, with bronze-colored hair spilling down over her shoulders, a haunted look in her hazel eyes.

"Skip," the woman said. "I'm going to have to call you back. Yes. Okay, tonight." She hung up, stood up from the desk. "Can I help you?"

Caitlyn took a deep breath. "Nora Kelly?"

"That's right."

Caitlyn pulled the press ID from her bag, held it open. "I'm Caitlyn Kidd, from the *West Sider*."

Nora Kelly abruptly flushed. "The author of that piece of garbage?" Her voice was sharp with anger and grief.

"Ms. Kelly—"

"That was quite a piece of work. Another one like that and you might get an offer from the *Weekly World News*. I suggest you leave before I call security."

"Did you actually read my story?" Caitlyn blurted out hastily.

A look of uncertainty crossed Nora's face. Caitlyn had guessed right: the woman hadn't read it.

"It was a good story, factual and unbiased. I don't write the headlines, I just report the news."

Nora took a step forward, and Caitlyn instinctively moved back.

For a moment, Nora stared at her, eyes flashing. Then she turned back toward the desk, picking up the phone.

"What are you doing?" Caitlyn asked.

"Calling security."

"Ms. Kelly, please don't do that."

She finished dialing and waited while it rang.

"You're only hurting yourself. Because I can help you find your husband's murderer."

"Yes?" Nora spoke into the phone. "This is Nora Kelly, in the anthro lab."

"We both want the same thing," Caitlyn hissed. "Please let me show you how I can help you. *Please.*"

A silence. Nora stared at her, and then said into the phone, "I'm sorry, I dialed the wrong number." She slowly replaced the phone in its cradle.

"Two minutes," she said.

"Okay. Nora—can I call you Nora? I knew your husband. Did he ever mention that? We used to run into each other at journalistic events, press conferences, crime scenes. Sometimes we were after the same story but, well . . . it was kind of hard for me, a cub reporter with a throwaway tabloid like the *West Sider,* to compete with the *Times.*"

Nora said nothing.

"Bill was a good guy. It's like I said: you and I have a common goal—find his murderer. We each have unique resources at our disposal; we should use them. You know him better than anyone. And I've got a paper. We could pool our talents, help each other."

"I'm still waiting to hear how."

"You know that story Bill was working on, the animal rights piece? He mentioned it to me a few weeks ago."

Nora nodded. "I already told the police about that." She hesitated. "You think it's connected?"

"That's what my gut tells me. But I don't have enough information yet. Tell me more about it."

"It was that business of animal sacrifice up in Inwood. There was a flurry of stories and then it got dropped. But it held Bill's interest. He kept it on the back burner, kept looking for new angles."

"Did he tell you much about it?"

"I just got the sense that some people weren't thrilled about his interest in the subject, but what else is new? He was never happier than when he was pissing off people. Unpleasant people in particular. And there was no one he hated more than an animal abuser." She glanced at her watch. "Thirty seconds left. You still haven't told me how you can help me."

"I'm a tireless researcher. Ask any of my colleagues. I know how to work the police, the hospitals, the libraries, the morgue—I mean, the newspaper's morgue. My press card gets me in places you can't go. I can devote my nights and my days to this, twenty-four/seven. It's true, I want a story. But I also want to do right by Bill."

"Your two minutes are up."

"Okay, I'll leave now. I want you to do something—for yourself as much as for me." Caitlyn tapped her head. "Get out his notes on that piece. The animal rights piece. Share them with me. Remember: we reporters look after our own. I want to get to the bottom of this almost as much as you do. Help me do that, Nora."

And with that, she smiled briefly, gave Nora her card, then turned and let herself out of the lab.

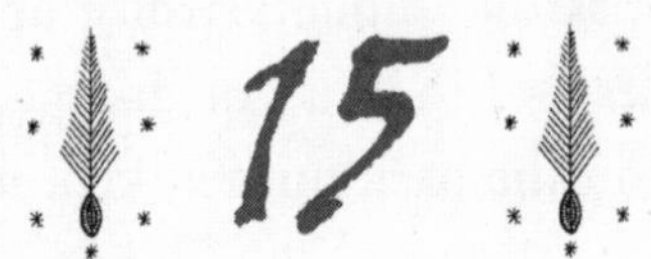

15

The Rolls passed through a pair of gates set into a faux-brick wall, decorated with plastic ivy stapled haphazardly across its front. A sign amid the ivy informed visitors that they had arrived at Whispering Oaks Cemetery and Mausoleum. Beyond the wall lay an expanse of green lawn, bordered by freshly planted oak trees kept vertical by guy wires. Everything was new and raw. The graveyard itself was virtually empty, and D'Agosta could still see the seams where the turf had been rolled down. Half a dozen gigantic, polished granite gravestones were clustered in one corner. Ahead, a mausoleum rose up from the center of the greensward, bone white, stark, and charmless.

Proctor guided the Rolls up the asphalt drive and came to a halt in front of the building. A strip of flower bed before the mausoleum was bursting with flowers, despite the fall season, and as he emerged from the car D'Agosta prodded one with his foot.

Plastic.

They stood in the parking lot, looking around. "Where is everybody?" D'Agosta asked, looking at his watch. "The guy was supposed to be here at noon."

"Gentlemen?" A man had emerged, ghost-like, from the rear of the mausoleum. D'Agosta was startled by his appearance: slender, wearing a well-cut black suit, his skin unnaturally white. The man hurried over, hands clasped obsequiously in front of him, and went straight up to Pendergast. "How may I help you, sir?"

"We are here with regard to the remains of Colin Fearing."

"Ah, yes, the poor fellow we interred, what, almost two weeks ago?" The man beamed, looking Pendergast up and down. "You must be in the business. I can always tell a man in the business!"

Pendergast slowly dipped a hand into his pocket.

"Yes, yes," the man went on, "I remember the interment well. Poor fellow, there was just his sister and the priest. I was surprised—the young ones usually draw a crowd. Well! What mortuary are you gentlemen from, and how can I be of service?"

Pendergast's hand had finally withdrawn a leather case from his pocket, which he held up, allowing it to drop open.

The man stared. "What—what's this?"

"Alas, we are not 'in the business,' as you so charmingly put it."

The man paled even further, saying nothing.

D'Agosta stepped up and handed him an envelope. "We're here about the court-ordered *exhumation* of Colin Fearing. The papers are all in there."

"Exhumation? I don't know a thing about it."

"I talked to a Mr. Radcliffe about it last night," said D'Agosta.

"Mr. Radcliffe didn't tell me anything. He *never* tells me anything." The man's voice rose in querulous complaint.

"That's too bad," said D'Agosta, the foul mood he had been in since the murder surfacing again. "Let's get this over with."

The man was clearly frightened. He seemed to sway in place. "We've . . . we've never had this sort of thing happen before."

"Always a first time, Mr.—?"

"Lille. Maurice Lille."

Now the M.E.'s much-abused van came rattling down the drive, laying down a cloud of blue smoke. It swung around the curve too fast—D'Agosta wondered why they always drove like maniacs—

and came to a halt with a little screech, the vehicle rocking back and forth on a bad suspension. A couple of med techs in white overalls got out, walked to the back, threw open the doors, and slid out a gurney on which lay an empty body bag. Then they approached across the parking lot, pushing the gurney in front.

"Where's the mort?" bawled the thinner of the two, a freckle-faced kid with carroty hair.

Silence.

"Mr. Lille?" D'Agosta asked after a moment.

"The . . . *mort*?"

"You know," said the tech. "The stiff. We don't got all day."

Lille shook himself out of his shock. "Yes. Yes, of course. Please, follow me into the mausoleum."

He led the way to the front door, punched a code into a keypad, and the faux-bronze door clicked open, revealing a high, white space with crypts rising from floor to ceiling on all four walls. Two enormous bunches of plastic flowers spilled out of a pair of gigantic Italianate plaster urns. Only a few of the crypts were marked with black, incised lettering giving names and dates. D'Agosta couldn't help but test the air for that smell he knew so well, but it was clean, fresh, perfumed. Definitely perfumed. *Place like this,* he thought, *must have one hell of a forced-air system.*

"I'm sorry. You did say it was Colin Fearing?" Despite the excessive air-conditioning, Lille was sweating.

"That's right." D'Agosta glanced with irritation at Pendergast, who had gone off on a stroll, hands behind his back, lips pursed, looking around the place. He always seemed to disappear at the wrong time.

"Just a moment, please." Lille went through a glass door that led to his office and came back out clutching a clipboard, looking up at the vast wall of crypts, his lips moving as if counting. After a moment, he stopped.

"There it is. Colin Fearing." He pointed at one of the marked crypts, then stepped back, the grimace of an attempted smile on his face.

"Mr. Lille?" said D'Agosta. "The key?"

"Key?" A look of panic took hold. "You want me to *open* it?"

"That's what an exhumation is all about, right?" said D'Agosta.

"But, you see, I'm not authorized. I'm just a salesman."

D'Agosta exhaled. "You'll find all the paperwork in that envelope. All you have to do is sign the top page—and get us the key."

Lille looked down and discovered, as if for the first time, the manila envelope he was clutching in his hand.

"But I'm not authorized. I'll have to call Mr. Radcliffe."

D'Agosta rolled his eyes.

Lille went back into his office, leaving the door open. D'Agosta listened. The conversation started off low, but soon Lille's shrill voice was echoing through the mausoleum like the cries of a kicked dog. Mr. Radcliffe, apparently, was not interested in cooperation.

Lille came back out. "Mr. Radcliffe is coming in."

"How long will that take?"

"An hour."

"Forget it. I already explained this to Radcliffe. Open the crypt. Now."

Lille wrung his hands, his face contorted. "Oh dear. I just . . . *can't.*"

"That's a court order in your hand, pal, not a permission request. If you don't open that crypt, I'll cite you for obstructing a police officer in the performance of his duty."

"But Mr. Racliffe will fire me!" Lille wailed.

Pendergast swung back around from his self-guided tour, strolling casually up to the group. He approached the face of Fearing's crypt and read aloud: "*Colin Fearing, age thirty-eight.* Sad when they die young, don't you think, Mr. Lille?"

Lille didn't seem to hear. Pendergast laid a hand on the marble, as if caressing it. "You say no one came to the funeral?"

"Just the sister."

"How sad. And who paid for it?"

"I'm . . . I'm not sure. The sister paid the bill, I think from the mother's estate."

"But the mother is non compos mentis." The agent turned to D'Agosta. "I wonder if the sister had a power of attorney? Worth looking into."

"Good idea."

Pendergast's white fingers continued to stroke the marble, drawing back a small, hidden plate, exposing a lock. His other hand dipped into his breast pocket and emerged with a small object, like a comb with only a few short teeth at one end. He inserted it into the lock, gave it a wiggle.

"Excuse me, what do you think you're . . . ?" Lille began, his voice dying away as the crypt door swung open noiselessly on oiled hinges. "No, wait, you mustn't do this—"

The med techs pushed the gurney forward, raising it with a little shake to the level of the crypt. A small flashlight appeared in Pendergast's hand, and he aimed it into the darkness, peering inside.

There was a short silence. Then Pendergast said: "I don't think we'll be needing the gurney."

The two med techs paused, uncertain.

Pendergast straightened up and turned to Lille. "Pray tell, who keeps the keys to these crypts?"

"The keys?" The man was shaking. "I do."

"Where?"

"I keep them locked up in my office."

"And the second set?"

"Mr. Radcliffe keeps them off site. I don't know where."

"Vincent?" Pendergast stepped back, motioned toward the open crypt.

D'Agosta stepped up and peered in the dark cavity, his eye following the narrow beam of the flashlight.

"The damn thing's empty!" he said.

"Impossible," quavered Lille. "I saw the body put in there with my own eyes . . ." His voice choked off and he clutched at his tie.

The carroty-haired med tech peered in, to see for himself. "Well fuck me twice on Sunday," he said, staring.

"Not *quite* empty, Vincent." Pendergast snapped on a latex glove and reached inside, gingerly withdrawing an object and displaying it to the others in the palm of his hand. It was a tiny coffin, crudely fashioned from papier-mâché and bits of cloth, its folded-paper lid ajar. Inside lay a grinning skeleton composed of tiny, white-painted toothpicks.

"There *is* an interment in here—of sorts," he said in his mellifluous voice.

There was a gasp, followed by a soft, collapsing sound. D'Agosta turned. Maurice Lille had fainted.

16

Midnight. Nora Kelly walked briskly through the dark heart of the museum's basement, her heels tapping softly against the polished stone floor. The corridors were on after-hours lighting, and shadows yawned from open doorways. There was nobody around: even the most hard-core curator had left for home hours ago, and most of the guards' rounds were through the museum's public spaces.

She came to a halt at a stainless-steel door labeled PCR LAB. As she'd hoped, the door's wire-covered window was dark. She turned to the keypad lock, typed in a sequence of numbers. An LED set into the pad turned from red to green.

She pushed open the door, ducked inside, and turned on the light, stopping to look around. She had been in the lab only a few times on casual visits, on the occasions she'd dropped off samples for testing. The thermal cycler for the PCR stood on a spotless stainless-steel table, shrouded in plastic. She stepped up, pulled away the plastic, folded it and laid it aside. The machine—an Eppendorf Mastercycler 5330—was made of white plastic, its ugly, low-tech appearance belying its sophisticated innards. She rummaged in her bag and removed a printed document she had downloaded from the Internet with directions on how to use it.

The door had locked behind her automatically. She took a deep breath, then hunted around behind the machine with one hand, at last locating the power switch and turning it on. The manual stated it would take a full fifteen minutes to warm up.

Laying her bag on the table, she removed a Styrofoam container, took off the lid, and began carefully withdrawing pencil-thin test tubes and racking them. One tube contained a bit of hair, another a fiber, another a piece of Kleenex, still another freeze-dried fragments of blood, all of which Pendergast had given her.

She passed a hand over her brow, noticing as she did so that her fingertips were trembling slightly. She tried not to think of anything beyond the lab work. She had to be finished and long gone by dawn. Her head pounded; she was dead tired; she hadn't slept since returning home two days before. But her anger and her grief gave her energy, fed her, kept her going. Pendergast needed the DNA results as soon as possible. She was grateful for the chance to be of use—any use—if it would help catch Bill's murderer.

From a lab refrigerator, she took out a strip of eight PCR tubes: tiny, bullet-shaped sealed plastic containers pre-filled with buffer solution, Taq polymerase, dNTPs, and other reagents. With exquisite care, she used a pair of sterilized tweezers to transfer minuscule samples of the biological material from her test tubes to the PCR tubes, quickly resealing each one as she did so. By the time the machine trilled its readiness, she had filled thirty-two: the maximum the PCR cycler could hold in a single run.

She slipped a few extra tubes into her pocket for later use, then went over the instructions for the third time. She opened the cycler, slotted in the reaction tubes, then closed and locked it down. Setting the controls, she gingerly pressed the start button.

It would take forty thermal cycles, each lasting three minutes, to complete the PCR reaction. Two hours. Then, she knew, she would have to submit the results to gel electrophoresis in order to identify the DNA.

The machine issued another soft chime, and a screen indicated that the first thermal cycle was in progress. Nora sat back, waiting. Only now did she realize how deathly silent it was in the lab. There wasn't even the usual sound of air moving through the circulation system. The room smelled of dust, mold, and the faint sweetness of para-dichlorobenzene from the nearby storage areas.

She glanced up at the clock: twelve twenty-five. She should have brought a book. In the silent lab, she found herself alone with her thoughts—and they were terrible thoughts.

She got up and paced across the lab, returned to the table, sat down, got up once again. She hunted through cupboards for something to read, finding only manuals. She thought of going up to her office, but there was always the danger of running into someone and having to explain why she was in the museum at such a late hour. She had no clearance to be in the PCR lab. She hadn't signed up for it, she hadn't recorded her presence in the log. Even if she had, she wasn't authorized to use the machine . . .

Suddenly she halted, listening. She had heard a noise, or thought she had. Outside the door.

She glanced over to the little window, but there was nothing to see except the dim hallway beyond, illuminated by a lightbulb in a metal cage. The LED in the door's keypad glowed red: it was still locked.

With a groan, she clenched her fists together. It was hopeless: horrible images kept coming, unbidden, sweeping into her consciousness without warning. She squeezed her eyes closed, tightened her fists still further, trying to think of anything but that first glimpse . . . *anything* . . .

Her eyes popped open again. There was that noise again, and this time she identified it: a soft scraping against the lab door. Glancing up quickly, she just caught a shape moving beyond the window. She had the distinct feeling that someone had just looked in on her.

One of the night watchmen? It was possible. With a stab of

anxiety, she wondered if they would report her unauthorized presence. Then she shook her head. If they'd suspected anything, they would have come in and confronted her. How would they know she wasn't supposed to be there? After all, she had her ID and was clearly a curator. It was her mind, playing tricks on her again. It had been doing that ever since . . . She turned her eyes away from the window. Maybe she *was* going crazy.

The sound came again, and her eyes shot back toward the window. This time, she saw a dark silhouette of a head bobbing in the hallway beyond, swaying a little, backlit and indistinct. It loomed in the little window—and then, as it pressed up against the glass, the light from the lab revealed its features.

She caught her breath, blinked, and stared again.

It was Colin Fearing.

17

Nora jumped back with a cry. The face vanished.

She felt her heart accelerate, thudding in her chest. There was no question this time. *This was no dream.*

She scrambled backward, looking around wildly for a place to hide, and ducked behind a lab table, gasping for breath.

There was no sound. The lab, and the hallway beyond, were utterly silent. She thought: *This is stupid. The door's locked. He can't get in.* A minute passed. As she crouched there, breathing fast, a strange thing happened. The fear that had instinctively gripped her melted away. Rage began to take its place.

Slowly, she stood up. The window remained empty.

Her hand moved across the tabletop, grasped a Pyrex graduated cylinder, and lifted it from its stand. Then, with a sharp rap, she knocked it against the edge of the stand, shattering its end. More quickly now, she moved to the door, shaking fingers trying to punch in the code. On the third try she got it, threw open the door, and stepped into the hall.

From around the far bend of the hall came the sound of a door closing.

"Fearing!" she cried.

She broke into a run, charging at top speed down the hall and around the corner. The hall was lined with doors, but only one was near the intersection. She seized its handle, found it unlocked, jerked it open.

She fumbled along the wall, felt the banks of light switches, and in two swipes of her hand turned them all on.

Ahead lay a room she had heard of but never seen, one of the museum's most legendary storage areas. It had once been the old power plant; now, the vast space contained the museum's collection of whale skeletons. The enormous bones and skulls, some as large as city buses, hung on chains from the ceiling; had they been set on the floor, their own weight would have caused them to deform and break. Each of the suspended skeletons was draped in plastic sheets that hung, shroud-like, almost to the floor, a seascape of draped bones. Despite the banks of fluorescent bulbs overhead, there were still too few for such a large room, and the lighting had a gauzy, almost submarine quality.

She glanced around, makeshift weapon at the ready. To the left, a few of the sheets were swaying, as if recently disturbed.

"Fearing!"

Her voice echoed weirdly in the cavernous vault. She ran toward the nearest shrouds, then slipped between them. The great skeletons cast strange shadows in the indistinct light, and the plastic sheets, dirty and stiff, formed a maze-like set of curtains that prevented her from seeing more than a few feet in any direction. She was almost gasping with mingled tension and rage.

She reached out and jerked aside a curtain of plastic. Nothing.

She stepped forward, pulled aside another, and then another. Now the plastic shrouds that surrounded her were swaying crazily, as if the giant skeletons within had come to restless life.

"*Bastard!* Show yourself!"

A rustle—and then she saw a shadow move swiftly against the plastic. She lunged forward, slashing with the cylinder.

Nothing.

Suddenly she could take it no longer and ran forward with a cry, batting aside curtain after curtain, sweeping the broken glass tube before her in wild arcs, until she became tangled in the heavy plastic and had to struggle to free herself. The fit passing, she took a few more steps, listening. At first all she heard were her own gasps of breath. But then she made out, quite distinctly, a shuffling sound to her right. She rushed toward it, slashing and lunging, preparing to call out again.

Then, abruptly, she stopped. A voice of reason began to penetrate her red haze of fury. This was stupid—very stupid. She had allowed her anger to cloud her judgment.

She stopped to listen again. A scrape, a flitting shadow, more swaying sheets. She spun toward it. Then she paused, licking lips that had suddenly gone dry. In the dim light, surrounded by countless hulking, shrouded skeletons, she asked herself a question: who was hunting . . . and who was the hunted?

Her anger dissipated abruptly, replaced by mounting anxiety as she realized what had happened. Fearing had been unable to get into her locked lab. Instead, he had drawn her out. And now she'd allowed herself to be lured into this maze.

Suddenly, a knife slashed through a nearby plastic curtain, creating a huge rend. A figure began coming through the gap. Nora whirled toward it, slashed at it with the jagged end of the cylinder, made glancing contact. But the figure struck her makeshift weapon away with his knife, sending the glass tube crashing to the floor.

She backed up, staring at him.

Fearing's clothes were tattered, stinking, stiff with old blood. One livid eye stared at her; the other was whitish, dead looking. The mouth yawned open, exposing a mouth packed with black, carious teeth. His hair was full of dirt and leaves. His skin was sallow and smelled of the grave. With a wet snoring sound, he took a step forward and slashed at her, the knife—a knife she recognized too well—moving in a glittering arc.

Nora twisted aside as the weapon swept past, losing her balance and falling to the ground. The figure advanced as she took up a large piece of broken glass and scrambled backward.

The mouth yawned wide, making a horrible, gurgling sound.

"Get away from me!" she screamed, brandishing the shard of glass and rising to her feet.

The figure shambled forward, slashing clumsily at her. Nora backed up, then turned and ran, thrashing through the curtains of plastic as she tried to fight her way to the rear of the room. Surely she would find a back door. Behind her, she could hear the figure cutting through the plastic, the knife almost shrieking as it nicked hanging bones.

Shhchrroooggggnnn. The figure made horrible sounds as it drew in ragged breaths through a wet windpipe. She cried out in fear and dismay, her voice echoing crazily in the cavernous gloom.

She was disoriented now, unsure she was going in the right direction. She fought against the plastic, struggling for breath, getting entangled again, finally throwing herself to the ground and crawling frantically under the rustling, swinging shrouds. She had become completely lost.

Sssshrrooogggnnn, came the awful, sucking noise behind her.

In desperation, she stood up underneath the plastic drape of a low-hanging skeleton, reached up and seized a whale's rib bone, then swung herself up, crawling into the rib cage as if it were some monstrous piece of playground equipment. She climbed frantically, the desiccated bones swaying and clacking together, until she had reached the top of the rib cage. Here a slot between two ribs was big enough to squeeze through. She slashed a hole in the covering plastic with the piece of glass, then hauled herself between the bones and through the plastic, clambering onto the back of the skeleton. For a moment, despite everything, she paused, frozen by the bizarre sight: a sea of whale skeletons, large and small, hanging in all directions beneath her, arranged so close together they were touching.

The skeleton beneath her feet began to sway again. She looked down. Fearing was below her, climbing up into the jungle gym of bones.

With a groan of fear, she ran as quickly as she dared along the top of the skeleton, crouched, then jumped to the next, grabbing on tight as it swayed crazily beneath her. She ran along the second backbone, jumping to a third skeleton. From here, she could just make out a door at the far end of the hall.

Please let it be unlocked.

The hideous figure appeared on top of a skeleton, rearing out of the rend in the plastic. It scuttled forward, leaping from one skeleton to the next, and Nora realized that despite its shambling movements it was more agile than she had realized. All she had accomplished by climbing atop the skeletons was to give it an advantage.

Slashing another hole in the plastic beneath her, she climbed back down, then dropped to the floor, crawling as fast as she could toward the rear of the vault. Behind, she could hear Fearing thrashing his way after her, the horrifying sucking sounds growing louder.

Suddenly she broke free of the mass of bones. There, no more than ten feet ahead of her, was the door: heavy and old-fashioned, without a security keypad. She ran for it, grasped the handle.

Locked.

With a sob of dismay she turned, setting her back against the door and clutching the sliver of glass, ready to make a last stand.

The skeletons swayed and creaked on their chains, the agitated curtains of plastic restlessly scraping the ground. She waited, preparing herself as best she could for the final struggle.

A minute went by, then another. Fearing did not appear. Gradually, the rustling and swaying of the skeletons settled down. Silence returned to the storage room.

She took one shuddering breath after another. Had he broken off the chase? Had he gone?

From the far side of the storage room, she heard the creak of a door, shuffling footsteps, and then silence.

No, no. He hadn't gone.

"Who's in here?" a voice rang out, quavering slightly with ill-suppressed anxiety. "Show yourself!"

It was a night guard. Nora almost sobbed with relief. Fearing must have heard approaching footsteps and been frightened off. But she held her breath. She couldn't reveal herself now; not while her DNA analysis was in process.

"Anybody here?" the guard called out, clearly reluctant to advance into that forest of whale skeletons. The feeble beam of a light played about the dimly lit room.

"Last call, I'm locking the door."

Nora didn't care. As a curator, she had the security code to the front door.

"All right, you asked for it."

A shuffling, the lights went out, and then the slamming of a door.

Slowly, Nora got her breathing under control. She dropped to her knees and peered forward in the dim light trickling in from the small window set into the door.

Was he, like her, still in the room? Was he waiting, ready to ambush? What did he want—to finish the job he'd failed to finish in the apartment?

Dropping to her hands and knees, she crawled under the now-still plastic, moving slowly, as quietly as possible, heading for the front door. Every few minutes, she stopped to peer around and listen. But there were no sounds, no shadows—just the great hanging whale bones in their shrouds.

As she reached the middle of the skeletons, she paused in her journey. She could see the faint glimmer of a scattering of broken glass. The rest of her makeshift weapon, broken to pieces. In the gloom, she made out a faint dark streak along the glistening edge of one large shard. So she *had* struck Fearing with the glass—and cut him. That was blood . . . *his* blood.

She drew in a breath, then another, trying to think as clearly as possible. Then, with shaking fingers, she withdrew one of the spare reaction tubes she'd shoved into her pocket. Carefully breaking the sterile seal, she picked up the glass, dipped it into the liquid, and resealed the tube. Pendergast had already given her DNA samples from Fearing's mother, and mother–son mitochondrial DNA were always identical. Now she could test his DNA and compare it directly with the unknown DNA recovered from the crime scene.

She slipped the tube back in her pocket and made her way—quietly and carefully—to the door. It responded to the code and opened. She closed and locked it quickly behind her, then walked on shaky legs down the corridor and back to the PCR lab. There was no sign of Fearing. Entering the code into the keypad, she slipped into the lab, shut the door behind her, and turned off the overhead light. She'd finish her work by the glow of the instrumentation.

The thermal cycler was halfway done with its pass. Her heart still thumping, Nora racked the tube with her attacker's blood next to the others, ready for the next run.

By tomorrow night, she would know for sure whether or not it was really Fearing who had killed her husband—and tried to kill her twice.

18

D'Agosta entered the waiting room for the morgue annex, careful to breathe through his mouth. Pendergast followed, taking in the room with a quick glance, then slipping cat-like into one of the ugly plastic chairs that lined the wall, flanking a table heaped with dog-eared magazines. The agent picked up the one with the lightest wear, flipped through the pages, then began to read.

D'Agosta made a circuit of the room, then another. The New York City morgue was a place full of horrible memories for him, and he knew he was about to undergo an experience that would lodge another in his head—perhaps the worst one of all. Pendergast's preternatural coolness irritated him. How could he remain so nonchalant? He glanced over and saw the agent was reading *Mademoiselle* with evident interest.

"What are you reading that for?" D'Agosta asked irritably.

"There is an instructive article on bad first dates. It reminds me of a case I once had: a particularly untoward first date that ended in murder-suicide." Pendergast shook his head at the memory and continued reading.

D'Agosta hugged himself, then took yet another turn around the room.

"Vincent, do sit down. Use your time constructively."

"I hate this place. I hate the smell of it. I hate the *look* of it."

"I quite sympathize. The intimations of mortality here are—shall we say—hard to ignore? *Thoughts that do often lie too deep for tears.*"

The pages rustled as Pendergast read on. A few dreadful minutes passed before the door to the morgue finally opened. One of the pathologists, Beckstein, stood there. *Thank God*, thought D'Agosta: they had pulled Beckstein for the autopsy. He was one of the best and—surprise—an almost normal human being.

Beckstein peeled off his gloves and mask, dropped them in a bin. "Lieutenant. Agent Pendergast." He nodded his greetings, not offering his hand. Shaking hands just wasn't done in the morgue. "I'm at your disposal."

"Dr. Beckstein," said D'Agosta, taking the lead, "thanks for taking the time to see us."

"My pleasure."

"Give us a rundown, light on the jargon, please."

"Certainly. Would you like to observe the cadaver? The prosector is still working on it. It sometimes helps to see—"

"No thank you," said D'Agosta decisively.

He felt Pendergast's gaze on him. *Screw it,* he thought determinedly.

"As you wish. The cadaver showed fourteen full or partial knife wounds, pre-mortem, some to the hands and arms, several in the lower back, and a final one, also with a posterior entry, that passed through the heart. I would be glad to provide you with a diagram—"

"Not necessary. Any postmortem wounds?"

"None. Death was almost immediate after the final, fatal blow to the heart. The knife entered horizontally, between the second and third posterior rib, at a downward angle of eighty degrees from the vertical, penetrating the left atrium, the pulmonary artery, and splitting the conus arteriosus at the top of the right ventricle, causing massive exsanguination."

"I get the picture."

"Right."

"Would you say that the killer did what he had to do to kill the victim, and no more?"

"That statement is consistent with the facts, yes."

"The weapon?"

"A blade ten inches long, two inches in width, very stiff, probably a high-quality kitchen knife or a scuba knife."

D'Agosta nodded. "Anything else?"

"Blood toxicology showed a blood alcohol level within legal limits. No drugs or other foreign substances. The contents of the stomach—"

"I don't need to know that."

Beckstein hesitated, and D'Agosta saw something in his eyes. Uncertainty, unease.

"Yeah?" he urged. "Something else?"

"Yes. I haven't written the report yet, but there was one thing, quite strange, that was missed by the forensic team."

"Go on."

The pathologist hesitated again. "I'd like to show it to you. We haven't moved it—yet."

D'Agosta swallowed. "What was it?"

"Please, just let me show it to you. I can't . . . well, I can't very well describe it."

"Of course," said Pendergast, stepping forward. "Vincent, if you'd prefer to wait here—?"

D'Agosta felt his jaw set. "I'm coming."

They followed the technician through the set of double stainless-steel doors into the green light of a large tiled room. They donned masks, gloves, and scrubs from nearby bins, then continued on, passing into one of the autopsy suites.

Immediately D'Agosta saw the prosector hunched over the cadaver, the whine of the Stryker saw in his hands like an angry mosquito. A diener lounged nearby, eating a bagel with lox. A second dissecting table was covered with various tagged organs. D'Agosta swallowed again, harder.

"Hey," the diener said to Beckstein. "You're just in time. We were about to run the gut."

A hard stare from Beckstein silenced the man. "Sorry. Didn't know you had guests." He smirked, rubbery lips crunching down on his breakfast. The room smelled of formalin, fish, and feces.

Beckstein turned to the prosector. "John, I'd like to show Lieutenant D'Agosta and Special Agent Pendergast the, ah, item we found."

"No problem." The saw powered down and the prosector stepped away. With huge reluctance, D'Agosta stepped slowly forward, then looked down at the cadaver.

It was worse than he had ever imagined it could be. Worse even than his worst nightmares. Bill Smithback: naked, dead, opened. His scalp was peeled back, the brown hair all bunched up at the base, bloody skull exposed, fresh saw marks running in a semicircle around the cranium. Body cavity yawning, ribs spread, organs removed.

He bowed his head and closed his eyes.

"John, would you mind fixing a spreader in the mouth?"

"Not at all."

D'Agosta kept his eyes closed.

"There."

He opened his eyes. The mouth had been forced open with a piece of stainless steel. Beckstein adjusted the overhead light to illuminate the interior. Hooked into Smithback's tongue was a fishhook, tied with feathers, like a dry fly. Against his will, D'Agosta bent forward for a closer examination. The hook had a knotted head of light-colored twine, on which had been painted a tiny, grinning skull. A miniature pouch, like a tiny pill, was attached to the hook's neck.

D'Agosta glanced over at Pendergast. The agent was staring down at the open mouth, his silvery eyes full of rare intensity. And it seemed to D'Agosta there was more than intensity in that look. There was regret, disbelief, sorrow—and uncertainty. Pendergast's shoulders slumped visibly. It was as if the agent had been hoping against hope he'd been wrong about something . . . only to learn with huge dismay that, in fact, he had been all too right.

The silence lasted minutes. Finally, D'Agosta turned to Beckstein. He suddenly felt very old and tired. "I want this photographed and tested. Remove it with the tongue—leave it embedded. I want forensics to analyze that thing, open up the tiny pouch, and report its contents to me."

The diener peered over D'Agosta's shoulder, chewing his bagel. "Looks like we got a real psychopath running around. Think what the *Post* would do with this one!" A loud crunch, followed by the sounds of mastication.

D'Agosta turned to him. "If the *Post* finds out," he growled, "I'll personally see to it you spend the rest of your life toasting bagels instead of eating them."

"Hey, sorry, man. Touchy, touchy." The diener backed away.

Pendergast's eyes flickered up at D'Agosta. He straightened up and stepped away from the corpse. "Vincent, it occurs to me that I haven't paid a visit to my dear aunt Cornelia in ages. Would you care to accompany me?"

19

Nora turned the key in the deadbolt and pushed her apartment door open. It was two in the afternoon, and the low-angle sunlight flooded through the blinds and illuminated—pitilessly—every last fragment of her life with Bill. Books, paintings, objets d'art, even carelessly thrown magazines: each brought back a flood of unwanted, painful memories. Double-locking the front door, she walked, eyes down, through the living room and into the bedroom.

Her work on the PCR machine was complete. The DNA samples supplied by Pendergast had each been multiplied by millions, and she had stashed the test tubes in the rear of the lab refrigerator where nobody would notice them. She had then put in a respectable day in the anthropology lab. No one minded that she'd left early. Tonight, at one, she would return for the second and final stage: the gel electrophoresis test. In the meantime, she desperately needed sleep.

Dropping her bag unceremoniously on the floor, she threw herself on the bed and covered her head with pillows. And yet, though she lay motionless, sleep refused to come. An hour went by, then two, and finally she gave up. She might as well have stayed at the museum. Perhaps she should return there now.

Nora glanced over at her answering machine: twenty-two messages. Additional expressions of sympathy, no doubt. She simply could not bear to hear any more. With a sigh, she pressed the replay button, deleting each message as soon as she heard a note of concern sound in the caller's voice.

The seventh message was different. It was from the *West Sider* reporter.

"Dr. Kelly? It's Caitlyn Kidd. Listen, I was just wondering if you'd found out anything more about those animal stories Bill was working on. I read the ones he published. They're very hard hitting. I was curious if he'd found out anything new that he hadn't had time to publish—or maybe that someone didn't *want* him to publish. Call me when you get the chance."

As the next message started, Nora pressed the stop button. She stared thoughtfully at the machine a moment. Then she rose from the bed, walked back into the living room, sat down at the desk, and booted up her laptop. She didn't know Caitlyn Kidd, didn't especially trust Caitlyn Kidd. But she'd work with the devil himself if he could help her track down the people behind Bill's death.

She stared at the screen, took a deep breath. Then—quickly, before she could reconsider—she logged into her husband's private account at the *New York Times.* The password was accepted: the account had not yet been deactivated. A minute later, she was staring at an index of articles he'd written over the last year. Sorting them chronologically, she moused back several months, then began scrolling forward through them, examining the titles. It was remarkable how many sounded unfamiliar, and now she bitterly regretted not being more involved in his work.

The first topical story on animal sacrifice had been published about three months back. It was primarily a background piece on how, far from being a thing of the distant past, animal sacrifice was still being actively—if secretly—practiced in the city. She continued moving forward. There were several other articles: an interview with somebody named Alexander Esteban, spokesman for Humans for Other Animals; an investigative piece on cockfighting in Brooklyn. Then Nora came upon the most recent article, published two weeks before, titled "For Manhattanites, Animal Sacrifice Hits Close to Home."

She brought up the text and scanned it quickly, her eye hovering over one paragraph in particular:

> The most persistent stories of animal sacrifice come from Inwood, the northernmost neighborhood of Manhattan. A number of complaints have reached police and animal welfare agencies from the Indian Road and West 214th Street neighborhoods, in which residents claim to have heard the sounds of animals in distress. These animal cries, which residents describe as coming from goats, chickens, and sheep, allegedly issue from a deconsecrated church building at the center of a reclusive community in Inwood Hill Park known familiarly as "the Ville." Efforts to speak to residents of the Ville and its community leader, Eugene Bossong, were unsuccessful.

With this discovery, it seemed that Bill had secured the paper's backing for still further investigation, because the article concluded with an italicized note:

> *This is one of a continuing series of articles on animal sacrifice in New York City.*

Nora sat back. Now that she thought about it, she did remember Bill coming home one evening a week or so ago, crowing about some minor coup he'd achieved in his ongoing work on the animal sacrifices story.

Perhaps the coup hadn't been so minor, after all.

Nora frowned at the screen. It had been around then that the strange little artifacts had begun showing up in their mailbox, and the creepy designs inscribed in dust started appearing outside their front door.

Closing the index of articles, she opened up Bill's information management software, scanning for the notes he always kept for upcoming stories. The most recent entries were what she was looking for.

> Concentrate on the Ville—follow up in next article. ARE THESE REALLY ANIMAL SACRIFICES? Need to PROVE IT—no allegations. Review police files. SEE with own eyes.
>
> Write up Pizzetti interview. Other neighbors who've complained? Schedule second interview with Esteban, animal rights guy? Local PETA chapter, etc.
>
> Where obtaining animals?
>
> What is history of Ville? Who are they? Check *Times* morgue for Ville backstory/history. Good color: rumors of zombies(zombiis?)/ cults/etc. (Check w/ copydesk correct spelling zombie/zombiis.)
>
> Possible article title: "Ville d'Evil?" Nah, *Times* would nix.
>
> *First anniversary—don't forget reservation at Café des Artistes & tickets to *The Man Who Came to Dinner* for the weekend!!!!

This final entry was so unexpected, so out of context with the others, that in a defenseless moment Nora felt hot tears spring to her eyes. She immediately closed the program and stood up from the desk.

She paced the living room once, then glanced at her watch: four fifteen. She could catch the train at 96th and Central Park West and be in Inwood in forty minutes. Firing up a new program on the computer, she typed briefly, examined the screen, then sent a document to the printer. Striding into the bedroom, she plucked her bag from the floor; took a quick look around; then headed for the front door.

A quarter of an hour before, she had felt rudderless, adrift. Now—suddenly—she found herself filled with overwhelming purpose.

20

D'Agosta had brought an entire squad along—twelve armed and uniformed officers—and the elevator was filled to capacity. He pressed the button for thirty-seven, then turned his gaze to the illuminated display above the doors. He felt calm and cool. No, that was wrong: he felt cold. Ice cold.

He believed he was basically a fair human being. If somebody treated him with even a modicum of respect, he'd reciprocate. But when somebody acted like a dick, that was a different story. Lucas Kline had been a dick—a Grade A, first-class, USDA Choice dick. And now he was going to learn what a bad idea it was to really piss off a cop.

He turned to the squad. "Remember the briefing," he said. "I want this thorough. Thorough and dirty. Work in teams of two—I don't want any problems with the chain of evidence. And if you encounter any shit, any obstructionism, anything at all, shut it down fast and hard."

A murmur rippled through the group, followed by a chorus of snaps and clicks as Maglites were checked and batteries slotted into cordless screwdrivers.

The elevator doors opened on the expansive lobby of Digital Veracity. It was late in the afternoon—four thirty—but D'Agosta noticed there were still a couple of clients seated on the leather sofas, waiting for appointments.

Good.

He stepped out of the elevator and into the center of the lobby, the team spreading out behind him. "I'm Lieutenant D'Agosta of the NYPD," he said in a loud, clear voice. "I have a search warrant to execute on these premises." He glanced toward the waiting clients. "I would suggest you come back some other time."

They stood quickly, white-faced, scooped up their jackets and briefcases, and scampered gratefully for the elevator bank. D'Agosta turned to the receptionist. "Why don't you go downstairs and get yourself a cup of coffee?"

In fifteen seconds, the lobby was empty except for D'Agosta and his squad. "We'll use this as a staging area," he said. "Leave the evidence boxes here and let's get started." He pointed to the sergeants. "I want you three with me."

It was the work of sixty seconds to reach Kline's outer office. D'Agosta glanced at the frightened-looking secretary. "Nothing more's going to get done here today," he said quietly, smiling at her. "Why don't you knock off early?"

He waited until she had gone. Then he opened the door to the inner office. Kline was once again on the phone, his feet on the broad desk. When he saw D'Agosta and the uniformed officers, he nodded, as if unsurprised. "I'll have to call you back," he said into the phone.

"Take all the computers," D'Agosta told the sergeants. Then he turned to the software developer. "I've got a search warrant here." He pushed it toward Kline's face, then let it drop to the floor. "Oops. There it is, you can read it when you've got time."

"I thought you might be back, D'Agosta," Kline said. "I've had a talk with my lawyers. That search warrant has to specify what it is you're looking for."

"Oh, it does. We're looking for evidence that Bill Smithback's murder was either planned, committed, or perhaps paid for by you."

"And why, precisely, would I plan, commit, or pay for such an act?"

"Because of a psychotic rage against high-profile journalists—such as the one that got you fired from your first job on a newspaper."

Kline's eyes narrowed ever so slightly.

"The information could be concealed in any of these offices," D'Agosta continued. "We'll have to search the entire suite."

"It could be anywhere," Kline replied. "It could be at my home."

"That's where we'll be going next." D'Agosta sat down. "But you're right—it *could* be anywhere. That's why I'll have to confiscate all CDs, DVDs, hard disks, PDAs, anything on the premises that can store information. You have a BlackBerry?"

"Yes."

"Now it's evidence. Hand it over, please."

Kline reached his hand into his pocket, pulled out the device, laid it on his desk.

D'Agosta glanced around. One of the sergeants was taking paintings off the cherrywood walls, carefully scrutinizing their backs, then placing them on the floor. Another was plucking books off the shelves, holding them by the spines and shaking them, then dropping them onto growing piles. The third was pulling the expensive rugs from the floor, searching underneath, then leaving them bunched up in a corner. Watching, D'Agosta reflected how convenient it was that no law required you to clean up after a search.

From other offices down the hallway, he could hear drawers slamming, dragging noises, crying, voices raised in protest. The sergeant had finished with the rugs and was starting in on the file cabinets, opening them, removing manila folders, leafing through them, then dumping the papers onto the floor. The sergeant who'd examined the oil paintings was now dismantling the PCs on the desk. "I need those for my business," Kline said.

"They're mine now. Hope you backed everything up." This reminded D'Agosta of something—something Pendergast had recommended. "Would you mind loosening your tie?" he asked.

Kline frowned. "What?"

"Indulge me, please."

Kline hesitated. Then, slowly, he reached up and tugged down his tie.

"Now unbutton the top button of your shirt and spread the collar."

"What are you up to, D'Agosta?" Kline asked, doing as instructed.

D'Agosta peered at the scrawny neck. "That cord—draw it out, please."

Even more slowly, Kline reached in and pulled out the cord. Sure enough: dangling from its end was a small flash drive.

"I'll take that, please."

"It's encrypted," Kline said.

"I'll take it anyway."

Kline stared. "You'll regret this, Lieutenant."

"You'll get it back." And D'Agosta held out his hand. Kline raised it over his head and placed it on the desk beside the BlackBerry. His expression, his manner, betrayed nothing. The only sign of what might be going on inside his head was a faint rising of pink on his acne-scarred cheeks.

D'Agosta looked around. "We'll need to take some of these African masks and statues, as well."

"Why?"

"They may relate to certain, ah, exotic elements of the case."

Kline began to speak, stopped, began again. "They are extremely valuable works of art, Lieutenant."

"We won't break anything."

The sergeant had finished with the books and was now unscrewing ceiling ducts with a screwgun. D'Agosta stood up, walked to the closet, opened the door. Today Chauncy was absent. He glanced back at Kline. "Do you have a safe?"

"In the far office."

"Let's take a walk, shall we?"

The journey down the hallway took in half a dozen scenes of devastation. His team was disassembling monitors, searching cabinets with Maglites, pulling drawers out of desks. Kline's employees had assembled in the lobby, where an ever-growing mountain of paper stood beside the evidence boxes. Kline looked left and right with hooded eyes. The pinkish cast to his face had deepened somewhat. "Vincent D'Agosta," he said as they walked. "Do your pals call you Vinnie?"

"Some of them do."

"Vinnie, I believe we might have friends in common."

"I don't think so."

"Well, the person I'm referring to isn't exactly a friend as of yet. But I feel as though I know her. Laura Hayward."

It took all the force of will D'Agosta could muster not to check his stride.

"You see, I've done quite a bit of looking into that girlfriend of yours—or ex-girlfriend, I should say. What's the matter, Viagra no longer working?"

D'Agosta kept his eyes locked straight ahead.

"Still, my sources say you two are close. Boy, does she have a great career. She could make commissioner someday, if she plays her cards right . . ."

At last, D'Agosta stopped. "Let me tell you something, Mr. Kline. If you think you can threaten or intimidate Captain Hayward, you're sadly mistaken. She could crush you like a roach. And if, in her infinite mercy, she decides to spare you—rest assured that I won't. Now, if you'd show me to the safe, please?"

Nora exited the subway at the 207th Street station. She walked to the north end of the platform, then climbed the stairs to street level, where she found a three-way confluence of streets: Broadway, Isham, and West 211th. This was a neighborhood she had never been in before, the northernmost tip of Manhattan, and she looked around curiously. The buildings reminded her of Harlem: prewar walkups, attractive and sturdily built. There were few brownstones or town houses: dollar stores, bodegas, and nail salons sat cheek-by-jowl with funky restaurants and whole-grain bakeries. Nearby, she knew, was Dyckman House: the last remaining Dutch Colonial farmhouse in Manhattan. It was a place she had always intended to visit with Bill some sunny weekend afternoon.

She pushed this thought from her mind. Checking the document she had printed earlier—a satellite view of the neighborhood, with the street names marked—she got her bearings and began making her way north and west, along Isham, climbing the rise toward Seaman Avenue and the setting sun.

She crossed broad, busy Seaman Avenue and continued down an asphalt path, tennis courts to her left and a large baseball diamond to her right. She paused. Ahead of her, across the fields, lay what appeared to be primeval forest. The map showed an extension of Indian Road passing through the northern end of Inwood Hill Park, which connected to a tight little unmarked neighborhood she assumed must be the Ville. The path was more direct and, she felt, perhaps more secure. It crossed the field and disappeared into a dark tangle of red oaks and tulip trees, their long shadows knitting together amid the rocky undergrowth. Their leaves glowed with autumnal glory, russet and yellow, with splashes of blood red, forming an almost impenetrable wall. She had heard this was the last wild forest in Manhattan, and it looked it.

Nora glanced at her watch: five thirty. Night was falling quickly and the air had taken on an almost frosty chill. She took a step forward, then stopped again, glancing uncertainly into the gloomy forest. She had never been in Inwood Hill Park before—in fact, she didn't know anybody who had—and she had no idea how safe it was after dark. Hadn't a jogger been murdered in here a few years back . . . ?

Her jaw set in a hard line. She hadn't come all this way just to turn back now. There was still plenty of light left. Shaking her head impatiently, she started forward, leaning toward the wall of trees almost as if challenging them to stop her.

The path curved gently to the right, running past a small grassy field before diving between the first massive trunks. Nora walked on quickly, feeling the shadow of the heavy boughs fall over her. The path split, then split again, the tarmac webbed with grassy cracks, plastered with fallen leaves, the bushes on either side crowding into the path. She passed an occasional gas lamp, once clearly elegant but now rusted and long disused. The oaks and tulip trees—some with trunks as massive as five feet across—were punctuated by dogwoods and ginkgos. Here and there, a rocky defile thrust up from the forest floor like the edge of a knife.

Soon the paved path gave way to a dirt track that wound its way sinuously among the trunks, climbing all the while. Through a gap in the trees, Nora could make out a steep slope plunging to a tidal basin, thick with mud and populated by noisy seabirds. Their cries followed her faintly as she continued climbing the winding path, her feet kicking aside drifts of fallen leaves.

After about fifteen minutes, she stopped at the foot of an ancient retaining wall, crumbling into ruin. The roar of Manhattan had receded to the sound of wind sighing in trees. The sun had fallen behind the rise of land, and an angry orange glow suffused the October sky. The chill of night was coming down. Nora glanced at the hardwoods crowding in around her, at the glacial boulders and kettle holes scattered treacherously about. It seemed almost impossible that two hundred acres of such wild forest existed here on the most urban of all islands. Nearby, she knew, were the remains of the old Straus mansion. Isidor Straus had been a congressman and co-owner of Macy's. After he and his wife died on the *Titanic,* their country house in Inwood Hill Park had gradually fallen into ruin. Perhaps this very retaining wall had once been part of the estate.

The path continued to drift westward, away from the direction she needed to go. She peered at the satellite map in the dying light and then, hesitating only a moment longer, decided to bushwhack northward. She left the trail and began pushing through the sparse undergrowth, away from the trail.

The land pitched sharply upward, shelves of exposed gneiss cropping out here and there. She scrambled up the defile, hands grabbing for purchase on bushes and small trunks. Her fingers were very cold now, and she bitterly regretted not bringing gloves. She slipped, falling onto a striated rib of rock. She clambered back to her feet with a curse, brushed the leaves off, slung her bag back over her shoulder, and listened. There were no sounds of birds or rustles of squirrels, only the gentle sigh of the wind. The air smelled of dead leaves and damp earth. After a moment, she scrambled on, feeling increasingly alone in the wooded stillness.

This was crazy. It was getting dark a lot faster than she'd thought.

Already the lights of Manhattan had drowned out the last of the twilight, casting an eerie glow across the sky, the black silhouettes of the half-bare trees outlined against it, giving the scene the unreality of a Magritte painting, bright above, dark below. Ahead, at the top of the defile, Nora could make out the ridgeline, studded with spectral trees. Quickly now, she half ran, half scrambled toward it. Gaining the height of land, she paused a moment to catch her breath. An old, rusting chain-link fence ran east to west, but it was bowed and twisted from neglect, and Nora soon found a loose section and ducked beneath easily. She took a few steps forward, angled her way around a set of massive boulders—and then stopped again abruptly.

The vista that lay ahead took her breath away. Before her feet, the ground fell away in a cliff, ramparts of rock dropping toward the tidal waters. She had reached the uttermost tip of Manhattan. Far below, the waters of the Harlem River were black, running westward around the Spuyten Duyvil to the great vast opening of the Hudson River, the color of dark steel in the dying light, a vast waterscape glittering beneath a rising gibbous moon. Beyond the Hudson, the high cliffs of the Jersey Palisades stood black against the final light of sunset; in the middle ground, the Henry Hudson Parkway arched over the Harlem River on a graceful bridge, arrowing northward into the Bronx. A solid stream of yellow headlights flowed over it, commuters heading home from the city. Directly across the water was Riverdale, almost as thickly wooded here as Inwood Hill Park itself. And to the east, beyond the Harlem River, lay the smoky flanks of the Bronx, pierced by a dozen bridges, afire with a million lights. The landscape formed a confusing, bizarre, and magnificent spectacle of geologic majesty: a sprawling tableau of the primeval and the cosmopolitan, thrown together with supreme capriciousness over the course of the city's centuries of growth.

But Nora admired it for only a moment. Because, looking down again, a quarter mile away and a hundred feet below, she saw—half hidden in a thick knot of woods—a cluster of grimy brick buildings, dotted with the faint twinkle of yellow lights. They sat on a flat shelf of land, perched halfway between a ragged, trash-strewn pebble beach along the Harlem River and her own vantage spot atop the ridge. It was unreachable from her cliff—in fact, she wasn't quite sure how it could be reached at all, although through the trees she could glimpse a ribbon of asphalt that, she thought, must connect to Indian Road. As she stared, she realized that the surrounding copse of trees would render the community invisible from almost any angle: from the parkway, from the riverbank, from the cliffs on the far shore. At the center of the cluster was a much larger structure, evidently an old church, which had been added on to indiscriminately, again and again, until the whole lost any architectural cohesion. This was tightly surrounded by a tangle of small, ancient timber-frame buildings, divided by deep alleyways.

The Ville: the target of Bill's most recent article. The place he believed to be the main source of animal sacrifice in the city. She stared at it in mingled dread and fascination. The huge structure at its heart looked almost as old as the Manhattan Purchase itself: extravagantly dilapidated, part brick, part chocolate-brown timber, with a squat, crudely built spire rising from behind a massive gambrel roof. While the lower windows were bricked over, the cracked glasswork of the upper stories flickered with a pale yellow glow she felt certain could only be candlelight. The place lay apparently somnolent in the silvery moonlight, now and then falling into deeper darkness as a cloud scudded past.

As she stood, staring at the flickering lights, the craziness of what she had done became clear. Why had she really come—to stare at a bunch of buildings? What could she hope to accomplish here by herself? What made her feel so certain that *the* secret lay within: the secret to her husband's murder?

The Ville remained wrapped in silence as a chilly night breeze stirred the leaves around her.

Nora shivered. Then—wrapping her coat more tightly around her—she turned and began to make her way as quickly as she could back through the dark woods toward the welcoming streets of the city.

22

Strange how there always seems to be fog out here," D'Agosta said as the big Rolls hummed along the one-lane road that crossed Little Governor's Island.

"It must come from the marshes," Pendergast murmured.

D'Agosta looked out the window. The marshes did indeed stretch away into the darkness, exhaling miasmic vapors that curled and moved among the rushes and cattails, the nocturnal skyline of Manhattan rising incongruously in the background. Passing a row of dead trees, they came to a set of iron gates and a bronze plaque.

THE MOUNT MERCY HOSPITAL
FOR THE CRIMINALLY INSANE

The car slowed at the little guardhouse and a uniformed man stepped out of its door. "Good evening, Mr. Pendergast," the guard said, apparently unsurprised by the late hour. "Here to see Miss Cornelia?"

"Good evening to you, Mr. Gott. Yes, thank you. We have an appointment."

A rumble, and the gates began to open. "Have a good night," the guard said.

Proctor eased the car through and they approached the main

house: an immense Gothic Revival building in brown brick, standing like a grim sentinel among dark, heavy fir trees, sagging under the weight of their ancient branches.

Proctor swung into the visitors' parking lot. Within minutes, D'Agosta found himself following a doctor down the hospital's long, tiled halls. Mount Mercy had once been New York's largest tuberculosis sanatorium. Now it had been converted into a high-security hospital for murderers and other violent criminals found not guilty by reason of insanity.

"How is she?" Pendergast asked.

"The same" came the terse answer.

Two guards joined them and they continued down the echoing corridors, finally stopping at a steel door with a barred window. A guard unlocked the door, and they entered the small "quiet room" beyond. D'Agosta remembered the room from his first visit here, with Laura Hayward, last January. It seemed like years ago, but the room hadn't changed an iota, with its plastic furniture bolted to the floor, its green walls devoid of pictures or decoration.

The two attendants disappeared through a heavy metal door in the rear of the room. A minute or two later, D'Agosta made out a faint creaking noise approaching, and then one of the guards pushed a wheelchair into the room. The old lady was dressed with Victorian severity, in deep mourning, her black taffeta dress and black lace rustling with every move, but D'Agosta could see underneath a white-canvas, five-point restraint.

"Raise my veil" came the querulous command. One of the attendants did as ordered. A remarkably seamed face, alive with malice, was revealed. A pair of small black eyes, which somehow reminded D'Agosta of the beady eyes of a snake, raked over him. She gave a faint smile of sardonic recognition. Then the glittering eyes fell on Pendergast.

The agent took a step forward.

"Mr. Pendergast?" came the edgy voice of the doctor. "I'm sure I don't have to remind you to respect your distance."

At the sound of the name, the old lady seemed to startle. "Why," she cried in a suddenly strong voice, "how are you, Diogenes, my dear? What a *charming* surprise!" She turned to the nearest attendant and rapped out in a shrill voice, "Bring out the best Amontillado. Diogenes has paid us a visit." She turned and smiled broadly, her face wrinkling grotesquely. "Or would you prefer tea, dearest Diogenes?"

"Nothing, thank you," said Pendergast, his voice cool. "It is Aloysius, Aunt Cornelia, not Diogenes."

"Nonsense! Diogenes, you bad thing, don't try to tease an old woman. Don't you think I know my own nephew?"

Pendergast hesitated a moment. "I never could fool you, Aunt. We were in the area and thought we'd drop in."

"How lovely. Yes, I see you brought my brother Ambergris with you."

Pendergast glanced over at D'Agosta briefly before nodding.

"I have a few minutes before I have to start preparing for the dinner party. You know how it is with servants these days. I should fire them all and do it myself."

"Indeed."

D'Agosta waited as Pendergast engaged his aunt in what seemed like interminable small talk. Slowly, the agent brought the conversation back to his own childhood in New Orleans.

"I wonder if you remember that, ah, *unpleasantness* with Marie LeBon, one of the downstairs servants," he asked at last. "We children used to call her Miss Marie."

"The one who looked like a broomstick? I never liked her. She gave me the heebie-jeebies." And Aunt Cornelia gave a delicious shudder.

"She was found dead one day, isn't that right?"

"It is most unfortunate when the servants bring scandal into the house. And Marie was the worst of the lot. Except, of course, for that dreadful, *dreadful* Monsieur Bertin." The old woman shook her head in distaste and muttered something under her breath.

"Can you tell me what happened with Miss Marie? I was just a child then."

"Marie was from the bayou, a promiscuous woman, like so many of the swamp folk. A mixture of French Acadian and Micmac Indian, and who knows what else besides. She got to fooling around with the groom, who was married—you remember, Diogenes, that groom with the pompadour who fancied himself a gentleman? The man was as common as dirt."

She looked around. "Where is my drink? Gaston!"

One of the attendants lifted a Dixie cup to her lips, and she sucked daintily through the straw. "I prefer gin, as you know," she said.

"Yes, ma'am," said the attendant, with a smirk at his partner.

"What happened?" Pendergast asked.

"The groom's wife—God bless her—didn't care for Marie LeBon congressing with her husband. She wreaked her revenge." She cackled. "Settled her hash with a meat cleaver. I didn't think she had it in her."

"The jealous wife's name was Mrs. Ducharme."

"Mrs. Ducharme! A big woman with arms like French hams. She knew how to swing that cleaver!"

"Mr. Pendergast?" said the doctor. "I have warned you about these types of interviews before."

Pendergast ignored him. "Wasn't there something strange about the . . . corpse?"

"Strange? What do you mean?"

"The . . . Vôdou aspects."

"Vôdou? Diogenes! It was not Vôdou, but Obeah. There's a difference, you know. Yes, but *of course* you know. Certainly more than your brother does, eh? Though he is no stranger to it, either—is he?" And here the old woman began chuckling unpleasantly.

"We were talking about the corpse—?" Pendergast said by way of encouragement.

"There was something strange, now that you mention it. A bit of gris-gris was pinned to her tongue—*oanga.*"

"*Oanga?* You seem to know a lot about Obeah, Aunt Cornelia."

Suddenly Aunt Cornelia's expression grew wary. "One hears servants talking. Besides, that's a fine thing to say, coming from *you*. Do you think I've forgotten your little—*experiment,* shall we say?—and the unfortunate reaction it provoked from the *mobile vulgus*—"

"Tell me about the *oanga,*" Pendergast interrupted, with the briefest of glances toward D'Agosta.

"Very well. The *oanga,* they said, was a fetish of a skeleton or corpse soaked in a broth made from Shrove Tuesday ashes; bile of a sow; water from a forge used to harden iron; blood of a virgin mouse; and alligator flesh."

"And its purpose?"

"To extract the dead person's soul, make him a slave. A zombii. You of all people know all this, Diogenes!"

"Still, I appreciate hearing it from you, Aunt Cornelia."

"After the corpse is buried, it is supposed to come back as the slave of the person who placed the *oanga*. And do you know what? Six months later, that boy died over on Iberville Street—found suffocated to death in a tied-up sack—and they said it was the zombii of Miss Marie, because the boy had pulled down Mrs. Ducharme's laundry. And then they checked Miss Marie's tomb and found it empty, or so they say. I hardly need add that the Ducharmes were discharged. You can't have servants embarrassing a genteel home."

"Time's up, Mr. Pendergast." The doctor rose with a sense of finality. The attendants sprang to their feet and took their places on either side of her wheelchair. The doctor nodded and they began turning her around, heading for the back door.

Suddenly, Aunt Cornelia swiveled her head back toward them, fixing her gaze on D'Agosta. "You were awfully silent today, Ambergris. Cat got your tongue? Next time, I'll be sure to prepare some of my lovely little watercress sandwiches for you. Your family always adored them."

D'Agosta could only nod. The doctor opened the door for the wheelchair.

"And lovely to see you again, Diogenes," said Aunt Cornelia over her shoulder. "You were always my favorite, you know. I'm so glad you finally did something about that horrid eye of yours."

As they drove past the gates, the headlights of the Rolls-Royce cutting through the drifting layers of fog, D'Agosta could stand it no longer. "Excuse me, Pendergast, but I have to ask: you don't actually believe that stuff about *oanga* and zombiis?"

"My dear Vincent, I don't *believe* anything. I am not a priest. I deal with evidence and probabilities, not beliefs."

"Yeah, I know. But I mean, Night of the Living Dead? No way."

"That is a rather categorical statement."

"But . . ."

"But what?"

"It's clear to me we're dealing with someone trying to mislead us with this voodoo shit, sending us off on a wild goose chase."

"Clear?" Pendergast quoted the word back to him, his right eyebrow elevating slightly.

D'Agosta said, exasperated, "Look, I just want to know if you think it's even *remotely* possible we're dealing with a real zombii. That's all."

"I'd prefer not to say what I think. However, there is a line of *Hamlet* you might do well to keep in mind."

"And what's that?"

"*There are more things in heaven and earth, Horatio*— Need I continue?"

"No." D'Agosta sat back in the plush leather seat, musing that sometimes it was better to leave Pendergast to his unknown thoughts than to try to force the issue.

At nine o'clock the next morning, Nora walked swiftly down the long hall of the museum's fifth floor, eyes resolutely downcast, past the doors of her colleagues. It was like running the gauntlet, but at least they didn't all come rushing out as they had the days before.

Reaching her own office, she turned the key and quickly entered, shutting and locking the door behind her. She turned and there, silhouetted against the window, stood Special Agent Pendergast, leafing casually through a monograph. D'Agosta sat in an overstuffed chair in the corner, dark circles under his eyes.

The agent glanced up. "Forgive our intrusion into your office, but I do not care to be seen loitering about the museum's halls. Given my past history with this institution, some might take exception to my presence."

She dropped her backpack on the desk. "I have the results."

Pendergast slowly laid down the monograph. "You look very tired."

"Whatever." After her trip to Inwood, she had managed a few hours of fitful sleep, but still she'd had to rise in the middle of the night to finish the gel electrophoresis of the DNA.

"May I?" Pendergast gestured toward a second empty chair.

"Please."

Pendergast settled himself. "Tell me what you found."

Nora pulled an expandable file out of her backpack and laid it on the table. "Before I give you this, I have to tell you something. Something important."

Pendergast inclined his head.

"The night before last, while I was doing the initial PCR work, Fearing showed his face at the lab window. I chased him down the hall and into one of the storage rooms."

Pendergast gazed at her intently. "Are you quite sure it was Fearing?"

"I have proof."

"You were ill advised to follow him," he said sharply. "What happened?"

"I know it was incredibly stupid. I reacted instinctively, didn't think. He was luring me out of the PCR lab. He had a knife, he stalked me through the storage room. If a guard hadn't come by . . . " She didn't finish the sentence.

D'Agosta had risen from his chair, like a coiled spring suddenly released. "Son of a *bitch,*" he said, scowling.

"And your proof?" Pendergast asked.

She smiled grimly. "I cut him with a piece of glass and tested a blood sample. It's Fearing, all right." She opened the folder, pulled out the electrophoresis pictures, thrust them toward the agent. "Take a look."

Pendergast took the pictures and began to leaf through them.

"To summarize," Nora said, "the bloods of two people were in the samples you secured from . . . from my apartment. One was my husband's. The other I will call X. The X sample matched the mitochondrial DNA of Fearing's mother perfectly. And the X sample was also identical to the person who chased me through the storage room. Q.E.D.: X is Fearing."

Pendergast nodded slowly.

"Just what I've said all along," D'Agosta said. "The son of a bitch is still alive. The sister was either mistaken or, more likely, lying when she ID'd the body—no surprise she disappeared. And the M.E. screwed up."

Pendergast said nothing as he examined the images.

"You can keep those," said Nora. "I've got another set. And I have the samples hidden in the back of the PCR lab refrigerator, if you need anything more. Mislabeled, of course."

Pendergast slipped the images back into the folder. "Nora, this is extremely helpful of you. And now I must reproach myself most severely for putting you in danger. I did not anticipate this attack, especially in the museum, and I am very sorry. From now on, you are to have nothing more to do with the case. We will handle it. Until the murderer is caught, you must take exceptional care with your person. No more late nights at the museum."

Nora looked into the agent's silvery eyes. "I've got more information for you."

One eyebrow raised in inquiry.

"I went through Bill's recent articles. He was doing a series of stories on animal abuse in New York—cockfighting, dogfighting . . . and animal sacrifice."

"Indeed?"

"There's a small community up in Inwood known as the Ville. It's deep inside Inwood Hill Park, cut off from the rest of the city. Apparently, some residents up on Indian Road had been complaining that they could hear animals being tortured inside the Ville. An animal rights group was up in arms—their spokesman, a man named Esteban, has spoken out against it more than once. The police did a cursory investigation but nothing's been proved. Anyway, Bill was looking into it. He'd written one article and was working on more. Apparently, his . . . well, his final interview was with an Inwood resident, one of the people who'd complained. Somebody named Pizzetti."

D'Agosta was taking notes.

She could see from the almost eager glitter in Pendergast's eyes that this news was being received with great interest. "The Ville," he repeated.

"Sounds like another search warrant just might be in order," D'Agosta muttered.

"I went up there last night," Nora said.

"Jesus, Nora!" said D'Agosta. "You can't just take this sort of thing upon yourself. Let us handle it."

Nora resumed as if she hadn't heard. "I didn't enter the community itself, which seems to have only one access road. I approached from the south, up a high ridge in the park overlooking the Ville."

"What did you see?"

"Nothing but a crumbling cluster of buildings. Except for a few lights, no signs of life. Creepy place."

"I'll look into it, talk to this Pizzetti," said D'Agosta.

"Anyway, thinking back, I realized that the weird stuff that began showing up at our door—the little fetishes, the inscribed dust—started right around the time Bill published his first article on the Ville. I don't know exactly how or why, but I think they may be involved in all this."

"Fearing's alleged suicide took place near there," said D'Agosta. "On the swinging trestle at Spuyten Duyvil, next to Inwood Hill Park."

"This is extremely important information, Nora," said Pendergast, holding her gaze intently. "Now please listen. I implore you to stop further investigations. You've done more than enough. I made a dreadful mistake asking for your help with the DNA work—it appears your husband's death has affected my judgment."

Nora stared back. "I'm sorry, it's *way* too late to stop me now."

Pendergast hesitated. "We can't protect you and solve your husband's murder both."

"I can look after myself."

"I urge you to follow my advice. I've already lost one friend in Bill—I don't want to lose another."

He held her gaze a moment longer. Then he thanked her again for the DNA results, nodded his good-bye, and followed D'Agosta out the door.

Nora stood at her desk as their footsteps receded. For a time she did nothing, merely tapping a pencil absently against the veneer of the desktop. Then at last she lifted the phone on her desk and dialed Caitlyn Kidd. "It's Nora Kelly," she said when the reporter answered. "I've got some information for you. Meet me at midnight tonight at the corner of Indian Road and West Two Hundred Fourteenth Street."

"Two Hundred Fourteenth?" came the reply. "What's all the way up there?"

"I'm going to show you a story—a *big* story."

D'Agosta settled himself into the deep leather seat of the Rolls as Proctor pulled out of Museum Drive and headed north on Central Park West. He watched Pendergast slip something out of his black suitcoat and was surprised to see it was an iPhone.

"Christ, not you too?"

The agent began typing rapidly on it with his long white fingers. "I find it surprisingly useful."

"What are we going to do about Nora?" D'Agosta asked. "It's obvious she's not going to pay any attention to what you said."

"I am aware of that. She is a very determined lady."

"I don't understand why this guy—Fearing or not—is after Nora. I mean, he got away once after killing Smithback. Why take the risk a second time?"

"Clearly, Fearing meant to kill them both. I believe the message is quite intentional: if you meddle in our affairs, we'll not only kill you, but your family as well." He leaned toward the front seat. "Proctor? Two forty-four East One Hundred Twenty-seventh Street, please."

"Where are we going?" D'Agosta asked. "That's Spanish Harlem."

"We're going to do something about Nora."

D'Agosta grunted. "We've started working on the Kline evidence."

"Ah," said Pendergast. "And?"

"I'm getting the goods on Kline—turns out all that African shit we hauled out of his office was eighteenth- and nineteenth-century Yoruba, worth a fortune. Get this: it's all connected to an extinct religion known as Sevi Lwa—a direct ancestor of voodoo that came into the islands with West African slaves."

Pendergast did not reply. A startled look briefly crossed his face before the studied neutrality returned.

"That's not all. The commissioner's taken an interest in our investigation of that bastard. He wants to meet with me this afternoon."

"Ah."

"What do you mean, *ah*? It shows that Kline knows all about voodoo—to the point of spending millions on voodoo art. There's your connection!"

"Indeed," Pendergast said vaguely.

D'Agosta settled back in his seat, irritated. Ten minutes later, the Rolls had turned off Lenox Avenue and was cruising down 127th Street toward the East River. It rolled to a stop in front of a tiny storefront with a hand-painted sign in Day-Glo colors, surmounted by an illustration of a staring eye.

Blanche de Grimoire la Magie

Underneath it hung a number of little wooden placards on hooks:

LES POUPÉES VAUDOU

MAGIE NOIR

MAGIE ZWARTE, MAGIE ROUGE

SORCELLERIE, HEXEREI MAGIE

RITUEL DE PROSPÉRITÉ FORMULES ET POTIONS MAGIQUES

The shop's filthy front window had a huge crack across it, repaired with duct tape. The rest was almost entirely obscured by bizarre hanging objects—bundles of hair, skin, feathers, canvas, straw, and other more obscure and vile-looking materials.

D'Agosta eyed the shop. "You're kidding, right?"

"After you, my dear Vincent."

D'Agosta got out, Pendergast following. The door to the shop opened with a groan of rusty hinges, setting off a tinkling of bells. D'Agosta was immediately overwhelmed with the cloying smell of patchouli, sandalwood, herbs, and old meat. An ancient African American looked up from behind the counter. Upon spying Pendergast in his black suit, the man's face abruptly shut down, like the slamming of a door. He had a tight helmet of gray hair, and his face was pockmarked and remarkably wrinkled.

"May I help you?" The flat tone and blank stare managed to convey the exact opposite sentiment.

"Are you Monsieur Ravel, the Obeahman?"

The man did not answer.

"I am Aloysius Pendergast, of the New Orleans Pendergasts. Very glad to make your acquaintance." He came forward, hand extended, employing his richest New Orleans parlance.

The man stared at the proffered hand, clearly unmoved.

"Pendergast, formerly of the Maison de la Rochenoire, Dauphine Street," the agent went on. His outstretched hand did not falter. D'Agosta was amazed at how quickly Pendergast could assume a completely new personality. This one appeared to be that of an affable, eccentric New Orleans aristocrat.

"Maison de la Rochenoire?" A glimmer of recognition kindled in the bloodshot eyes. "The one that was burned back in '71?"

Now Pendergast leaned forward and said, in a low voice, *"Oi chusoi Dios aei enpiptousi."*

A long silence, and then Ravel raised an enormous hand. Pendergast clasped it in his.

"Welcome."

"This is my associate, Mr. D'Agosta."

The man inclined his head.

"The others—they are frauds," said Pendergast. "Thieves and scroungers. You—you are different. I know I can trust your rootwork and merchandise."

The man inclined his head in agreement and said nothing, but D'Agosta could see he was grudgingly pleased by the compliment.

"May I?" Pendergast gestured with an ivory hand around the interior of the shop.

"Look, but please do not touch."

"Naturellement."

As Pendergast began one of his leisurely strolls, hands clasped behind his back, peering into everything, D'Agosta glanced around the shop. It was packed with hanging bundles; cabinets that ran from floor to ceiling with hundreds of tiny drawers; perfume containers; tins and small boxes; shelves of glass bottles containing herbs, colored earths, liquids, twisted roots, and dried insects. Everything had tiny labels, meticulously handwritten in French.

Pendergast returned to the shopkeeper. "Most impressive. And now, Monsieur Ravel, I must make a purchase. A rather unfortunate purchase. It seems a friend of mine has been made the target of *magie noir*. I need to make a preparation, an *arrêt.*"

"Tell me the ingredients, and I will get them." Ravel placed a tightly woven basket on the counter.

"Bois-caca leaf."

The man came from around the counter and darted a hand at a high drawer, pulled it out, removed a wrinkled leaf, and placed it in the basket. It gave off a fearful smell.

"Bones of a white cockerel and flesh of a curly cock, crushed with its feathers."

Another swift procurement from an obscure corner of the shop.

D'Agosta watched the process with mounting incredulity. Pendergast was acting a little strangely. He wondered if it had anything to do with the agent's extended trip to Tibet last summer, or the difficult ocean crossing he'd endured. Or maybe it was yet another hidden facet of Pendergast's personality that he was glimpsing for the first time.

"Alligator's tooth and champagne verte."

A small vial of liquid was added to the growing pile.

"Powdered human bone."

At this, Ravel hesitated, went into the back of the shop, emerged with a small stepladder, reached up above one of the cabinets, and brought down a glassine packet of the kind used by drug dealers. It was filled with ivory powder. He added it to the basket, eyes on Pendergast.

"Water used to wash a corpse."

A longer pause before Ravel returned with the requested item.

"Holy water."

At this, Ravel stopped, staring at Pendergast. Then, once again, he went into the back and returned with a tiny ampoule. "Will that be all, I hope?"

"One thing more."

Ravel waited.

"A consecrated host."

A long, hard stare. "Monsieur Pendergast, it seems your friend . . . is facing something a bit more dangerous than mere black magic."

"True."

"Perhaps this is out of my league, monsieur."

"I had so hoped you could help me. My friend's life is in danger—grave danger."

Ravel gazed at Pendergast sadly. "You are aware of the consequences to you, monsieur, for employing the *envoi morts arrêt*?"

"I am well aware."

"This friend must be very dear to you."

"She is."

"*She*. Ah, I see. This . . . host you ask for, it's going to cost."

"Expense is no object."

Ravel dropped his eyes and seemed to think for a long time. Then, with a long sigh, he turned and disappeared out a side door. After several minutes, he returned with a small glass disk made from two large watch-glasses, fitted together and sealed with silver trim, inside which was a single wafer. He laid it carefully in the basket.

"That will be one thousand two hundred and twenty dollars, monsieur."

D'Agosta watched in disbelief as Pendergast slipped his hand into his jacket, removed a thick sheaf of crisp bills, and peeled them off.

As soon as they were back in the Rolls, Pendergast cradling the basket of items, D'Agosta exploded. "What in heck was that all about?"

"Careful, Vincent, do not jar the merchandise."

"I can't believe you just shelled out a thousand bucks for that woo-woo crap."

"There are many reasons, and if you could transcend your emotions you would see why. First, we have established our bona fides with Monsieur Ravel, who might in the future turn out to be an informant of no little importance. Second, the individual pursuing Nora may well believe in Obeah, in which case the *arrêt* we are about to fashion could be a deterrent. Finally"—and here he lowered his voice—"our *arrêt* might work."

"Might *work*? You mean, if a real zombii is after Nora?" D'Agosta shook his head in disbelief.

"I prefer to call it an *envoi mort.*"

"Whatever. The idea is ridiculous." D'Agosta stared at Pendergast. "You told that guy your house in New Orleans was burned by a mob. Your aunt Cornelia made some reference to it, as well. Was that where you learned about this voodoo and Obeah? Were you involved with that shit when you were young?"

"I'd prefer not to answer that. Instead, let me ask a question: have you ever heard of Pascal's Wager?"

"No."

"A lifelong atheist is on his deathbed. He suddenly asks for a priest so he can confess and be absolved. Is he behaving logically?"

"No."

"On the contrary: it doesn't matter what he believes. The atheist realizes that if there is even the slimmest chance he is wrong, he should act as if there is a God. If God exists, he will go to heaven rather than hell. If God does not, he loses nothing."

"Sounds pretty calculating to me."

"It is a wager with an infinite upside and no downside. And, I might add, it is a wager every human being must make. It is not optional. Pascal's Wager—the logic is impeccable."

"What does this have to do with Nora and zombiis?"

"I am sure if you consider the matter long enough you will see the logical connection."

D'Agosta screwed up his face, thought about it, and finally grunted. "I guess I can see your point."

"In that case: excellent. I am not normally in the habit of explaining myself, but for you I sometimes make an exception."

D'Agosta looked out the window as Spanish Harlem passed by. Then he turned back to Pendergast.

"What was that you said?"

"I'm sorry?"

"To the shopkeeper. You said something to him in a foreign language."

"Ah, yes. *Oi chusoi Dios aei enpiptousi*—the dice of God are always loaded." And he sat back in the seat with a half smile.

25

Rocker saw D'Agosta immediately, less than a minute after he'd arrived in the commissioner's outer office at the very top of One Police Plaza. D'Agosta took this summons to be a good sign. The Smithback homicide was high profile—very high profile—and he had no doubt Rocker was following his progress in the case with interest. As he passed Rocker's assistant, Alice, a grandmotherly woman with a pile of gray hair, he gave her a wink and a smile. She did not smile back.

He strode into the grand paneled office with all its accoutrements of power, the huge mahogany desk with the green leather top, the wainscoted oak paneling, the Persian rug, all solid and traditional. Like Rocker.

Rocker was already standing at the window, and he didn't turn as D'Agosta entered. Nor, uncharacteristically, did he ask D'Agosta to take a seat in one of the overstuffed sofa-chairs that graced the sitting area opposite his desk.

D'Agosta waited a moment before venturing a small "Commissioner?"

The man turned around, hands clasped behind his back. On seeing the man's dark red face, D'Agosta felt sudden nausea in his gut.

"So what's this Kline business?" the commissioner asked abruptly.

D'Agosta did a quick mental backpedaling. "Well, sir, it's related to the Smithback homicide—"

"I'm aware of that," the commissioner rapped out. "What I mean is, why the heavy-handed search? You trashed the man's office."

D'Agosta took a deep breath. "Sir, Mr. Kline had made direct, verifiable threats to Smithback shortly before his death. He's a prime suspect."

"Then why didn't you charge him with threatening the deceased?"

"The threats were very careful, they stopped just this side of the law."

The commissioner stared at him. "And that's all you have against Kline? Vague threats to a journalist?"

"No, sir."

Rocker waited, his arms crossed.

"In the raid we netted Kline's collection of West African art—art that we can tie directly to an old voodoo-style religion. Similar to the objects found at the murder scene and on the victim's corpse."

"Similar? I thought they were masks."

"Masks, yes, but from the same tradition. We have an expert from the New York Museum examining them now."

The commissioner stared at him, tired eyes rimmed with red. It wasn't like him to be so brusque. *Jesus,* thought D'Agosta, *Kline got to Rocker. Somehow, Kline got to him.*

Rocker finally said, "I repeat: that's all?"

"The man's issued threats, he's a collector of voodoo items—I think that's a solid beginning."

"*Solid?* Lieutenant, let me tell you what you have. You have shit."

"Sir, I respectfully disagree." D'Agosta wasn't going to knuckle under. His entire team was behind him on this.

"Can't you understand we're dealing with one of the wealthiest men in Manhattan, a friend of the mayor, a philanthropist all over town, sitting on a dozen Fortune Five Hundred boards? You can't trash his office without a damn good reason!"

"Sir, this is just the beginning. I believe we have enough to justify continuing the investigation, and I intend to do just that." D'Agosta tried to keep his voice mild, neutral, but firm.

The commissioner stared at him. "Let me just say this: until you get a smoking gun on the man—and I mean *smoking*—you back off. That search was improper. It was harassment. And don't feign innocence. I was a homicide cop once, just like you. I know why you tossed his place, and I don't approve of those methods. You don't pull that drug-bust crap on a well-known, respected member of this city."

"He's a scumbag."

"That's the bad attitude I'm talking about, D'Agosta. Look, I'm not going to tell you how to run a homicide investigation, but I am warning you that the next time you want to pull something like that on Kline, think again." He stared long and hard at D'Agosta.

"I hear you, sir." D'Agosta had said what he had to say. No point in provoking the commissioner further.

"I'm not taking you off the Smithback homicide. Not yet. But I'm watching you, D'Agosta. Don't go native on me again."

"Yes, sir."

The commissioner waved a hand dismissively as he turned back to the window. "Now get out of here."

26

Although the New York Public Library had closed ninety minutes before, Special Agent Pendergast had unusual visiting privileges and never permitted the formality of business hours to incommode him. He glanced around with approval at the empty rows of tables in the cavernous Main Reading Room; nodded to the guard in the doorway whose nose was deep in *Mont Saint Michel and Chartres;* then ducked into the receiving station and made his way down a steep set of metal stairs. After descending four flights, he exited into a low-ceilinged basement vault that seemed to stretch ahead endlessly, filled floor-to-ceiling with stack after stack of books on cast-iron shelves. Making his way down a transverse corridor, he opened a dingy, unmarked gray door. Beyond, another set of stairs—narrow and even steeper—led farther downward.

Another three flights and he emerged into a bizarre and semi-ruined bookscape. In the dim light, stacks of ancient and decomposing books leaned against one another for support. Tables littered with unbound book signatures, razor blades, jars of printer's glue, and other paraphernalia of manuscript surgery stood everywhere. Blizzards of printed material receded on all sides to an unguessable distance, forming a labyrinth of literature. There was an intense silence. The stuffy air smelled of dust and decay.

Pendergast placed the bundle he had been carrying on a nearby stack and cleared his throat.

For a moment, the silence remained unbroken. Then—from some remote and indeterminate distance—there was a faint scurrying. It grew slowly louder. And then an old man emerged from between two columns of books, tiny and frighteningly gaunt. A miner's hard hat rested atop a blizzard of white hair.

The man reached up and snapped off the headlamp. *"Hypocrite lecteur,"* he said in a voice as thin and dry as birch bark. "I've been expecting you."

Pendergast gave a small bow. "Interesting fashion statement, Wren," he said, indicating the hard hat. "Quite the rage in West Virginia, I understand."

The old man gave a silent laugh. "I've been—shall we say—spelunking. And down here in the Antipodes, working lightbulbs can be hard to come by."

Whether Wren was actually employed by the public library, or whether he'd simply decided to take up residence here on its lowest sub-level, was anybody's guess. What was uncontestable, however, was his unique talent for esoteric research.

Wren's eyes fell hungrily on the bundle. "And what goodies have you brought me today?"

Pendergast picked it up and proffered it. Wren reached greedily, tearing away the wrappings to reveal three books.

"Early Arkham House," he sniffed. "I'm afraid I was never one for the literature of the weird."

"Take a closer look. These are the rarest, most collectible editions."

Wren examined the books one after the other. "Hmm. A prepublication *Outsider,* with the trial green dustwrapper. *Always Comes Evening*"—he plucked off the jacket to examine the cover—"with the variant spine. And a leather-bound *Shunned House* . . . containing Barlow's signature on the front pastedown. Dated

Mexico City, not long before his suicide. A remarkable association copy." Wren raised his eyebrows as he carefully put down the books. "I spoke too rashly. A noble gift indeed."

Pendergast nodded. "I'm glad you approve."

"Since your call, I've managed to do some preliminary research."

"And?"

Wren rubbed his hands together. "I'd no idea Inwood Hill Park had such an interesting history. Did you know it has remained an essentially primeval forest since the American Revolution? Or that it was once the site of Isidor Straus's summer estate—until Straus and his wife died on the *Titanic*?"

"So I've heard."

"Quite a story. The old man refused to board the lifeboat before the women and children, and Mrs. Straus refused to leave her husband. She put her maid into the lifeboat instead, and the couple went down together. After they died, their 'cottage' up in Inwood fell into ruin. But my research indicates that, in the years before, a groundskeeper was murdered, and there were other unfortunate events that kept the Strauses away from—"

"And the Ville?" Pendergast interjected gently.

"You mean the Ville des Zirondelles." Wren grimaced. "A more shadowy, secretive bunch is hard to imagine. I'm afraid my examination of them is still in its infancy—and under the circumstances I'm not sure I'll ever be able to learn a great deal."

Pendergast waved his hand. "Just let me know what you've discovered so far, please."

"Very well." Wren laid the tip of one bony index finger against the other, as if to tick off points of interest. "It seems that the first building of the Ville—as it's now known—was originally constructed in the early 1740s by a religious sect that fled England to avoid persecution. They ended up on the north end of Manhattan, in what is now the park in question. As was so often the case, this band of pilgrims had more idealism than pragmatism. They were city people—writers, teachers, a banker—and were intensely naive about making a living off the land. It seemed they had peculiar views regarding communal living. Believing the entire community should live and work together as a single unit, they had their ship's carpenters build a vast structure out of local stone and planking. It was part dwelling place, part workplace, part chapel, part fortress."

He ticked off the next finger. "But the tip of the island they'd chosen for their settlement was rocky and inhospitable for farming or animal husbandry—even for those knowledgeable about such things. There were no more local Indians around to give them advice—the Weckquaesgeek and the Lenape had long since left—and the closest European settlement was at the other end of Manhattan, two days' journey. The new settlers proved to be indifferent fishermen. There were a few farmers scattered around who had already chosen the best farming spots, and though they were willing to sell some crops for hard cash, they weren't inclined to provide free sustenance for an entire community."

"So the folly of their plan soon became clear," Pendergast murmured.

"Precisely. Disappointment and internecine squabbling followed quickly. Within a dozen years or so the colony was dissolved, its residents moving elsewhere in New England or returning to Europe, and the structure was abandoned: a testament to misplaced hopes. Their leader—I haven't been able to discover his name, but he was the one who secured the ship and purchased the site—moved to southern Manhattan and became a gentleman farmer."

"Go on," Pendergast said.

"Fast-forward a hundred years. Around 1858 or 1859, a ragtag group reached New York from points south. By period accounts it was a motley assemblage. At its core was a charismatic Baton Rouge preacher, the Reverend Misham Walker, who had gathered around him a small number of French Creole craftsmen shunned by their community for some reason I haven't discovered, along with several West Indian slaves. Along the way they were joined by others: Cajun, some Portuguese heretics, and a number of bayou dwellers who had fled Brittany for allegedly practicing paganism, druidism, and witchcraft. Theirs wasn't voodoo or Obeah in any traditional sense. Instead, it seems to be an entirely new belief system, built from various pieces of what came before. Their journey from the Deep South to New York was fraught with difficulty. Wherever they tried to settle, the locals objected to the group's religious rituals; they were repeatedly forced to move on. Nasty rumors were spread: that the group stole babies, sacrificed animals, brought people back from the dead. The band was secretive by nature; the treatment they received seems to have made them positively reclusive. Walker and his band ultimately discovered the remote structure the religious pilgrims had abandoned at the northern tip of Manhattan a century earlier and took it for their own, bricking up the windows and fortifying the walls. There was talk of mob action against them, but nothing came of it beyond several peculiar confrontations confusedly described in the local press. As years passed, the Ville grew more and more insular."

Pendergast nodded slowly. "And in more recent times?"

"Complaints of animal sacrifice have persisted over the years." Wren paused, then a dry smile hovered about his lips. "It seems they were—are—a celibate community. Like the Shakers."

Pendergast's eyebrows shot up in surprise. "Celibate? And yet they continue to persist."

"Not only persist, but—apparently—always maintain the same number: one hundred forty-four. All male, all adult. It is believed they recruit. Rather vigorously, when necessary, and always at night. They are said to prey on the disaffected, the mentally unstable, the fringe dwellers: ideal candidates for press-ganging. When one member dies, another must be found. And then there were the *rumors.*" Wren's dark eyes glittered.

"Of what?"

"A murderous creature wandering at night. A *zombii,* some said." He gave a little hiss of amusement.

"And the history of the land and buildings?"

"The surrounding land was acquired by the New York City Department of Parks in 1916. Some other decaying structures in the park were demolished, but the Ville was passed over. It appears the parks department was reluctant to force the issue."

"I see." Pendergast glanced at Wren, a strange look on his face. "Thank you; you've made an excellent start. Keep at it, if you please."

Wren returned the look, dark eyes alight with curiosity. "What is it exactly, *hypocrite lecteur*? What's your interest in all this?"

Pendergast did not answer immediately. For a moment, his expression seemed to go far away. Then he roused himself. "It's premature to discuss it."

"At least tell me this: is your interest . . . in matters iniquitous?" Wren repeated.

Pendergast made another small bow. "Please let me know when you've discovered more." And then he turned and began the long ascent back to the surface world.

27

Nora added a final entry to her database of samples, then terminated the program, sealed the bag of potsherds, and put it aside. She stretched, glanced at her watch. It was almost ten PM, and the museum offices were silent and watchful.

She looked around her lab: at the shelves of artifacts, the files and papers, the locked door. This was the first day she'd really been able to concentrate a little, get some work done. Partly, this was because the stream of sympathizers knocking at her door had finally subsided. But there was more to it than that. It was because she knew she was doing something—something concrete—about Bill's death. The DNA sequencing for Pendergast had been a start. But now, this very evening, she'd be taking the fight to the enemy.

She took a deep breath, exhaled slowly. Strange how she felt no fear. There was only a grim determination: to get to the bottom of Bill's death, restore a modicum of order and peace to her fractured world.

Picking up the bag of potsherds, she returned it to its storage rack. Earlier that afternoon she had paid a visit to her new boss, Andrew Getz, head of the anthropology department. She'd requested—and received—a written guarantee of funding for her expedition to Utah the coming summer. She wanted to have a long-term plan already in place, something to keep her going through what promised to be a long, dark winter.

Very faintly, she heard what sounded like a childish shout echo through the corridors. The museum had taken to allowing groups of schoolchildren to attend weekend sleepovers in certain heavily chaperoned halls. She shook her head: anything to generate a little hard cash, it seemed.

As the echo died away, another sound took its place: a single rap on her door.

She froze, turning toward the noise. Amazing, how fast her heart could start beating wildly. But almost as quickly, she reminded herself: Fearing would not have knocked.

The knock came again. She cleared her throat. "Who is it?"

"Agent Pendergast."

It was his voice, all right. She moved quickly to the door, unlocked it. The agent stood in the hallway, leaning against the doorjamb, wearing a black cashmere coat over the usual black suit. "May I enter?"

She nodded, stepped away. The agent glided in, pale eyes quickly scanning the lab before returning to her. "I wanted to thank you again for your assistance."

"Don't thank me. Anything I can do to help bring the killer to justice."

"Indeed. That's what I wanted to speak with you about." He closed the door, turned back to her. "I suppose there's nothing I can say that will stop you from pursuing your own investigation."

"That's right."

"Entreaties to leave things to the professionals—reminders that you are putting your own life in grave danger—will fall on deaf ears."

She nodded.

He regarded her closely for a moment. "In that case, there's something you must do for me."

"What's that?"

Pendergast reached into his pocket, retrieved something, and pressed it into her hand. "Wear this around your neck at all times."

She looked down. It was a charm of some kind, made of feathers and a small piece of chamois, sewn into a ball and attached to a fine gold chain. She pressed the chamois gently: it seemed to contain something powdery.

"What is this?" she asked.

"It is an *arrêt.*"

"A what?"

"In common parlance, an enemy-be-gone charm."

She glanced at him. "You can't be serious."

"Highly useful against all save immediate family. There is something else." He reached into another pocket and plucked out a bag of red flannel, cinched tight by a drawstring of multicolored thread. "Keep this on your person, in a pocket or purse."

She frowned. "Agent Pendergast . . ." She shook her head. She didn't know what to say. Of all the people she knew, Pendergast had always seemed an immovable rock of logic and pragmatism. Yet here he was, giving her charms?

Looking at her, his eyes flashed slightly, as if reading her thoughts. "You're an anthropologist," he said. "Have you read *The Forest of Symbols,* by Victor Turner?"

"No."

"What about Émile Durkheim's *Elementary Forms of Religious Life*?"

She nodded.

"Then you know that certain things can be analyzed and codified—and certain things cannot. And certainly, as one who studied anthropology, you understand the concept of phenomenology?"

"Yes, but . . ." She fell silent.

"Because our minds are trapped within our bodies, we cannot

determine ultimate truth—or untruth. The best we can do is describe what we see."

"You're losing me . . ."

"There is a wisdom on this earth, Nora, which is mysterious, which is very old, and with which we must not quarrel. Is it true? Untrue? We cannot know. Therefore, will you do as I ask? Keep these on your person?"

She glanced at the objects in her hand. "I don't know what to say."

"Say yes, if you please. Because that is the only condition I shall *permit.*"

Slowly, she nodded.

"Very good." He turned to go, then stopped, looked back at her. "And Dr. Kelly?"

"Yes?"

"It is not enough merely to possess these things. One must *believe.*"

"Believe what?"

"Believe they work. Because those who wish you ill most certainly believe." And with that he slipped out of the office, closing the door silently behind him.

28

Midnight. Nora paused at the corner of Indian Road and 214th Street to check her map. The air was cool and smelled of fall. Beyond the low apartment houses, the dark treetops of Inwood Hill Park rose black against a luminous night sky. The lack of sleep made her feel light-headed, almost as if she had taken a stiff drink.

As she pored over the map, Caitlyn Kidd looked curiously over her shoulder.

Nora stuffed the map back in her pocket. "Up another block."

They continued along Indian Road. It was a quiet, residential street, bathed in yellow sodium light, the brick buildings on either side somber and plain. A car passed slowly, turning onto 214th Street, its headlights lancing the dark. Where Indian curved into 214th, an unmarked road, little more than an abandoned driveway, branched off, heading west between an apartment building and a shuttered dry cleaners. A rusty iron chain was draped across it, fixed to old iron posts set into each side of the lane. Nora looked down the narrow road, which headed past some baseball diamonds and disappeared into the darkness. The asphalt was cracked, heaving up in chunks. Tufts of grass and even the occasional small sapling poked up here and there through the gaps. She checked the newly printed map once again—her earlier excursion had clearly shown her the best route of approach.

"This is it."

They ducked under the chain. Ahead, past the playing fields, the old road crossed an expanse of fallow ground, then vanished into the forest of Inwood Hill Park. Only a few cast-iron lampposts remained, and they were dark; looking up, Nora thought she could see bullet holes in the glass coverings.

Somewhere in the darkness ahead lay the Ville.

She started forward, Caitlyn hurrying to keep up. The paved road narrowed and the trees closed in. The smell of damp leaves filled the air.

"You brought a flashlight, right?" Caitlyn asked.

"Yes, but I'd rather not use it."

The lane rose, gently at first, then steeply, to a rise that afforded views of the Henry Hudson Parkway and Columbia's Baker Field. They paused, gaining their bearings. Ahead, the path descended toward an embayment in the Harlem River. As they proceeded, Nora began to make out, through a screen of trees, a faint scattering of yellow lights about a quarter mile away.

She felt Caitlyn nudge her side. "Is that it?"

"I think so. Let's find out."

After a moment's hesitation, they continued down the hill, following the lane as it curved to take advantage of the topography. The trees grew denser, shutting out the faint glow of the city. The thin drone of traffic on the parkway receded. The lane curved again and something dark loomed ahead: an ancient chain-link fence, much abused, barred further access. A large hole in the fence had been patched with a crisscrossing mass of razor wire. In the center of the fence stood a gate, a crudely lettered sign affixed to it:

Private Property
No Trespassing
Do Not Enter

"This is a city street," said Nora. "This isn't legal. Be sure you put that in your article."

"Not much of a street though, is it?" Caitlyn replied. "Anyway, the whole complex isn't strictly legal. They're squatters."

Nora examined the gate. It was wrought iron, black paint peeling from it, the metal underneath pitted and bubbling with rust. A row of spikes ran across the upper edge of its frame, but half of the spikes had either broken or fallen off. Despite the appearance of antiquity, Nora noticed that the gate's hinges were well oiled and its chain and padlock were quite new. No sound came through the trees.

"Easier to climb over the fence than the gate," Nora said.

"Yeah."

Neither moved.

"You really think this is a good idea?" asked Caitlyn.

Before she had a chance to change her mind, Nora took the initiative, grasping the rusted chain link with her hands and jamming her toes into the gaps, pulling herself up as quickly as she could. The fence was about ten feet tall. Brackets along the upper edge indicated that it had once been topped by strands of barbed wire, which had disappeared long ago.

In half a minute, she was over. She dropped to the soft leaves on the other side, panting. "Your turn," she said.

Caitlyn grasped the links and did the same. She wasn't in nearly as good shape as Nora, but managed to struggle over, sliding down the far side with a quiet rattle of metal. "Whew," she said as she brushed away leaves and rust.

Nora peered into the dimness ahead. "Better to go through the woods than follow the road," she whispered.

"No argument here."

Moving gingerly, trying not to rustle the leaves, Nora moved off the road to the right, where a dark gully ran downhill through oak trees toward the edge of a cleared area. She could hear Caitlyn behind her, moving cautiously. The gully soon became steep, and Nora paused from time to time to peer ahead. It was dark in the woods, but she knew they couldn't use the flashlight. She had every reason to believe the people inside the Ville were alert to intruders and might investigate a light bobbing in the woods.

The gully gradually leveled out as they approached the flat area marking the edge of a field around the Ville itself. Abruptly, the trees ended and the dead field stretched before them, ending at the rear of the massive, ancient church, attached to—and perhaps even held up by—its helter-skelter accretion of dependent buildings. A chill wind blew across the field, and Nora could hear the rattle of dry weeds.

"My God," she heard Caitlyn murmur beside her.

This time, Nora had approached the Ville from the opposite side. From the closer perspective, she could see that the bizarre structure was even more rough-hewn than she'd thought. In the pale glow reflected from the night sky, she could almost make out the adze marks on the massive timbers that made up the ribs of the fortress. The central church seemed to have been built in successive layers, each higher layer slightly overhanging that below it, forming an inverted ziggurat that looked perverse and menacing. The vast majority of windows were far up in its flanks. Those not bricked up were filled with old ship's glass, pale green, though some appeared to be covered in oilcloth or waxed paper. This close, the impression of candlelight from the far side of the windows was unmistakable. A single window—small and rectangular—was placed at eye level, as if just for them.

"Unbelievable that a place like this could still exist in Manhattan," she said.

"Unbelievable it could still exist at all. What do we do?"

"Wait. See if anyone's around."

"How long?"

"Ten, fifteen minutes. Enough time for a guard, if there is one, to make his rounds. Then we might move in closer. Be sure to take note of everything. We want *West Sider* readers to really get an eyeful."

"Right," said Caitlyn, her voice quavering, her hand clutching her notebook.

Nora settled down to wait. As she shifted, she felt the rough charm around her neck scratch her skin. She drew it out, looked at it. It looked as strange as the fetishes that had been left outside her apartment: tufts of feathers, the bundle of chamois. Pendergast had pressed it upon her, made her promise to wear it, promise to keep the flannel bag always on her person. New Orleans bred or not, he didn't seem like the type to believe in voodoo—did he? She let it drop back, feeling faintly silly, glad the reporter hadn't noticed.

A faint noise put her on high alert. It had just started out of the darkness, a low drone like the sound of monstrous cicadas, and it took her a moment to realize it was coming from the church. It grew louder and clearer: the sound of deep singing. No, not singing exactly—more like chanting.

"You hear that?" Caitlyn asked, voice suddenly tight.

Nora nodded.

The sound swelled, growing in volume while deepening in timbre. It quavered, rising and falling in a complex rhythm. Nora saw Caitlyn shiver, draw her jacket more tightly around her shoulders.

As they waited, listening intently, the chanting grew faster, more insistent. Now it began to rise in pitch, little by little.

"Oh shit, I don't like this at all," said Caitlyn.

Nora put an arm around the reporter's shoulders. "Just sit tight. Nobody knows we're here. We're invisible in the dark."

"I shouldn't have agreed to come. This was a bad idea."

Nora could feel the woman shaking. She marveled at her own lack of fear. She had Bill's death to thank for that. It wasn't fearlessness, exactly, so much as feeling dead to fear. After his death, what could be worse? Her own death would be a kind of release.

The chanting grew in urgency, faster and faster. And then a new noise intruded—the bleating of a goat.

"Oh, no," Nora muttered. She tightened her arm around Caitlyn.

Another plaintive bleat. The chanting was now high and fast, almost like a machine, the humming of a huge dynamo.

Two more bleats cut through the drone: higher, frightened. Nora knew what was coming; she wanted to cover her ears but knew she couldn't.

"This needs a witness." She began to rise.

Caitlyn clutched at her. "No. Wait, please."

Nora shook her off. "This is what we came for."

"*Please*. They'll see you."

"Nobody's going to see me."

"Wait—!"

But Nora was up and running across the field at a crouch. The grass was wet and slick underfoot. She flattened herself against the back wall of the old church; crept along it toward the small yellow window; paused; then glanced in, heart pounding.

Porcelain sink, brown with age; broken china chamber pot; commode of splintered wood. An ancient, empty privy.

Damn. She slid down, face against the cold, rough timber. The fabric of the ancient place seemed to exude an unusual odor: musky, smoky. Close as she was now, the sounds within were a lot louder. She pressed her ear to the wall, listening intently.

She couldn't make out the words, couldn't even tell what language, although it was clearly not English. French? Creole?

Along with the chanting, she could hear what seemed like the soft slap of bare feet, fast and rhythmical. A lone voice rose above the insistent ostinato: wavering, shrill, tuneless, yet clearly part of the ritual.

Another long, frightened bleating: high, terrified. Then sudden, total silence.

And then the shriek came, cutting the air, a pure animal expression of surprise and pain. The sound was almost immediately choked off by a thick gargling, followed by a long, drawn-out rattling cough, and then silence.

Nora didn't have to see to know exactly what had happened.

Just as suddenly, the chanting resumed, fast, exultant, with the voice of what was certainly a kind of priest rising above, wailing with glee. Mingled with that were the sounds of something else: something grunting, breathy, and wet.

Nora gulped down mouthfuls of air, feeling suddenly nauseated. The sound had cut her to the bone and unexpectedly revived that terrible moment when she saw her husband, motionless, in a spreading pool of blood on their living room floor. She felt paralyzed. The earth whirled around her, and spots danced before her eyes. Caitlyn was right: this was a bad idea. These people, whoever they were, would not take kindly to an intrusion. She gripped the brick wall for a minute or two, until the feeling passed, and then she realized: they had to get out—now.

As she turned, she caught sight of something moving in the dark, at the corner of the farthest building. A lurching, shambling movement; a blur of sallow flesh in the spectral moonlight; and then it was gone.

With a thrill of dread she blinked hard, opened her eyes again. All was silent and dark; the chanting had ceased. Had she really seen something? Just when she was concluding she hadn't, it appeared again: glabrous, strangely bloated, dressed in tatters. It moved toward her with a motion that seemed somehow both random and yet full of horrible purpose.

As she stared, Nora was irresistibly reminded of the thing that had chased her through the room of whale skeletons two nights before. With a gasp, she lurched to her feet and ran across the field.

"Caitlyn!" she gasped, stumbling into the reporter and grabbing her jacket, her lungs burning. "We've got to get the hell out of here!"

"What happened?" She was instantly terrified by Nora's terror, cowering on the ground.

"Go!" Nora grasped her shirt and hauled her bodily to her feet. Caitlyn stumbled as she tried to get up, and Nora caught her.

"Oh, my God," said Caitlyn, staring back, suddenly paralyzed. "Dear God."

Nora looked back. The thing—its face puffy and distorted, impossible to make out in the dim light—was now moving toward them with a horrible disjointed motion.

"Caitlyn!" Nora screamed, pulling her around. "Go!"

"What—?"

But Nora was already running up the dark gully, pulling the reporter along by her arm. Caitlyn seemed drugged by fear, slipping and falling on the leaves, turning to look back again and again.

Now the thing was moving more swiftly, coming at them with a loping motion that was full of sinister design. She could hear its slobbering, eager breathing.

"It's coming," said Caitlyn. "It's coming after us."

"Shut up and run!"

Oh, God, Nora thought as she ran. *Oh, my God. It can't be Fearing—can it?*

But she was all too sure that it could be.

They reached the top of the gully. The gate and fence lay just ahead.

"Haul ass!" Nora cried as Caitlyn slipped and came dangerously close to falling. She was sobbing and gasping for air. Behind, the sound of something treading the ground came up swiftly through the dark. Nora pulled Caitlyn back up.

"Oh, Jesus . . ."

Nora hit the fence, pulling Caitlyn after her, throwing her

against the fence and heaving her upward with as much strength as she could manage. The reporter scrabbled against the chain link, finding a purchase and pulling herself up. Nora followed. They slipped over the top, dropped to the leaves, began running again.

Something crashed into the fence behind them. Nora stopped, turned. Despite the hammering of her heart, she had to know. She *had* to know.

"What are you doing?" Caitlyn cried, still running like hell.

Nora jammed her hand into her shoulder bag, yanked out the flashlight, turned it on, aimed it at the fence . . .

. . . Nothing—except a convex bulge in the rusted steel where the thing had hit, and the faint residual motion of the fence from the blow, creaking back and forth, until silence reigned.

The thing was gone.

She could hear Caitlyn running, her footfalls receding up the old lane.

Nora followed at a jog, and soon caught up with the heaving, exhausted reporter. Caitlyn was doubled over, heaving and gasping, and then she vomited. Nora held her shoulders while she was sick.

"Who . . . what was *that*?" she finally managed to choke out.

Nora said nothing, and helped Caitlyn to her feet. Ten minutes later, they were walking down Indian Road, back in familiar Manhattan, but Nora—unconsciously fingering the charm around her neck—could not shake the feeling of horror, of the thing that had chased them, and of the death-cough of the doomed goat. One terrible thought kept recurring, a single irrational, useless, sickening thought:

Did Bill sound like that when he died?

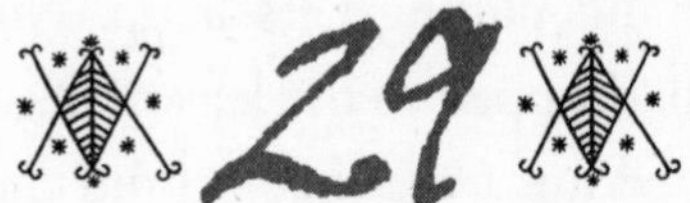

Lieutenant D'Agosta sat in his cubbyhole office at One Police Plaza, staring at the glow of the computer screen. He was an author, he'd published two novels. The books had gotten great reviews. So why was it that writing an interim report was so damn difficult? He was still burning from the reaming-out that the commissioner had given him the prior afternoon. Kline had gotten to him, no doubt about that.

He turned from the screen, rubbing his eyes. Feeble morning light came in the room's single window, from which he could glimpse a sliver of sky. He took a slug from his third cup of coffee, tried to clear his mind. After a certain point, coffee seemed to make him more tired.

Was it really only a week since Smithback was murdered? He shook his head. Right now, he was supposed to be in Canada, visiting his son and signing paperwork for his impending divorce. Instead, he was chained to New York and a case that only grew more bizarre with every passing day.

The phone on his desk rang. That's all he needed: another distraction. He plucked it from the cradle, sighing inwardly. "Homicide, D'Agosta speaking."

"Vincent? Fred Stolfutz."

Stolfutz was the assistant US attorney helping D'Agosta draft the search warrant affidavit for the Ville. "Hi, Fred. So what do you think?"

"If you're trying to get in there looking for homicide evidence, you're going to be out of luck. The evidence is too thin, no judge will approve a warrant. Especially after what you pulled on Kline the other day."

"Christ, how'd you hear about that?"

"Vinnie, it's all over the place. Not to mention how the commissioner—"

D'Agosta interrupted impatiently. "So what are the options?"

"Well, you said this place is deep in the woods, right?"

"Right."

"That rules out plain-use doctrine: you can't get close enough to, say, see evidence of a crime in plain view or smell marijuana smoke. And there won't be any exigent circumstances, somebody screaming for help or something."

"There's been plenty of screaming—by animals."

"See, that's what I was thinking. You'll never get in there on a homicide rap, but I could probably draft something about cruelty to animals. That's a statute we could make stick. If you go in there with an animal control officer, you can keep your eyes out for the other evidence you're looking for."

"Interesting. Think it'll fly?"

"Yes, I do."

"Fred, you're a genius. Call me back when you know more." D'Agosta hung up the phone and returned to the problem at hand.

On the surface, it wasn't complicated. Good witnesses, *excellent* witnesses, had seen Fearing enter and leave the building. And even though the results weren't official, and couldn't be used in court, the man's DNA had been found at the scene, something the official results would eventually confirm. Fearing was stalking Nora and, again, there was the proof of his DNA. His crypt was empty—no body. That was the proof on one side.

On the other side? An overworked, sloppy asshole of a medical examiner who couldn't admit he'd made a mistake. A tattoo and a birthmark, either of which could be faked or mistaken, given the time the body was in the water. A sister's ID, but false IDs had happened before when a family member was too distraught, or the body too changed. Maybe it was insurance fraud, with the sister in on it. The fact that she had disappeared afterward just added to the suspicion.

No: Colin Fearing was alive, of that D'Agosta was sure. And he was no frigging zombii, either. Was Kline behind it, or the Ville? He'd keep up the pressure on both.

D'Agosta picked up his coffee, stared at it, then poured it into the wastebasket, following it with the cup. Enough of that shit. He thought about the crime itself. It just didn't look to him like a rape gone bad. And the guy had *stared* at the camera going in. The man knew he was being recorded—yet he *didn't care.*

Pendergast was right. This was no disorganized killing: there was a plan here. But what plan? He swore under his breath.

The phone rang again.

"D'Agosta."

"Vinnie? It's Laura. Have you seen the *West Sider* this morning?"

"No."

"You'd better get yourself a copy."

"What does it say?"

"Just get yourself a copy. And . . ."

"And what?"

"Expect a call from the commissioner. Don't tell them I told you, just be ready."

"Shit, not again." D'Agosta re-cradled the phone. Then he stood up and headed for the nearest bank of elevators. He could probably scrounge a copy up on the floor, but if Laura was right, he needed to carve out some time to digest whatever it was before the commissioner called.

The elevator bell rang, and a set of doors opened. A few minutes later, D'Agosta approached the newsstand in the lobby. He could see the *West Sider* hung prominently on the upper left rack, as usual. He dropped his two bits on the counter, slid one off the top of the pile, and tucked it under his arm. Stepping into the Starbucks across the lobby, he ordered a single shot of espresso, took it to the table, and opened the newspaper. The lead article practically yelled out at him:

Animal Sacrifice!

Ritual Death at "the Ville"
Possible Ties to Voodoo and Smithback Murder

By Caitlyn Kidd

D'Agosta stared at the espresso, which barely covered the bottom of the paper cup. Whatever happened to the preheated demitasses they used to serve it in? He shot it down, barely tasting it, snapped the paper flat, and began to read.

He had to admit, for a shit-piece of a story it was effective. Nora Kelly and the reporter had gone up to the Ville at night, jumped the fence, and heard the whole thing. Then they'd been chased away, by who or what was left vague, but the reporter insinuated it had the appearance of a zombii. The reporter went on to wonder how the city could have allowed a public road to be closed, and whether animal cruelty laws were being broken. There were quotes from Smithback's article on the Ville, descriptions of the *vévé* left at his apartment door prior to the murder, as well as the weird stuff left at the murder scene itself. There was a pithy quote from the head of an animal rights group. While the reporter made no direct assertions of a connection between the Ville and Smithback's murder, the thrust of the article was unmistakable: Smithback had started writing about animal sacrifices, and he'd been planning to do more. And then there was a line that particularly burned him, typical of this kind of reportage. "Repeated attempts to reach Lieutenant Detective Vincent D'Agosta, in charge of the Smithback homicide investigation, were unsuccessful."

Repeated attempts. His cell phone was on night and frigging day, and his office number rolled over to it after hours. Now that he thought about it, he had gotten a call or maybe two from that woman, Kidd, but who has time to return every call? *Repeated attempts, my ass.* Twice, more like it. Well, okay, maybe three times.

Now he knew exactly why Laura Hayward had called.

The previous article, about voodoo, had been a joke. But this one had some real meat, and the piteous description of the bleating animal being killed was all too effective. Animal lovers, he knew, could be damn near rabid.

The theme song from *The Good, the Bad, and the Ugly* rang out in the coffee shop. D'Agosta quickly grabbed his cell phone, flipped it open, and walked out into the lobby.

The commissioner.

"We speak again," said the commissioner.

"Yes, sir."

"I assume you've seen the *West Sider* piece?"

"Yes, sir, I have." He tried to keep his tone respectful, as if yesterday had never happened.

"It seems that you might be barking up the wrong tree with Kline—eh, Lieutenant?" The voice had a cold edge to it.

"I'm keeping all lines open in this investigation."

A grunt. "So what do you think? Ville or Kline?"

"As I said, we're pursuing both leads."

"This thing has really exploded. The mayor's concerned. I just got calls from the *News* and the *Post*. This business about you being unavailable for comment . . . Look, you need to be out there, reassuring people, giving answers."

"I'll schedule a press conference."

"You do that. Two o'clock would be a good time. Focus on the Ville—and leave Kline out of it." A crackle as the connection was cut.

D'Agosta headed back into Starbucks. "Give me four shots of espresso," he said. "To go."

30

At the best of times, D'Agosta hated press conferences. And this was hardly the best of times. There was little to tell—and what there was to tell seemed to beggar belief. As he peered through the doorway into the briefing room—every seat taken, the reporters and cameramen and officials all shouting over each other—Commissioner Rocker came up beside him. "Ready with your statement, Lieutenant?"

"Yes, sir." D'Agosta glanced at him. Rocker wore his usual dark suit, a small NYPD pin set into one lapel. The commissioner returned the glance, looking even wearier than usual.

"You remember what I said: no Kline."

D'Agosta swallowed. Forget all the coffee—he could use a double bourbon right about now. He hadn't planned to mention Kline anyway; he didn't want to get sued for defamation.

As they walked out into the briefing room and ascended the podium, the volume of noise grew even louder. Explosions of light peppered the room as a dozen flash units went off. The commissioner stepped toward the lectern and put out his hands for silence. It took a good thirty seconds for the crowd to settle down. At last, the commissioner cleared his throat.

"Detective Lieutenant D'Agosta, who is in charge of the Smithback homicide, will say a few words about the current state of his investigation. We will then open the floor for questions. Before Lieutenant D'Agosta speaks, I would just ask all of you to please be responsible in how you report this case to the public. This is an exceptionally sensational crime, and the city is already on edge as a result. Causing additional unrest can only lead to further damage. And now, Lieutenant, if you would?"

"Thank you." D'Agosta approached the microphone with trepidation. He gazed out over the sea of faces, swallowed painfully. "As you are all aware," he began, "William Smithback, a resident of the Upper West Side, was the victim of a homicide one week ago. Members of law enforcement, under my direction, have been aggressively investigating the case. As a result, numerous lines of inquiry have been opened. We are pursuing several leads, and we feel confident that those responsible will be identified and apprehended in the very near future. In the meantime, we would ask that if anybody has any information of value to the investigation, they contact the NYPD immediately." He paused. "I'll take your questions now."

Instantly, the hubbub resumed. D'Agosta held up his hands for order. "Quiet, please!" he said into the microphone. "Quiet!" He stepped back, waiting for a semblance of order to return. "Thank you. You, in front." He nodded at a middle-aged woman in a yellow blouse.

"What can you tell us about this Ville? Are they really performing animal sacrifices?"

"There have been several complaints about animal noise emanating from that location. This is one of the areas under active investigation. I might add that we have found no direct connection between the Ville and the Smithback homicide."

"Speaking of the Smithback homicide," the woman went on, "are the autopsy results back? What was the cause of death?"

"The cause of death was a stab wound to the heart."

He surveyed the crowd: the hands straining in the air, the lights and cameras and digital recorders. It seemed strange not to see Smithback among the eager faces, shouting and gesticulating, cowlick bobbing.

"Yes," he said, pointing to a man in the third row wearing a large, gaudy bow tie.

"Have you confirmed the identity of Smithback's killer? Was it Fearing, his neighbor?"

"Fearing wasn't a neighbor. He lived in the same building. Tests are still ongoing, but at present all evidence indicates that, yes, Fearing is definitely a person of interest in our investigation. He is currently at large and considered a fugitive from justice." *If a possible stiff can be considered a fugitive, that is.*

"What's Fearing's connection to the Ville?"

"We have not established a connection between Fearing and the Ville."

This was going better than he'd hoped: under the circumstances, the press seemed controlled, almost respectful. He nodded at another upraised hand.

"What about the search of Kline's office. Is he a suspect?"

"He's not a suspect at this time." D'Agosta avoided glancing at Rocker. Jesus, how did the press always seem to know everything?

"Then why the search?"

"I'm sorry, I can't go into that aspect of the investigation."

He began to point to another reporter, but suddenly one voice cut over the others. D'Agosta turned toward it, frowning. A man had stood up near the front: tall and preppie looking, with short sandy hair, a repp tie, and a chin cleft you could park a truck in.

"I want to know what *real* progress has been made," he said in a loud, stentorian voice. The question was so vague, yet so aggressive, that for a moment D'Agosta was stunned into silence.

"Excuse me?" he said.

"I'm Bryce Harriman," the man said. "Of the *Times*. A fellow member of the New York journalist corps—my *good friend* Bill Smithback—has been brutally murdered. A week has gone by. So let me put it a different way: why has so little real progress been made?"

A murmur ran through the crowd. A few heads nodded their agreement.

"We have made real progress. Obviously, I am not at liberty to go into all the details." D'Agosta knew how lame it sounded, but it was the best he could do.

But Harriman paid no attention. "This was an attack on a journalist for doing his job," he said with a flourish. "An attack on us, on our profession."

The assenting murmurs increased. D'Agosta began to call on another, but Harriman refused to be silent. "What's going on at the Ville?" he said, raising his voice.

"As I said, there is no evidence implicating the Ville in—"

Harriman cut him off. "Why are they allowed to keep openly torturing and killing animals—and maybe not just animals? Lieutenant, surely you must be aware that a lot of New Yorkers are asking the same question: *Why have the police done absolutely nothing?*"

All at once the crowd was in full cry—demanding, gesticulating, their expressions angry. And—as one by one they rose to their feet—Harriman sat back down again, a look of smug satisfaction creasing his patrician face.

31

The Rolls passed through a large white gate and continued up a cobbled driveway, which ran among ancient oaks before opening suddenly onto a grand mansion surrounded by outbuildings: a carriage house, a gazebo, a greenhouse, and a vast, shingled red barn built on ancient stone foundations. Beyond, a sweep of manicured lawn led down to the waters of Long Island Sound, sparkling in the morning light.

D'Agosta whistled. "Jesus, what a spread."

"Indeed. And we can't even see the caretaker's house, helipad, and trout hatchery from our current vantage point."

"Remind me why we're here again," D'Agosta said.

"Mr. Esteban is one of the people who complained most vocally about the Ville. I'm curious to hear his sentiments on the place firsthand."

At a word from Pendergast, Proctor brought the vehicle to a stop before the barn. Its doors were wide open, and without a word the agent stepped quickly out of the Rolls and disappeared into the cavernous structure.

"Hey, the house is that way . . ." D'Agosta's voice faltered. He looked around nervously. What on earth was Pendergast up to this time?

He could hear the sound of chopping wood. The noise stopped

and a moment later, a man emerged from behind the woodshed, ax in one hand. At the same time, Pendergast reappeared from the darkness of the barn.

The man came over, still holding the ax.

"Looks like we got a real Paul Bunyan here," D'Agosta murmured as the agent rejoined him.

The man was tall, with a short salt-and-pepper beard, longish hair falling below his collar, bald spot on top. Despite the Hispanic surname, he looked as Anglo as they came—in fact, except for the hairstyle, he could have been a walking advertisement for Lands' End, dressed in neatly pressed chinos, checked shirt, work gloves—lean and fit. He brushed a few wood chips off his shirt, slung the ax over his shoulder, and pulled off a glove to shake hands.

"What can I do for you?" he asked, his melodious voice bearing no trace of accent.

Pendergast slipped out his badge. "Special Agent Pendergast, Federal Bureau of Investigation. Lieutenant Vincent D'Agosta, NYPD homicide."

The eyes narrowed, the lips pursed, as he examined the badge carefully. His eyes finally glanced up and past them at the Rolls. "Nice squad car you've got there."

"Budget cuts," Pendergast replied. "One makes do as best one can."

"Right."

"You are Alexander Esteban?" D'Agosta asked.

"Correct."

"We'd like to ask a few questions, if you don't mind."

"Do you have a warrant?"

"We're looking for some help with the homicide of William Smithback, the *Times* journalist," Pendergast said. "I'd consider it a favor if you would answer our questions."

The man nodded, stroked his beard. "I knew Smithback. I'll do whatever I can to help."

"You produce films, is that correct?" Pendergast asked.

"I used to. These days I spend most of my time in philanthropic pursuits."

"I saw the article about you in *Mademoiselle*. The one that called you the 'modern DeMille.'"

"History's my passion." Esteban gave a light laugh of false modesty. It didn't work.

D'Agosta suddenly remembered: Esteban was that guy who made the splashy, cheesy historical epics. He'd gone to see the most recent with Laura Hayward, *Breakout Sing Sing,* about the famous breakout of thirty-three inmates back in the early sixties. Neither of them had liked it. There was another he vaguely recollected: *The Last Days of Marie Antoinette*.

"But more to our purpose is the organization you run. Humans for Other Animals, is that correct?"

He nodded. "HOA, right. Although I'm primarily the mouthpiece, as it were. A well-known name assigned to the cause." He smiled. "Rich Plock is the guy in charge."

"I see. And you were in touch with Mr. Smithback about the series he was planning to write on the Ville des Zirondelles, known popularly as the Ville?"

"Our organization has been concerned about reports of animal sacrifices there. It's been going on for a long time, and nothing's been done. I contacted all the papers, including the *Times,* and finally Mr. Smithback got back to me."

"When was that?"

"Let's see—it was about a week or so before he published his first article, I believe."

Pendergast nodded, then seemed to lose interest in the questioning.

D'Agosta took over. "Tell us about it."

"Smithback called me up and I met with him in the city. We had gathered some information on the Ville—complaints from neighbors, eyewitness reports of live animals being delivered, bills of sale, that sort of thing—and I gave him copies."

"Did they contain any proof?"

"Lots of proof! People in Inwood have heard animals being tortured and killed up there for years. The city hasn't done a damn thing, because of some politically correct ideas about religious freedom or some such rot. Don't get me wrong, I'm all for religious freedom—but not if it means torturing and killing animals."

"Did Smithback make any enemies that you know of by publishing that first article on animal sacrifice?"

"I'm sure he did—just as I have. Those people at the Ville are fanatics."

"Do you have any *specific* information about that? Something that was said to him, threatening phone calls or e-mails to you or him, anything like that?"

"I got something in the mail once, some charm or other. I threw it away. I don't know if it came from the Ville or not—although the package was postmarked from Upper Manhattan. Those people keep to themselves. A very, *very* strange group. Clannish and insular, to put it mildly. Been there forever, too, on that bit of ground."

D'Agosta scuffed his foot on the cobbles, thinking of what else to ask. The man wasn't telling them much they didn't already know.

Pendergast suddenly spoke again. "A lovely estate you have here, Mr. Esteban. Do you keep horses?"

"Absolutely not. I don't condone animal slavery."

"Dogs?"

"Animals are meant to live in the wild, not be demeaned in the service of man."

"Are you a vegetarian, Mr. Esteban?"

"Naturally."

"Are you married? Children?"

"Divorced, no children. Now, look—"

"Why are you a vegetarian?"

"Killing animals for the gratification of our appetites is unethical. Not to mention bad for the planet, wasteful of energy, and morally atrocious while millions are starving. Like that disgusting car of yours—sorry, I don't mean to offend you, but there's no excuse for driving a car like that." Esteban's lips pursed in disapproval, and for a moment his face reminded D'Agosta of one of the nuns who used to smack his hand with a ruler for talking in class. He wondered how Pendergast was going to take this, but the agent's face remained smoothly untroubled.

"There are quite a number of people in New York City who practice religions in which animals may be sacrificed," the agent said. "Why focus on the Ville?"

"It's the most egregious and longest-lived example. We have to start somewhere."

"How many people belong to your organization?"

Esteban seemed embarrassed. "Well, Rich is the man to give you the definitive number. I think we have a few hundred."

"You've read the recent stories in the *West Sider,* Mr. Esteban?"

"I have."

"What do you think?"

"I think that reporter is on to something. Like I said, those people are crazy. Voodoo, Obeah . . . I understand they're not even there legally, that they're squatters of some kind. The city should evict them."

"Where would they go?"

Esteban gave a short laugh. "They can go to hell for all I care."

"So you think it's okay to torture humans in hell, but not animals on earth?"

The laugh died in Esteban's throat. He looked carefully at the agent. "That's just an expression, Mister—?"

"Pendergast."

"Mr. Pendergast. Are we through here?"

"I don't think so."

D'Agosta was surprised to hear the sudden edge in Pendergast's voice.

"Well, I am."

"Do you believe in Vôdou, Mr. Esteban?"

"Are you asking if I believe people *practice* voodoo, or do I believe that it actually works?"

"Both."

"I believe those zealots up in the Ville practice voodoo. Do I think they're bringing people back from the dead? Who knows? I don't care. I just want them gone."

"Who finances your organization?"

"It's not my organization. I'm just a member. We get a lot of small donations, but if the truth be told, I'm the major source of support."

"Is it a 501(c)(3) tax-exempt organization?"

"Yes."

"Where do you get your money?"

"I did well in the movie business—but frankly, I don't see how that's any of your business." Esteban eased the ax off his shoulder. "Your questions seem rambling and pointless, Mr. Pendergast, and I'm getting tired of answering them. So would you please climb back into your carbon monster and remove yourself from my property?"

"I would be delighted." Pendergast half bowed and, with a faint smile on his face, climbed back into the Rolls, D'Agosta following.

As they were heading back into the city, D'Agosta shifted in his seat and scowled. "What a self-righteous prig. I'll bet he sinks his teeth into a bloody steak when no one's around."

Pendergast had been gazing out the window, absorbed in some private rumination. At this he turned. "Why, Vincent, I do believe that is one of the most insightful comments I've heard you make today." He pulled a thin Styrofoam tray from his suit pocket, removed the cover, and handed it to D'Agosta. Inside was a bloody absorbent pad, folded twice, along with a label affixed to a torn piece of plastic wrap. It smelled of rancid meat.

D'Agosta recoiled and handed it back quickly. "What the hell's that?"

"I found it in the trash in the barn. According to this label, it once contained a crown roast of lamb, at twelve ninety-nine the pound."

"No shit."

"Excellent price for that cut. I was tempted to ask Mr. Esteban who his butcher was." And Pendergast covered the tray, placed it on the leather seat between them, leaned back, and resumed his perusal of the passing scenery.

32

Nora Kelly turned the corner of Fifth Avenue and headed down West 53rd Street with a feeling of dread. Ahead of her, brown and yellow leaves swirled past the entrance to the Museum of Modern Art. It was dusk, and in the sharpness of the air there was a portent of the coming winter. She had taken a circuitous route from the museum—first a crosstown bus through the park, then the subway—perversely hoping for a breakdown, a traffic jam, anything that would give her an excuse to avoid what lay ahead. But public transportation had been depressingly efficient.

And now here she was, mere steps from her destination.

Of their own accord, her feet slowed, then stopped. Reaching into her bag, she pulled out the cream-colored envelope, hand-addressed to WILLIAM SMITHBACK, JR., AND GUEST. Plucking out the card inside, she read it for perhaps the hundredth time.

You are cordially invited to the
One Hundred and Twenty Seventh Annual
Press Awards Ceremony
Gotham Press Club
25 West 53rd Street, New York City
October 15, 7:00 PM

She'd attended her share of these events—typical Manhattan affairs with lots of drinking, gossip, and the usual journalistic one-upmanship. She'd never learned to like them. And this one would be worse than normal: infinitely worse. The pressed hands, the whispered condolences, the looks of sympathy . . . she felt herself becoming queasy at the mere thought. She'd done all she could to avoid precisely such things at the museum.

And yet she had to do it. Bill was getting—*would* have been getting—an honorable mention for one of the awards. And he loved these elbow-rubbing drink-fests. It seemed a dishonor to his memory to skip it. Taking a deep breath, she stuffed the invitation back into her bag and strode on. She was still shaken up by their visit to the Ville the night before last: the terrible cries of the goat, the thing that had chased them. Had it been Fearing? Nora, unsure, hadn't mentioned it to D'Agosta. But the memory haunted her, made her jumpy. Maybe this is what she needed: to get out, mingle, put it behind her.

The Gotham Press Club was a narrow building vexed by a façade of extravagantly rococo marble. Nora ascended the stairs and passed through the cast-bronze doors, surrendering her coat at the check stand and receiving a ticket in return. Ahead, from the direction of the Horace Greeley Banquet Hall, she could hear music, laughter, and the tinkling of glasses. The feeling of dread increased. Adjusting the strap of her shoulder bag, she climbed the plush red carpet and passed into the oak-paneled hall.

The event had started an hour before, and the vast space was packed. The noise was deafening, everyone talking over one another to ensure no bon mot went unappreciated. At least half a dozen bars were arrayed along the walls: journalistic events like this were notorious bacchanals. Along the right wall, a temporary stage had been erected, supporting a podium festooned with microphones. She threaded her way through the crowds, moving away from the door toward the back of the hall. If she could park herself in an out-of-the-way corner, maybe she could watch the proceedings in peace without having to endure a lot of . . .

As if on cue, a nearby man made a point with a broad gesture, sending his elbow into her ribs. He turned, glaring at her briefly before his face broke into recognition. It was Fenton Davies, Bill's boss at the *Times*. Standing in a half circle around him were a group of Bill's co-workers.

"Nora!" he exclaimed. "How good of you to come. We're all so terribly, *terribly* sorry for your loss. Bill was one of the best—a fine reporter and a stellar human being."

A chorus of agreement came from the circle of reporters.

Nora looked from face to sympathetic face. It was all she could do not to bolt. She forced herself to smile. "Thank you. That means a lot."

"I've been trying to get in touch with you. Have you gotten my calls?"

"I have, sorry. There've been so many details to clear up—"

"Of course, of course! I understand. No rush. It's just—" Here Davies lowered his voice, put his lips to her ear. "—we've been approached by the police. They seem to think it might have had something to do with his work. If that's the case, then we at the *Times* must know."

"I'll make it a point to call you when . . . when I'm a little better able to cope."

Davies straightened up, resumed his normal voice. "Also, we've been talking about organizing a memorial in Bill's name. The William Smithback award for excellence, or something along those lines. We'd like to talk to you about that, too, when you have a chance."

"Certainly."

"We're getting the word out, soliciting contributions. Maybe it could even become a part of this annual event."

"That's really great. Bill would have appreciated it."

Davies touched a hand to his bald pate and nodded, pleased.

"I'm just going to grab a drink," Nora said. "I'll catch up with you all later."

"Would you like me to—" several voices began.

"That's all right, thanks. I'll be back." And with one more smile Nora slipped away into the crowd.

She managed to gain the back of the room without encountering anyone else. She stood near the bar, trying to get her breathing under control. She never should have come. She was about to order a drink when she felt somebody touch her arm. With a sinking feeling she looked around only to see Caitlyn Kidd.

"Wasn't sure you'd be here," the reporter said.

"You've recovered from the excitement?"

"Sure." Caitlyn didn't exactly look recovered, though—her face was pale and a little drawn.

"I'm presenting the first award on behalf of the *West Sider,*" said Caitlyn, "so I've got to go up now. Let's try to hook up before you leave. I have an idea for our next move."

Nora nodded, and with a smile and a little wave the reporter disappeared into the milling crowd.

Turning back to the bartender, Nora ordered a drink, then retreated to a nearby spot against the bookcases lining the rear wall. There, standing between a bust of Washington Irving and an inscribed photograph of Ring Lardner, she watched the raucous gathering, quietly sipping her cocktail.

She glanced over at the stage. It was interesting that the *West Sider* was sponsoring one of the awards. No doubt the scrappy tabloid was trying to buy itself some respectability. Interesting, too, that Caitlyn was presenting . . .

She heard her name being called over the babel of voices. She scanned the crowd, frowning, searching for the source. There it was: a man of about forty, waving at her. For a moment, she drew a blank. Then, suddenly, she remembered the patrician features and yuppie haberdashery of Bryce Harriman. He had been her husband's nemesis during Bill's years at both the *Post* and the *Times*. There were at least a dozen people between them, and it would take a minute or two for him to wade over.

She was willing to put up with a lot, but this was too much. Placing her half-empty drink on a nearby table, she ducked behind a portly man hovering nearby and then moved away into the crowd, out of Harriman's sight.

Just then, the lights dimmed and a man took the stage. The music ceased and the crowd noise died down.

"Ladies and gentlemen!" the man cried, hands grasping the podium. "Welcome to the Gotham Press Club's annual awards ceremony. My name's McGeorge Oddon and I'm in charge of this year's nominating committee. I'm delighted to see all of you here. We have a wonderful evening in store for you tonight."

Nora braced herself for a rambling introduction, full of self-referential anecdotes and lame jokes.

"I'd love to stand here, crack bad jokes, and talk about myself," Oddon said. "But we have a lot of awards to hand out this evening. So let's get right to it!" He plucked a card from his jacket pocket, scanned it quickly. "Our first award is a new one for this year: the Jack Wilson Donohue Prize for Investigative Journalism, sponsored by the *West Sider*. And here to present the five-thousand-dollar award on behalf of the *West Sider* is that paragon of community journalists herself: Caitlyn Kidd!"

As Nora watched, Caitlyn took the stage to a chorus of applause, raucous cheers, and a few wolf whistles. She shook hands with Oddon, then plucked one of the microphones from its stand. "Thanks, McGeorge," she said. She looked slightly nervous in front of the large crowd, but her voice was strong and clear. "*West Sider* is as young as this club is old," she began. "Some people say too young. But the fact is, our newspaper couldn't be happier to be a part of this evening. And with this new award, we're putting our money where our mouth is!"

A deluge of cheers.

"There are plenty of awards for journalistic excellence," she continued. "Most of them concentrate on the quality of the printed word. Or maybe its timeliness. Or—dare I say—political correctness."

Jeers, moans, catcalls.

"But what about an award for sheer guts? For sheer doggedness of doing whatever it takes to get the story, get it *right,* get it *now.* For having—oh, all right—a set of brass balls!"

This time, the yells and applause shook the room itself.

"Because that's what *West Sider* is all about. Sure, we're a new paper. But that makes us all the hungrier."

Even as the last round of cheers died away, there was a fresh commotion at one end of the hall.

"And so it's only right that the *West Sider* is sponsoring this new award!"

A strange shudder—half gasp, half moan—rippled through the room. Nora frowned, looking over the sea of heads. Over by the entranceway, the crowds were surging backward, clearing an area. There were gasps, scattered cries of dismay.

What the hell was happening?

"With that said, I—" Caitlyn stopped in midsentence as she noticed it, too. She glanced toward the entrance. "Um, just a moment . . ."

The strange ripple in the crowd grew, parting in the direction of the stage. There was something at its center, a figure that people seemed to be recoiling from. Screams, more incoherent cries. Then—most bizarre of all—the hall fell quiet.

Caitlyn Kidd spoke into the silence. "Bill? *Smithback?*"

The figure had lurched forward and was approaching the foot of the stage. Nora stared—then felt herself physically staggered by disbelief.

It was Bill. He was dressed in a loose green hospital smock, open at the back. His skin was hideously sallow, and his face and hands were covered with caked blood. He was dreadfully, horribly changed, an apparition from someplace *beyond*—an apparition horribly similar to the one that had chased her from the Ville. And yet there was no mistaking the cowlick that reared from the mass of matted hair; no mistaking the rangy limbs.

"God," Nora heard herself groan. "Oh, *God*—"

"Smithback!" Caitlyn cried, voice shrill.

Nora couldn't move. Caitlyn screamed—a wail that cut through the air of the hall like a straight razor. "It's *you*!" she cried.

The figure was mounting the stage. His movements were shuffling, erratic. His hands hung loosely at his sides. One of them held a heavy knife, the blade barely visible beneath a heavy accumulation of gore.

Caitlyn backed up, screaming in sheer terror now.

As Nora stared, unable to move, the figure of her husband lurched up the last step, shambled across the stage.

"Bill!" Caitlyn said, shrinking back against the podium, her voice half lost in the rising cry of the crowd. "Wait! My God, no! Not me! *NO—!*"

The knife hand hesitated, shaking, in the air. Then it plunged down—into Caitlyn's chest, rose again, plunged, a sudden fountain of blood spraying across the scabby arm that slashed down, up, down. And then the figure turned and fled behind the stage, and Nora felt her knees give way and a blackness engulf her, blotting out everything, overwhelming her utterly.

33

The hallway smelled of cats. D'Agosta walked along it until he found apartment 5D. He rang the buzzer, listened as it echoed loudly inside. There was a shuffling of slippers, then the peephole darkened as an eye pressed against it.

"Who is it?" came the quavering voice.

"Lieutenant Vincent D'Agosta." He held up his shield.

"Hold it closer, I can't read it."

He held it up to the peephole.

"Step into view, I want to look at you."

D'Agosta centered himself before the peephole.

"What do you want?"

"Mrs. Pizzetti, we spoke earlier. I'm investigating the Smithback homicide."

"I don't have anything to do with no murders."

"I know, Mrs. Pizzetti. But you agreed to talk to me about Mr. Smithback, who interviewed you for the *Times*. Remember?"

A long wait. Then came the unbolting of one, two, three bolts, a chain being pulled back, and a brace being removed. The door opened a crack, held in place by a second chain.

D'Agosta held up his badge again, and a pair of beady eyes gave it a twice-over.

With a rattle, the final chain was pulled back and the door

opened. The little old lady that D'Agosta had imagined materialized before him, frail as a bone-china teacup, bathrobe clutched tightly in one blue-veined hand, lips compressed. Her eyes, black and bright as a mouse's, looked him up and down.

He quickly stepped inside to avoid having the door shut in his face. It was an old-fashioned apartment, heated to equatorial standards, large and cluttered, with overstuffed wing chairs and lace antimacassars, fringed lamps, knickknacks and bric-a-brac. And cats. Naturally.

"May I?" D'Agosta indicated a chair.

"Who's stopping you?"

D'Agosta chose the least stuffed looking of the chairs, and yet his posterior still sank down alarmingly, as if in quicksand. A cat immediately jumped up on the arm and began purring loudly, arching its back.

"Get down, Scamp, and leave the man alone." Mrs. Pizzetti had a heavy Queens accent.

Naturally, the cat did not listen. D'Agosta did not like cats. He gave it a gentle push with his elbow. The cat only purred louder, thinking it was about to get petted.

"Mrs. Pizzetti," said D'Agosta, removing his notebook and trying to ignore the cat, which was shedding hairs all over his brand-new Rothman's suit, "I understand you spoke to William Smithback on . . ." He consulted his notes. "October third."

"I don't remember when it was." She shook her head. "It just gets worse and worse."

"Can you tell me what it was you talked about?"

"I had nothing to do with no murder."

"I know that. You certainly aren't a suspect. Now, your meeting with Mr. Smithback . . . ?"

"He brought me a little present. Let's see . . ." She began poking around in the apartment, her palsied hand finally settling on a small china cat. She brought it over to D'Agosta, tossed it in his lap. "He brought me this. Chinese. You can get them down on Canal Street."

D'Agosta turned the knickknack over in his hand. This was a side of Smithback he hadn't known, bringing presents to little old ladies, even sour ones like Pizzetti. Of course, it was probably to secure an interview.

"Very nice." He set it down on a side table. "What did you talk about, Mrs. Pizzetti?"

"Those horrible animal killers over there." She gestured toward the nearest window. "There at the Ville."

"Tell me what you said to him."

"Well! You can hear the screams at night, when the wind is from the river. Horrible sounds, animals getting cut up, getting their throats cut!" Her voice rose and she said the last with a certain relish. "Someone should cut *their* throats!"

"Was there anything specific, any incidents in particular?"

"I told him about the van."

At this D'Agosta felt his heart quicken. "The van?"

"Every Thursday, like clockwork. Out the van goes at five. In it comes at nine at night."

"Today is Thursday. Did you see it today?"

"I certainly did, just like every Thursday evening."

D'Agosta stood and went to the window. It looked west, out over the back of the building. He'd walked there himself, doing a quick recon of the area prior to the interview. An old road—apparently leading to the Ville—could be seen below, running along the fields and disappearing into the trees.

"From this window?" he asked.

"What other window is there? Of course from that window."

"Any markings on the van?"

"None that I could see. Just a white van."

"Model, make?"

"I don't know about those things. It's white, dirty. Old. Piece of junk."

"You ever see the driver?"

"From up here, how could I see anyone inside? But when my window's open at night, I can sometimes hear sounds from the van. That's what made me notice it in the first place."

"Sounds? What kind?"

"Bleating. Whimpering."

"Animal sounds?"

"Certainly, animal sounds."

"May I?" He indicated the window.

"And let the cold air in? You should see my heating bills."

"Just for a moment." Without waiting for the woman to reply, he lifted the double-hung—it went up easily—and leaned out. The fall evening was cool and quiet. It was believable she'd hear something in the van, if it was loud enough.

"Look here, if you need fresh air, do it on somebody else's dime."

D'Agosta shut the window. "How's your hearing, Mrs. Pizzetti? Do you wear a hearing aid?"

"How's your hearing, Officer?" she snapped back. "Mine is perfect."

"Anything else you remember telling Smithback—or anything else about the Ville?"

She seemed to hesitate. "People talk about seeing something wandering around over there, inside the fence."

"Something? An animal?"

She shrugged. "And then they sometimes come out at night. In the van. Gone all night and come back in the morning."

"Often?"

"Two or three times a year."

"Any idea what they're up to?"

"Oh yes. Recruiting. For their cult."

"How do you know?"

"That's what people around here say. The old-timers."

"What people, specifically, Mrs. Pizzetti?"

She shrugged.

"Can you give me any names?"

"Oh no. I'm not dragging my neighbors into this. They'd kill me."

D'Agosta found himself becoming exasperated with this difficult old lady. "What else do you know?"

"I don't remember anything else. Except cats. He was very fond of cats."

"Excuse me, who was fond of cats?"

"That reporter, Smithback. Who else?"

Fond of cats. Smithback was good at his job, knew how to gain people's trust, establish a connection with them. D'Agosta recollected that Smithback loathed cats. He cleared his throat, checked his watch. "So the van is due back in an hour?"

"Never fails."

D'Agosta exited the building, breathing deep of the night air. Quiet, leafy. Hard to believe it was still Manhattan Island. He checked his watch: just after eight. He'd seen a diner down the street; he'd grab a cup of coffee and wait.

The van came right on schedule, a '97 Chevy Express with windows in front only, deeply tinted, and a ladder running up to the roof. It eased slowly onto Indian Road from West 214th, cruised the length of the block, then turned into the stem road leading to the Ville. It stopped at the padlocked chain.

D'Agosta timed his steps so that he was just crossing behind the van as the driver's door opened. A man got out, went up to the padlock, and unlocked it. D'Agosta couldn't get a clear view in the dim light, but he seemed to be extraordinarily tall. He wore a long coat that looked almost antique, like something out of a Western movie. D'Agosta paused to fish out and light a cigarette, keeping his head down. Chain down, the man came back, got in the cab, drove the van across the chain, stopped again.

Dropping the cigarette, D'Agosta darted forward, keeping the van between himself and the man. He listened as the man raised the chain again, padlocked it, and returned to the driver's door. Then, keeping low, D'Agosta slid around to the rear, stepping onto the bumper and grabbing hold of the ladder. This was public land, city land. There was no reason why an officer of the law couldn't enter, as long as he didn't trespass inside any private buildings.

The van crept forward, the driver cautious and slow. They left the dim lights of Upper Manhattan behind and were soon among the dark, silent trees of Inwood Hill Park. Although the windows were closed tight, the sounds Mrs. Pizzetti had mentioned were all too plain to D'Agosta: a chorus of crying, bleating, meowing, barking, clucking, and—even more horrifying—the terrified whinny of what could only be a newborn colt. At the thought of the pitiful menagerie within, and the fate that they seemed all too clearly destined for, D'Agosta felt white-hot anger boil up inside him.

The van crested a hill, descended, then stopped. D'Agosta heard the driver get out. As he did so, D'Agosta leapt from the rear of the van and sprinted into the nearby woods, diving into the dark leaves. Rolling into a crouch, he glanced back in the direction of the van. The driver was unlocking an old gate in a chain-link fence, and for the briefest of instants the face passed through the glow of the headlights. His skin was pale, and there was something strikingly refined, almost aristocratic, about it.

The van went through the gate; the man emerged once again and relocked it; then, getting back in, he drove on. D'Agosta rose and brushed off the leaves, his hands trembling with fury. Nothing was going to keep him out now, not with all those animals at risk. He was an officer of the law in performance of his duty. As a homicide detective, he didn't normally wear a uniform; taking his badge out and pinning it to his lapel, he scaled the chain-link fence and set off down the road, where the taillights of the van had disappeared. The road curved and ahead he could faintly make out the spire of a large, rudely built church, surrounded by a disorganized cluster of dim lights.

After a minute, he stopped in the middle of the road and turned, peering into the darkness. Some cop instinct told him he wasn't alone. He pulled out his Maglite and played it about the tree trunks, the dead bushes with their rustling leaves.

"Who's there?"

Silence.

D'Agosta turned off the Maglite and slipped it back into his pocket. He continued staring into the darkness. There was the faint light of a quarter moon, and the trunks of the beech trees seemed to float in the darkness like long scabby legs. He listened intently. There *was* something there. He could feel it—and now he could hear it. A faint crush of damp leaves, the crack of a twig.

He reached for his service revolver. "I'm a New York City police officer," he rapped out. "Step into the roadway, please." He left the torch off—he could see farther into the gloom without it.

Now he could see, just barely, a pale shape moving with a strange, lurching gait through the trees. It ducked into a stand of deep brush and he lost it. A strange moaning floated out from the woods, inarticulate and sepulchral, as if from a mouth yawning wide and slack: *aaaaahhhhhuuuu* . . .

He slipped the torch out of his holster, turned it on, flashed it through the trees. Nothing.

This was bullshit. Some kids were playing a game with him.

He strode toward the area of brush, playing the light about. It was a large tangle of overgrown azaleas and mountain laurel stretching for hundreds of feet—he paused, and then pushed in.

In response, he heard the rustling of brush to his right. He flashed the light toward it, but the bright beam striking the tightly packed brush prevented him from seeing deeper. He switched off the light and waited, his eyes adjusting. He spoke calmly. "This is public property and I'm a police officer—show yourself now or I'll charge you with resisting arrest."

The single crack of a twig came, once again from his right. Turning toward it, he saw a figure rear up out of the bracken: pallid, sickly green skin; slack face smeared with blood and mucus; clothes hanging from knobby limbs in rags and tatters.

"Hey, you!"

It reared back, as if temporarily losing its balance, then lurched forward and began to approach with an almost diabolical hunger. One eye swiveled toward him, then moved away; the other eye was hidden in a thick crusting of blood or perhaps mud. *Aaaaahhuuuu . . .*

"Jesus Christ!" D'Agosta yelled, leaping backward, dropping the flashlight and fumbling for his service piece, a Glock 19.

Abruptly, the thing rushed him, bulling through the brush with a crashing sound; he raised his gun but at the same moment felt a stunning blow to his head, a humming sound, and then nothing.

34

Monica Hatto's eyes flew open and she straightened at her desk, squaring her shoulders, trying to look alert. She glanced around nervously. The big clock against the tiled wall opposite her indicated it was half past nine. The last night-desk receptionist in the morgue annex had been fired for sleeping on the job. Adjusting the papers on the desk, she looked about once again, relaxing somewhat. The fluorescent lights in the annex cast their usual pall over the tiled floors and walls, and the air smelled of the usual chemicals. All was quiet.

But *something* had woken her up.

Hatto rose and smoothed her hands down her sides, adjusting her uniform over her copious love-handles, trying to look neat, alert, and presentable. This was one job she couldn't afford to lose. It paid well and, what's more, came with health benefits.

There was a muffled sound, almost like a commotion, somewhere upstairs. A "mort" was on its way, perhaps. Hatto smiled to herself, proud of her growing command of the lingo. She slipped a makeup mirror from her handbag and touched up her lips, adjusted her hair with a few deft pats, examined her nose for that horrid oily shine.

She heard a second sound, the faint boom of an elevator door closing. Another once-over, a dab of scent, and the mirror went back into the bag, the bag back over the arm of her chair, the papers once more squared on the desk.

Now the sound of pounding of feet came, not from the bank of elevators, but from the stairwell. That was odd.

The feet approached rapidly. Then the stairwell door flew open with a crash and a woman came tearing down the corridor, wearing a black cocktail dress, running in high-heeled shoes, her copper hair flying.

Hatto was so surprised she didn't know what to say.

The woman came to stop in the middle of the annex, her face gray in the ghastly fluorescent light.

"Can I help you—?" Hatto began.

"Where is it?" the woman screamed. "I want to see it!"

Monica Hatto stared. "It?"

"My husband's body! William Smithback!"

Hatto backed up, terrified. The woman was crazy. As she waited for an answer, sobbing, Hatto could hear the rumble of the slow, slow elevator starting up.

"The name's Smithback! *Where is it?*"

On the desk behind her, a voice suddenly bawled out of the intercom. "Security breach! We've got a security breach! Hatto, you read?"

The voice broke the spell. Hatto punched the button.

"There's a—"

The voice on the intercom overrode hers. "You got a nutcase coming your way! Female, might be violent! Don't engage her physically! Security's on its way!"

"She's already—"

"Smithback!" the woman cried. "The journalist who was murdered!"

Hatto's eyes involuntarily flickered toward Morgue 2, where they had been working on the famous reporter's cadaver. It was a big deal, with a call from the police commissioner and front-page stories in the newspaper.

The woman broke for the Morgue 2 door, which had been left open by the night cleaning crew. Too late, Hatto realized she should have closed and locked it.

"Wait, you're not allowed in there—!"

The woman disappeared through the door. Hatto stood, rooted by panic. There was nothing in the employment manual about what to do in this kind of situation.

With a *ding!* the elevator doors creaked open. Two portly security guards came huffing out into the annex. "Hey," *gasp,* "where'd she go—?" *gasp.*

Hatto turned, pointed mutely to Morgue 2.

The two heaving guards stood for a moment, trying to catch their breath. A crash came from the morgue, the slamming of steel, the screech of a metal drawer being flung open. There was a tearing sound and a cry.

"Oh, Jesus," one of the guards said. They lumbered back into motion, across the annex toward the open door of Morgue 2. Hatto followed on unwilling legs, morbid curiosity aroused.

A scene greeted her eyes that she would never forget as long as she lived. The woman stood in the center of the room, her face like a witch's, hair wild, teeth bared, eyes flashing. Behind her, one of the morgue drawers had been pulled out. She was shaking a body bag, bloodied and empty, with one hand; the other hand held up what looked like a small bundle of feathers.

"Where's his body?" she screamed. *"Where's my husband's body? And who left* this *here?"*

35

D'Agosta parked the squad car under the porte-cochere of 891 Riverside Drive, got out, and pounded on the heavy wooden door. Thirty seconds later it was opened by Proctor, who gazed at him silently for a moment and then stood aside.

"You'll find him in the library," he murmured.

D'Agosta staggered down the length of the refectory, across the reception hall, and into the library, all the while pressing a cloth tight against the cut on his head. He found Pendergast—and the strange old archivist named Wren—sitting in leather wing chairs on either side of a blazing fire, a table between them laden with papers and a bottle of port.

"Vincent!" Pendergast rose with haste and came over. "What happened? Proctor, the man needs a chair."

"I can get my own chair, thanks." D'Agosta sat down, dabbing gingerly at his head. The bleeding had finally stopped. "Had a little accident up at the Ville," he said in a low voice. He didn't know what made him angrier: the thought of those animals being butchered, or the fact that he'd allowed some wino to get the drop on him. At least, he sure as hell hoped it was a wino. He wasn't prepared to think about the alternative.

Pendergast bent over to examine the cut but D'Agosta waved

him away. "It's only a scratch. Heads always bleed like a stuck pig."

"May I offer you some refreshment? Port, perhaps?"

"Beer. Bud Light, if you've got it."

Proctor left the room.

Wren was sitting in his wing chair as if nothing untoward were happening. He was sharpening a pencil by hand with a tiny pocketknife: examining the tip, blowing on it, pursing his lips, sharpening a bit more.

The frosty can soon arrived on a silver salver, along with a chilled glass. Ignoring the glass, D'Agosta grabbed the beer and took a long pull. "Needed that, big-time," he said. He took another pull.

Pendergast had returned to his own wing chair. "My dear Vincent, we are all ears."

D'Agosta told the story of his interview with the woman on Indian Road and the events that followed. He didn't mention the fact that he'd almost walked into the Ville single-handedly in his rage—something he'd thought better of upon reviving. Pendergast listened intently. Vicent also decided to bypass the fact that he'd lost his cell phone and pager in the attack. When he had finished, a silence gathered in the library. The fire crackled and burned.

At last, Pendergast stirred. "And this—this man? He moved erratically, you say?"

"Yes."

"And he was covered with blood and gore?"

"That's what it looked like in the moonlight, anyway."

Pendergast paused. "Was there a resemblance to the figure we saw in the security video?"

"Yes, there was."

Another pause, longer this time. "Was it Colin Fearing?"

"No. Yes." D'Agosta shook his throbbing head. "I don't know. I didn't see the face all that well."

Pendergast was silent for a long time, his smooth forehead creasing slightly. "And this happened when, precisely?"

"Thirty minutes ago. I was only out for a moment. Since I was uptown already, I came straight here."

"Curious." But the expression on Pendergast's face wasn't curious. It looked more like alarm.

After a moment, Pendergast glanced toward the wizened old man. "Wren was just about to share the fruits of his recent research on the very place you were attacked. Wren, would you care to continue?"

"Delighted," said Wren. Two heavily veined hands reached into the pile of papers and deftly extracted a brown folder. "Shall I read from the articles—?"

"You may recapitulate succinctly, if you please."

"Of course." Wren cleared his throat, carefully arranged the papers in his lap, sorted through them. "Hmm. Let us see . . ." Shuffling and examination of papers; many eyebrow movements, grunts, and tappings. "On the evening of June eleven, 1901 . . ."

"*Succinctly* is the operative word," murmured Pendergast, his tone not unfriendly.

"Yes, yes! Succinctly." A great clearing of phlegm. "It seems that the Ville has been, shall we say, *controversial* for some time. I have collected a series of articles from the *New York Sun,* dating from around the turn of the century—the turn of the twentieth century, that is—describing complaints of neighbors not dissimilar to the ones being made today. Strange noises and smells, headless animal carcasses found in the woods, carryings-on. There were many unconfirmed reports of a 'wandering shadow' divagating about the woods of Inwood Hill."

The liver-spotted hand removed a yellowed clipping with exquisite care, as if it were the leaf of an illuminated manuscript. He read.

> According to sources this paper has spoken with, this apparition—described by eyewitnesses as a shambling, seemingly mindless being—has been preying on Gotham citizenry unlucky or unwise enough to be caught in the environs of Inwood Hill after dark. Its attacks have often been lethal. The corpses that have been left behind have been found draped in dreadful attitudes of repose, mutilated in the most grievous manner imaginable. Others have merely disappeared—never to be seen again.

"How exactly were they mutilated?" D'Agosta asked.

"Disemboweled, with certain digits cut off—most frequently, middle fingers and toes—or so the paper says. The *Sun,* Lieutenant, was not known for its probity. It was the originator of 'yellow journalism.' You see, it was printed on yellowish paper, as it was the cheapest available at the time. Bleaching and sizing added a good twenty percent to the cost of newsprint in those days—"

"Very interesting," Pendergast interjected smoothly. "Pray continue, Mr. Wren."

More shufflings and tappings. "If you believe these stories, it appears that four people may have been killed by this so-called mindless being."

"Four people? That's the extent of the 'Gotham citizenry'?"

"As I told you, Lieutenant, the *Sun* was a sensationalist paper. Exaggeration was its stock in trade. The reports must be read with a grain of salt."

"Who were the citizens killed?"

"The first, who had been decapitated, was unidentified. The second was a landscape architect named Phipps Gormly. The third was a member of the parks commission, also a highly respectable citizen, apparently out for an evening's constitutional. One Cornelius Sprague. The murder of two respectable citizens back-to-back raised an uproar. The fourth killing, almost immediately on the heels of the third, was a groundskeeper at a local estate: the Straus summer cottage on Inwood Hill. The strange part of this last killing was that the groundskeeper had disappeared a few months before his body was found. But he had been freshly killed."

D'Agosta shifted in his chair. "Disemboweled? And fingers and toes cut off, you say?"

"The others, yes. But the groundskeeper was not disemboweled. He was found covered in blood, a knife in his chest. According to the papers, the wound might have been self-inflicted."

"What was the upshot?" D'Agosta asked.

"It appears the police raided the Ville and arrested several people, who later had to be released for lack of evidence. Searches turned up nothing, and the cases were never solved. Nothing definitely connected the killings with the Ville, beyond the proximity of the village to the crime scenes. Stories of shambling, mindless creatures died away, and reports of animal sacrifices grew relatively spotty—the Ville seems to have lain low. Until now, of course. But here's the most interesting thing of all, something I managed to turn up by cross-checking a variety of other old records. It seems that in 1901, the Straus family wanted to clear-cut a large northern section of Inwood Hill, affording them a better view of the Hudson River. They hired a landscape architect to design the new plantings in the finest of taste. Guess what his name was?"

There was a brief silence. "Not Phipps Gormly?" Pendergast said.

"The same. And would you care to guess the park commissioner involved in clearing the necessary variances?"

"Cornelius Sprague." Pendergast sat in his chair, leaning forward, hands clasped. "If those plans to clear the park had gone through, would the Ville have been affected?"

Wren nodded. "It stood directly in the path. It would have undoubtedly been torn down."

D'Agosta looked from Pendergast to Wren and back again. "Are you saying the Ville murdered those people to discourage the family from going ahead with their landscaping plans?"

"Murdered—or *arranged* for them to be murdered. The police were never able to establish a connection. However, the message clearly got through. Because the plan to re-landscape the park was obviously abandoned."

"Anything else?"

Wren shuffled through his papers. "The articles talk about a 'devilish cult' at the Ville. The members are celibate, and they keep their numbers steady by recruitment or press-ganging street people and the less fortunate."

"Curioser and curioser," murmured Pendergast. He turned to D'Agosta. "'Mindless apparition' . . . Not so very different from what attacked you, eh, Vincent?"

D'Agosta scowled.

The elegant white hands unclasped and reclasped as Pendergast sank into deep thought. Somewhere, in the bowels of the great mansion, came the old-fashioned ringing of a phone.

Pendergast roused himself. "It would be useful to get one's hands on the remains of one of those victims."

D'Agosta grunted. "Gormly and Sprague are probably buried in family plots. You'll never get a warrant."

"Ah. But the fourth victim, the Straus family groundskeeper—the supposed suicide—it's just possible he'll yield up his secrets more easily. And if so, we shall be in luck. Because of all the bodies, *his* is the one of greatest interest to us."

"Why is that?"

Pendergast smiled faintly. "Why, my dear Vincent, why do you think?"

D'Agosta frowned in exasperation. "Damn it, Pendergast, my head hurts. I'm not in the mood to play Sherlock Holmes!"

A pained look briefly appeared on the agent's face. "Very well," he said after a moment. "Here are the salient points. Unlike the others, the body was not disemboweled. It was covered in blood, the clothes in rags. It was a possible suicide. And it was *the last to be found.* After its discovery, the killings ceased. And I might point out that he had disappeared several months before the murders began—where was he? Living at the Ville, perhaps." He sat back in his chair.

D'Agosta felt gingerly at the bump on his skull. "What are you saying?"

"The groundskeeper wasn't a victim—he was the *perpetrator.*"

Despite himself, D'Agosta felt a tingle of excitement. "Go on."

"At great estates such as the one in question, it was common practice for the servants and workers to have their own family plot, where the deceased were interred. If such a plot exists at the old Straus summer house, we might find the groundskeeper's remains there."

"But you're only going on an account in a newspaper. There's no connection. Nobody's going to issue an exhumation order on such flimsy evidence."

"We can always freelance."

"Please don't tell me you intend to dig him up at night."

A faint affirmative incline of the head.

"Don't you ever do anything by the book?"

"Only infrequently, I'm afraid. A very bad habit, but one that I find hard to break."

Proctor appeared in the doorway. "Sir?" he said, his deep voice studiously neutral. "I heard from one of our contacts downtown. There have been developments."

"Share them with us, if you please."

"There was a killing at the Gotham Press Club; a reporter named Caitlyn Kidd. The perpetrator vanished, but many witnesses are swearing the killer was William Smithback."

"Smithback!" said Pendergast, rising suddenly.

Proctor nodded.

"When?"

"Ninety minutes ago. In addition, Smithback's body is missing from the morgue. His wife went looking for it there, caused a scene when it was gone. Apparently, some, ah, voodoo ephemera was left in its place." Proctor paused, his large hands folded in front of his suit coat.

D'Agosta was seized with horror and dread. All this had come down—and he was without beeper or cell phone.

"I see," murmured Pendergast, his face suddenly as sallow as a corpse's. "What a dreadful turn of events." He added in almost a whisper, to nobody in particular: "Perhaps the time has come to call in the help of Monsieur Bertin."

36

D'Agosta could see a gray dawn creeping through the curtained windows of the Gotham Press Club. He was exhausted, and his head pounded with every beat of his heart. The scene-of-crime unit had finished up their work and gone; the hair and fiber guys had come and gone; the photographer had come and gone; the M.E. had collected the corpse; all the witnesses had been questioned or scheduled for questioning; and now D'Agosta found himself alone at the sealed crime scene.

He could hear the traffic on 53rd Street, the early delivery vans, the crack-of-dawn garbage pickups, the day-shift taxi drivers beginning their rounds with the usual wake-up ritual of horn blaring and cursing.

D'Agosta remained standing quietly in the corner of the room. It was very elegant and old New York; the walls covered with dark oak paneling, a fireplace with carved mantelpieces, a marble floor tiled in black and white, a crystal chandelier above and tall mullioned windows with gold-embroidered drapes. The room smelled of old smoke, stale hors d'oeuvres, and spilled wine. Quite a lot of food and broken glass was strewn about the floor from the panic at the time of the murder. But there was nothing more for D'Agosta to see, no lack of witnesses or evidence. The killer had committed murder in front of more than two hundred people—not one lily-livered journalist had tried to stop him—and then escaped out the back kitchen, through several sets of doors left unlocked by the catering group whose van was parked in a lane behind the building.

Had the killer known that? Yes. All the witnesses reported that the killer had moved surely—not swiftly, but deliberately—straight for one of the room's rear service doors, down a hall, through the kitchen, and out. He knew the layout of the place, knew the doors were unlocked, knew the gates blocking the back lane would be open, knew that it led to 54th Street and the anonymity of the crowd. Or a waiting car. Because this had all the appearance of being a well-planned crime.

D'Agosta rubbed his nose, trying to breathe slowly, to reduce the pounding in his temples. He could hardly think. Those bastards at the Ville were going to realize they had made a serious mistake in assaulting a police officer. They were involved in this, one way or another, he felt sure. Smithback had written about them and paid dearly for it; now the same fate had befallen Caitlyn Kidd.

Why was he still here? There was nothing new he could extract from the crime scene, nothing that hadn't already been examined, recorded, photographed, picked over, tested, sniffed, eyeballed, and noted for the record. He was utterly exhausted. And yet he couldn't bring himself to leave.

Smithback. That, he knew, was the reason he couldn't leave.

The witnesses all swore it was Smithback. Even Nora, whom he had interviewed—sedated but lucid enough—at her apartment. Nora had seen the killer from across the room, so she was less reliable—but there were others who had seen the killer up close and swore it was him. The victim herself had shouted out his name as he approached her. And yet a few days earlier, D'Agosta had seen with his very own eyes Smithback's dead body on a gurney, his chest opened, his organs removed and tagged, the top of his skull sawed open.

Smithback's body gone . . . How could some jackass just walk into the morgue and steal a body? Maybe it wasn't so surprising—Nora had charged right in and nobody stopped her. There was only one night receiver, and people in that position seemed to have a history of sleeping on the job. But Nora had been chased, and ultimately caught, by security. And charging into a morgue was a lot different than leaving with a body.

Unless the body left on its own . . .

What the hell was he thinking? A dozen theories were swimming in his head. He'd been certain the Ville was involved somehow. But of course he couldn't dismiss that software developer, Kline, who had threatened Smithback so openly. As he'd told Rocker, certain pieces of his African sculpture had been identified by museum specialists as voodoo artifacts with particularly dark significance. Although that brought up the question of why Kline would want to kill Caitlyn Kidd. Had Kidd written about him, too? Or did something about her remind him of the journalist who had once destroyed his budding career? That was worth looking into.

And then, there was that other theory that Pendergast, despite all his dissembling, seemed to take seriously: that Smithback, like Fearing, had been raised from the dead.

"Son of a *bitch,*" he muttered out loud, turning and walking out of the reception hall into the foyer. The cop guarding the front door signed him out, and he stepped into a chill, gray October dawn.

He glanced at his watch. Six forty-five. He was due to meet Pendergast downtown at nine. Leaving his squad car parked on Fifth, he walked down 53rd to Madison, stepped into a coffee shop, eased himself into a chair.

By the time the waitress arrived, he was already asleep.

37

At ten after nine in the morning, D'Agosta gave up waiting for Pendergast and made his way from the lobby of City Hall to an anonymous office on a high floor of the building, which took him another ten minutes to find. At last he stood before the closed office door, reading its engraved plastic plaque:

MARTY WARTEK
DEPUTY ASSOCIATE DIRECTOR
NEW YORK CITY HOUSING AUTHORITY
BOROUGH OF MANHATTAN

He gave the door a double rap.

"Come in," came a thin voice.

D'Agosta entered. The office was surprisingly spacious and comfortable, with a sofa and two easy chairs on one side, a desk on the other, and an alcove containing an old bag of a secretary. A single window looked into the forest of towers that constituted Wall Street.

"Lieutenant D'Agosta?" asked the office's occupant, rising from behind his desk and indicating one of the easy chairs. D'Agosta took the sofa instead: it looked more comfortable.

The man came around the desk and settled himself in a chair.

D'Agosta took him in quickly: small, slight, ill-fitting brown suit, razor-burned, tufts of thinning hair springing from the middle of a bald head, nervous shifty brown eyes, small trembly hands, tight mouth, self-righteous air.

D'Agosta started to remove his shield, but Wartek quickly shook his head. "Not necessary. Anyone can see you're a detective."

"That so?" D'Agosta was somehow offended. He realized he was hoping to be offended. *Vinnie-boy, just take it easy.*

A silence. "Coffee?"

"Thank you. Regular."

"Susy, two regular coffees, please."

D'Agosta tried to organize his thinking. His mind was shot. "Mr. Wartek—"

"Please call me Marty." The guy was making an effort to be friendly, D'Agosta reminded himself. No need to be an asshole in return.

"Marty, I'm here to talk about the Ville. Up in Inwood. You know it?"

A cautious affirmative nod. "I've read the articles."

"I want to know how the hell it is these people can occupy city land and block off a public access road—and get away with it." D'Agosta hadn't meant to be so blunt, but it just came out that way. He was too damn tired to care.

"Well, now." Wartek leaned forward. "You see, Lieutenant, there's a point of law called a 'proscriptive easement' or 'right of adverse possession'"—he indicated the quotation marks with nervous darts of his fingers—"which states that if a piece of land has been occupied and used in an 'open and notorious' manner for a certain specific period of time without the permission of the owner, then the using party acquires certain legal rights to the property. In New York, that specific period of time is twenty years."

D'Agosta stared. What the man had said was just so much noise in his ear. "Sorry. I didn't follow you."

A sigh. "It seems the residents of the Ville have occupied that land since at least the Civil War. It was an abandoned church with numerous outbuildings, I believe, and they simply squatted there. There were a lot of squatters in New York City at the time. Central Park was full of them: little kitchen farms, pigpens, shacks, and so forth."

"They're not in Central Park now."

"True, true—the squatters were evicted from Central Park when it was designated a park. But the northern tip of Manhattan was always something of a no-man's-land. It's rocky and rugged, unsuited to farming or development. Inwood Hill Park wasn't created until the thirties. By that time, the residents of the Ville had acquired a right of adverse possession."

The man's insistent, lecture-hall tone of voice was starting to grate. "Look, I'm no lawyer. All I know is, they don't have title to the land and they've blocked a public way. I'm still waiting to hear how that's possible." D'Agosta folded his arms and sat back.

"Lieutenant, please. I am *trying* to explain this to you. They've been there for a hundred and fifty years. They *have* acquired rights."

"Rights to block a city street?"

"Perhaps."

"So you mean, if I decide to barricade Fifth Avenue, it's okay? I have a right to do it?"

"You'd be arrested. The city would object. The law of adverse possession would never apply."

"All right then, I break into your apartment while you're away, live there rent free for twenty years, and then it's mine?"

The coffees arrived, milky and lukewarm. D'Agosta drank half his down. Wartek sipped his with poked-out lips.

"In point of fact," he continued, "it would be yours, if your occupation of the apartment were open and notorious and if I never gave you permission to be there. You would eventually acquire a right of adverse possession, because—"

"What the hell—are we Communist Russia, or what?"

"Lieutenant, I didn't write the law but I have to say it's a perfectly reasonable one. It's to protect you if you, say, accidentally build a septic system that encroaches on a neighbor's land and that neighbor doesn't notice or complain for twenty years—do you think you should have to take it away if he notices it then?"

"An entire village in Manhattan is not a septic system."

Wartek's voice had climbed a notch as he became excited, a rashy splotch spreading over his neck. "Septic system or entire village, it's the same principle! If the owner doesn't object or notice, and you are using the property openly, then you *do* acquire certain rights. It's as if you abandoned the property, not so different from the marine law of salvage."

"So you're telling me the city never objected to this Ville?"

A silence. "Well, I don't know."

"Yeah, well maybe the city *did* object. Maybe there are letters on file. I'll bet—"

D'Agosta fell silent as a black-clad figure glided into the room.

"Who are you?" Wartek asked, his voice high with alarm. D'Agosta had to admit that Pendergast was a rather disturbing presence at first notice—all black and white, his skin so pale he almost looked dead, his silver eyes like newly minted dimes.

"Special Agent Pendergast, Federal Bureau of Investigation, at your service, sir." Pendergast gave a little bow. He reached into his suit and produced a manila file, which he laid on the desk and opened. Inside were photocopies of old letters on New York City letterhead.

"What's this?" Wartek asked.

"The letters." He turned to D'Agosta. "Vincent, please forgive my tardiness."

"Letters?" Wartek asked, frowning.

"The letters in which the city objected to the Ville. Going back to 1864."

"Where did you get these?"

"I have a researcher at the library. An excellent fellow, I recommend him highly."

"So," said D'Agosta. "There you have it. No right of possession or whatever the hell it was you said."

The rash on Wartek's neck deepened. "Lieutenant, we are *not* going to institute eviction proceedings against these people just because you or this FBI agent want us to. I suspect this crusade of yours might have something to do with certain religious practices you find objectionable. Well, there is a question of religious freedom here, as well."

"Freedom of religion—to torture and kill animals . . . or worse?" D'Agosta said. "To clobber policemen in the performance of their duty? To disturb the peace and tranquility of the neighborhood?"

"There has to be due process."

"Of course," said Pendergast, interjecting smoothly. "Due process. That is where your office comes in—to institute the due process. And that is why we are here, to suggest that you do so with all dispatch."

"This kind of decision takes long and careful study. It takes legal consultations, staff meetings, and documentary research. It can't happen overnight."

"If only we had the time, my dear Mr. Wartek! Popular opinion is moving against you even as we speak. Did you see the papers this morning?"

The rash had overspread most of Wartek's face and he was beginning to sweat. He rose to his full five-foot-three-inch height. "As I said, we'll study the issue," he repeated, ushering them to the door.

On the way down in a crowded elevator full of somnolent gray suits, Pendergast turned to D'Agosta and said, "How lovely, my dear Vincent, to see New York City bureaucracy in vibrant, full-throated action!"

38

The waiting area at JFK's Terminal 8 was at the bottom of a wide bank of escalators. Pendergast and D'Agosta stood along with a gaggle of portly men in black suits, holding up little signs with people's names on them.

"Tell me again," said D'Agosta. "Who is this guy? And what's he doing here?"

"Monsieur Bertin. He was our tutor when we were youths."

"We? You mean, you and . . ."

"Yes. My brother. Monsieur Bertin taught us zoology and natural history. I was rather taken with him—he was a charming and charismatic fellow. Unfortunately, he had to leave the family employ."

"What happened?"

"The fire."

"Fire? You mean, when your house burned down? Did he have something to do with it?"

There was a sudden, freezing silence from Pendergast.

"So this man's expertise is . . . zoology? And you call him in on a murder case? Am I missing something here?"

"While Monsieur Bertin was hired to teach us natural history, he was also extremely knowledgeable about local lore and legend: Vôdou, Obeah, rootwork, and conjure."

"So he branched out. And taught you more than how to dissect a frog."

"I'd prefer not to dwell on the past. The fact is, Monsieur Bertin knows as much about the subject as anyone alive. That's why I asked him to fly up from Louisiana."

"You really think voodoo is involved?"

"You don't?" Pendergast turned his silvery eyes on D'Agosta.

"I think some asshole is trying to make us *think* voodoo is involved."

"Is there a difference? Ah. Here he is now."

D'Agosta turned, then started despite himself. Approaching them was a tiny man in a swallowtail coat. His skin was almost as pale as Pendergast's, and he wore a floppy, broad-brimmed white hat. What looked like a shrunken head dangled from a heavy gold chain around his neck. One hand gripped an ancient, travel-stained BOAC flight bag; the other was tapping a massive, fantastically carved cane before him. *Cane* didn't do it justice, D'Agosta decided; *walking stick* was more like it. *Cudgel* was even better. He looked like some faith healer from a traveling medicine show, or one of the nutcases who wandered about JFK because it was warmer inside than out. In a place like New York City, where people had seen just about everything, this weirdo was getting a lot of stares. The man was trailed by a skycap burdened down with an alarming number of suitcases.

"Aloysius!" He came bustling over on bird-like legs and kissed Pendergast on both cheeks in the French style. "*Quelle plaisir!* You haven't aged a day."

He turned and stared at D'Agosta, looking him swiftly up and down with a fierce black eye. "Who is this man?"

"I'm Lieutenant D'Agosta." He held out his hand, but it was ignored.

The man turned back to Pendergast. "A *policeman*?"

"I'm also a policeman, *maître.*" Pendergast almost seemed amused by the excitable little fellow.

"Pah!" The white hat flopped up and down with disdainful disapproval. A pack of cigarillos appeared in Bertin's hand, and he shucked one out and fitted it into a mother-of-pearl cigarette holder.

"I'm sorry, *maître,* but there's no smoking in here."

"Barbarians." Bertin put the thing in his mouth anyway, unlit. "Show me to the car."

They went out to the curb, where Proctor was waiting. "What, a Rolls-Royce? How vulgar!"

While the skycap loaded the suitcases into the trunk, D'Agosta was dismayed to see Pendergast slip into the front seat, leaving him to share the back with Bertin. Once inside, the man immediately produced a gold lighter and set the cigarillo aflame.

"Excuse me—do you mind?" D'Agosta said.

The man turned his bright black eyes toward him. "I *do* mind." He inhaled deeply, cracked the window with a look askance at D'Agosta, and exhaled a thin stream through pursed lips. He leaned forward. "Now, Aloysius, I've been mulling over the information you gave me. The photographs you sent of the charms found at the murder scene—they are *mal, très mal*! The doll of feathers and Spanish moss; the needles wrapped in black thread; the name inscribed on parchment; and that powder—saltpeter, I assume?"

"Correct."

Bertin nodded. "There can be no question. A death conjure."

"Death conjure?" D'Agosta said in disbelief.

"Also known as a 'killing hurt,'" Bertin said in full-throated lecture-hall style. "That is flat-out hoodoo. That could have been dealt with more easily. But this—this *revenant,* this dead man walking. That is serious. That is Vôdou proper. Especially . . ." Here he dropped his voice. ". . . now that the victim has returned as well." He looked at Pendergast. "He has a wife, you say?"

"Yes."

"She is in serious danger."

"I've put in a request for police protection," D'Agosta said.

Bertin scoffed. "Pah!"

"I purchased her an enemy-be-gone charm," said Pendergast.

"That may be of use against the *first* one, but he I am not so worried about. Such charms are useless against family or kin—including husbands."

"I also prepared a charm bag and urged her to keep it in her pocket."

Bertin's expression brightened. "A mojo hand! *Très bien*. Tell me: what did it contain?"

"Protection oil, High John the Conqueror root, vervain, and wormwood."

D'Agosta scarcely believed what he was hearing. He looked from Pendergast to Bertin and back again.

Bertin sat back. "This will continue unless we can find the conjure-doctor. Turn the trick."

"We're working on a search warrant for the Ville now. And we spoke to the city yesterday about possible eviction proceedings."

Bertin muttered to himself, then issued another stream of smoke. D'Agosta had once enjoyed cigars, but they had been normal, man-size things. The Rolls was filling up with disgusting clove-scented smoke.

"I heard about this guy once," said D'Agosta. "He used to smoke those skinny little sticks."

Bertin looked at him sideways.

"Got cancer. Had to cut off his lips."

"Who needs lips?" Bertin asked.

D'Agosta could feel the man's beady eyes on his face. He opened his window, crossed his arms, and sat back, closing his eyes.

Just when he was about to drift off, his newly replaced cell phone went off. He glanced down, read the text message. "The search warrant finally came through for the Ville," he told Pendergast.

"Excellent. How broad?"

"Pretty limited, actually. The public areas of the church itself, the altar and tabernacle—assuming there is one—but not the sacristy or the other non-public areas, or the outlying buildings."

"Very well. It's enough to get us in—and introduce us to the people there. Monsieur Bertin will accompany us."

"And how are we going to justify that?"

"I have engaged him as a special consultant to the FBI on the case."

"Yeah, right." D'Agosta ran a hand through his thinning hair, sighed, and leaned back in the seat, closing his eyes again, hoping for a few minutes of nap. Unbelievable. Just frigging unbelievable.

39

Nora stared at the ceiling of her bedroom, her gaze traveling back and forth along a crack in the plaster. Back and forth, back and forth, her eye following its meanderings as one would follow river tributaries on a map. She remembered Bill volunteering to plaster and repaint that crack, saying it drove him crazy when he lay down and tried to nap during the day—which he often did, forced as he was to keep journalistic hours. She had said it was a waste, sinking money into a rental apartment, and he'd never mentioned it again.

Now it was driving *her* crazy. She couldn't take her eyes off it.

With a sharp effort she turned her head and stared out the open window beside her bed. Through the bars of the fire escape beyond she could see the apartment building across the alley, pigeons strutting along the wooden water tank atop its roof. Sounds of traffic—horns, the blat of a diesel, the grinding of gears—filtered up from the adjacent street. Her limbs felt heavy, her senses unreal. Unreal. Everything had become unreal. The last forty-four hours had been bizarre, obscene, unbearable. Bill's body missing; Caitlyn dead, dead at the hands of . . . She squeezed her eyes closed for a moment, forcing the thought away. She had given up trying to make sense of anything.

She focused on the alarm clock next to the bedside table. Its red

LED glowed back at her: three PM. This was stupid, lying in bed in the middle of the day.

With a huge effort she sat up, her body feeling as dull and soft as lead. For a moment the room spun around, then stabilized a little. She plumped up her pillow and eased back against it, sighing as her gaze drifted unwillingly back to the crack in the ceiling.

There was a creak of metal outside the window. She glanced toward it, saw nothing but the bright light of an Indian summer afternoon.

Tomorrow was supposed to have been Bill's funeral. Over the last several days she'd been doing her best to ready herself for the ordeal: it would be painful, but it would at least bring an end of sorts, maybe allow her to move on a little. But now even that bit of closure was denied her. How could there be a funeral with no body? She closed her eyes, groaned softly.

Another groan—low, guttural—echoed her own.

Her eyes flew open. A figure was crouching on the fire escape just outside her window—a grotesque figure, a monster: hair matted, pale skin crudely stitched up, its crabbed form covered by a bloody hospital gown sticky with bodily fluids and clotted blood. One bony hand gripped a truncheon.

The face was puffy and malformed, and covered with dried clots of blood—yet it was still recognizable. Nora felt her throat close with utter horror: the monster was her husband, Bill Smithback.

A strange sound filled the bedroom, a soft, high keening noise, and it took her a moment to realize it was coming from her own lips. She was filled with revulsion—and a sick longing. Bill—alive. Could it be? Could it possibly be him?

The figure slowly shifted position, moving forward on crouched hams.

White spots began to dance before her eyes and a sensation of heat bloomed throughout her body, as if she was about to faint, or her grip on sanity was loosening. He was gaunt, and his skin had a sickly pale cast—not unlike that of the thing that had chased her through the woods outside the Ville.

Was that Bill? Was it even possible?

The figure lurched forward again, still at a crouch, raised a hand, tapped one finger on the window. *Tap, tap, tap.*

It—he—Bill—stared at her through rheumy, bloodshot eyes. The sagging mouth opened wider, the tongue lolled. Vague, half-formed sounds emerged.

Is he trying to speak to me? Alive . . . *is it possible?*

Tap, tap, tap.

"Bill?" she croaked, her heart a jackhammer in her chest.

The crouching form jerked. The eyes opened wider, rolling before fixing on her once again.

"Can you talk to me?" she said.

Another sound, half moan, half whine. The claw-like hands flexed and unflexed; the desperate eyes locked on hers imploringly. She stared at him, utterly paralyzed. He was repulsive, feral, barely human. And yet, beneath the caking of blood and the matted hair, she recognized a puffy caricature of her husband's features. This was the man whom she had loved like no other on earth, who had completed her. This was the man who, before her eyes, had killed Caitlyn Kidd.

"Speak to me. Please."

Fresh sounds issued from the ruined mouth now, sounds of increased urgency. The crouching figure brought its hands together, lifted them toward her in a beseeching gesture. Despite everything, Nora felt her heart break with the piteous gesture, with the deep longing and sorrow that overwhelmed her.

"Oh, Bill," she said, as for the first time since the attack she began to weep openly. "What have they done to you?"

The figure on the fire escape groaned. It sat for a moment, looking at her intently, motionless save for the spastic gestures that occasionally racked its frame. Then, very slowly, one of its claw-like hands reached out, grasping the lower edge of the window sash.

And then lifted it.

Nora watched, the sobs dying in her throat, as—slowly, slowly—the window inched up until it was half open. The figure bent low, easing itself beneath the frame. The hospital gown caught on a protruding nail and ripped with a sharp sound. Something about the unexpectedly sinuous movement reminded her of a wolverine sneaking into a rabbit's den. The head and shoulders were inside now. The mouth yawned wider again, a thin rope of saliva swinging from the lower lip. A hand reached for her.

Instinctively—without conscious thought—Nora shrank away.

The extended arm paused. Smithback looked up at her from his position half in, half out of the window. Another whine emerged from the muddy mouth. He lifted his arm again, more forcefully this time.

At the gesture, a stench of the charnel house wafted toward Nora. Terror rose in her throat and she backed up on the bed, drawing her knees to her chin.

The red-rimmed eyes narrowed. The whine turned to a low growl. And suddenly, with a violent thrust, the figure forced itself through the half-open window and into the room. There was a splintering of wood, a crash of glass. Nora fell back with a cry, tangling herself in the bedsheets and falling to the floor. Quickly, she struggled out of the sheets and rose. Bill was there with her, in the room.

He gave a cry of rage, lurching toward her and swinging the truncheon.

"No!" she cried. "It's me, Nora—!"

It was a clumsy move and she dodged it, backing up through the doorway into the living room. He followed, reeling forward and raising the truncheon again. Close up, his eyes were whitish, cloudy, their surface dry and wrinkled. His mouth opened wide again, the lips cracking, exhaling a dreadful reek that mingled with the sharp odor of formalin and methyl alcohol.

Nnnngghhhhaaaah!

She kept backing up through the living room. He lurched toward her, one hand reaching out, fingers spastically jerking. Straining toward her, reaching, closer and closer.

She took another step backward, felt her shoulder blades touch the wall. It was as if the figure was threatening and pleading with her at the same time, the left hand reaching out to touch her as the right hand raised the truncheon to strike. He threw his head back, exposing a neck with huge raw cuts sewn up with twine, the skin gray and dead.

Nnnnggggghhhhhaaaaah!

"No," she whispered. "No. Stay back."

The hand reached out, trembling, touched her hair, caressed it. The smell of death enveloped her.

"No," she croaked. "Please."

The mouth opened wider, foul air streaming out.

"Get away!" she said with a rising shriek.

The twitching hand traced a dirty finger down her cheek to her lips, caressed them. She pressed her back against the wall.

Nnngah . . . Nnngah . . . Nnngah . . . The figure began to pant as the convulsive, twitching finger rubbed her lips. Then the finger tried to push inside her mouth.

She gagged, turning her head away. "No . . ."

A pounding came at the door—her screams must have brought someone.

"Nora!" came a muffled voice. "Hey, are you all right? Nora!"

As if in reaction, the upraised hand clutching the truncheon began to shake.

Nnngah! Nnngah! Nnngah! The panting turned into an urgent, lascivious grunting.

Nora was paralyzed, speechless with horror.

The right hand swept down in one spastic motion, the truncheon crashing onto her skull—and the world ended.

40

D'Agosta sat in the passenger seat of the squad car, the black mood that had settled over him refusing to dissipate. If anything, it seemed to grow darker the closer they got to the Ville. At least he didn't have to sit in the back with the annoying little French Creole, or whatever the hell he was. He glanced at the man covertly in the rearview mirror, lips tightening in disapproval. There he was, perched on the seat, looking like an Upper East Side doorman in his swallowtail coat.

The driver halted the cruiser where Indian Road turned into 214th, the crime-scene van following them coming to a rattling stop behind. D'Agosta glanced at his watch: three thirty. The driver popped the trunk and D'Agosta got out, hefted out the bolt cutters, and snapped the padlock, letting the chain drop to the ground. He chucked the bolt cutters back into the trunk, slammed it, and slid back into the car.

"Motherfuckers," he said to no one in particular.

The driver gunned the Crown Vic, the tires giving a little screech as the car lurched forward.

"Driver," said Bertin, leaning forward, "watch those starts, if you please."

The driver—a homicide detective named Perez—rolled his eyes.

They halted again at the iron gate in the chain-link fence, and D'Agosta took another small joy in cutting off the lock and tossing it into the woods. Then, to make sure the job was done well, he cut through both sets of hinges, kicked the iron gate down, and dragged the two pieces off the road. He got back in the car, puffing slightly. "Public way," he said in explanation.

Another screech of tires and the Crown Vic jerked forward, jostling the passengers. It climbed, then descended, through a dark, twilight wood, ultimately nosing out into a dead field. The Ville rose up ahead, bathed in the crystalline light of a fall afternoon. Despite the sun, it looked dark and crooked, wreathed in shadow: a haphazard jumble of steeples and roofs like some nightmare village of Dr. Seuss. The entire construction had accreted around a monstrous, half-timbered church, impossibly old. The front part was surrounded by a tall wooden stockade fence, into which was set a single wooden door of oak, banded, plated, and riveted in iron.

The vehicles pulled up to a dirt parking area beside the oak door. A few shabby cars were parked to one side, along with the panel truck that D'Agosta had seen earlier. Just the sight of it sent a fresh stab of anger through him.

The place appeared to be deserted. D'Agosta looked around, then turned to Perez. "Bring the kayo and pro-bar. I'll carry the evidence locker."

"Sure thing, Lieutenant."

D'Agosta threw open the door again and stepped out. The van had pulled up behind and the animal control officer got out. He was a timid fellow with an unfortunate blond mustache, red-faced, thin arms, potbelly. Nervous as hell, never executed a warrant before. D'Agosta tried to dredge up his name. Pulchinski.

"Did we call ahead?" Pulchinski asked in a quavering voice.

"You don't 'call ahead' with a no-knock search warrant. The last thing you want to do is give someone time to destroy evidence."

D'Agosta opened the trunk, pulled out the locker. "You got the papers in order?"

Pulchinski patted a capacious pocket. The man was already sweating.

D'Agosta turned to Perez. "Detective?"

Perez hefted the kayo battering ram. "I'm on it."

Meanwhile, Pendergast and his weird little sidekick Bertin had gotten out of the squad car. Pendergast was inscrutable as usual, his silvery eyes hooded and expressionless. Bertin—incredibly enough—was sniffing flowers. Literally.

"By heaven," he exclaimed, "this is a splendid example of sandplain gerardia, *Agalinis acuta* 'Pennell'! An endangered species! A whole field of them!" He cupped a flower in his hand, inhaled loudly.

Perez, who was massive and compact, placed himself before the door; took tight hold of the battering ram's front and rear grips; balanced it a moment at hip level; swung it back; then heaved it forward with a grunt. The forty-pound ram slammed into the oaken door with a booming sound, the door shuddering in its frame.

Bertin jumped like he had been shot. "What's this?" he shrilled.

"We're executing a warrant," said D'Agosta.

Bertin retreated hastily behind Pendergast, peering out like a Munchkin. "No one said there would be *violence*!"

Boom! A second hit, then a third. The rivets on the old door began to work their way out.

"Hold it." D'Agosta picked up the pro-bar and jammed the forked end under a rivet, leveraging it up. With a crack, the rivet popped out. He pulled out four more rivets and stepped back, nodding to the detective.

Perez swung the ram again and again, the heavy door splitting with each blow. An iron band sprang loose and fell to the ground with a clank. A long vertical crack opened in the oak, splinters flying.

"A few more should do it," D'Agosta said.

Boom! Boom!

Suddenly D'Agosta became aware of a presence behind them. He turned. A man stood watching them, ten paces back. He was a striking individual, dressed in a long gray cloak with a velvet collar, and a strange, soft medieval-style cap on his head with two flaps over his ears, his face in shadow. His long, bushy white hair was pulled back in a ponytail. He was very tall—at least six foot seven inches—about fifty years old, lean and muscular, with a disquieting stare. His skin was pale, almost as pale as Pendergast's, but the eyes were as black as coals, his face chiseled, nose thin and aquiline. D'Agosta recognized him immediately as the driver of the van.

The man stared at D'Agosta with his marble-like eyes. Where he had come from, how he had approached without alerting them, was a mystery. Without saying a word, he dipped into his pocket and removed a large iron key.

D'Agosta turned to Perez. "Looks like we got a key."

The key disappeared back into the robe. "Show me your warrant first," the man said, approaching, his face impassive. But the voice was like honey, and it was the first time D'Agosta had heard anyone speak with an accent remotely like Pendergast's.

"Of course," said Pulchinski hastily, dipping into his pocket and pulling out a mass of papers, which he began to sort through. "There you are."

The man took it with a large hand. *"Warrant of Search and Seizure,"* he read out loud, in his sonorous voice. The accent *was* like Pendergast's, and yet it was also very different—with a trace of French and something else D'Agosta couldn't identify.

The man looked at Pulchinski. "And you are?"

"Morris Pulchinski, animal control." He nervously stuck out his hand, and then, when he was stared down, let it drop. "We've had reliable reports of animal cruelty, animal torture, perhaps even animal sacrifice up here, and that warrant allows us to search the premises and collect evidence."

"Not the premises. The warrant specifies only the church proper. And these other people?"

D'Agosta flashed his shield. "NYPD homicide. You got some ID?"

"We do not carry identification cards," the man said, his voice like dry ice.

"You'll have to identify yourself, mister, one way or another."

"I am Étienne Bossong."

"Spell it." D'Agosta took out his notebook, flipping the pages.

The man spelled it slowly, dryly, enunciating each letter, as if to a child.

D'Agosta wrote it down. "And your position here?"

"I am the leader."

"Of what?"

"Of this community."

"And what exactly is 'this community'?"

A long silence followed, as Bossong stared at D'Agosta. "NYPD Homicide? For an animal control issue?"

"We're tagging along for fun," said D'Agosta.

"These other storm troopers haven't yet identified themselves."

"Detective Perez, NYPD homicide," D'Agosta said. "Special Agent Pendergast, Federal Bureau of Investigation. And Mr. Bertin, FBI consultant."

Everyone in turn flashed their shields, except for Bertin, who merely stared at Bossong, his eyes narrowing to slits. Bossong flinched, as if in recognition, then stared back equally hard. Something seemed to pass between the two: something electric. It made the hair on D'Agosta's neck stand on end.

"Open the door," D'Agosta said.

After a long, tense moment, Bossong broke off eye contact with

Bertin. He took the massive iron key out of his pocket and fitted it into the iron lock. He turned it with a violent twist, the tumblers clacking loudly, and hauled open the mangled door.

"We do not seek confrontation," he said.

"Good."

Beyond lay a narrow alleyway, curving around to the right. Small wooden structures lined both sides, the upper floors overhanging the lower. The buildings were so old they listed toward one another, the steeply pitched gables of their penthouse projections almost meeting above the alley. Dying autumn light filtered down, but the empty doorways and blown-glass windows remained shrouded in gloom.

Bossong silently led the group along the alleyway. As they rounded the curve, D'Agosta saw the church itself rear up ahead of them: rambling, countless dependent structures fixed to its sides like limpets. Huge, ancient timbers spiked out from its flanks, attached to even heavier, fantastically carven vertical beams that were driven into the ground like primitive flying buttresses. Bossong led the way between two of the beams, opened a door in the outer wall of the church, and entered. As he did so, he called out something into the darkness in a language D'Agosta didn't recognize.

D'Agosta hesitated on the threshold. The interior was in utter blackness. It exhaled a sour smell of dung, burned wood, candlewax, frankincense, fear, and unwashed people. An ominous creaking sound came from the timbers above, as if the place was about to come down.

"Turn on the lights," said D'Agosta.

"There is no electricity," said Bossong from the darkness within. "We do not allow modern conveniences to defile the inner sanctuary."

D'Agosta pulled out his Maglite, switched it on, aimed it inside. The place was cavernous. "Perez, bring up the portable halogen lamp from the van."

"Sure thing, Lieutenant."

He turned to the animal control officer. "Pulchinski, you know what you're looking for, right?"

"To tell you the truth, Lieutenant—"

"Just do your job, please."

D'Agosta glanced over his shoulder. Pendergast was looking around with his own flashlight, Bertin at his side.

Perez returned with a halogen light, connected by a coiled wire to a large battery in a canvas pouch on a sling.

"Let me carry it." D'Agosta slung the battery over his shoulder. "I'll go first. The rest of you, follow me. Perez, bring the evidence locker. You understand the rules, right? We're here on an *animal control* issue." His voice carried a heavy weight of irony.

He stepped into the darkness, switched on the light.

He almost jumped back. The walls were completely lined with people, silent, staring, all dressed in rough brown cloth.

"What the *fuck*?"

One of the men came forward. He was shorter than Bossong and just as thin, but unlike the others his brown robes were decorated with spirals and complex curlicues of white. His face was coarse and rough, as if shaped by a hatchet. He carried a heavy staff. "This is sacred ground," he said in a quavering preacher's voice. "Words of vulgar language will not be tolerated."

"Who are you?" D'Agosta asked.

"My name is Charrière." The man almost spit the words.

"And who are these people?"

"This is a sanctuary. This is our flock."

"Oh, your *flock*? Remind me to skip the Kool-Aid after the service."

Pendergast came gliding up behind D'Agosta and leaned over. "Vincent?" he murmured. "Mr. Charrière would seem to be a *hungenikon* priest. I would avoid antagonizing him—or these people—more than necessary."

D'Agosta took a deep breath. It irritated him, Pendergast giving him advice. But he recognized that he was angry, and a good cop should never be angry. What was the matter with him? It seemed he'd been angry since the beginning of the case. He'd better get over it. He took a deep breath, nodded, and Pendergast backed away.

Even with the halogen light, the space was so large that he felt swallowed by the darkness. It was made worse by a kind of miasma hanging in the air. The silent congregation, standing against the walls, all staring silently at him, gave him the creeps. There must be a hundred in there, maybe more. All adults, all men, white, black, Asian, Indian, Hispanic, and about everything else. All with dull, staring faces. He felt a twinge of apprehension. They should have come in with more backup. A whole lot more.

"All right, listen up, folks." He spoke loudly, so all could hear, trying to pitch confidence into his voice. "We've got a search warrant for the interior of this church, and it states we can search the area and the physical person of any individual present on the scene. We have the right to take anything deemed of interest under the terms of the warrant. You'll get a full accounting and everything will be duly returned to you. You all understand?"

He paused, his voice echoing and dying away. Nobody moved. Their eyes glowed red in the flashlight beams, like animals at night.

"So, please: nobody move, nobody interfere. Follow the directions of the officers. Okay? That's the way to get this over with as quickly as possible."

He looked around again. Was it his imagination, or had they moved in slightly, narrowed the circle? It must be his imagination. He hadn't heard or seen any of them move. In the silence, he could feel the presence of the brooding, ancient timbers lowering above, their creaking and shifting.

The people themselves made no noise at all. None. And then a small sound came from the far end of the church: the pathetic bleating of a lamb.

"All right," said D'Agosta, "start at the back and work toward the door."

They walked down the center of the church. The floor was laid in large, square blocks of foot-polished stone, and there were no chairs, no pews. Their ceremonies and rites—and D'Agosta couldn't even begin to imagine what they must be like—must be done standing. Or maybe kneeling. He noticed strange designs painted on the walls: curlicues and eyes and fronded plants, all linked by elaborate series of lines. They reminded him strongly of the priest's garb—and even more of the bloody design that had been painted on the wall of Smithback's apartment.

He motioned to Perez. "Take a picture of that design."

"Right."

The flash caused Pulchinski to jump.

The lamb bleated again. Hundreds of eyes watched them, and now and again D'Agosta was sure he saw the gleam of honed metal tucked into the folds of their robes.

At length the small group reached the rear of the structure. Where the choir would normally be, there was instead an animal pen, surrounded by a wooden fence, with straw matting covering the ground. In the middle stood a post with a chain dangling from it, and attached to the chain was a lamb. Damp straw, splattered with dark stains, covered the floor. The walls were dribbled with hardened blood, gore, and bits of feces. The post had once been carved like a totem pole, but it was so layered in offal and dung that the carvings had become unrecognizable.

Behind stood a brickwork altar, on which were placed pitchers of water, polished stones, fetishes, and bits of food. Above, on a small pedestal, were some implements of a vaguely nautical cast that D'Agosta didn't recognize: coiled, hooked pieces of metal set into wooden bases, almost like oversize corkscrews. They were highly polished, displayed like holy relics. Next to the altar sat a horsehair chest, padlocked.

"Nice," said D'Agosta, as he played the light over the scene. "Real nice."

"I've never seen Vôdou like this," murmured Bertin. "In fact, I would not call this Vôdou. Oh, the foundations are there, certainly, but this has gone in a completely different, more *dangerous*, direction."

"This is *horrible,*" said Pulchinski. He took out a video camera and began taping.

The appearance of the device caused a shuffling sound to rise from the massed people, a collective rustle.

"This is a sacred place," said the high priest, his voice resonating in the enclosed space. "You are *defiling* it. Defiling our faith!"

"Get it all on tape, Mr. Pulchinski," said D'Agosta.

Moving as swiftly as a bat, his robes suddenly flaring, the high priest swooped in, swung his staff, and knocked the video camera out of Pulchinski's hands, sending it crashing to the floor. Pulchinski stumbled back, neighing in terror.

D'Agosta had his service revolver out in a flash. "Mr. Charrière, keep your hands in sight and turn around—I said, *turn around*!"

The high priest did nothing. The gun was trained on him, but the man seemed unfazed.

Pendergast—who had been flitting around, scraping samples off various artifacts and altar items and dropping them into tiny test tubes—swiftly appeared in front of D'Agosta. "Just a moment, Lieutenant," he said quietly, then turned. "Mr. Charrière?"

The high priest's eyes swiveled toward him. "Befoulers!" he cried.

"Mr. Charrière." Pendergast spoke the name again with a most peculiar emphasis, and the man fell silent. "You have just assaulted an officer of the law." He turned to the animal control officer. "Are you all right?"

"No problem, fine," said Pulchinski, putting on a brave front.

The man's knees were practically knocking together. D'Agosta glanced around uneasily. It was not his imagination this time: the crowd *had* moved in closer.

"That was a very foolish thing to do, Mr. Charrière," Pendergast continued, his voice not loud yet somehow penetrating. "You have now put yourself in our power." He glanced over. "Isn't that right, Mr. Bossong?"

A smile spread over the priest's features. For most people, smiles lighten their faces; the smile disfigured Charrière, revealing scar tissue that wasn't previously evident. "The only power comes from the gods of this place, the power of the *Loa* and their *hungan*!" He pounded his staff on the floor as if to emphasize the point. And then, in the electric silence, a muffled answering sound came from below their feet.

Aaaaaahhuuuu . . .

D'Agosta jumped in recognition—it was the sound he had heard in the bushes the other night. "What the hell was that?"

No answer. The crowd seemed to be poised, electric, waiting.

"I want to search below."

Now Bossong, the community leader, stepped forward. He had been watching the confrontation from one side, an inscrutable look on his face. "Your warrant doesn't extend there," he said.

"I have probable cause. There's an animal or something down there."

Bossong frowned. "You shall not pass."

"The fuck I won't."

Now the priest, Charrière, took up the cry. He turned and spoke to the crowd. "He shall not pass!"

"He shall not pass!" they called back, in unison. Their sudden, thunderous cry—after such silence—was almost terrifying.

"We will finish our work up here first," Pendergast continued calmly. "Any further efforts to impede us will be met with disfavor. Perhaps even unpleasantness."

Charrière pressed a finger against Pendergast's coat, the grimacing smile frozen on his face. "*You* have no power over me."

Pendergast stepped back from the man's touch. "Lieutenant? Shall we proceed?"

D'Agosta holstered his weapon. Pendergast had somehow bought them a minute or two more. "Pulchinski, take the lamb and the post. Perez, cut the lock off that chest."

Perez cut a padlock off the horsehair chest, lifted the lid. D'Agosta shined the light inside. It was filled with instruments wrapped in pieces of leather. D'Agosta picked up one, unrolled it—a recurved knife.

"Take the chest and everything in it."

"Yes, sir."

The crowd was muttering to itself now, the people shuffling closer. The high priest's face, split by a grimace, stared at them as they worked, his lips drawn back and working, as if he was chanting silently to himself.

D'Agosta caught a glimpse of Bertin out of the corner of his eye. He'd almost forgotten about the bizarre little man. He was poking in a transept-like corner, where dozens of leather strips hung from the ceiling, with fetishes pinned to them. Next, he moved to a bizarre construction of sticks, thousands of them, tied up into a crooked three-dimensional quincunx. His face looked drawn and worried.

"Take that, too," said D'Agosta, pointing to a fetish lying on the ground. "And that, and that." He shined the light into the corners, searching for doorways or closets, trying to see behind the masses of people.

"May the *Loa* rain disaster on the filthy *baka* who defile the sanctuary!" cried the high priest. He now held a strange charm in his other hand—a small, dark rattle topped by a desiccated knob the size of a golf ball—and he was shaking it at the intruders.

"Take the fetishes off the altar," said D'Agosta. "And those instruments, and that other shit over there. All of it."

Quickly, Perez loaded the stuff into the plastic evidence locker.

"Thief!" thundered Charrière, shaking the charm. The crowd shuffled forward.

"Cool it, you'll get everything back," D'Agosta said. They'd better finish up—quick—and then check out downstairs.

"Lieutenant, don't forget the objects on the *caye-mystère*." Pendergast nodded toward another shrine set into a dark alcove, fringed by stripped palm leaves, on which were piled a number of little pots, fetishes, and food offerings.

"Right."

"*Baka* swine!"

Abruptly, a noise like a rattlesnake came from the circle of acolytes. It sounded first from one place, then another, and then it was multiplying everywhere. D'Agosta swept his light toward the circle and saw the people—closer still now—each thrusting forward a carven bone handle with what could only be rattlesnake rattles tied to the end.

"That should wrap it up," said D'Agosta, feigning nonchalance.

"Perhaps," Pendergast murmured, "the search below can wait."

D'Agosta nodded. Jesus, they really had to get out of there.

"Dog-eating *baka*!" the priest shrilled.

D'Agosta turned to leave. Their exit corridor through the nave was now completely blocked with people.

"Hey, folks, we're done. We're leaving now." Pulchinski was clearly only too ready to go, as was Perez. Pendergast had returned to collecting his tiny specimens. But where the hell was Bertin?

At that moment a noisy scuffle erupted in a dark corner. D'Agosta turned to see Bertin rushing at the high priest with a scream, throwing himself on the man like a wild animal. Charrière staggered back, the two locked in struggle over the charm the high priest clutched in his hand.

"Hey!" D'Agosta shouted. "What the hell?"

The crowd pressed forward, the rattling becoming a low hissing roar.

The two assailants fell to the floor, becoming entangled in Charrière's robes. In a flash Pendergast had joined the scuffle. A moment later he emerged, holding Bertin by the arms.

"Let me get him!" cried Bertin. "I will kill him! You, you will die, *masisi*!"

Charrière merely rearranged his robes, dusted himself off, and smiled another hideous, disfiguring smile. "It is you who will die," he said quietly. "You and your friends."

Bossong, the community leader, looked quickly at the priest. "Enough of this!"

Bertin struggled, but Pendergast held him fast, whispering something urgently into his ear.

"No!" Bertin cried. *"No!"*

The crowd moved in, rattles shaking maniacally. D'Agosta caught more glimpses of honed steel in the dark folds of their clothing. Bertin abruptly fell silent, his face pale and trembling.

The crowd pressed in.

D'Agosta swallowed. Confrontation was out of the question. They just might, with luck, be able to shoot their way out, assuming none of the mob had guns; but then they'd spend the rest of their lives in court. "We're leaving," he managed to say. He turned to the others. "Let's go."

Charrière stepped in front of him, blocking his way. The crowd tightened around them like a vise.

"We're not looking for a fight," said D'Agosta. He let his hand rest lightly on his service piece.

"It is too late for that now," said the high priest, his voice suddenly increasing in volume. "You are defilers, filth. Only a complete cleansing will remove the stain."

"Cleanse the church!" cried a voice, echoed by others. *"Cleanse the church!"*

D'Agosta's finger undid the keeper on his holster, and he did a quick mental calculation. The Glock 19 had a fifteen-round magazine; that would be enough to clear a path to the door through any normal crowd. But this crowd was far from normal. He tightened his grip on the pistol butt, took a deep breath.

Suddenly, Pendergast stepped toward Charrière. "What's this?" Like lightning, his hand darted forward, ripping something from the high priest's sleeve. He held it up, shining his flashlight beam on it. "Look at this! An *arrêt,* with a false twine twist, done in a reverse spiral. The false-friend amulet! Mr. Charrière, why are you wearing this if you're the minister of these people? What do you fear from them?"

He turned to the crowd, shaking the little tufted fetish. "He's suspicious of you! Do you see?"

He swung back toward Charrière. "Why don't you trust these folk?" he asked.

With a roar, Charrière leapt forward to strike with his staff, cloak billowing; but the FBI agent twisted so adroitly that the man swung through air, whirling, and a short kick sent him sprawling to the dirt. An angry roar rippled through the crowd. Bossong stepped in quickly, putting a restraining hand on the high priest as he rose, a look of anger and hatred contorting his face.

"You! Bastard!" he said to Pendergast.

"Without a doubt, time to leave," murmured Pendergast.

D'Agosta grasped the forward handle of the coffin-size evidence box, Perez took the rear, and they dashed forward, wielding it like a battering ram, the surprised crowd scattering. With his free hand, D'Agosta plucked the Glock from his holster and fired into the air, the sound echoing and re-echoing in the vaulted space. "Let's go! *Go!*" Holstering his gun, he literally grabbed Bertin by the collar and hauled him along as they rushed the entrance, knocking people down as they went. A knife flashed but with a sudden movement Pendergast sent the would-be attacker sprawling.

They burst through the doors, the crowd boiling out after them. D'Agosta fired into the air a second time. "Get back!"

Dozens of knives were now out, flashing dully in the fading light.

"Into the vehicles!" D'Agosta shouted. "*Now!*"

They piled in, throwing the evidence into the back of the van and hoisting the lamb in after it, the van screeching off almost before they'd had a chance to shut the doors, followed by the cruiser, peppering gravel over the screaming mob just behind them. As they sped off, D'Agosta heard a groan from the backseat. He turned to find the Frenchman, Bertin, white and shaking, clutching Pendergast's lapel. Pendergast took something out of his own suit pocket: one of the strange, hooked implements that had lain on the altar. He must have purloined it during the melee.

"You hurt?" D'Agosta gasped to Bertin. His heart was hammering in his chest, and he couldn't seem to catch his breath.

"That *hungan,* Charrière . . ."

"What?"

"He collected samples . . ."

"He *what*?"

"Samples from me, from all of us . . . hair, clothing—you didn't see? You heard him, heard his threats. *Maleficia,* death conjuring. We're going to know it, *feel* it. Soon." The man looked like he was dying.

D'Agosta turned around brusquely. The shit he had to put up with, working with Pendergast.

41

What'll it be, hon?" the harassed-looking waitress asked, elbow balanced on hip, pad open, pen at the ready.

D'Agosta pushed his menu aside. "Coffee, black, and oatmeal."

The waitress glanced across the table. "And you?"

"Blueberry pancakes," said Hayward. "Warm the syrup, please."

"Will do," the waitress replied, flipping her pad closed and turning away.

"Just a second," said D'Agosta.

This bore consideration. In his experience during the time they lived together, Laura Hayward ordered—or cooked—blueberry pancakes for one of two reasons. She felt guilty about overworking and ignoring him. Or she was feeling amorous. Either option sounded good. Was she sending a signal? Breakfast had, after all, been her idea.

"Make that two orders of pancakes," he said.

"You got it." And the waitress moved off.

"Did you see the *West Sider* this morning?" Hayward asked.

"I did. Unfortunately." The scandal sheet seemed hell-bent on whipping the entire city into a state of hysteria. And it wasn't just the *West Sider*—all the tabloids had now picked up the hue and cry. The Ville was being depicted in ever more ghoulish terms, with plenty of not-so-subtle hints that it was behind the killing of the *West Sider*'s "star reporter," Caitlyn Kidd.

But it was on Bill Smithback himself that the papers lingered with the greatest morbidity. The high-profile murder of Kidd by Smithback, after being pronounced dead and undergoing an autopsy; his corpse missing from the M.E.'s office—everything had been sifted and speculated on with the greatest relish. And, of course, with more dark hints that the Ville was ultimately responsible.

As far as D'Agosta was concerned, the Ville *was* responsible. Still, despite his own mounting anger, he knew the last thing the city needed was vigilante justice.

The waitress returned with his coffee. He sipped it gratefully, stealing a glance at Hayward. Their eyes met. Her expression didn't seem particularly guilty, or particularly amorous. It seemed troubled.

"When did you visit Nora Kelly?"

"Last evening, as soon as I heard. Right after we finished searching the Ville."

"What happened to the protection you arranged for her?"

D'Agosta frowned. "The handoff was botched. Each of the two teams assigned thought the other had things covered. Fucking idiots."

"How is Nora?"

"Banged up here and there, some cuts and abrasions. Of greater concern is the second concussion she suffered. She'll be in the hospital at least a couple more days for observation."

"The neighbors broke it up?"

D'Agosta took another sip of coffee, nodded. "Her screams brought them running. They kicked down the door."

"And Nora insists it was Smithback?"

"Sure enough to testify to it in court. Same with the neighbors."

Hayward's eyes were on the faux marble of the tabletop. "This is too weird. I mean, what's going on?"

"The goddamn Ville is what's going on." Just thinking of Nora brought the anger back with a vengeance. It seemed he was always mad these days: mad at the Ville; mad at Kline and his oily threats; mad at the commissioner; mad at all the bureaucratic red tape that tied his hands; mad even at Pendergast with his irritating coyness and his insufferable little French Creole adviser.

Hayward was looking at him again. The troubled look was more pronounced. "What about the Ville, exactly?"

"Don't you see? They're behind everything. They *have* to be. Smithback was right."

"May I point out that you haven't yet made good the connection. Smithback wrote about their alleged animal killings—that's it."

"They weren't alleged. I heard the animals in the back of the van. I *saw* the knives, the bloodied straw. If you could have seen the place, Laura. My God, the robes, the hoods, the chanting . . . Those people are fanatics."

"That doesn't make them murderers. Vinnie, you need a *direct connection.*"

"And they've got the motive. That head priest of theirs, Charrière . . ." He shook his head. "A real piece of work, that one. Capable of murder? You bet."

"And what about this Bertin I read about in the report. Who's he?"

"Pendergast brought him in. Expert in voodoo or something. A quack, if you ask me."

"Voodoo?"

"Pendergast's pretty damn interested in it. He pretends not to be, but he is. Hell, he can start sticking pins into dolls for all I care—as long as it will bring down the Ville."

Their plates arrived, smelling delightfully of fresh blueberries. Hayward drizzled maple syrup over her plate, picked up her fork, set it down again. She leaned forward. "Vinnie, listen to me. You're too angry to be in charge of this case."

"What are you talking about?"

"You can't be objective. You loved Smithback. You're a great cop, but you need to consider passing this on to someone else."

"You've got to be kidding. I'm all over this case, twenty-four/ seven."

"That's what I mean. You're on a witch hunt, you're convinced it's the Ville."

D'Agosta took a deep breath, consciously held off on replying until he'd taken a bite of his pancake. "Aren't we supposed to follow up on our convictions, our gut feelings? Whatever happened to investigating the most likely suspect?"

"What I'm talking about is being so blinded by anger, by emotion, that you fail to investigate other possibilities."

D'Agosta opened his mouth, shut it again. He didn't know what to say. Deep down, he sensed she was right. No, he *knew* she was right. The hell of it was, part of him just didn't care. Smithback's death had shocked him, left a hole he never could have predicted. And he wanted those responsible to burn.

"And what are you doing with Pendergast? Every time he comes into the picture, he causes trouble. He's no good for you, Vinnie—stay away from him. Work on your own."

"That's bullshit," D'Agosta snapped. "He's brilliant. He gets results."

"Yes, he does. And you know why? Because he's too impatient to go through the process. So he goes outside the system. And he drags you along on his extralegal escapades. And who ends up taking the fall? You do."

"I've worked with him on half a dozen cases. He's gotten to the bottom of every one, brought the killers to justice."

"To Pendergast's justice, you mean. The way he goes about gathering evidence, I doubt Pendergast could ever convict his perps in a court of law. Maybe it's no coincidence they end up dead before trial."

D'Agosta didn't reply. He just pushed his full plate aside. This breakfast hadn't gone as he'd hoped. He felt weary—weary and confused.

Then Hayward did something he didn't expect. She reached across the table, took his hand. "Look, Vinnie. I'm not trying to give you a hard time. I'm trying to help you."

"I know that. And I appreciate it, I really do."

"It's just that you came so close to losing everything on that last case of Pendergast's you were involved with. The commissioner's got his microscope on you now. I know how important your career is to you, I don't want to see it jeopardized again. Will you at least promise me you won't let him draw you into any more illegal expeditions? You're in charge of this case. In the end, you're the guy who's going to be testifying up there on the witness stand about what you did—and didn't do."

D'Agosta nodded. "Okay."

She squeezed his hand, smiled.

"Remember when we first met?" he asked. "I was the seasoned veteran, the big bad NYPD lieutenant."

"And I was the rookie sergeant, fresh from the transit police."

"That's right. Seven years ago, if you can believe it. Back then, I kind of looked after you. Watched your back. Funny how the roles have reversed."

Her eyes dropped back to the tabletop. A faint color rose in her cheeks.

"But you know what, Laura? I kind of like it this way."

An urgent, breathless voice intruded from over Hayward's shoulder. "Is that *him*?"

He looked past Hayward to the next booth. A skinny woman in a white blouse and black dress had turned around and was staring directly at him, a cell phone pressed against her cheek. For a moment, he couldn't tell who she was talking to—him, a breakfast companion, or the person on the other end of the cell.

"It *is* him! I recognize him from last night's news!" Dropping the phone into her purse, the woman slipped out of her own booth and came over. "You're the lieutenant investigating the zombii murders, right?"

The waitress, overhearing this, came over. "He is?"

The skinny woman leaned toward him, manicured nails gripping the edge of the table so hard her knuckles went white. "Please tell me you're going to solve this soon, put those horrible people behind bars!"

Now an elderly woman, catching wind of the conversation, stepped forward. "*Please,* Officer," she implored, as a rat-sized Yorkshire terrier peeped out from a basket cradled in her arms. "I haven't slept in days. Neither have my friends. The city's doing nothing. You've *got* to put a stop to this!"

D'Agosta looked from one to the next in amazement, temporarily speechless. Nothing like this had happened before, even in high-profile cases. New Yorkers were usually jaded, worldly, dismissive. But these people—the fear in their eyes, the urgency in their voices, was unmistakable.

He gave the skinny woman what he hoped was a reassuring smile. "We're doing our level best, ma'am. It won't be long now, I promise you that."

"I hope you keep that promise!" The women retreated, talking animatedly, joined in common cause.

D'Agosta glanced back at Hayward. She returned the gaze, as nonplussed as he was. "That was interesting," she finally said. "This issue is getting really big, really fast, Vinnie. Take care."

"Shall we?" he asked her, indicating the door.

"You go ahead. I think I'll stay and finish my coffee."

He slipped a twenty onto the table. "See you at the evidence annex this afternoon?"

When she nodded, he turned and—as gently as he could—pressed his way through the small huddle of anxious faces.

D'Agosta dreaded having anything to do with the new evidence annex in the basement at One Police Plaza. The space, and all the procedures related to it, had been overhauled after yet another case was thrown out of court on a chain-of-evidence error, and now entering the annex was like gaining access to Fort Knox.

D'Agosta presented the paperwork to a secretary behind bulletproof glass and then he, Hayward, Pendergast, and Bertin cooled their heels in the waiting area—no chairs, no magazines, just a portrait of the governor—while the paperwork was processed. After fifteen minutes, a brisk woman, as wrinkled as a mummy and yet remarkably animated, a radio in one hand, appeared and presented them all with badges and cotton gloves.

"This way," she said in a clear, clipped voice. "Stay together. Touch nothing."

They followed her down a stark, fluorescent hallway lined with painted and numbered steel doors. After an interminable walk, she halted before one of the doors, swept a card through its key slot, and punched a code into the security pad with machine-like precision. The door sprang ajar. In the room beyond, evidence cabinets lined three of the walls and a Formica table stood in the center beneath a set of bright lights. In the old days, the evidence would already have been laid out on the table. Now, photographs of the evidence were there, next to a corresponding list. They had to make specific requests for items—no more browsing.

"Stand behind the table," came the brisk voice.

They filed in and did as instructed, Hayward, Pendergast, and the annoying Bertin. D'Agosta could already feel disapproving vibes radiating from Hayward. She had protested Bertin's presence—the swallowtail coat and cudgel-cane hadn't gone over well at all—but his temporary FBI credentials were in order. The little man looked disheveled, his face pale, beads of sweat standing out on his temples.

"All right now," said the woman, standing behind the table. "Have we done this before?"

D'Agosta said nothing. The rest murmured, "No."

"You can request only one evidence set at a time. I'm the only one allowed to touch the evidence, unless you need to perform a close examination—which, I should add, needs to be pre-approved. Tests may be ordered through written requests. Now, this piece of paper here lists all the evidence collected under the warrant, as well as other evidence assembled in the case. As you can see, there are photographs of everything. Now—" She smiled, her face almost cracking. "—what would you like to examine?"

"First," said Pendergast, "can you bring out the evidence we retrieved from Colin Fearing's crypt?"

After a delay, the tiny paper coffin and its faux-skeletal contents were retrieved. "What next?" the woman said.

"We'd like to see the trunk from the Ville and its contents." D'Agosta pointed. "That picture, there."

The woman ran a lacquered finger down the list, tapped a number, turned, moved to one of the evidence cabinets, opened a drawer, slid out a tray. "It's rather too big for me," she said.

D'Agosta stepped forward. "I'll help you."

"No." The woman made a call on her handheld radio, and a few minutes later a burly man came in and helped her lift the trunk onto the table, then took up a position in the corner.

"Open it, please, and lay out the contents," said D'Agosta. He hadn't had a good look at it when they'd taken it from the Ville.

With maddening care, the woman opened the lid and removed the leather-wrapped contents, laying them out with excessive precision.

"Unwrap them, please," D'Agosta said.

Each item was untied and unwrapped as if a museum object. A set of knives was revealed, each stranger, more exotic, and more unsettling than the last. Their blades were elaborately curved, serrated, and notched, the bone and wooden handles inlaid with odd curlicues and designs. The last item to be unwrapped wasn't a knife but a thick piece of wire bent and curled into a most fantastical design, with a bone handle at one end and a hook at the other, the hook's outer edge honed to a razor-like sharpness. It was precisely like the one Pendergast had snagged.

"Sacrifice knives with *vévé,*" said Bertin, taking a step back.

D'Agosta turned on him with irritation. "Vay-vay?"

Bertin covered his mouth, coughed. "The handles," he said in a weak voice, "have *vévé* on them, the designs of the *Loa.*"

"And what the hell's a 'loa'?"

"A demon, or spirit. Each knife represents one of them. The circular designs represent the inner dance or *danse-cimetière* of that particular demon. When animals or . . . other living things . . . are sacrificed to the *Loa,* you must use the *Loa*'s knife."

"In other words, voodoo shit," said D'Agosta.

The little man plucked out a handkerchief, dabbed at his temples with a shaking hand. "Not Vôdou. Obeah."

Bertin's French pronunciation of *voodoo* was a fresh irritation for D'Agosta. "What's the difference?"

"Obeah is the real thing."

"The real thing," D'Agosta repeated. He glanced at Hayward. Her face was closed.

Pendergast removed a leather kit from his suit coat, opened it, and began removing things—a small rack, test tubes, tweezers, a pin, several eyedropper bottles of reagents—placing each item on the table in turn.

"What's this?" Hayward asked, sharply.

"Tests," was the clipped answer.

"You can't set up a lab in here," she said. "And you heard the lady—you need pre-approvals."

A white hand slipped into the black suit coat, reappeared with a piece of paper. Hayward took it and read it, her face darkening.

"This is highly irregular—" the mummified woman began. Before she could finish, a second paper appeared and was held up before her. She took it, read it, did not offer to return it.

"Very well," she said. "What object would you like to begin with?"

Pendergast pointed to the wire hook, bent into elaborate curlicues. "I shall need to handle it."

The woman glanced at the sheet of paper again, then nodded.

Pendergast fitted a loupe to his eye, picked the hook up in gloved hands, turned it over, examining it closely, then laid it down. Using the pin with excessive care, he removed some flakes of material encrusted near the handle and put them in a test tube. He took a swab, moistened it in a bottle, swiped it along part of the hook, then sealed the swab in another test tube. He repeated this process with several of the knives, handles, and blades, each swab going into its own tiny test tube. Then, using an eyedropper, he added reagents to each tube. Only the first tube turned color.

He straightened up. "How unusual." Just as swiftly as the equipment had appeared, it disappeared back into the leather kit, which was folded, zipped up, and tucked back in the suit.

Pendergast smoothed and patted down his suit, and folded his hands in front. Everyone was staring at him. "Yes?" he asked innocently.

"Mr. Pendergast," said Hayward, "if it isn't too much *trouble,* would you mind sharing with us the fruits of your labors?"

"I'm afraid I've struck out rather badly."

"What a pity," said Hayward.

"You're familiar with Wade Davis, the Canadian ethnobotanist, and his 1988 book, *Passage of Darkness: The Ethnobiology of the Haitian Zombie*?"

Hayward continued glaring at him, saying nothing, her arms crossed.

"A most interesting study," said Pendergast, "I recommend it highly."

"I'll be sure to order it from Amazon," said Hayward.

"Davis's investigation showed, in essence, that a living person can be zombified by the application of two special chemicals, usually via a wound. The first, *coup de poudre,* has tetrodotoxin as its primary ingredient—the same toxin found in the Japanese delicacy fugu. The second involves a datura-like dissociative. A particular combination of these substances, applied in doses approaching the LD-50, can keep a person in a state of near-death for days, yet mobile, with minimal brain function and no independent will. In short, according to theory, with certain chemical compounds you can create an actual zombii."

"And you found these chemical compounds?" asked Hayward, in a clipped voice.

"That's the surprise. I did not—neither here, nor in independent tests I conducted while at the Ville. I must confess myself surprised—and disappointed."

She turned away brusquely. "Bring out the next batch of evidence. We've wasted enough time on this as it is."

"I did find, however," added Pendergast, "that human blood is present on that hook."

There was a silence.

D'Agosta grunted, turned to the evidence mummy. "I want a DNA test on that hook, run it through the databases, test for presence of human tissue as well. In fact, I want all these instruments tested for both human and animal blood. Make sure the handles are fingerprinted—I want a record of who handled them." He turned to Pendergast. "Got any idea what that crazy hook is for?"

"I confess I am baffled. Monsieur Bertin?"

Bertin had been looking increasingly agitated. Now he gestured for Pendergast to step to one side. "*Mon frere,* I cannot continue," he said in a low, urgent whisper. "I am sick, I tell you—sick! It is the work of that *hungan,* Charrière. His death conjure—you don't feel it at work yet?"

"I feel fine."

Hayward looked from the two of them to D'Agosta. She shook her head.

"We must leave," Bertin said. "We must return home. I need the syrup—sipping syrup. 'Lean'—I know you have some! Nothing else will calm me."

"*Du calme, du calme, maître.* Very soon." Then, turning back to the group, Pendergast said in a louder voice: "Now if you'd please examine this hook, *monsieur*?"

After a moment Bertin stepped forward most unwillingly, bent warily over the item, sniffed. He was sweating copiously now and his face was sallow. His breathing sounded like the wheezing of old bagpipes in the small room. "How very strange. I've never seen anything like this before."

Another sniff.

"And the miniature coffin we retrieved from Fearing's crypt. Is it the work of the same sect?"

Bertin took a cautious step closer to the little coffin. Its lid was in place now: made of cream-colored paper, hand-decorated with skulls and long bones in black ink. It had been elaborately folded, origami-fashion, to fit snugly over the papier-mâché coffin.

"The *vévé* drawn on that paper lid," said Pendergast. "With what *Loa* is that identified?"

Bertin shook his head. "This *vévé* is quite unknown to me. I would guess this is private, secret, known only to a single Obeah sect. Whatever it is, it is very strange. I've never seen anything like it." He stretched out his hand—pulled it back when the ancient woman clucked her desiccated tongue—then stretched it out again and picked up the lid.

"Put that down," the woman said immediately.

Bertin turned it gently around and around in his hands, staring at it very closely and muttering to himself.

"Mr. Bertin," Hayward said warningly.

Bertin seemed not to hear. He turned the little paper construct over in his hands, first one way then another, still quietly muttering. And then—with a sudden flick of his fingers—he tore it in two.

A grayish powder poured from beneath the folds down over Bertin's pants and shoes.

Several things happened at once. Bertin cartwheeled backward, neighing in dismay and terror, the strips of paper fluttering away. The old lady grabbed for them as she began shouting imprecations. The burly man took hold of Bertin's collar and dragged him out of the evidence room. Pendergast knelt with the speed of a striking snake, plucked a small test tube from his suit pocket, and began sweeping grains of the gray powder into it. And Hayward stood in the midst of it all, arms folded, looking at D'Agosta as if to say: *I warned you. I warned you.*

43

Proctor pulled the Rolls into a deserted parking lot behind the baseball fields at the edge of Inwood Hill Park and killed the lights. As Pendergast and D'Agosta stepped out of the car, Proctor walked to the trunk, opened it, and hauled out a long canvas bag holding tools, a plastic evidence box, and a metal detector.

"You think it's okay to just leave the car?" D'Agosta asked dubiously.

"Proctor will watch it." Pendergast took the canvas bag and handed it to D'Agosta. "Let us not dally here, Vincent."

"No shit."

He slung the bag over his shoulder and they set off across the empty baseball diamonds toward the woods. He glanced at his watch: two AM. What was he doing? He had just promised Hayward he wouldn't let Pendergast drag him into any more sketchy activity—and now here he was, in the middle of the night, on a body-snatching expedition in a public park without permit or warrant. Hayward's phrase rang in his head: *The way he goes about gathering evidence, I doubt Pendergast could ever convict his perps in a court of law. Maybe it's no coincidence they end up dead before trial.*

"Remind me again why we're sneaking around like grave robbers?" he asked.

"Because we *are* grave robbers."

At least, D'Agosta thought, Bertin wasn't along. He'd dropped out at the last minute, complaining of palpitations. The little man was all in a panic because Charrière had managed to get a few of his hairs. It seemed unlikely the high priest got any of *his* hairs, at least, D'Agosta thought with grim satisfaction: one advantage to going bald. He thought of the little scene that had played out in the evidence annex and frowned.

"What the hell was your pal Bertin demanding?" he asked. "Sipping syrup?"

"It's a cocktail he prefers when he gets, ah, overly excited."

"A cocktail?"

"Of sorts. Lemon-lime soda, vodka, codeine in solution, and a Jolly Rancher candy."

"A *what*?"

"Bertin prefers the watermelon-flavored variety."

D'Agosta shook his head. "Christ. Only in Louisiana."

"Actually, I understand the concoction originated in Houston."

Past the playing fields they ducked through a gap in a low, chain-link fence, crossed some fallow ground, and entered the woods. Pendergast switched on a GPS, the faint blue glow of its screen casting a ghastly light on the agent's face.

"Where's the grave, exactly?"

"There's no marker. But thanks to Wren I know the location. It seems that, since the groundskeeper was a suspected suicide with no family to speak of, his remains couldn't be buried in the consecrated ground of the family plot. So he was buried close to where his body was found. An account of the burial says it took place near the Shorakkopoch monument."

"The what?"

"It's a marker commemorating the place where Peter Minuit purchased Manhattan from the Weckquaesgeek Indians."

Pendergast took the lead, D'Agosta following. They headed through the dense trees and underbrush, the rocky ground underfoot growing increasingly rugged. Once again, D'Agosta marveled that they were still on the island of Manhattan. The ground rose and fell, and they crossed a small brook, just a trickle of water running in its bed, then some rocky outcroppings. The woods grew thicker, blotting out the moon, and Pendergast produced his flashlight. Another half a mile of gradual descent over very rocky terrain, and suddenly a large boulder loomed up in the circle of yellow light.

"The Shorakkopoch monument," said Pendergast, checking his GPS. He directed his light to a bronze plaque screwed into the boulder, which described how at this spot, in 1626, Peter Minuit had bought Manhattan Island from the local Indians for sixty guilders' worth of trinkets.

"Nice investment," said D'Agosta.

"A very poor investment," said Pendergast. "If the sixty guilders had been invested in 1626 at five percent compound interest, a sum would have accumulated many times the value of the land of Manhattan today." Pendergast paused, shining his torch into the darkness. "According to our information, the body was buried twenty-two rods due north of the tulip tree that once stood near this monument."

"Is the stump still around?"

"No. The tree was cut in 1933. But Wren found me an old map giving the location of the tree as eigthteen yards southwest of the monument. I've already entered the data into the GPS unit."

Pendergast walked southwest, keeping a careful eye on the device. "Here." He turned south. "Twenty-two rods, at sixteen point five feet the rod, is three hundred sixty-three feet." He punched some buttons on the GPS. "Follow me, please."

Pendergast set off again into the darkness, almost spectral in his black suit. D'Agosta followed, hoisting the heavy bag higher onto his shoulder. He could smell the marshes and mudflats along the Spuyten Duyvil and soon he could make out, filtering through the trees, the lights of the tall apartment buildings perched on the bluffs of Riverdale, just across the river. Abruptly, they came to the edge of the trees, which opened onto an expanse of matted grass, dropping down to a half-moon pebbled beach. Beyond, the river swirled and eddied, the lights of the Henry Hudson Parkway arching overhead and the apartment buildings across the water caught in the swirling tide, glittering and dimpling as the water flowed past. A low-lying mist drifted in patches across the water; the rumble of a boat could be heard.

"Wait a moment," Pendergast murmured, pausing at the verge of the trees.

A police boat came slowly churning down the Spuyten Duyvil, its ghostly form sliding in and out of the mist, a spotlight mounted on the hardtop sweeping the shore. They crouched just as the light passed over them, lancing through the woods.

"Christ," muttered D'Agosta, "I'm hiding from my own damn men. This is crazy."

"This is the only solution. Have you any idea how long it would take to get the proper permissions to exhume a body buried, not in a cemetery, but on public land, without a death certificate, and with only a few newspaper articles as supporting evidence?"

"We've been through that."

Rising, Pendergast walked out of the trees and down through the sea grass to the edge of the cobbled beach. To the east, halfway up the cliffs, D'Agosta could just make out the vast ramshackle structure of the Ville's central church, rising like a fang above the trees, a faint yellow glow peeking from upper-story windows.

Pendergast stopped. "Right here."

D'Agosta looked around the shingle beach. "No way. Who would bury a body here, in such an exposed location?"

"Easier digging. And a hundred years ago, none of those buildings on the other side of the river had been built."

"Nice. How are we supposed to dig up a body with the whole world watching?"

"As quickly as possible."

With a sigh, D'Agosta dropped the bag, unzipped it, and hauled out the shovel and pick. Pendergast screwed the rods of the metal detector together, donned a pair of earphones and plugged them into the device, then turned it on. He began sweeping the ground.

"A lot of metal here," he said.

He swept the detector back and forth, back and forth, walking slowly forward. After proceeding about five feet he turned, came back. "I'm getting a consistent signal here, two feet down."

"Two feet? That seems awfully shallow."

"Wren tells me the general erosion of the ground level in this area would be about four feet since the time of the interment." He laid the metal detector aside, removed his jacket and hung it on a nearby tree, grasped the pick, and with surprising vigor began to break up the ground. D'Agosta pulled on a pair of work gloves and began shoveling out the loose dirt and pebbles.

Another rumble heralded the return of the police boat. D'Agosta hit the deck as the spotlight licked the shore, Pendergast quickly falling prone beside him. When the boat had passed, Pendergast rose. "How inconvenient," he said, dusting himself off and grasping the pick once again.

The rectangular hole deepened—twelve inches, eighteen. Pendergast tossed the pick aside, knelt, and began working with a trowel, scraping off layers of dirt that D'Agosta then shoveled out of the way. The pit exhaled the cloying smell of brackish seawater and rotting humus.

When the grave had deepened to about twenty inches, Pendergast swept it again with the metal detector. "We're almost there."

Five more minutes of work and the trowel scraped across something hollow. Pendergast quickly brushed the loose dirt away, revealing the back of a skull. More scraping revealed the posterior side of a scapula and the end of a wooden handle.

"Our friend appears to have been buried facedown," Pendergast said. He cleared around the wooden handle, exposing a guard and rusted blade. "With a knife in his back."

"I thought he was stabbed in the chest," said D'Agosta. The moon broke through the mist, and he glanced from the corpse to Pendergast. The agent's face had gone very grim and wan.

They worked together, gradually exposing the back of the skeleton. Rotting clothing came to light: a pair of shriveled shoes peeling off the foot bones, a rotting belt, old cufflinks, and a buckle. They cut the earth down around the skeleton, exposing the sides, whisking dirt off the old, brown bones.

D'Agosta rose—one eye toward the river and any sign of the police boat—and shined his light around. The skeleton lay facedown, arms and legs arranged neatly, toes bent inward. Pendergast reached in and lifted off a few rotting pieces of clothing that clung to the bones, first exposing the upper part of the skeleton, then pulling pieces of canvas off the legs, laying everything in the locker. The knife stuck out of the back, having been driven to the hilt through the left blade of the scapula, directly above the heart. Peering more closely, D'Agosta could see what looked like a severe depressed fracture on the back of the skull.

Pendergast bent low over the makeshift grave, taking a series of photographs of the skeleton from various angles. Then he rose. "Let's remove it," he said.

While D'Agosta held the flashlight, Pendergast pried up the bones one by one with the tip of his trowel, starting with the feet and working upward, handing them to D'Agosta for stowing in the evidence box. When he reached the chest, he slowly worked the knife out of the soil and handed it over.

"Do you see that, Vincent?" he asked, pointing. D'Agosta shined his light over a piece of wrought iron, like a long spike or rod, with an end that curved over the bones of the victim's upper arm. The long end of the spike was buried deep in the ground. "Pinned into the grave."

Pendergast pulled the spikes out and set them with the rest of the remains. "Curious. And do you see this?"

Now D'Agosta shined the light on the victim's neck. The remains of a thin, twisted hemp cord could still be seen, horribly constrictive around the neck bone.

"Strangled so hard," said D'Agosta, "it must have half decapitated him."

"Indeed. The hyoid bone is nearly crushed." Pendergast continued with his grisly task.

Soon all that was left to be exposed was the skull, which remained facedown in the dirt. Pendergast undermined it and the jaw with a small penknife, wiggling them loose, then freeing them as a single unit. He turned them over with the blade of his penknife.

"Oh, shit." D'Agosta took a step back. The skull's mouth was closed, but the space behind the teeth, where the tongue had been, was packed with a chalky, greenish white substance. A curled-up thread lay in a tangle in front, one end clamped between the teeth.

Pendergast picked out the thread and looked at it, then carefully placed it in a test tube. He then leaned in gingerly, sniffed the skull, pinched up a minuscule amount of the powder, and rubbed it between thumb and forefinger. "Arsenic. The mouth was filled with it and the lips sewn shut."

"Jesus. So what's a suicide doing strangled, with a knife in his back and a mouth sewn full of arsenic? You'd think the people who buried him would have noticed."

"The body wasn't originally buried like this. Nobody buries their kin facedown. After the relations buried the body, someone else—those who had presumably, ah, 'reanimated' it—came back, dug it up, and prepared it in this special manner."

"Why?"

"A common enough Obeah ceremony. To kill him a second time."

"What the hell for?"

"To make sure he was very, very dead." Pendergast stood up. "As you've already noticed, Vincent, this was no suicide. Or victim. In fact, since he was killed twice, the second time with arsenic and a knife in the back, there can be no doubt at all. After his initial burial, this man was dug up—dug up *for a purpose*—and, when that purpose was accomplished, buried again, facedown. This is the perpetrator—the 'reanimated corpse' of the *New York Sun*—of the Inwood Hill murders of 1901."

"You're saying the Ville kidnapped or recruited him, turned him into a zombii, made him kill that landscape architect and parks commissioner—all to keep their church from being razed?"

Pendergast waved at the corpse. *"Ecce signum."*

44

D'Agosta took a swig of coffee and shuddered. It was his fifth cup of the day and it wasn't even noon. The expense of drinking Starbucks was becoming ruinous, and so he'd switched back to the black tar produced by the ancient coffee machine in the break room down the hall. As he sipped, he gazed at Pendergast, sitting in the corner, lost in thought, his fingers tented—apparently no worse the wear for the previous night's gravedigging antics.

Suddenly, he heard a querulous voice raised in the hallway—someone demanding to see him. It sounded familiar, but D'Agosta couldn't immediately place it. He rose and poked his head out the door. A man in a corduroy jacket was arguing with one of the secretaries.

The secretary glanced up and saw him. "Lieutenant, I keep telling this man he needs to make his report to the sergeant."

The man turned. "There you are!"

It was that movie-producer-with-a-cause, Esteban. With a fresh bandage on his forehead.

"Sir," the secretary said, "you *must* make an appointment to see the lieutenant—"

D'Agosta waved him over. "Shelley, I'll go ahead and see him. Thanks."

D'Agosta stepped back into his office, and Esteban followed.

When he caught sight of Pendergast, sitting silently in the corner, he frowned; the two hadn't exactly become best buddies during their first encounter, out at Esteban's Long Island estate.

D'Agosta sat down wearily behind his desk, and the man took a chair in front. There was something about Esteban that D'Agosta didn't like. Basically, the man was a self-righteous prig.

"What is it?" D'Agosta asked.

"I was attacked," said Esteban. "Look at me! Attacked with a knife!"

"Did you report it to the police?"

"What the hell do you think I'm doing now?"

"Mr. Esteban, I'm a lieutenant in the homicide division. I'll be happy to refer you to an investigating officer—"

"It's an *attempted* homicide, isn't it? I was attacked by a zombii."

D'Agosta halted. Pendergast slowly raised his head.

"Excuse me . . . a zombii?" D'Agosta said.

"That's what I said. Or someone acting like a zombii."

D'Agosta held up a hand and pressed down his intercom. "Shelley? I need an investigating officer in here right away, ready to take a statement."

"Sure thing, Lieutenant."

The man tried to speak again but D'Agosta held up his hand. In a minute an officer came in with a digital recorder, and D'Agosta nodded him toward the lone remaining empty chair.

The officer snapped on the recorder and D'Agosta lowered his hand. "All right, Mr. Esteban. Let's hear your story."

"I stayed late in my office working last night."

"Address?"

"Five thirty-three West Thirty-fifth Street, near the Javits Convention Center. I left about one AM. That area of town is pretty dead at night, and I was walking east on Thirty-fifth when I realized someone was behind me. I turned and he looked like some kind of bum, drunk or maybe high, dressed in rags, lurching along. He looked out of it, so I didn't pay much attention. Just before I reached the corner of Tenth Avenue, I heard this rush behind me; I spun around and was struck in the head with a knife. It was just a glancing blow, thank God. The man—or man-thing—tried to stab me again with the knife. But I keep myself in good shape and I was a boxer in college, so I parried the strike and hit him back. Hard. He made another swipe at me but by that time I was ready and knocked him down. He got up, grabbed the knife, and went lurching away into the night."

"Can you describe the assailant?" Pendergast asked.

"All too well. His face was all puffy and swollen. His clothes were ragged and covered with splotches, maybe blood. His hair was brown, all matted and sticking up from his head, and he made this sound, like . . ." Esteban paused, thinking. "Almost like water being sucked down a drain. Tall, angular, thin, gawky. Around thirty-five. His hands were spotted, streaked with what looked like old blood."

Colin Fearing, thought D'Agosta. *Or Smithback.* "Can you give a precise time?"

"I checked my watch. It was one eleven AM."

"Any witnesses?"

"No. Look, Lieutenant, I *know* who's behind this."

D'Agosta waited.

"The Ville has been out to get me ever since I raised the issue of animal sacrifice. I was interviewed by that reporter, Smithback—then he was murdered. By a zombii or someone dressed like one, according to the papers. Then I was interviewed by that other reporter, Caitlyn Kidd—and then *she's* killed by a so-called zombii. Now they're after me!"

"The zombiis are after you," D'Agosta repeated, in as neutral a tone as possible.

"Look, I don't know if they're real or fake. The point is—*they're coming from the Ville*. Something's got to be done—right away. Those people are way out of control, cutting the throats of innocent animals, and now using unholy ceremonies to murder people who object to their practices. Meanwhile, New York does nothing while these killers squat on city-owned land!"

Now Pendergast, who had been unusually quiet through this exchange, came forward. "I'm so sorry about your injury," he said as he bent solicitously, examining Esteban's bandage. "May I—?" He began detaching the tape.

"I would rather you didn't."

But the bandage was off. Underneath was a two-inch cut with half a dozen stitches. Pendergast nodded. "Lucky for you it was a sharp knife and a clean cut. Rub it with a little Neosporin and it won't even leave a scar."

"Lucky? The thing nearly killed me!"

Pendergast reattached the bandage and stepped back behind the desk.

"There's no mystery to why the attack came now, either," Esteban said. "It's well known I've been planning a march protesting animal cruelty at the Ville—I've got a parade permit for this afternoon, and it's been reported in the papers."

"I'm aware of that," said D'Agosta.

"Obviously, they're trying to silence me."

D'Agosta leaned forward. "Do you have any *specific* information connecting the Ville with this attack?"

"Any idiot can see everything points to the Ville! First Smithback, then Kidd, and now me."

"I'm afraid it's not obvious at all," said Pendergast.

"What do you mean?"

"I'm puzzled why they didn't come for you first."

Esteban gave him a hostile stare. "How so?"

"You've been the instigator from the beginning. If it were me, I'd have killed you right away."

"Are you trying to be a wise guy?"

"By no means. Just pointing out the obvious."

"Then allow me to point out the obvious—that you've got a bunch of murderous squatters up there in Inwood, and that neither the city nor the cops are doing anything about it. Well, they're going to be sorry they came after *me*. Come this afternoon, we're going to raise such a stink that you'll have no choice but to take action." He rose.

"You'll need to read and sign the statement," said D'Agosta.

With an irritated exhalation of breath, Esteban waited while the statement was being printed, read through it fast, scribbled a signature. He stepped to the door, then turned and pointed a finger at them. It was trembling with outrage and anger. "Today, everything changes. I'm sick and tired of this inaction, and so are a lot of other New Yorkers."

Pendergast smiled, touching a finger to his forehead. "Neosporin, once a day. Works wonders."

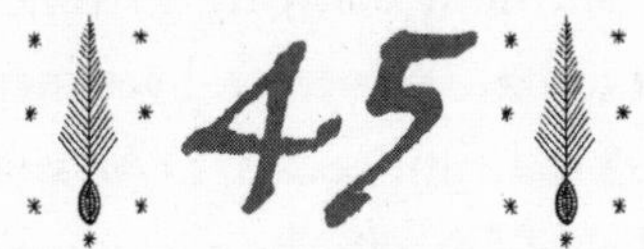

D'Agosta and Pendergast stood on the corner of 214th Street and Seaman Avenue, watching the progress of the march. D'Agosta was surprised at the minuscule turnout—he estimated a hundred people, maybe less. Harry Chislett, the deputy chief for this district, had shown up and then, when he saw the size of the crowd, had left. It was proving an orderly affair, sedate, placid, almost somnolent. No angry shouting, no pressing against the police barricades, no rocks or bottles flying out of nowhere.

"Looks like an ad for the L. L. Bean catalog," said D'Agosta, squinting through the sunlight of the crisp fall day.

Pendergast was leaning against a lamppost, arms folded. "L. L. Bean? I'm not familiar with that brand."

The marchers flowed around the corner at West 214th Street, heading toward Inwood Hill Park, waving placards and chanting in unison. Leading the fray was Alexander Esteban, bandage still on his forehead, along with another man.

"Who's the guy holding hands with Esteban?" D'Agosta asked.

"Richard Plock," Pendergast replied. "Executive director of Humans for Other Animals."

D'Agosta looked curiously at the man. Plock was young, no more than thirty, soft, white, and overweight. He walked with determination, his short legs earnestly pumping, toes pointed outward, his plump arms swinging, the hands flapping at the apex of each swing, his face set with determination. Even in a short-sleeved shirt in the chill fall air, he was sweating. Where Esteban had charisma, Plock seemed to have none. And yet there was an aura about him of solemn belief that impressed D'Agosta: here was clearly a man with an unshakable faith in the rightness of his cause.

Behind the two leaders came a line of people holding up a huge banner:

Evict the Ville!

Everyone seemed to have his own agenda. There were many signs accusing the Ville of murdering Smithback and Kidd. Beyond that, the protesters were all over the map: vegetarians, the anti-fur and anti–drug-testing crowd, religious extremists protesting voodoo and zombiis, even a scattering of anti-war protesters. MEAT IS MURDER, read one sign; FRIEND NOT FOOD, FUR IS DEAD, ANIMAL TORTURE IS NOT SPIRITUAL. Some held up blown-up photographs of Smithback and Kidd, side by side, with the caption MURDERED underneath.

D'Agosta looked away from the blurry photographs. It was getting on toward one PM. His stomach growled. "Not much happening here."

Pendergast did not reply, his silvery eyes scanning the crowd.

"Lunch?"

"I suggest we wait."

"Nothing's going to happen—these people don't want to wrinkle their button-down pinpoint oxfords."

Pendergast gazed at the passing crowd. "I would prefer to remain here at least until the speechifying is over."

Pendergast never seems to eat, thought D'Agosta. In fact, he couldn't remember a single time when they had shared a meal outside of the Riverside Drive mansion. Why did he even bother to ask?

"Let's follow the crowd to Indian Road," said Pendergast.

This isn't a crowd, D'Agosta thought. *It's a damn Sunday gathering.* He followed Pendergast down the sidewalk, feeling disgruntled. The "crowd" was beginning to gather in the field at the edge of the baseball diamonds, along the road to the Ville. So far, all according to permit. The police hung back, watching, the riot gear, pepper spray, and batons already stowed back inside the vans. Of the two dozen squad cars originally dispatched, more than half had already left the scene to return to their normal patrols.

As the group milled about, chanting and waving their placards, Plock climbed onto the baseball bleachers. Esteban stepped up and positioned himself behind him, hands folded respectfully across his chest, listening.

"Friends and other animals!" Plock cried. "Welcome!" He used no megaphone, but his strident, high-pitched voice carried all too well.

A hush fell on the crowd, the ragged chanting dying away. This crowd of yuppies and Upper West Siders, D'Agosta thought, was no more likely to riot than the ladies at a Colonial Dames tea. What he really needed right now was a cup of coffee and a bacon cheeseburger.

"My name is Rich Plock, executive director of the organization Humans for Other Animals. It is my honor and privilege to present to you our organization's chief spokesman. Please give a warm welcome to Alexander Esteban!"

This seemed to rouse the crowd somewhat, and as Esteban stepped to the top of the bleachers the clapping and chanting intensified. Esteban smiled, looking this way and that over the small crowd, letting the noise continue for a minute or two. At last, he put out his hands for quiet.

"My friends," he said, his deep rich voice the polar opposite of Plock's, "instead of giving a speech, I want to try something different. Call it a cognitive exercise, if you will."

There was a shuffling of the crowd, a ripple of feeling that they were here to protest, not listen to a lecture.

D'Agosta smirked. "*Cognitive exercise*. Look out, here comes the riot."

"I want all of you, every one of you, to close your eyes. Take yourself out of your human body for a moment."

A silence.

"And put yourself into the body of a little lamb."

More shuffling.

"You were born in the spring on a farm in upstate New York—green fields, sun, fresh grass. For the first weeks of life, you're with your mother, you're free, you're snuggled in the protective embrace of your flock. Every day you gambol about the fields, following your mother and siblings, and every night you're led back to the safe enclosure of the barn. You're happy, because you are living the life God meant you to live. That is the very definition of happiness. There is no fear. No terror. No pain. You don't even know that such things exist.

"Then one day a diesel truck arrives—huge, noisy, foreign. You are roughly separated from your mother. It is a terrifying, almost inconceivable, experience. You're driven with prods into the back of the truck. The door slams. Inside, it stinks of dung and fear. It is dark. The truck lurches off with a roar. Can you try—try with me now—to imagine the terror that helpless, tiny animal feels?"

Esteban paused, looking around. The crowd had gone silent.

"You bleat pitifully for your mother, but she doesn't come. You call and call, but she is not there. She won't come. In fact . . . she will *never* come again."

Another pause.

"After a black journey, the truck stops. All the lambs are taken off the truck—except for you. Becoming a rack of lamb is not your fate. No, something far worse is in store.

"The truck drives on. Now you are completely alone. You collapse in terror, in the dark. The loneliness is overwhelming; it is, in a very real sense, *biological.* A lamb separated from the flock is a dead lamb—always. And you feel it, you feel a terror more powerful than death itself.

"The truck stops again. A man climbs in, wraps a stinking, blood-encrusted chain around your neck. You are dragged out, into a dark, dark place. It is a church, at least of a kind—but of course you do not know this. It is crowded with humans, and it stinks. You can hardly see in the gloom. The people crowd around, chanting and beating drums. Strange faces loom out of the darkness. There are calls, hissing, rattles shaken in your face, the stomping of feet. Your terror knows no bounds.

"You are led to a post and chained to it. The pounding of drums, the stamping of feet, the closeness of the dead air—all these surround you. You bleat out in terror, still calling for your mother. For this is the one thing you still have: hope. Hope that your mother will come and take you from this place.

"A shape approaches. It is a man, a tall, ugly man in a mask, holding something long and bright in his hand. He comes at you. You try to escape, but the chain around your neck chokes you as you try to flee. The man grabs you and throws you to the ground, pins you on your back. The chanting grows faster, louder. You squeal and struggle. The man seizes your head by the fur and yanks it back, exposing the delicate underside of your neck. The bright shiny thing gets closer, flashes in the dim light. You feel it pressing against your throat . . ."

He paused again, letting a silence build. "I'm going to ask you all again to close your eyes and make a sustained effort to *put yourselves* into the body of this helpless lamb."

More silence.

"The shiny thing is pressing against your throat. There is a sudden movement, a horrifying flash of pain—pain that you never even knew existed in the world. Your breath is suddenly choked off by a flood of hot blood. Your small, gentle mind cannot begin to fathom the cruelty of this. You try to make one last pitiful cry for your mother, for your lost flock—those sunny green fields of your childhood—you cry for your dead brothers and sisters . . . But nothing comes. Only a gurgle of air through blood. And now your life rushes out over the dung-encrusted floor, into the dirty hay. And the final thought in your mind isn't hatred, isn't anger, isn't even fear. It is simply: *Why?*

"And then—*mercifully*—it is over."

He stopped. The crowd was deathly silent. Even D'Agosta felt a lump in his throat. It was maudlin, it was mawkish, but *damn* if it wasn't affecting.

Without speaking—adding no commentary of his own to Esteban's speech, no call to action—Rich Plock stepped down and began walking across the field with that same determined walk.

The crowd hesitated, watching Plock walk away. Esteban himself seemed taken by surprise, not quite sure what Plock was doing.

Then the crowd began to move, following Plock. The short man cut across the field and reached the road to the Ville. He turned and headed down it, accelerating his determined pace.

"Uh-oh," said D'Agosta.

"To the Ville!" cried a voice in the now surging crowd.

"To the Ville! To the Ville!" came the response, already louder, more urgent.

The murmuring in the crowd became a rumble that became a roar. "To the Ville! Confront the killers!"

D'Agosta suddenly looked about. The cops were still half asleep. Nobody expected this. In a split second, it seemed, the crowd had become electrified and was in determined motion. Small or not, this group meant business.

"To the Ville!"

"Evict the Ville!"

"Avenge Smithback!"

D'Agosta unholstered his radio, tuned it. "This is Lieutenant D'Agosta. Wake up, people, get your asses in gear! The protest is *not authorized* to approach the Ville."

But the crowd continued to move—like the tide, not quickly, but inexorably—down the road. And now Esteban, a look of alarm on his face, belatedly joined the moving crowd, pushing his way through, trying to get to the front.

"Confront the murderers!"

"If they reach the Ville," D'Agosta shouted into the radio, "the shit's really going to hit the fan. There'll be violence!"

There was a burst of talk on the radio as the diminished knot of police belatedly tried to equip their riot gear, to move into position and stop the crowd. D'Agosta could see that they were too few and too late—they had been caught completely off guard. A hundred or a hundred thousand, it didn't matter—he could see blood in these people's eyes. Esteban's speech had roused them in a way nothing else could have. The group was streaming past the baseball diamonds onto the Ville road, moving faster now, blocking any possibility of police cruisers getting ahead of the march.

"Vincent, follow me." Pendergast set off at a swift pace, cutting across the baseball diamonds toward the trees. D'Agosta immediately saw his plan—to take a shortcut through the woods and get ahead of the mob moving down the road.

"Pity that someone took down the gate to the Ville . . . eh, Vincent?"

"Don't give me shit, Pendergast—not now." D'Agosta could hear, at some distance, the chanting of the group, the shouting and yelling as they marched down the road.

Within moments they emerged onto the road a little ahead of the crowd. The chain-link fence was to their left, the gate still down. The crowd was moving at a rapid clip, the front ranks almost jogging, Plock leading the way. Esteban was nowhere to be seen. The crowd control cops had fallen far behind and there was no way to get ahead of the mob in a squad car. The press, on the other hand, were keeping up nicely, half a dozen running alongside with handheld video cameras, accompanied by still photographers and print journalists. This disaster was going to be all over the news that night.

"Looks like it's up to us," D'Agosta said. He took a deep breath, then stepped into the road and pulled out his shield, Pendergast beside him.

He turned to face the crowd, led by Plock. It was unnerving, like staring down a herd of charging bulls. "Folks!" he said in his loudest voice. "I'm Lieutenant D'Agosta, NYPD! You are not authorized to proceed!"

The crowd kept coming. *"To the Ville!"*

"Mr. Plock, don't do this! It's illegal and, believe me, you *will* be arrested!"

"Evict them!"

"Get the hell out of the way!"

"Step past me and you're under arrest!" He grabbed Plock and, though the man put up no resistance, the gesture was hopeless. The rest came like the tide, sweeping toward him, and he couldn't arrest a hundred people single-handedly.

"Stand your ground," Pendergast said beside him.

D'Agosta gritted his teeth.

As if by magic, Esteban appeared beside them. "My friends!" he cried, stepping out to face the approaching crowd. "My fellow sympathizers!"

At this, the advancing front faltered, slowed.

"To the Ville!"

In a surprise move, Esteban turned and embraced Plock, then turned to face the crowd again, holding up his hands. "*No!* My friends, your bravery touches me deeply—deeply! But I beg you: *do not proceed!*" He suddenly dropped his voice, speaking privately to Plock. "Rich, I need your help. This is premature—you know it is."

Plock looked at Esteban, frowning. Seeing this apparent disagreement between the leaders, the front line of marchers began to falter.

"Thank you for your big hearts!" Esteban cried out again to the crowd. "Thank you! But please—listen to me. There is a time and place for everything. Rich and I agree: now is *not* the time and place to confront the Ville! Do you understand? We've made our point, we've demonstrated our resolve. We've shown the public face of our just anger! We've shamed the bureaucrats and put the politicians on notice! We've done what we came to do! But no violence. Please, *no violence!*"

Plock remained silent, his face darkening.

"We came to stop the killings, not to talk!" shouted a voice.

"And we *are* going to stop these killings!" Esteban said. "I ask you, what will confrontation accomplish? Don't kid yourselves, those people will meet us with violent resistance. They might be armed. Are you prepared? There are so few of us! My friends, the time is soon coming when these animal torturers will be evicted, these murderers of lambs and calves—not to mention journalists—will be scattered to the four winds! But not now—not yet!"

He paused. The sudden, listening silence was remarkable.

"My fellow creatures," Esteban continued, "you have demonstrated the courage of your convictions. Now we will turn around and march back to our gathering point. There we will talk, we will make speeches, and we will show the entire city what is happening here! We will bring justice—even to those who show none themselves!"

The crowd seemed to be waiting for Plock to affirm Esteban. At long last, Plock raised his hands in a slow, almost unwilling gesture. "Our point is made!" he said. "Let us go back—*for now!*"

The press crowded forward, the evening news cameras running, boomed mikes swinging about, but Esteban waved them off. D'Agosta watched amazed as—at Esteban's urging—the mob reversed direction, flowing back up the road, slowly subsiding into the same peaceable group as before, some even picking up signs that had been discarded along the way during their blitzkrieg toward the Ville. The transformation was shocking, almost awe inspiring. D'Agosta looked on with astonishment. Esteban had fired up the crowd and put it in motion—and then, at the last possible moment, he had thrown cold water on it.

"What's with this guy, Esteban?" he asked. "You think he chickened out at the last minute, got cold feet?"

"No," murmured Pendergast, his eyes fixed on Esteban's retreating back. "It is very curious," he said, almost to himself, "that our friend eats meat. Lamb, in point of fact."

46

When D'Agosta showed up at Marty Wartek's office, the nervous little bureaucrat took one look at his angry demeanor and rolled out the red carpet: took his coat, escorted him to the sofa, fetched him a cup of tepid coffee.

Then he retreated behind his desk. "What can I do for you, Lieutenant?" he asked in his high, thin voice. "Are you comfortable?"

Actually, D'Agosta wasn't especially comfortable. He'd felt increasingly lousy since breakfast—flushed, achy—and wondered if he wasn't coming down with the flu or something. He tried not to think about how poorly Bertin was supposedly doing, or how the animal control officer, Pulchinski, had left work early the day before, complaining of chills and weakness. Their complaints weren't related to Charrière and his magic tricks . . . they couldn't be. But he wasn't here to talk about comfort.

"You know what happened at the march yesterday afternoon, right?"

"I read the papers."

In fact, D'Agosta spied copies of the *News*, *Post,* and *West Sider* on the deputy associate director's desk, poorly concealed beneath folders of official-looking paperwork. Clearly, the man had kept up on what was happening at the Ville.

"I was there. We came *this* close to a riot. And we're not talking a bunch of left-wing agitators, Mr. Wartek. These are regular law-abiding citizens."

"I had a call from the mayor's office," Wartek said, his voice even higher. "He, too, expressed his concern—in no uncertain terms—about the inflammatory situation in Inwood Hill Park."

D'Agosta felt slightly mollified. It seemed Wartek was finally getting with the program—or at least getting the message. The man's mouth was pursed more tightly than ever, and his razor-burned wattles quivered faintly. He looked exactly like someone who'd just been administered a Grade A reaming-out. "Well? What are you going to do about it?"

The administrator gave a small, bird-like nod and removed a piece of paper from his desk. "We've consulted with our lawyers, looked into past precedents, and discussed this issue at the highest levels of the housing authority. And we've determined that the right of adverse possession does not apply in this case, where the greater public good might be compromised. Our position is, ah, bolstered by the fact that the city is on record as having objected to this occupation of public land as far back as a hundred forty years ago."

D'Agosta relaxed deeper into the sofa. It seemed the call from the mayor had finally lit a fire. "I'm glad to hear it."

"There are no clear records as to exactly when that occupation began. As best we can tell, it was shortly before the outbreak of the Civil War. That would put the city's initial objection well within the legal window."

"No problems, then? They're going to be evicted?" The man's legal circumlocutions had a slippery feel to them.

"Absolutely. And I haven't even mentioned to you our legal fall-back position: even if they had gained some sort of rights to the property, we could still acquire it by eminent domain. The commonweal must take priority over individual needs."

"The what?"

"Commonweal. The common good of the community."

"So what's the timetable?"

"Timetable?"

"Yeah. When are they out?"

Wartek shifted uncomfortably in his seat. "We've agreed to put the matter before our lawyers to draw up the legal case for eviction, on an expedited schedule."

"Which is?"

"With the legal preparation and research, then a trial, followed by an appeal—I can only assume these people will appeal—I would think we could have this case concluded within, perhaps, three years' time."

There was a long silence in the room. "Three years?"

"Maybe two if we fast-track it." Wartek smiled nervously.

D'Agosta rose. It was unbelievable. A joke. "Mr. Wartek, we don't have three *weeks*."

The little man shrugged. "Due process is due process. As I told the mayor, keeping the public order is the function of the police, not the housing authority. Taking away someone's home in New York City is a difficult and expensive legal process. As it should be."

D'Agosta could feel the anger throbbing in his temples, his muscles tensing. He made an effort to control his breathing. He was going to say *You haven't heard the end of this,* then decided against it—no point in making threats. Instead, he simply turned and walked out.

Wartek's voice echoed out into the hall as he exited the office. "Lieutenant, we're going to have a press conference tomorrow to announce our action against the Ville. Perhaps that will help calm things down."

"Somehow," D'Agosta growled, "I doubt it."

47

Laura Hayward stood in the ladies' room on the thirty-second floor of One Police Plaza, examining herself in the mirror. A grave, intelligent face looked back. Her suit was immaculate. Not a strand of blue-black hair was out of place.

Except for the year she'd taken off to complete her master's at NYU, Hayward had been a police officer her entire career—first with the transit police, then NYPD. At thirty-seven, she was still the youngest captain—and only female captain—on the force. She knew that people talked about her behind her back. Some called her an ass kisser. Others said she'd risen so high, so quickly, precisely because she was a woman, a poster girl for the department's progressive stance. She'd long since ceased to care about such talk. The fact was, rank really didn't matter that much to her. She simply loved being on the job.

Glancing away from the mirror, she consulted her watch. Five minutes to twelve. Commissioner Rocker had asked to see her at noon.

She smiled. All too frequently, life was a bitch. But every now and then it had its moments. This promised to be one of them.

She exited the ladies' room and walked down the hall. While it was true she didn't care much about promotions, this was different. This task force the mayor was putting together was the real thing, not some bit of fluff cobbled together for the media. For years there had been too little trust, too little high-level cooperation between the commissioner's office and the mayor's. The task force, she'd been assured at the highest levels, would change that. It could mean a lot less bureaucracy, a chance to dramatically improve department efficiency. Sure, it would also mean a huge career boost—fast track to deputy inspector—but that wasn't important. What mattered was the opportunity to make a real difference.

She stepped through the double glass doors of the commissioner's suite and announced herself to the secretary. Almost immediately, an aide appeared and led the way back, past offices and conference rooms, to the commissioner's inner sanctum. Rocker was seated behind his large mahogany desk, signing memos. As always, he looked exhausted: the dark rings beneath his eyes were even more pronounced than usual.

"Hello, Laura," he said. "Have a seat."

Hayward took one of the chairs before the desk, surprised. A stickler for protocol and formality, Rocker almost never called anyone by his first name.

Rocker glanced over the desk at her. Something in his expression instantly put her on her guard.

"There's no easy way to say this," he began. "So I'll just tell you straight. I'm not appointing you to the task force."

For a moment, Hayward couldn't believe she had heard right. She opened her mouth to speak, but no sound came. She swallowed painfully, took a deep breath.

"I—" she managed, then stopped. She felt confused, stunned, unable to form a coherent sentence.

"I'm very sorry," Rocker said. "I know how much you were looking forward to the opportunity."

Hayward took another deep breath. She felt a strange heat blooming through her limbs. Only now—when the job had so unexpectedly slipped from her grasp—did she realize how important it had been to her.

"Who are you appointing in my place?" she asked.

Rocker glanced away briefly before replying. He looked uncharacteristically abashed. "Sanchez."

"Sanchez is a good man." It was as if she were in a dream, and somebody other than her was speaking the lines.

Rocker nodded.

Hayward became aware that her hands were hurting. Looking down, she saw she was gripping the arms of the chair with all her strength. She willed herself to relax, to maintain her composure—with little success. "Is it something I've done wrong?" she blurted.

"No, no, of course not. It's nothing like that."

"Have I let you down somehow? Come up short?"

"You've been an exemplary officer, and I'm proud to have you on the force."

"Then *why*? Inexperience?"

"I consider your master's in sociology ideal for the task force. It's just that—well—an appointment like this is all about politics. And it turns out Sanchez has seniority."

Hayward didn't answer right away. She hadn't realized seniority was a factor. In fact, this was the one appointment she'd believed free of such bullshit.

Rocker shifted in his chair. "I don't want you to feel this is any reflection on your performance."

"Surely you were aware of our respective seniority rankings before you gave me reason to hope," Hayward said quietly.

Rocker spread his hands. "Fact is, seniority formulas can be rather arcane. I made an honest mistake. I'm sorry."

Hayward said nothing.

"There will be other opportunities—especially for a captain of your caliber. Rest assured I'll see to it that your hard work and commitment are rewarded."

"Virtue is its own reward, sir. Isn't that what they say?" Hayward stood and—seeing from Rocker's face there was nothing more—walked on slightly unsteady legs to the door.

By the time the elevator doors opened onto the lobby, she had regained her composure. The echoing space was full of noise and lunch-hour bustle. Hayward passed the security checkpoint, then pushed her way out the revolving doors onto the broad steps. She had no real destination in mind: she just needed to walk. Walk and not think.

Her reverie was interrupted when someone collided heavily with her. She glanced over quickly. It was a man: thin and youthful looking, with acne-pitted cheeks.

"Pardon me," he said. Then he stopped and drew himself up. "Captain Hayward?"

She frowned. "Yes."

"What a coincidence!"

She looked at him more closely. He had dark, cold eyes that belied the smile on his face. She did a quick mental cross-check—acquaintances, colleagues, perps—and satisfied herself he was a stranger.

"Who are you?" she asked.

"The name's Kline. Lucas Kline."

"What coincidence are you talking about?"

"Why, the fact I'm going to the very place you've just been."

"Oh? And where would that be?"

"The commissioner's office. You see, he wants to thank me. In person." And before Hayward could say anything more, Kline reached into his pocket, took out an envelope, removed the letter within, and held it open before her.

She reached for it but Kline held it back, out of reach. "Uh-uh. No touching."

Hayward glanced at him again, eyes narrowing. Then she turned her attention to the letter. It was indeed from Commissioner Rocker, on official letterhead, dated the day before, and thanking Kline—as head of Digital Veracity, Inc.—for his just-announced five-million-dollar donation to the Dyson Fund. The Fund, sacred among the NYPD rank and file, was named for Gregg Dyson, an undercover cop who'd been killed by drug dealers ten years before. It had been established to provide financial and emotional assistance to families of New York cops killed in the line of duty.

She looked at Kline once again. Streams of people were leaving the building, stepping around them. The smile was still on his face. "I'm very happy for you," she said. "But what does this have to do with me?"

"It has everything to do with you."

She shook her head. "You've lost me."

"You're a smart cop. You'll figure it out." He turned toward the revolving doors, then stopped and glanced back. "I can tell you a good place to start, though."

Hayward waited.

"Ask your boyfriend Vinnie." And when Kline turned away again, the smile was gone.

Nora Kelly's eyes flew open. For a moment she struggled to understand where she was. Then it all came back: the smell of rubbing alcohol and bad food; the beeping and murmuring; the distant sirens. The hospital. *Still.*

She lay there, head throbbing. The IV, hanging on its rack next to the bed, was swaying in the bright moonlight, creaking back and forth like a rusty sign in the wind. Had she caused it to move like that? Perhaps a nurse had bumped it while checking on her just now, administering more of the tranquilizers she kept insisting she didn't need. Or maybe the cop that D'Agosta stationed outside had looked in. She glanced over; the door was shut.

The IV bottle swayed and creaked unceasingly.

A strange feeling of dissociation began creeping over her. She was more tired than she'd realized. Or else perhaps it was a side effect of the second concussion.

The concussion. She didn't want to think about that. Because that would take her back to what caused it: to her darkened apartment, the open window, and . . .

She shook her head—gently; squeezed her eyes tightly closed; then began taking deep, cleansing breaths. When she was calm again, she opened her eyes and looked around. She was in the same double room she'd been in the last three days, her bed nearest to the window. The blinds of the windows were closed, and the privacy curtain had been drawn around the bed nearest the door.

She turned, looking more closely at the drawn curtain. She could see the outline of the sleeping person within, backlit by the glow filtering out of the bathroom. But was that really the outline of a person? Hadn't the bed been empty when she'd fallen asleep? This was her third night here now—the doctors kept promising it was just for observation, that she'd be released tomorrow—and that bed had always been empty.

A horrible sense of déjà vu began to steal over her. She listened and could just hear the breathing, a faint, ragged sighing. She looked around again. The whole room looked strange, the angles wrong, the dark television above her bed crooked as the lines of a German Expressionist film.

I must still be sleeping, she thought. *This is just a dream.* The torpor of dreamscape seemed to surround her, swaddling her in its gauzy embrace.

The outline stirred; a sigh came. A faint gurgle of phlegm. Then an arm reached up slowly, its silhouette imprinted against the curtain. With a shudder of dread Nora gripped her sheets, trying to shrink away. But she felt so weak . . .

The curtain slid back with a slow, terrible deliberation, making a faint *eeeee* as the metal loops ran along the cold steel rail. She watched, paralyzed with terror, as the dark outline of a person emerged, first in shadow—then into moonlight.

Bill.

The same bloated face, matted hair, blackened, sagging eyes, gray lips. The same dried blood, dirt, foulness. She couldn't move. She couldn't cry out. She could only lie and stare as the nightmare to end all nightmares unfolded.

The figure got out of bed and stood up, staring down at her. Bill . . . and yet *not* Bill, living and yet dead. He took a step forward. His mouth opened and there were worms. The claw-like hand reached out, its nails long and cracked, while the head slowly bent down toward her—to *kiss* . . .

She sat up in bed with a cry.

For a moment she just sat there, shaking with terror, until relief flooded through her as she realized it had, in fact, been a dream. A dream like the last one—only worse.

She lay back in bed, bathed in sweat, her heart slowing, feeling the nightmare recede like a tide. Her IV bottle wasn't swaying; the television looked normal. The room was dark: there was no bright moonlight. The modesty curtain was drawn around the next bed, but there was no sound of breathing. The bed was empty.

Or was it?

She stared at the curtain. It was swaying just slightly. The curtain was opaque and she could not see inside.

She willed herself to relax. Of course there was no one in there. It was just a dream. And on top of that, D'Agosta had told her the room would remain private. She closed her eyes but sleep didn't come—nor did she really want it to come. The dream had been so dreadful that she feared falling asleep.

That was silly. Despite her enforced time in the hospital, sleep had been hard to find. She desperately needed rest.

She closed her eyes, yet felt so awake she almost couldn't make her eyelids shut. One minute passed. Two.

With an irritated sigh she opened her eyes again. Against her will, she found her gaze sliding once more toward the adjacent bed. The curtains were moving again, ever so slightly.

She sighed. It was stupid, her overactive imagination. No wonder, really, after a nightmare like that.

But when she'd gone to sleep, had those curtains been drawn?

She couldn't be sure. The longer she pondered it, though, the more convinced she became that the curtains had been open. Yet she'd been in a fog, still concussed—how could she rely on her memory? She turned away, stared resolutely at the far wall, tried to close her eyes again.

And once more, against her will, her eyes were drawn back to the closed curtains, still gently swaying. It was just air currents, the forced-air system: a breeze too faint for her to feel but enough to stir those curtains.

Why were the curtains shut? Had they been shut while she was asleep?

She sat up abruptly, her head throbbing in protest. It was silly to be worrying about this when a simple action would solve the problem once and for all. She swung her legs over the side of the bed and stood up, careful not to tangle her IV line. Two quick steps, then she reached out, grasped the modesty curtain—and hesitated. Her heart was suddenly pounding in fear.

"Oh, Nora," she said out loud, "don't be such a coward."

She yanked the curtain back.

A man lay on the bed, utterly still. He was dressed in the starched white of an orderly's uniform, his arms crossed on his chest, his ankles crossed, laid out almost like an Egyptian mummy—except his eyes were wide open, gleaming in the light. Staring directly at her. *Toying* with her.

In that moment of frozen fear, the figure leapt up like a cat, slapped a hand over her mouth, forced her back on her bed, and pinned her.

She struggled, kicking, trying to make a sound, but he was very strong, and she was trapped. He forced her head to the side and she saw, in his free hand, a glass syringe with a steel hypodermic needle attached, long and cruel looking, a drop of liquid trembling at its tip. A swift motion and she felt it sting deep into her thigh.

How hard she tried to struggle, to move, to scream—but paralysis enrobed her like a succubus, no dream this time but horribly and undeniably real, wrapping her in an irresistible embrace, and then it was as if she were falling, falling, falling down a bottomless well that shrank to a terminal point—and then blinked out.

49

Marty Wartek folded his sweaty hands over the edges of the podium and looked out over the crowd assembled in the plaza before the New York City Housing Authority's Batchelder Building. It was his first press conference and it was an experience both daunting and, if truth be known, rather thrilling. To his left and right stood a few subordinates—whom he had hastily corralled for appearance's sake—and a couple of uniformed cops. The podium had been set up on the lower steps, wires duct-taped up its rear edge.

His eye slid over to the small group of protesters huddled in one corner of the plaza, held at bay by a scattering of cops. Their chanting had a diffident air that encouraged him to think they would stop as soon as he began to speak.

He cleared his throat, heard the reassuring amplification over the PA system. He looked around as the crowd quieted. "Good afternoon," he began. "Ladies and gentlemen of the press, I will read from a prepared statement."

He began to read, and as he did so even the protesters fell silent. The legal process, he explained, was in motion. Action would be taken if warranted against the Ville. Everyone's rights would be respected. Due process would be observed. Patience and calm were the order of the day.

His voice droned on, the platitudes having a soporific effect on the gaggle of press. It was a short statement, not more than a page, which had been written by committee and vetted by half a dozen lawyers. It had the virtue of saying nothing, conveying no information, making no promises, while at the same time giving the impression that everyone's agenda was being dealt with. At least, that was the idea.

Halfway through the page he heard a vulgar noise, conveyed by bullhorn, from the knot of protesters. He ploughed on, without hesitation, not even looking up. Another noise.

"What a load of crap!"

He raised his voice, riding over the shouting.

"What about the animals?"

"What about the killing of Smithback?"

"Stop the murderers!"

He continued in a slightly louder monotone, eyes on the page, his bald head bowed over the podium.

"Talk, all talk! We want action!"

He could see, out of the corner of his eye, the boomed mikes and cameras swinging away from him toward the protesters. There were a few more shouts, arguing, a waving sign pushed aside by a cop. And that was it. The disturbance was contained; the protesters intimidated. There weren't enough of them to trigger mob mentality.

Wartek finished, folded the paper in half, and at last glanced up. "And now I will take questions."

The cameras and mikes were all back on him. The questions came slowly, desultorily. Disappointment seemed to hang in the air. The protesters remained in their corner, waving their signs and chanting, but their voices were now subdued and mostly drowned by the rush of traffic on Chambers Street.

The questions were predictable and he answered them all. Yes, they were bringing action against the Ville. No, it would not be tomorrow; the legal process would determine the schedule. Yes, he was aware of the allegations of homicide against the group; no, there was no proof, the investigation was proceeding, no one had been charged with a crime. Yes, it did appear that the Ville had no valid deed to the site; in fact, it was the opinion of city attorneys that they had not established a right of adverse possession.

The questions began to die, and he checked his watch: quarter to one. He nodded to his aides, raised his tufted head to the press one last time. "Thank you, ladies and gentlemen, that concludes this press conference."

This was greeted with a few more catcalls from the protesters: *All talk, no action! All talk, no action!*

Feeling pleased with himself, Wartek slipped the paper back into his suit pocket and walked up the steps. It had gone just as he'd hoped. He could almost see the evening news: a few sound bites from his speech, a question or two answered, a few moments devoted to the protesters, and that would be it. He had covered all the bases, thrown a bone to every constituency, and displayed the sober, dull face of New York City officialdom. As New York protesters went, this had been a pretty anemic group. Clearly this was a sideshow to whatever else the main group was planning. He had heard of a second Ville protest in the works, much bigger than the first, but thank God it wouldn't be in his sandbox. As long as they didn't protest here, he didn't really care. If they ended up burning down the Ville—well, that would be a convenient solution to his problem.

He reached the top of the stairs and headed toward the revolving glass doors, two aides at his side. It was lunch hour, and streams of municipal office workers were leaving the large building and pouring down the stairs. It was like swimming against the tide.

As he and the aides worked their way upstream against the flow, Wartek felt a passerby strike him hard with his shoulder.

"Excuse *me!*" Wartek began to turn in irritation, when he felt the most surprising sensation in his side. He jerked back, instinctively clutching his midriff, and was even more astonished to feel—and observe—a very long knife being extracted from his body, right through his clutched hands. There was a sudden feeling of heat and ice at once; ice inside him, in the depths of his guts; heat rushing outside and down. He looked up and had a brief glimpse of a swollen, scabrous face; foul sticky hair; cracked lips drawing back over rotten teeth.

And then the figure was gone.

Speechless, Wartek clutched his side, staggered forward. The crowd streaming past seemed to hesitate, bunch up, collide into one another.

A woman screamed in his ear.

Wartek, still unable to comprehend, his mind a blank, took a second staggering step. "Ouch," he said quietly, to no one in particular.

Another scream, and then a chorus of noise, a roar like Niagara Falls, filled the air. His legs began to buckle and he heard incoherent shouting, saw a rush of blue uniforms: policemen madly fighting their way through the crowd. There was another sudden explosion of chaos around him: people going this way and that, back and forth.

With a supreme effort he took another step and then folded; he was caught and eased to the ground by many hands. More confused shouting, with a few persistent words penetrating the hubbub: *Ambulance! Doctor! Stabbed! Bleeding!*

He wondered what all the confusion was about as he lay down to sleep. Marty Wartek was so very, very tired, and New York was such a noisy city.

50

Slowly she drifted in and out of dark dreams. She slept, half woke, slept again. At last, full consciousness returned. It was pitch-black and smelled of mold and wet stone. She lay there for a moment, confused. Then it all came back to her and she groaned in terror. Her hands groped damp straw over a cold concrete floor. When she tried to sit up, her head protested fiercely and she lay back down with a wave of nausea.

She struggled with an impulse to scream, to cry out, and mastered it. Once again, after a few moments, she made the effort to sit up—more slowly—and this time she succeeded. God, she felt weak. There was no light, nothing, just darkness. Her arm was sore where the IV had been, and there was no bandage covering the injection site.

The realization settled in that she'd been kidnapped from the hospital room. By whom? The man in the orderly's uniform had been a stranger. What had happened to the cop guarding her room?

She rose unsteadily to her feet. Holding her arms out, shuffling cautiously, she made her way forward until her hands touched something—a wet, clammy wall. She felt around it. It was constructed of rough, mortared stones, powdery with efflorescence. She must be in some kind of cellar.

She began feeling along the wall, shuffling her feet. The floor was bare and free of obstructions except for patches of straw. She reached a corner, continued on, counting the distance in foot-lengths. Ten feet more and she came to a niche, which she followed—hitting a door frame, and then a door. Wood. She felt up, then down. Wood, with iron bands and rivets.

The faintest gleam of light shined through a crack in the door. She plastered her eye to the crack, but the tongue-and-groove construction defied her attempts to see through it.

She raised her fist; hesitated; then brought it down hard on the door: once, twice. The door boomed and echoed. There was a long silence, and then the sound of footsteps approaching. She leaned her ear against the door to listen.

Quite suddenly, there was a scraping noise above her head. As she looked up, a sudden blinding light burst over her. Instinctively she covered her face and stepped back. She turned away, narrowing her eyes to slits. After a long moment she began to adjust to the dazzling light. She glanced back.

"Help me," she managed to croak.

There was no reply.

She swallowed. "What do you want?"

Still no reply. But there was a sound: a low, regular whir. She peered into the brilliance. Now she could make out a small rectangular slit, set high into the door. The light was coming from there. And there was something else: the lens of a video camera, fat and bulky, thrust through the slit and aimed directly at her.

"Who . . . are you?" she asked.

Abruptly, the lens was withdrawn. The whirring noise stopped. And a voice, low and silky, replied. "You won't live long enough for my name to make any difference."

And with that the light was extinguished, the slit closed heavily, and she was once more in darkness.

51

Kenny Roybal, high school dropout, sat on the baseball bleachers and gave the weed a quick cleaning, combing through it, flicking out the seeds and rolling the rest into a fat doobie. He fired it up and inhaled sharply, then passed it on to his friend, Rocky Martinelli.

"Next year," said Martinelli, accepting the joint and nodding at the field beyond the dark baseball diamond, "we'll harvest the pot growing down there."

"Yeah," said Roybal, with a sharp exhale. "It's premium grade, too."

"Fuck, yeah."

"Word, homeboy."

"Word."

Roybal took another hit, passed it back, then exhaled noisily. He waited while Martinelli took a hit, the joint crackling and popping, the tip brightening momentarily, Martinelli's long, dopey face illuminated a dull orange. Roybal took back the joint, carefully tipped off the ash and reshaped the end. He was about to light it again when he saw, through the gathering dusk, a squad car oozing into the far parking lot like a cruising shark.

"Five-O. Heads up." He dropped down behind the bleachers, Martinelli following. They peered out through the metal and wooden supports. The cop car stopped and a headlamp swiveled around, playing across the diamonds.

"What's he doing?"

"Who the fuck knows?"

They waited, crouching, while the light slowly slid over the bleachers. It seemed to hesitate as it passed by them.

"Don't move," came Roybal's low voice.

"I'm *not* moving."

The light continued on, then came slowly back. It was blinding, shining through the bleachers. Could the cops see them crouching here in the back? Roybal doubted it, but they seemed uncommonly interested in the bleachers.

He heard a grunt and there was fucking Martinelli running like a jackass across the diamond and into the field, heading for the woods. The light jumped up, spotlighting him.

"Shit!" Roybal took off after Martinelli. Now the light fixed on him. It felt as if he were running to catch his shadow. He vaulted the low chain-link fence and pounded across the field into the woods, following Martinelli's dim fleeing form.

They ran and ran until they could run no more. At last Martinelli began to flag, then dropped, flopping heavily onto a log, his sides heaving. Roybal fell down beside him, gulping for air.

"They coming?" Martinelli finally gasped.

"You didn't need to flake out on me, man," Roybal replied. "That cop wouldn't have seen us if you hadn't jumped up."

"He'd already seen us."

Roybal stared into the wall of trees but could see nothing. Martinelli had run a long way. He felt in his shirt pocket. It was empty.

"You made me drop the blunt."

"I'm telling you, we were *made,* man."

Roybal spat. It wasn't worth arguing about. He fished out the

Zig-Zag papers from his pocket, along with the rest of the lid. He stuck two papers together, sealed them, and poured a little pot into the groove. "I can't see a freaking thing."

Nevertheless, there was enough faint moonlight filtering through the trees to allow him to tease out a couple of seeds, roll up the blunt, light it, and take a toke. He bogarted it for a moment, exhaled, took another hit, held the smoke in hard, exhaled again, then passed it along. He began to laugh, wheezing. "Man, you took off like a rabbit chased by a hound dog."

"Dude, the fuzz saw us." Martinelli took the joint and looked around. "You know what? That weird-ass place, the Ville, is around here somewhere."

"It's way over by the mudflats."

"Naw, man. It's straight down by the river."

"So? You gonna run again? Woo-woo, here come the zombiis!" Roybal waved his hands over his head. *"Brains! Braaaaaaaains!"*

"Shut the fuck up."

They passed the joint back and forth in silence, until at last Roybal carefully trimmed the roach and put it in a tin lozenge box. Suddenly the muffled sounds of "Smack My Bitch Up" floated into the darkness.

"I bet it's your mom," said Roybal.

Martinelli fished the ringing cell phone out of his pocket.

"Don't answer."

"She gets mad if I don't answer."

"That blows."

"Hello? Yeah. Hey."

Roybal listened sourly to the conversation. He had already left home, had his own crib. Martinelli still lived with his mother.

"No, I'm at the library annex. Kenny and I are studying for the trig test . . . I'll be careful . . . There're no muggers in here . . . Yo, Mom, it's only eleven o'clock!"

He snapped the phone shut. "Gotta go home."

"It's, like, not even midnight. Uncool, man."

Martinelli rose and Roybal followed. His legs were already getting stiff from their stupid run. Martinelli started back through the trees, walking fast, his gangly legs barely visible in the dark. He soon stopped.

"I don't remember this fallen tree," he said.

"How could you remember anything? You were shagging ass." Roybal wheezed again.

"I'd have remembered jumping it or something."

"Keep going." Roybal prodded him in the back.

They came to another fallen tree. Martinelli stopped again. "Now I *know* we didn't come this way."

"Just keep going."

But Martinelli didn't move. "What's that smell? Dude, did you just blast the butt trumpet?"

Roybal sniffed loudly. He looked around, but it was too dark to see the ground well.

"I'll lead." He stepped over the log and his foot sank into something firm yet yielding. "What the hell?" He withdrew his foot and bent down to look.

"Fuck!" he screamed, stumbling backward. "A body! Holy shit! I just stepped on a body!"

Now they both looked down. A bar of moonlight illuminated a face—pale, ruined, bloody, sightless eyes staring glassily.

Martinelli coughed. "Oh, my God!"

"Call nine-one-one!"

Martinelli, staggering back, fumbled his cell phone out, stabbed at it maniacally.

"I can't believe it, it's a body!"

"Hello? Hell—?" Martinelli suddenly bent double and vomited all over the phone.

"Oh fuck, man—!"

Martinelli continued puking, the cell phone dropping to the ground now, slick with vomit.

"Get back on the phone!"

More puking.

Roybal took another step back. Incredibly, he could hear a voice coming from the cell phone. "Who is this?" the tiny voice demanded. "Is that you, Rocky? Rocky! Are you all right?"

Still more puking. Roybal's eyes turned once more to the body, lying on its side, twisted, one arm thrown up, pale and ragged in the moonlight. This was messed up. Then he turned and ran through the trees: away, away, away, away . . .

52

It was four o'clock in the morning when D'Agosta and Pendergast arrived at the waiting room of the morgue annex. Dr. Beckstein was already waiting for them, looking strangely chipper. Or maybe, D'Agosta thought, he was just used to hanging around a morgue in the dead of night. D'Agosta felt like hell; he wanted nothing more than to go home and crawl into bed.

And yet that was the very last thing he could do. Things were happening almost faster than he could process them. Of all the recent events, by far the worst—to him, anyway—was the kidnapping of Nora Kelly, not a clue to her whereabouts, the officer assigned to protect her drugged with spiked coffee and his body locked in Nora's bathroom. Once again, he'd failed her.

And now, this.

"Well, well, gentlemen," Beckstein said, snapping on a pair of gloves. "The mystery deepens. Please, help yourselves." And he nodded toward a nearby bin.

D'Agosta tied on scrubs, donned a mask and surgical cap, and slipped on a pair of gloves. The feeling of dread increased as he tried to ready himself for the fresh ordeal he was about to endure. He had a hard time viewing morgue stiffs under the best of circumstances. Something about the mix of dead cold flesh, the clinical lights, and the gleam of steel made his stomach churn. How was he going to handle this one—when descriptions of the man while still ambulatory were enough to bring up anyone's lunch? He glanced over at Pendergast, now swathed in green and white, looking more like a morgue customer than a visitor. He was right at home.

"Doctor, before we go in"—D'Agosta tried to keep his voice casual—"I have a few questions."

"Of course," said Beckstein, pausing.

"The body was found in Inwood Hill Park, right? Not far from the Ville?"

Beckstein nodded. "Two teenage boys made the discovery."

"And you're certain about the ID on the victim? That the corpse is Colin Fearing?"

"Reasonably certain. The doorman of Fearing's building gave us a positive identification, and I consider him a credible witness. Two tenants who knew Fearing well also identified the body. It displays the correct tattoo and birthmark. Just to be sure, we've ordered DNA tests, but I'd stake my career on this being Colin Fearing."

"So the first corpse—the suicide, the bridge jumper? The one Dr. Heffler identified as Fearing? How'd that happen?"

Beckstein cleared his throat. "It would seem Dr. Heffler made a mistake—an understandable mistake, under the circumstances," he added hastily. "I certainly would have accepted the identification of a sister as definitive."

"Intriguing," murmured Pendergast.

"What?" asked D'Agosta.

"It makes one wonder what body Dr. Heffler did, in fact, autopsy."

"Yeah."

"The misidentification," said Beckstein, "is not so uncommon. I've seen it several times. When you combine grief and shock of the loved ones with the inevitable changes that death brings to the body—especially immersion in water or decomposition in the hot sun . . ."

"Right, right," said D'Agosta hastily. "Except external evidence points to this being a deliberate fraud. And on top of that, Dr. Heffler was slovenly in establishing the *sister's* identity, too."

"Mistakes happen," said Beckstein lamely.

"I have found that arrogance, of which Dr. Heffler suffers no paucity," intoned Pendergast, "is the fertilizing manure for the vineyard of error."

D'Agosta was still parsing this last sentence when Beckstein gestured for them to follow him into the autopsy room. Inside, the body of Fearing lay on a gurney under a harsh light, and D'Agosta was hugely relieved to find that a white plastic sheet covered it.

"I haven't started working on it yet," said Beckstein. "We're waiting for the arrival of a pathologist and diener. My apologies for the delay."

"Think nothing of it," said D'Agosta a little hastily. "We're grateful for the rush job. The body was only brought in around midnight, right?"

"That's correct. I've done the preliminaries and there are some—ah—curious things about the cadaver." Beckstein fingered the corner of the sheet. "May I?"

Curious. D'Agosta could just imagine what those things might be. "Well—"

"Delighted!" said Pendergast.

D'Agosta steeled himself, breathing through his mouth and relaxing the focus of his eyes. This was going to be hideous: a blackened, puffy corpse, flesh separating from the bones, fat melting, fluids draining . . . God, how he hated corpses!

There was a brisk ripple of plastic as Beckstein flicked off the sheet. "There," he said.

D'Agosta forced himself to focus on the cadaver. And was amazed.

It was the body of a normal-looking person: neat, spotless, and so fresh it could have been asleep. The face was clean-shaven, the hair combed and gelled, the only evidence of death being a nasty bullet wound above the right ear and a few twigs and leaves stuck to the gel on the back of the head.

D'Agosta looked at Pendergast and saw that the FBI agent seemed as astonished as he was.

"Well!" said D'Agosta, awash with relief. "So much for your zombiis and walking dead, Pendergast. Like I've been saying all along, this whole thing's a hoax—concocted by the Ville. The guy was probably returning there from a night's fake zombifying and got capped by a mugger."

Pendergast said nothing, just observed the corpse with glittering, silvery eyes.

D'Agosta turned to Beckstein. "You got time of death?"

"An anal probe indicates he'd been dead about two and a half hours when he was found in Inwood Hill Park. That was at eleven, give or take, which would put the time of death around eight thirty."

"Cause of death?"

"Most likely the prominent gunshot wound over the right ear."

D'Agosta squinted. "No exit wound. Looks like a .22."

"I believe that's right. Of course, we won't know for sure until we open him up. My preliminary examination indicates he was shot from behind, at point-blank range. No signs of a struggle or coercion, no evidence of bruising, scratching, or binding."

D'Agosta turned. "What do you make of that, Pendergast? No voodoo, no Obeah, just a piece-of-shit gunshot murder like half the others in this town. Dr. Beckstein, was he killed in situ or the body dumped?"

"I don't have any information on that, Lieutenant. The first responders rushed the body to the hospital. It was still warm, and they weren't making any assumptions."

"Right, of course. We'll have to check with the evidence-gathering teams when they're finished." D'Agosta just couldn't keep the note of triumph out of his voice. "It's pretty clear to me that we're dealing with a lot of mumbo-jumbo, rigged up by those sons of bitches in the Ville to scare people away."

"You mentioned some curious aspects?" Pendergast asked Beckstein.

"I did. The first one you might find familiar." Beckstein took a pair of tongue depressors from a jar, tore off the sterile coverings, and used them to open the corpse's mouth. There, pinned to the tongue, was a tiny bundle of feathers and hair. It matched, almost exactly, the one found in Bill Smithback's mouth.

D'Agosta peered at it, disbelieving.

"And then there was something else. I'm going to need a little help turning over the cadaver. Lieutenant?"

With huge reluctance, D'Agosta helped Beckstein roll the corpse over. Scrawled between the shoulder blades in thick Magic Marker was a complex, stylized design of two snakes surrounded by stars, X's and arrows, and coffin-like boxes. A weird, spidery drawing of a plant filled the small of the back.

D'Agosta swallowed. He recognized these drawings.

"Vévé," murmured Pendergast, "similar to what we saw on the wall of Smithback's apartment. Strange . . ." He paused.

"What?" D'Agosta asked instantly.

Instead of answering directly, Pendergast slowly shook his head. "I wish Monsieur Bertin could see this," he murmured. Then he straightened up. "My dear Vincent, I do not think this gentleman was 'capped by a mugger,' as you put it. This was a deliberate, execution-style killing, for a very specific purpose."

D'Agosta stared at him for a moment. Then he turned his gaze back to the body on the table.

Alexander Esteban settled himself into an inconspicuous place at the large Formica table in the shabby "boardroom" of Humans for Other Animals on West 14th Street. There was a bright fall morning outside, but little of it penetrated the room through the one grimy window that looked out on an airshaft. He folded his arms and watched the other board members take their places, accompanied by the scraping of chairs, murmured greetings, the clattering of BlackBerries and iPhones. The smell of Starbucks cinnamon dolce lattes and pumpkin spice Frappuccino crèmes filled the room as everyone set down their venti-size coffee cups.

The last to enter was Rich Plock, accompanied by three people Esteban didn't know. Plock took up a position at the far end of the room, clasped arms disguising the gravid-like swell of a paunch beneath the ill-fitting suit, his red face sweating behind aviator glasses. He immediately launched into a speech in his high, self-important voice.

"Ladies and gentlemen of the board, I am delighted to present to you three very distinguished guests. Miles Mondello, president of The Green Brigade; Lucinda Long-Pierson, chairwoman of Vegan Army; and Morris Wyland, director of Animal Amnesty."

The three stood there, looking to Esteban as if they were straight out of central casting. Rabid idealists, desperate for a cause, completely clueless.

"These three organizations are co-sponsoring tonight's demonstration, along with HOA. Let us welcome them to our meeting."

Applause.

"Please, everyone sit down. This special session of the HOA board is hereby convened."

A shuffling of papers, many sips of coffee, pencils and legal pads and laptops brought out. There was a call for a quorum. Esteban waited through it all.

"There is one and only one item on the agenda: the protest march this evening. In addition to the founding organizations, we have twenty-one other groups on board. That's right, ladies and gentlemen, you heard me: *twenty-one more!*" Plock beamed and looked around. "The reaction's been unbelievable. We're expecting maybe three thousand people—but I'm continuing to interface with other interested organizations and there may be more. Many more." He shuffled a stack of papers out of a folder and began passing them around. "Here are the details. The small diversionary group will convene at the baseball diamonds. Other groups—all listed on the sheet—will gather at the soccer field, the park alongside West Two Hundred Eighteenth Street, along the promenade by the mudflats, and several other nearby locations. As you know, I've secured a permit. We wouldn't be let near the Ville otherwise."

A murmur, nods.

"But of course the city authorities have no idea—*no* idea—just how big a group is going to be assembling uptown. I've made sure of that."

Some knowing chuckles.

"Because, ladies and gentlemen, this is an emergency! These sick, depraved people, squatters in our city, aren't just killing animals, but they're obviously behind the brutal murder of Martin

Wartek. They're responsible for the murder of two reporters, Smithback and Kidd, and the kidnapping of Smithback's wife. What's the city doing? Nothing. *Absolutely nothing!* It's up to us to act. So we're going in tonight at six PM. We're going to end this thing. Now!"

Plock was sweating, his voice was high and his physical presence unimpressive, and yet he possessed the charisma of true belief, of passion and genuine courage. Esteban was impressed.

"The detailed plan of the demonstration is on your sheets. Guard them carefully—it would be disastrous if one fell into the hands of the police. Go home, start calling, start e-mailing, start organizing! This is a tight schedule. We gather at six. We move at six thirty." He looked around. "Any questions?"

No one had questions. Esteban cleared his throat, raised his finger.

"Yes, Alexander?"

"I'm a little confused. You're planning to actually march on the Ville?"

"That's right. We're stopping this: here and now."

Esteban nodded thoughtfully. "It doesn't say what you plan to do when you get there."

"We're going to break into that compound and we're going to liberate those animals. And we're going to drive out those squatters. It's all covered in the plan."

"I see. It's of course true that they are killing—torturing—animals in cold blood. They've probably been doing it for years. But consider: they're likely to be armed. We already know they've murdered at least three people."

"If they choose violence, we'll respond in kind."

"You plan to go armed?"

Plock folded his arms. "I will say this: no one will be discouraged from acting in self-defense—with whatever means they may have brought with them."

"In other words," said Esteban, "you're recommending that people come armed."

"I'm not recommending anything, Alexander. I am merely stating a fact: violence is certainly a possibility—and everyone has the right of self-defense."

"I see. And the police? How will you handle them?"

"That's why we're gathering at different points and moving in from multiple directions, like an octopus. They'll be overwhelmed before they even know what's going on. Thousands of us, moving en masse through those woods—how are they going to stop us? They can't set up barricades or block our route. They don't have vehicular access except down a single road, and that'll be wall-to-wall with marchers."

Esteban shifted uncomfortably. "Now, don't get me wrong—I'm against the Ville, you've known that from the start. They're despicable, inhuman. I mean, look at this poor luckless Fearing. Brainwashed into murder, and then shot in the head—probably by the Ville—while trying to crawl back to the very sadists who made him a zombii in the first place. If they can do this kind of thing to Fearing, they can do it to anyone. But if you move in like this, in such an uncontrolled fashion, people might be hurt. Even killed. Have you considered that?"

"People have *already* been killed. Not to mention animals—hundreds, perhaps even thousands of them, their throats cut in the most horrific ways. No, sir: we're ending this. Tonight."

"I'm not sure I'm ready," said Esteban. "This is a pretty radical move."

"Alexander, we were happy to have you join our organization. We are glad that you've taken a strong interest in our work. We were happy to elect you a member of the board. Your financial generosity is much appreciated, as is your high visibility. But personally, I strongly believe there comes a time when a man or a woman must make a stand. Talk is no longer sufficient. That time is *now*."

"Once you break into the Ville," said Esteban, "and liberate the animals—what then?"

"Just what I said. We'll drive the animal murderers out. Where they go is their business."

"And then?"

"And then we burn the place, so they can't return."

At this, Esteban slowly shook his head. "With thousands of people milling outside *and* inside the Ville, and no access by firefighters, any fire you start may cause dozens of deaths. That place is a firetrap. You'll be killing your own, perhaps, as well as them."

An uncomfortable silence.

"I would strongly urge against fire. Just the opposite—I would assign fire control to selected protesters, to guard *against* that possibility. What if the inhabitants are like those nutcases in Waco and set fire to the place themselves, while you're all inside?"

Another pause. "Thank you, Alexander," said Plock. "I must admit you've made a good point. I retract what I said about fire. We'll tear the place down with our bare hands. The goal is to render it uninhabitable."

Murmurs of agreement.

Esteban frowned, then shook his head. "I still can't support this. I'm a well-known figure with a reputation to uphold. I'm sorry, I just can't be associated with an attack like this."

A shifting of chairs and a faint hiss. "That is of course your right, Alexander," said Plock, his voice cool. "And I must say I'm not entirely surprised, given the way you dashed cold water on our last encounter with the Ville. Anyone else wish to join Mr. Esteban in bailing out?"

Esteban looked around. Nobody else moved. He could read the disrespect, even scorn, in their eyes.

He stood up and walked out.

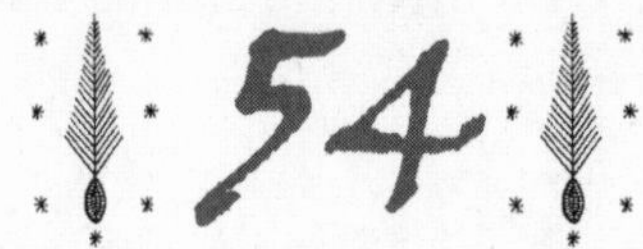

As the morning sun streamed in the windows, D'Agosta sat behind his desk, fingers on his computer keyboard, staring at the screen before him. He had been in this position, motionless, for perhaps ten minutes. There were a million things to be done and yet he felt something akin to paralysis. It was as if he were in the eye of a hurricane: all around was frantic activity, but here at the very epicenter of the howling storm there was nothing.

Suddenly the door to his office opened. He turned to see Laura Hayward step quickly in. He immediately rose to his feet.

"Laura," he said.

She closed the door behind her, stepped up to the desk. Seeing the icy look on her face, D'Agosta felt his stomach do an uncomfortable flip-flop.

"Vinnie, sometimes you can be a selfish bastard," she said in a low voice.

He swallowed. "What is it?"

"What is it? I've had my promotion snatched away from me at the last moment. And it's your fault."

For a moment he looked at her with incomprehension. Then he remembered the conversation he'd had in the corridor of Digital Veracity; the implied threat of the software developer. "Kline," he said, slumping against the desk.

"You're damn right, Kline."

D'Agosta looked at her for a moment. Then he lowered his eyes. "What did he do?"

"He donated five million to the Dyson Fund. On the condition that I be passed over for the task force."

"He can't do that. It's bribery. It's against the law."

"Oh, please. You know how this town works."

D'Agosta sighed. He knew what he should feel—righteous indignation, even rage—but all he felt, suddenly, was weary.

"Rocker's no fool," Hayward said bitterly. "He knows they'd crucify him if he turned down a donation like that—especially for a political hot potato like the Dyson Fund. And I'm the one who gets the shaft."

"Laura . . . I'm so sorry. You're the last person I wanted to see get victimized by this. But I was only doing my job. What was I supposed to do—give this joker Kline a pass? He's a person of interest. He threatened Smithback."

"What you were *supposed* to do was act professional. Ever since Smithback's murder, you've been out of control. I heard about that ham-fisted search warrant of yours, how you rubbed Kline's nose in it. You knew the man had a short fuse and you provoked him anyway. And to get revenge, he lashed out at me."

"It's true—I *was* trying to provoke him, trigger a false move. He's the kind of guy who can't stand to lose face. If I'd known he'd take it out on you I would never have done it." He hung his head, massaging his temples with his fingers. "What can I say?"

"That job meant more to me than *anything*."

Her words hung in the air. D'Agosta looked up slowly, met her glance.

There was a low rap on his office window. D'Agosta looked over to see a desk sergeant standing in the doorway.

"Excuse me, sir," he said. "I think you should turn on channel two."

Wordlessly, D'Agosta strode to the television mounted high on one wall, pressed the power button. An amateurish video filled the screen, grainy, shaky—but he immediately recognized the woman in the camera frame as Nora Kelly. She was dressed in a flimsy hospital robe, her face ashen, her hair askew. She seemed to be in a dungeon: rough-hewn rock walls, a scattering of straw on a cement floor. He watched as she stepped uncertainly toward the lens.

"Help me," she said.

Abruptly the picture went black.

D'Agosta turned back to the desk sergeant. "What the *hell*?"

"It came into the network about fifteen minutes ago. They're messengering the original over right now."

"I want our best forensic people on it. *Right away*—got that? Where was it dropped off?"

"Came in by e-mail."

"Trace it."

"Yes, sir." The sergeant disappeared.

D'Agosta slumped back into his seat, rested his head in his hands, closed his eyes. A minute passed as he collected himself. Then he licked his lips, spoke quietly. "I'm going to find her, Laura—if it's my last act as a law enforcement officer. Whatever it takes—*whatever*—I'll make it my personal business to see that Nora Kelly doesn't die. And that the people responsible pay dearly for it."

"There you go again," Hayward said. "That's just what I'm talking about. If you want to save Nora Kelly, you're going to have to get your emotions under control. You're going to have to start acting like a professional cop again. Or next time it won't be just me who ends up getting hurt."

And without another word she turned and left the office, closing the door firmly behind her.

55

As the morning sun gilded the cream-colored walls and soaring terra-cotta spandrels of the Dakota, a curious processional played itself out before the building's 72nd Street entrance. Two valets emerged from between the black wrought-iron gates, each holding three suitcases. They were followed by a woman in a white nurse's uniform, who stepped out from the gloom of the courtyard tunnel and took up a position beside the doorman's pillbox. Next came Proctor, who walked to the Rolls-Royce waiting at the curb, opened the rear door, and stood beside it expectantly. After a long moment, another figure emerged from the gate: a rather small figure, reclining in a wheelchair being pushed by a second nurse. Despite the warmth of the Indian summer day, the figure was so heavily wrapped in blankets, muffs, and scarves that its features and indeed its very sex were hard to discern. The face was obscured by a large and floppy white hat. A mother-of-pearl cigarette holder jutted out from beneath a pair of dark glasses.

The nurse wheeled the invalid up to the waiting Proctor. As she did so, Pendergast emerged from the entranceway and ambled over to the Rolls, hands in pockets.

"I can't persuade you to stay a little longer, *maître*?" he asked.

The person in the wheelchair sneezed explosively. "I wouldn't stay here a minute longer even if Saint Christopher himself asked me!" came the petulant response.

"Let me help you in, Mr. Bertin," said Proctor.

"One minute." A pale hand, holding a bottle of nasal spray, emerged from beneath the blanket. The bottle was applied to one quivering nostril, squeezed, then tucked away again beneath the blanket. The dark glasses were removed and slipped into the BOAC flight bag that never seemed to leave the little man's side. "You may proceed. *Doucement, pour l'amour du ciel—doucement!*"

With some effort Proctor and the nurse managed to shift Bertin from the wheelchair and—under a stream of imprecations—slide him into the rear of the vehicle. Pendergast came forward and leaned into the window.

"Are you feeling any better?" he asked.

"No, and I won't until I have returned to the back bayou—if then." Bertin peered out from between his wraps, clutching his huge cudgel-cane, his black eyes glistening like beads. "And you need to have a care, Aloysius—the death conjuring of that hungan is strong: old and strong."

"Indeed."

"How do you feel?"

"Not bad."

"You see!" Bertin declared with something like triumph. The hand reappeared again, rummaged in the battered bag, produced a tiny sealed envelope. "Dissolve this in six ounces of sarsaparilla and add a little flaxseed oil. Twice a day."

Pendergast pocketed the envelope. "Thank you, *maître*. I'm sorry to have caused you such trouble."

For a moment, the glittering black eyes softened. "Pah! It was good to see you after so many years. Next time we meet, however, it will be in New Orleans—I will not return to this place of darkness again!" He shuddered. "I wish you best of luck. This *Loa* of the Ville—it is truly evil. Evil."

"Is there anything more you should tell me before you leave?"

"No. Yes!" The little man coughed, sneezed again. "I almost forgot amid all my sufferings. That tiny coffin you showed me—the one in the evidence room—it is strange."

"The one from Colin Fearing's crypt? The one you, ah, damaged?"

Bertin nodded. "It took me some time to realize it. But the arrangement of skulls and bones on the lid . . ." He shook his head. "The ratio is unusual, self-conflicting. It should follow the True Pattern: two to five. A subtle difference, but a difference nonetheless. It doesn't match the rest." He gave a disdainful flick of his fingers. "It is crude, strange."

"I analyzed the grayish powder that was inside of it. It appears to be simple wood ash."

Another disdainful flick. "You see? It does not match the other Obeah of Charrière and the Ville. Those are infinitely worse. Why this one item doesn't match the pattern is a mystery."

"Thank you, *maître*." And Pendergast straightened up, a thoughtful look settling onto his face.

"Not at all. And now *adieu,* my dear Aloysius—*adieu!* Remember: dissolve in six ounces of sarsaparilla, twice a day." Bertin tapped the roof of the car with the head of his cane. "You may drive on, my good sir! And don't spare the horses, I beg you!"

56

The Multimedia Services Unit at One Police Plaza reminded D'Agosta of a submarine's control room: hot, overstuffed with electronics, ripe with the smell of humanity. At least twenty people were packed into the low-ceilinged space, hunched over terminals and workstations. Somebody was eating an early lunch, and the pungent smell of curry hung in the air.

He paused and looked around. The biggest group was concentrated in the rear, where John Loader, chief forensic tech, had his cubicle. D'Agosta began making his way toward it, his feeling of frustration mounting when he saw that Chislett was already here. The deputy chief turned, saw D'Agosta, turned back.

Loader was sitting at his digital workstation, a hulking CPU beneath the desk and dual thirty-inch flat-screen monitors atop it. Despite D'Agosta's pressuring, the forensic technician had insisted he'd need at least two hours to process and prep the video. So far he'd had ninety minutes.

"Give me an update," D'Agosta said as he drew near.

Loader pushed away from the workstation. "It's an MPEG-four file that was e-mailed to the network's news department."

"And the trace?"

Loader shook his head. "Whoever did it used a remailing service out of Kazakhstan."

"Okay, what about the video, then?"

The technician pointed at the matching screens. "It's in the forensic video analyzer."

"This is what took ninety minutes?"

Loader frowned. "I've striped in a time code, field-aligned and frame-averaged the entire clip, removed noise and brightened each frame, and applied digital image stabilization."

"Did you remember to put a cherry on top?"

"Lieutenant, cleaning up the file not only smooths and sharpens the image, but it also reduces distractions and can highlight evidence that would otherwise go unnoticed."

D'Agosta felt like pointing out that there was a human life at stake here and every minute counted, but decided against it. "Fair enough. Let's see it."

Loader pulled the jog shuttle closer—a round black device the size of a hockey puck—and the video flickered into life on the left-hand monitor. It was less grainy and muddy than when he'd seen it on the news. There was a rattle, then a feeble light stabbed into the darkness: and there was Nora. She stared at the camera; her face, illuminated by the light source, looked like a white ghost floating in darkness. Behind her, D'Agosta could just barely make out patches of straw on a cement floor, rough mortared stones forming the walls.

"Help me," Nora said.

The camera shook; lost focus; gained focus again.

"What do you want?" Nora asked.

No answer, no sound. And then something like a muffled scratch or creak. The light swiveled away, the darkness returned, and the clip ended.

"So you can't trace it," D'Agosta said, trying to keep his voice steady. "Is there anything else about the file that you can tell me? Anything at all?"

"It wasn't multiplexed."

"Which means?"

"It wasn't from a CCTV. The source was most likely a standard consumer digital camcorder, probably an older handheld model given the degree of image shake."

"And there was no communication in the e-mail? No ransom demand, no message of any kind?"

Loader shook his head.

"Play it again, please."

As it played, D'Agosta looked around at what little was visible of the room, searching for something, anything, that might help identify it.

"Can you zoom in on that wall?" he asked.

With the jog shuttle, Loader scrubbed back a second or two into the clip; highlighted a section of the wall close to Nora; then magnified it.

"It's too grainy," D'Agosta said.

"Let me apply the unsharp mask tool. That should clear it up." A few clicks of a mouse and the wall sharpened significantly—flat stones stacked and cemented into place.

"Basement," said D'Agosta. "An old one."

"Unfortunately," said Chislett, speaking for the first time, "there's nothing identifiable about it."

"What about the geology of the rocks?"

"Impossible to identify their specific mineral composition," said Loader. "Could be shale, could be basalt . . ."

"Run it again."

Silently, they watched the playback. D'Agosta could feel his anger filling the room. He wondered why he was even bothering to control it anymore: the bastards had kidnapped Nora.

"That sound in the background," he said. "What is it?"

Loader pushed the jog shuttle to one side. "We've been working on that. I'll bring up the audio enhancement software."

Now a window popped up on the second screen, a thin, wide window containing an audio waveform: a rough, squiggly band that looked like a sine curve on steroids.

"A little silence, please!" Loader called out. The room quieted, and Loader clicked a play button at the bottom of the window.

The squiggly curve began striping across the window like a spool of tape running through a recorder. D'Agosta could hear the muffled movements of the person apparently carrying the camera through the darkness, the little click as the camera light went on, a grating sound, as if the camera was resting on something—or the lens was being slid through bars or a hole. Nora spoke once, then again. And then there was the sound. A creak? A scratch? It was too low, there was too much background hiss, to make it out.

"Can you enhance it?" he asked. "Isolate it?"

"Let me add some parametric EQ to the signal path." More windows popped open, complex-looking graphs were dragged onto the audio waveform. Loader played the sound file again. It was clearer but still muddy.

"I'll apply a brick wall filter. High-pass, to block out that low-end hum." More clicks, more adjustments of the mouse, then Loader played the waveform once more.

"That's an animal sound," said D'Agosta. "The sound of an animal getting its throat cut."

"I'm afraid I don't hear it," said Chislett.

"Oh no?" D'Agosta turned to Loader. "What about you?"

The forensic tech scratched his cheek a little nervously. "Hard to say." He opened another window. "According to this spectrum analyzer, there's a mix of very high frequencies, some higher than the human ear can hear. I'd guess it's the creaking of a rusty door hinge."

"Bullshit!"

"With all due respect—" Loader began.

"With all due respect, that's the scream of an animal. The basement is old, crude. Let me tell you something: this tape came from the Ville. We need to raid the place. Now." He turned and stared aggressively at Chislett. "Right, Chief?"

"Lieutenant," Chislett intoned, his voice the very embodiment of calm and reason, "you're obfuscating the situation rather than clarifying it. There's no evidence—none—on that tape indicating its source. That sound could be any of myriad things."

Obfuscating rather than clarifying. Myriad things. How like the pretentious Chislett to turn a simple meeting into a spelling bee. D'Agosta tried to keep himself under control. "Chief, you're aware there's going to be a demonstration tonight against the Ville."

"They've got a parade permit, it's all quite legit. We'll have plenty of men this time, we'll keep things orderly."

"Yeah? There's no way to be sure of that. If the demonstration gets unruly, it might freak out the Ville—and cause them to kill Nora. We've got to raid them now, today, *before* the demonstration. Use the element of surprise, go in fast and hard and grab her."

"Lieutenant, haven't you been listening? Where's the evidence? No judge will authorize a raid based on that one sound—even if it is an animal. You know that. Especially," he sniffed, "after your heavy-handed search of Kline's offices."

D'Agosta straightened up. He finally felt the dam breaking, his anger and frustration pouring out. He didn't care. "Look at all of you," he said loudly, "sitting around here, fiddling with your equipment."

Everyone paused in their work to turn and look.

"While you're playing with your toys, a woman's been kidnapped, two journalists and a housing official murdered. What we need is a massive, multiple SWAT team raid on those scumbags up there."

"Lieutenant," said Chislett, "it would behoove you to get your emotions under control. We're well aware of the stakes and we're doing all we can."

"No, I won't, and no, you aren't." D'Agosta turned and stalked out of the room.

Pendergast sat in an overstuffed leather armchair in the salon of his Dakota apartment, one leg thrown over the other, chin resting on tented fingers. In a matching armchair across an expanse of Turkish rug sat Wren, his bird-like figure almost swallowed up in the burgundy-colored leather. Between them stood a table on which sat a pot of A-Li-Shan Jin Xuan tea, a basket of brioche, a tub of butter, and crocks of marmalade and gooseberry jam.

"To what do I owe the pleasure of this unexpected visit, in daylight no less?" Pendergast asked. "It would take something rather momentous to entice you out of your den at such an hour."

Wren gave a sharp nod. "True, I am no fan of the daytime. But I've discovered something I thought you ought to know."

"Fortunately it is rarely daytime in my apartment." Pendergast poured two cups of tea, placed one before his guest, raised the other to his lips.

Wren glanced at his cup but did not touch it. "I keep meaning to ask. How is the fetching Constance?"

"I've been getting regular reports from Tibet. Everything is proceeding on schedule—or as much as such things can run on schedule. I hope to travel there in the not-too-distant future." Pendergast took another sip. "You said you've discovered something. By all means, proceed."

"In my research into the history of the Ville and its occupants—and its predecessors—I naturally have made use of a large number of period accounts, newspaper reports, surveys, manuscripts, incunabula, and other documents. And the more that I have done so, the more I've noticed a curious pattern."

"And what might that be?"

Wren sat forward. "That I am not the first person to have made this particular journey."

Pendergast put down his cup. "Indeed?"

"Everybody who examines rare or historic documents is issued an identification number by the library. I began to notice that the same ID number was appearing in the accessions database for the documents I was withdrawing for examination. At first I thought it was just a coincidence. But after this happened a number of times, I went to the database and looked up that ID. Sure enough: every document of the Ville, its inhabitants, its history, the history of its prior occupants—with particular emphasis, it seems, on the founders—had also been examined by this other researcher. He was quite diligent—in fact, he had thought to examine a few papers it had not occurred to me to search." Wren chuckled, shook his head ruefully.

"And who is this mysterious researcher?"

"That's just the thing—his or her file has been wiped clean from the library's records. It was as if he didn't want anybody to know he'd been there. All that was left were the traces, so to speak, of his passing. I know he was a professional researcher—that's indicated by the prefix of his identification number. And I'm convinced this was a job for hire, not something of particular interest to him. It was done too quickly and in too orderly a fashion, over too short a period of time, to have been a hobby or a personal study."

"I see." Pendergast took a sip. "And when did this take place?"

"He began examining library materials about eight months ago. The withdrawals continued, on a more or less weekly basis. And then the trail ended rather abruptly about two months ago."

Pendergast looked at him. "He completed his research?"

"Yes." Wren hesitated. "There is, of course, one other possibility."

"Indeed. And what is that?"

"He was searching for something—something very particular. And the abrupt halt to his work meant that he'd found it."

After his guest had left, Pendergast rose from the chair, exited the salon, and walked down the apartment's central corridor until he came to a small and rather old-fashioned laboratory. He removed his black suit coat and hung it on a hook behind the door. The room was dominated by a soapstone lab table on which stood chemical apparatuses and a Bunsen burner. Old oaken cabinets lined the walls, glass bottles competing for space with tattered journals and well-worn reference books.

He slipped a key out of his pocket and unlocked one of the cabinets. From it, he removed various supplies: a pair of latex gloves, a polished walnut instrument case, a rack of glass test tubes with labels and stoppers, and a brass magnifying glass. He arranged everything on the soapstone table. Striding across the room, he snapped on the gloves and unlocked a second cabinet. A moment later a skull came to light, cradled in his hands—the skull that he and D'Agosta had recovered from the riverbank burial. Dirt still clung to the jaws and eye sockets. He gently placed the skull on the table and opened the case to reveal a set of nineteenth-century dental tools with ivory handles. With great care he cleaned the skull, removing bits of dirt, some of which he placed in various test tubes, affixing numbered labels. Samples of whitish powder clinging to the inside of the jaws and teeth also went into test tubes, along with fragments of skin, hair, and adipocere.

When he was done, he set the skull down and stared at it. Seconds passed, then minutes. The room was perfectly silent. And then Pendergast slowly rose. His silvery eyes glittered with an inner enthusiasm. He picked up the magnifying glass and examined the skull at close range, focusing at last on the right ocular cavity. Putting down the glass and lifting the skull, he examined the eye socket, rotating it, squinting at it from every direction. There were several thin, curved scratches on the inside of the cavity, as well as similar scratches on the inner rear wall of the cranial dome.

Laying the skull down on the table again, he walked to a third cabinet and unlocked it. From it he removed the strange implement pilfered from the Ville altar: a sharp, twisted piece of metal protruding from a wooden handle, looking like an extended, bizarre corkscrew. He carried it to the laboratory table and placed it next to the skull. Leaning on the table with both hands, he stared down at the two objects for some time, his eyes moving restlessly from one to the other.

Finally, he took a seat beside the table. He picked up the skull in his right hand and the implement in his left. More time passed as he stared at each object in turn. And then, with exquisite slowness, he brought the two together, placing the curved end of the hook into the eye socket. Slowly, carefully, he slid the hook along the faint scratch marks and manipulated it in such a way as to insert it through the superior orbital fissure—the gap in the back of the eye socket. The tip slid perfectly into the hole. As if working out a puzzle, Pendergast manipulated the hook into the brain cavity, worming it ever deeper, again following the scratch marks on the bone until a notch in the metal tool caught on the orbital fissure, bringing the hooked end to rest deep within the brain cavity.

With a sudden deft manipulation—a small twist of the handle—Pendergast caused the hooked end of the tool to make a circular cutting motion. Back and forth he twisted—and back and forth went the little sharpened hook inside the brain cavity, in a precise little arc.

A mirthless smile illuminated the face of Special Agent Pendergast, and he murmured a single word: "Broca."

58

Nora Kelly lay in the dark, listening. The room was as silent as the grave. No matter how hard she tried, she could not detect the normal, reassuring background sounds of the outside world: cars, voices, footsteps, wind in the trees. There weren't even the sounds of mice or rats in the damp basement.

Once she had recovered her wits and gained control of her fear, she had performed a minute exploration of her prison: first once, and then twice. It had taken hours. She had to work by feel—the only glimpse she'd had of her cell was when she'd been videotaped, and at the time she'd been too disoriented and upset to use the opportunity to memorize her surroundings.

Nevertheless, her tactile explorations had given her a clear impression of her cell—almost too clear. The floor was poured concrete, and it was very fresh and damp, with a strong cement smell. It was covered by straw. The dimensions of her prison, which she had measured by several meticulous pacings-off, were approximately ten feet by sixteen. The walls were rough mortared stone, probably granite, and absolutely solid, with no opening of any kind except the door. That was of heavy wood, massively plated and riveted with iron (which she determined by taste); she had the impression it was a new door, custom-built for the cellar, since its frame was lower and narrower than standard. The ceiling was a low vault of cemented brick, which she could touch around the edges, rising to a higher point in the middle. There were some rusty iron hooks on the wall and ceiling, indicating that the room had perhaps once been used for curing meat.

There were two things in the cell: a bucket in one corner to serve as a latrine, and a gallon plastic jug filled with water. She had been given no food at all during the time she had been imprisoned. In the pitch-dark it was hard to tell the passage of time, but she felt certain it had been at least twenty-four hours. Strangely enough, she didn't mind being hungry; it had the effect of sharpening her mind.

You won't live long enough for my name to make any difference. That was all her captor had said, and Nora knew he meant it. No effort was being made to keep her alive, to supply her with fresh air, to make sure she was returned to the land of the living in acceptable physical condition. More than that: the tone of voice had been so casual, and yet so quietly certain, that she felt in her bones it was the truth.

It seemed unlikely she would be rescued. Cooperation was not an option—she would merely be cooperating with her own death. She had to escape.

As methodically as if she was classifying potsherds, Nora explored every possible avenue of escape she could think of. Could she somehow dig through the not-fully-cured concrete floor? The plastic bucket and jug offered nothing to work with. She had no shoes or belt: she was still dressed in her flimsy hospital robe. The hooks were firmly attached to the ceiling. She had nothing but her fingernails and teeth to scrape with, and that was impossible.

Next she considered the mortared walls. She went over them with great care, testing each stone, probing the mortar in between. No luck. The stones were solid; none felt loose. The stones and the bricks in the ceiling seemed to have had been freshly repointed, and there wasn't even a crack in which she could insert a fingernail.

The door was equally impossible: immobile and immensely strong. There was no lock on the inside, or even a keyhole: it was probably bolted and padlocked on the far side. There was a small window in the door, barred on the inside, with a metal shutter that remained closed and locked. The room was so silent, it was clearly underground and soundproof.

This left only one option: overpower her jailer when he returned. To do that, she had to have a plan. And she had to have a weapon.

She thought first of the rusty hooks in the walls and ceiling; but they were of thick iron and too strong to work loose or break off. Even the bucket had no handle. She had her hands, feet, nails, and teeth to use as weapons. They would have to do.

He needed her alive, as least for now. Why? He had to prove to someone that she was alive. Was it for ransom? Possibly. Or was it to serve as a hostage? There was no way to know. She only knew that, once he had what he needed, he would kill her.

Simple.

She marveled at her own calmness. Why wasn't she more afraid? That was simple, too. After Bill's death, there was nothing left to fear. The worst had already occurred.

She sat up, did thirty sit-ups to get her blood flowing. The sudden exercise, combined with the lack of food and the concussion, made her momentarily dizzy. But when her head cleared, she felt more alert than ever.

A plan. Could she could feign sickness, draw him into the room, pretend to be unconscious—and then attack? But that wouldn't work: it was a lame trick, and he wouldn't fall for it.

His next appearance might be to kill her. She had to make sure that, when her jailer returned, he couldn't just execute her with a shot through the door slot. No; she would have to position herself such that he'd need to open the door and step inside if he wanted to kill her. That place was obviously behind the door. The darkness would be her ally. When he came in—that would be her only moment. She had to be ready to explode into action. She would go straight for the eyes. This was the man who had killed her husband—she was sure of it. She allowed her hatred for him to fill her with energy.

She began running through the steps in her mind, previsualizing the door opening, her leap, his falling back, her thumbs in his eyes. And then she would go for his gun, pull it, and kill him . . .

A sound interrupted her, a tiny sound, unidentifiable. Like a cat she leapt to the far side of the door and crouched in the dark, placing one foot forward, balancing herself almost like a runner in blocks, preparing to spring. She heard a padlock unlocking, a heavy bolt shooting back. The door opened slightly and a dim light fell across the floor. The door hit her foot and stopped.

"Movie time," said the voice. "I'm coming in." The light from the camcorder switched on, illuminating her cell in a brilliant white light that temporarily blinded her. She waited, tensing, struggling to focus her eyes.

The bright light suddenly swung around the door, shining directly in her face. She lunged at it, thumbs grasping and stiffening toward her captor's head. But the dazzling light blinded her and with a grunt the man caught her wrists in a vise-like grip, dropping the light. She felt herself wrenched aside with great force and thrown to the floor, kicked hard in the stomach. The light had clattered to the floor but the man immediately swept it up again and retreated a couple of steps.

She stared up from the floor, gasping, trying to recover her breath. The light focused on her afresh, the lens beneath winking; the man behind remained completely invisible in the dark. Again the unbearable thought flashed through her mind: *This is the man who murdered my husband.*

With a shuddering intake of air she rose and ran once again at the man behind the light, clawing at him, but he was ready. A blow struck the side of her head and the next thing she knew she was lying on the floor, her ears ringing afresh, points of light dancing across her field of vision.

The video light blinked off; the figure withdrew; the door began to close. Nora struggled to her knees, suddenly weak, her head pounding, but the bolt shot home before she could stand. She grasped the door, hauled herself painfully upward.

"You're a dead man," she gasped, pounding her fist on the door. "I swear I'll kill you."

"It's vice versa, you little vixen," came the voice. "Expect me—soon."

59

D'Agosta stood in the back of the squad room, arms folded across his chest, staring at the rows of seated officers before him, listening as Harry Chislett magisterially briefed the troops about the impending "parade event"—that's how the pompous prick referred to it—about to take place outside the Ville. *Parade, my ass,* thought D'Agosta impatiently. Just because Esteban and Plock had secured a parade permit didn't mean they were planning to march past the Ville with measured pace singing "Give Peace a Chance." D'Agosta had seen how ugly that first crowd had grown, and how quickly. Chislett hadn't—he'd left practically before the damn protest started. And now here he was, gesturing grandly at diagrams on a whiteboard, talking about protection, crowd control, and various tactical nuances as calmly as if he were mapping out a DAR cotillion.

As he listened to the lame plans unfold, D'Agosta felt his hands balling into fists. He'd tried to explain to Chislett that there was a good chance Nora Kelly was being held by the Ville, and that any outburst of violence from the protesters might mean her death. There was more to this than logistics; with any large crowd, violence and mob mentality were a mere heartbeat away. Nora Kelly's life might hang in the balance. But the deputy chief didn't see it that way. "The burden of proof rests on your shoulders," he'd intoned pompously. "Where's your evidence that Nora Kelly is in the Ville?" It was all D'Agosta could do not to sink his fist in the man's adipose tissue.

"We'll have three control points, here, here, and here," Chislett intoned, with another tap of his pointer. "Two at the central nodes of ingress and egress, one at the entrance to Inwood Hill Park. Chain of command will flow from those down to the forward field positions."

"Allemande left with your left hand," D'Agosta muttered to himself. "Right to your partner, right and left grand."

"It does seem that Deputy Chief Chislett is rather missing the point," said a familiar voice at his elbow.

D'Agosta turned to see Pendergast standing beside him. "Good afternoon, Vincent," the agent drawled.

"What are you doing here?" D'Agosta asked in surprise.

"I came looking for you."

"Where's your pal, Bertin?"

"He has retreated to the safety of the back bayou. It's just you and me once again."

D'Agosta felt a surge of hope go through him—something he hadn't felt in days. At least Pendergast understood the gravity of the situation. "Then you know we can't wait any longer," he said. "We have to get the hell in there and rescue Nora, now."

"I quite agree."

"If that riot takes place while Nora's being held in the Ville, there's a good chance she'll be killed immediately."

"Again, I would agree—assuming she is at the Ville."

"Assuming? Where else could she be? I had the soundprint on the video analyzed."

"I'm aware of that," Pendergast said. "The experts didn't seem to agree with you that it was an animal."

"Then to hell with the experts. I can't take this waiting anymore. I'm going in."

Pendergast nodded, as if he'd expected this. "Very well. But one thing, Vincent—we *must not* divide our strength. The Ville is involved in some way, yes. But how? That is the puzzle. There's something going on here I don't yet have a finger on—something that feels wrong to me."

"You're damn right it's wrong. Nora Kelly is about to die."

The special agent shook his head. "That's not what I mean. Do I have your word, Vincent—we do this together?"

D'Agosta looked at him. "You got it."

"Excellent. My car is waiting downstairs."

60

Richard Plock stood across from the parking lot of the 207th Street Subway Yard, looking out over the serried ranks of train cars parked in the glow of the late-afternoon sun. The yard was quiet, almost somnolent: a workman picked his way across the tracks and disappeared into the blacksmith's shop; an engineer slowly ferried a line of cars onto a siding beside the inspection shed.

Plock looked up and down the street beyond the fence. West 215th Street was quiet, too. He grunted his satisfaction, glanced at his watch: six fifteen.

One of the color-coded cell phones in his jacket pocket began to ring. He pulled it out, noticed it was the red one. That would be Traum, over at the Cloisters.

He flipped it open. "Give me an update."

"They've been arriving for the last twenty minutes or so."

"How many so far?"

"Two hundred, maybe two fifty."

"Good. Keep them thinned out, looking as disorganized as possible. We don't want to tip our hand prematurely."

"Got it."

"Keep the updates coming. We'll be moving out in fifteen minutes." Plock gently closed the phone and slipped it back into his pocket. It was almost time for him to join his own unit, which was gathering on the south side of the subway yard.

He was aware he looked like nobody's idea of a born leader. And if he admitted it to himself, he lacked a leader's charisma, as well. But he had the passion, the conviction—and that's what mattered most. The fact was, people had underestimated him all his life. They'd underestimate him today, too.

Rich Plock was counting on that.

Since the first, abortive rally, Plock had been ceaselessly at work, covertly reaching out to organizations across the city, the state, and even the country, assembling the most zealous group of people for the evening's action that he could. And now it was all about to come to fruition. Over two dozen different organizations—Humans for Other Animals, Vegan Army, Amnesty Without Borders, The Green Brigade—were converging on the West Side at that very moment. And it wasn't just vegetarians and animal sympathizers anymore: the killing of the two journalists and the city official, along with the kidnapping of Nora Kelly, had galvanized people in a remarkable way. With that publicity in hand, Plock had coaxed a few fringe groups with truly serious agendas to come out of the woodwork. Some, in fact, would normally have viewed one another with suspicion—for example, Guns Universal and Reclaim America were now involved—but thanks to Plock's incendiary rhetoric, they had all found a common enemy in the Ville.

Plock was taking no chances. He'd choreographed everything perfectly. In order to avoid being prematurely dispersed or bottled up by the cops, the various groups were congregating in ten different pre-arranged spots: Wien Stadium, the Dyckman House, High Bridge Park. That way, they wouldn't attract too much official attention . . . until Plock gave the order and they all merged smoothly into one. And by that point, it would be too late to stop them. There would be no more backing down—not this time.

As he recalled the first rally, Plock's face hardened. In retrospect, it was a very good thing that Esteban funked out. The man had outlived his usefulness. He'd done what needed to be done: acted as celebrity figurehead, increased their visibility, given them badly needed funds which had empowered Plock to gather a force sufficient for this job. If Esteban had been around today, he would probably advise caution, remind everybody that there was no proof a hostage was involved, no proof that the Ville was behind the killings.

Esteban's weak stomach had undercut their last action—but by God it wouldn't undercut this one. The Ville would be stopped, once and for all. The wanton cruelty, the murder of helpless animals, and the killing of journalists sympathetic to their cause would never happen again.

Plock had grown up on a farm in northern New Hampshire. Every year, as a young boy, he'd gotten physically sick when the time came to slaughter the lambs and hogs. His father had never understood, beating him and calling him a shirker, a mama's boy, when he tried to avoid helping. He'd been too small to fight back. He remembered watching his dad decapitate a chicken with a hand ax and then laugh as the luckless bird danced a strange, faltering tattoo in the dusty lane, blood shooting from the severed neck. The image had haunted his dreams ever since. His father insisted on eating their own animals, meat with every dinner, and demanded that Rich eat his fair share. When Plock's favorite pet pig was killed, his father forced him to eat her greasy ribs; he snuck out afterward and vomited endlessly behind the barn. The very next day, Plock had left home. He didn't even bother to pack, just took his few books—*Brave New World, Atlas Shrugged, 1984*—and pointed his feet south.

And never looked back. His father had given him no love, no support, no teaching—nothing.

That's not quite true, he thought, his mind turning to the Ville. His father had taught him one thing. He'd taught him to hate.

Another of his cell phones began to ring. It was the blue phone: McMoultree, outside Yeshiva University. As Plock went to answer it, he saw a curious thing: a Lincoln Town Car, tearing up Tenth Avenue on its way northward, a medic in full emergency gear at the wheel. But the phone was still ringing, and he stared after it for only a moment. Clearing his throat quietly, Plock opened the cell phone and pressed it confidently against his ear.

61

The Rolls coasted to a stop at the end of West 218th Street, pulling into a parking place between a shabby panel truck and a late-model Jeep. To their left sat a line of undistinguished low-rise co-ops; to their right lay the green oval of Columbia's Baker Field. Roughly two hundred people were scattered around the field and bleachers, seemingly disorganized, but D'Agosta felt sure they were part of the imminent protest. He'd seen similar suspicious groups as they drove through Inwood. The gloriously ignorant Chislett was about to find himself out of his depth.

"We'll head in laterally, through Isham Park," Pendergast said, grabbing a canvas bag from the rear seat.

They jogged across baseball diamonds and well-tended fields before abruptly crossing into the wilderness of Inwood Hill Park. The Ville itself was still invisible beyond the trees. Pendergast had chosen a good approach route: the Ville's attention would be directed elsewhere, allowing them to slip in unseen. D'Agosta could hear the sounds wafting out of the south on the evening breeze: the buzz of megaphones, the distant cries, the air horns. Whoever had planned this was very clever—allowing one raucous group to attract the attention of the police so that the other groups could organize and then descend en masse. If they didn't get Nora out before the main force made its move . . .

Ahead, Pendergast stopped, placed the duffel on the ground, opened it, and drew out two sets of coarse brown robes. D'Agosta, already sweating in the body armor he'd donned, felt glad it was a cold day. Pendergast passed him one of the robes, and he immediately pulled it over his head and tucked the hood up around his face. The FBI agent followed suit, examined himself in a pocket mirror, then held it up so D'Agosta could do the same. Not bad, if he kept the hood on and his head down. He watched as the agent pulled other supplies from the duffel—a small flashlight with extra batteries, a knife, a cold chisel and hammer, a set of lockpicks—and stowed them in a hip bag, which he then tucked beneath his robes. D'Agosta patted his own waist, satisfying himself that his Glock 19 and its extra magazines were within easy access.

Pendergast stowed the now-empty backpack under a fallen log, scraped some leaves over it, then nodded for D'Agosta to follow him up the embankment that lay directly ahead. They crawled up the steep slope, peered over the top. The Ville's chain-link fence stood about twenty yards off, this stretch of it rusted and decrepit, several gaping holes clearly visible. Fifty yards beyond lay the misshapen cluster of buildings, shadowy in the dying light of evening, the vast form of the old church dominating all.

D'Agosta remembered the first time he had been in these woods, clobbered on the head for his pains. He removed the Glock and kept it in his hand as he rose. That wouldn't happen again.

Following Pendergast, he darted to the chain-link fence, slipped through one of the gaps, and jogged at a crouch to the base of the outer walls of the Ville. They moved around the curve until they reached a small, rotting door set into the wall, locked with a padlock. A sharp blow of Pendergast's chisel wrenched it off, padlock, hinges, and all. The agent pushed it open to reveal a narrow, trash-strewn alley, almost completely enclosed by overhanging roofs, running along one side of the massive church. He ducked inside and D'Agosta followed, shutting the door behind them. Pendergast pressed his ear against the back wall of the church, and D'Agosta followed suit. Inside, he could hear a singsong voice rising and falling, a priestly tone full of quaverings and denunciations and exhortations, but too muffled and faint to discern any words—assuming it was English to begin with. Periodically a multivoiced response would come in unison, like the drone of a mindless chorus, and then the crazed chant would begin again.

Mingled with it came the faint, high-pitched whinnying of a frightened colt.

D'Agosta tried to push that horror out of his mind and focus on what they were doing. He moved down the alley at Pendergast's heels, ducking from doorway to darkened doorway, keeping his head bent and his face hidden. No one seemed about; most likely everyone was in the church for the vile ceremony. The alley made a sharp dogleg into a crazy complex of ancient, rickety buildings, then passed by a larger building attached to the church that looked like it might be the old parsonage or rectory.

The first door they came to in the parsonage was locked, but Pendergast had it open in less than five seconds. Stepping quickly inside, they found themselves in a room that was dark, the air stifling. As his eyes adjusted to the dimness, D'Agosta saw that it was a dining room, with an old oak table, chairs, and many candles in candelabra with massive accumulations of drippings. The only light came from the CRT terminal of an old DOS-era computer, hugely out of place among the ancient furniture. Doorways to the east, south, and west led to even more shadowy rooms.

The sound of the priest's ranting was louder here, filtering in from an indeterminate direction.

All at once the problem that they faced—finding Nora in this vast asylum of buildings—seemed insurmountable. He immediately shook off the thought. One step at a time.

"The kitchens in these old houses always had a way down to the basement storerooms," Pendergast whispered. He chose a doorway seemingly at random—the one to the east—and walked through it. D'Agosta followed suit. They were in a pantry, stacked with burlap sacks that appeared to be full of grain. There, at the end, was an ancient, primitive dumbwaiter. Stepping past Pendergast, D'Agosta walked over, slid open the door, switched on the light, and peered down—*way* down.

Suddenly, he heard a voice from behind them, loud and sharp.

"You two. *What are you doing here?*"

62

Deputy Chief Harry Chislett slid out of the rear seat of the unmarked Crown Vic and walked briskly across the sidewalk to where his personal aide, Inspector Minerva, was surveying the crowd through a pair of binoculars. *Crowd,* Chislett reflected, was something of an overstatement: there were two hundred, two fifty at most, scattered across the baseball diamond at the park's entrance, waving placards and chanting. They looked like the same tree-hugging types that had assembled the last time. As he watched, a ragged cheer went up, dying out almost as soon as it started.

"Do you see that bearded fellow?" he asked. "The movie director, the one who whipped them up last time?"

Minerva scanned the field with his binoculars. "Nope."

"The control points and forward field positions?"

"We've got teams in place at each location."

"Capital." Chislett listened as another halfhearted cheer went up. The protesters sounded a lot more apathetic than they had the last time. And without that speaker to whip them up, this affair would no doubt fizzle in short order. Even if it didn't, he was prepared.

"Sir." He turned and, to his surprise, saw a woman with captain's bars on her collar standing beside him. She was petite and dark-haired, and she returned his gaze with a cool self-confidence that he immediately found both irritating and a little intimidating. She wasn't part of his staff, but he recognized her nevertheless: Laura Hayward. Youngest female captain on the force. And Lieutenant D'Agosta's girlfriend—or, if gossip was correct, ex-girlfriend. Neither attribute endeared her to him.

"Yes, Captain?" he said in a clipped voice.

"I was at your briefing earlier. I tried to get in to see you afterward, but you left before I could reach you."

"And?"

"With all due respect, sir, given the field plan you described, I'm not sure you have sufficient manpower to control this crowd."

"*Man*power? Crowd? Observe them for yourself, Captain." Chislett swept his hand over the baseball diamond. "Don't you detect a paucity of protesters? They'll turn tail and run from the first cop who says boo to them."

Listening, Inspector Minerva grinned.

"I don't believe this is all of them. There may be others coming."

"And just where would they come from?"

"There are any number of rallying places in this neighborhood where a sizable assembly could gather," Hayward replied. "And, in fact, I've noticed quite a lot of people gathering in various spots up here—especially for a weekday evening in the fall."

"That is precisely why we have our men in forward positions. It gives us the flexibility we need to act quickly." He tried to keep the note of irritation out of his voice.

"I saw your diagram, sir. Those forward positions consist of only half a dozen officers each. If your line is breached, the protesters have a straight shot at the Ville itself. And if Nora Kelly is being held hostage inside—as seems possible—her captors may panic. Her life will be in jeopardy."

This was just the line of crap that D'Agosta had been spewing. Maybe he'd even been the one to put her up to it.

"Your concern is noted," Chislett replied, no longer bothering to hide the sarcasm in his tone, "although I note for the record that a judge earlier today stated there was absolutely no evidence that Nora Kelly was there and refused to grant a search warrant of the Ville. Now, would you kindly tell me just what you're doing here, Captain? The last time I checked, Inwood Hill Park wasn't part of your jurisdiction."

But Hayward didn't reply. He noticed she was no longer looking at him, but rather at something over his shoulder.

He turned. Another group of protesters was approaching from the east. They carried no placards but looked like they meant business, walking quickly and very quietly toward the baseball diamond, closing ranks as they approached. It was a motley, rougher-looking group than the one already assembled on the field.

"Let me have those glasses," he said to Minerva.

Scanning the group with the binoculars, he saw it was headed by the young, plump guy who'd helped lead the charge last time. For a moment, as he stared at the determined look on the man's face, at the hardened features of his followers, Chislett felt a tingle of anxiety.

But it passed as quickly as it came. What were one or two hundred more? He had the manpower to handle four hundred protesters—and then some. Besides, his plan for containment was a masterpiece of both economy and versatility.

He handed the binoculars back to Minerva. "Pass the word," he said in his most martial tone, ignoring Hayward. "We're starting the final deployment now. Tell the forward positions to stand ready."

"Yes, sir," Minerva replied, unshipping his radio.

63

D'Agosta froze. Pendergast, his head cowled, mumbled something and shuffled toward the man, wavering a little, like an old man unsteady on his feet.

"What are you doing here?" the man asked again in his strange, exotic accent.

Pendergast rasped, *"Va t'en, sale bête."*

The man backed up a pace. "Yes, but . . . you're not supposed to be here."

Pendergast shuffled closer, and with a flicker of his eye cautioned D'Agosta to be ready.

"I'm just an old man . . . ," he began, his voice quiet and wheezy, one trembling hand reaching upward solicitously. "Can you help me . . . ?"

The man leaned forward, straining to hear, and D'Agosta stepped smartly around and whacked him across the temple with the butt of his gun. The figure slumped, unconscious.

"A hit, a very palpable hit," Pendergast said as he deftly caught the sagging body.

D'Agosta could hear other voices, excited voices, in the rooms beyond; not everyone, it seemed, was attending the ceremony in the central church. There was no back door to the pantry—it was a cul-de-sac, and they were trapped with the unconscious man.

"Into the dumbwaiter," whispered Pendergast.

They bundled the man into the dumbwaiter, slid the door shut, and lowered him into the basement. Almost immediately afterward, three men appeared at the entrance to the pantry. "Morvedre, what are you doing?" one of them asked. "Come with us. You, too."

They passed by and D'Agosta and Pendergast fell into place behind them, trying to imitate their slow, hushed walk. D'Agosta felt his frustration and tension mount. There was no way they could keep up this deception for very long; they had to get away and begin searching the basement. Time was running out.

The men turned, followed a long, narrow passage, went through a set of double doors, and then they were in the church itself. The air was suffused with the smell of candle wax and heavy incense; the crowd jostled and murmured urgently, moving like the sea to the cadences of the high priest, Charrière, standing at the front. Two banks of burning candles provided light as four men labored over a flat stone set into the floor. Beyond, in the waxy darkness, stood many others, dozens of them, silent, the whites of their eyes like flickering pearls in the massed darkness of their hooded forms. And to one side stood Bossong, drawn up almost regally to full height, observing the proceedings from the shadows, his expression unreadable.

As D'Agosta watched, the four men threaded ropes through iron rings embedded into the corners of the large flagstone, tied them off, then laid the ropes on the stone floor and took up positions beside them. Silence descended as the high priest moved forward, holding a small candelabrum in one hand and a rattle in the other. Cloaked in rough brown, he moved with great deliberation, placing one bare foot after the other, toes pointed downward, until he stood in the center of the stone.

He agitated the rattle, softly: once, twice, three times as he slowly turned in a circle, the wax from the candles dripping onto his arm and splattering onto the stone. One hand reached into the pocket of his cloak, withdrew a small feathered object, and dropped it as he turned. Another soft rattle, another slow-motion turn. And then Charrière raised his bare foot high, held it, and brought it down with a slap on the stone.

A sudden silence, and then, from below, came a faint sound, a rasp of air, a fricative breath.

The silence in the chancel became absolute.

The high priest gave another rattle, slightly louder, and circled once more. Then he raised his foot and brought it down once again on the cold stone.

Aaaaaahhhuuuuu . . . came a mournful sound from below.

D'Agosta glanced sharply at Pendergast, his heart quickening, but the FBI agent was watching the proceedings intently from beneath the heavy, concealing hood.

Now the priest began to dance in lazy circles, his hoary feet pattering lightly, tracing a circle around the feathered object. Every once in a while a step would be much louder, a slap, and at those times an answering moan would sound from below. As the dance got faster, the slaps more frequent, the moaning grew in length and intensity. They were the vocalizations of someone or something prodded to irritation by the tattoo of sound above. With a thrill of dismay, D'Agosta recognized them all too well.

Aaaaiihhhhuuuuuuuuuuuuuuu came the forlorn call as Charrière danced, *aaaiihuuuuu* . . . *aaaiihuuuu* . . . the drawn-out vocalizations never falling into a rhythmic pattern but expressed with increasing excitement and shorter duration. As they grew in volume and urgency, the gathered crowd began to mirror them with a low chanting of their own. It started as a bare whisper, but gradually grew in intensity until the single word they chanted became evident: *envoie! envoie! envoie!*

The priest's dance quickened, his feet now a blur of movement, the rhythmic slap keeping time like a fleshy drum. *Aiihuuuuu!* grunted the thing below; *envoie!* chanted the group above.

Suddenly Charrière stopped dead. The chanting ceased, the voices echoing and dying in the church. But noises below continued, blending into each other, groans and stertorous breathing, along with the sounds of restless shuffling.

D'Agosta watched breathlessly from the shadows.

"Envoie!" cried the high priest, backing off from the stone. *"Envoie!"*

The four men at each corner of the stone slab seized their ropes, turned, slung them over their shoulders, and began to pull. With a grating sound, the stone tilted up, wobbled, and rose.

"Envoie!" cried the priest yet again, raising his flat palms upward.

The men stepped sideways, dragging the stone away to expose an opening in the floor of the chancel. They brought the slab to a standstill, dropped the ropes. The circle of men closed in tighter, all waiting in silence. The room was suspended, in stasis. Bossong, who had not moved, stared at them in turn with dark eyes. A faint exhalation rose from the opening—the perfume of death.

Now the pit below was filled with the noises of restless movement; scratchings and skitterings; mucous, anticipatory slurpings.

And then it appeared out of the darkness, gripping the lip of stone: a pale, desiccated hand, a skinny forearm in which the muscles and tendons stood out like cords. A second hand appeared, and with a scrabbling sound a head came into view: the hair matted and dank, the expression empty save for a vague hunger. One eye rolled in its socket; the other was obscured by clots of dried blood and matter. With a sudden thrust, the thing hoisted itself up from the pit and fell heavily onto the floor of the church, its nails scratching the floor. Gasps arose from the congregation, along with a few approving murmurs.

D'Agosta stared in disbelief and horror. It was a man—or, at least, it had been a man. And there was no doubt in his mind—no doubt at all—this was what had chased him, attacked him, outside the Ville precisely seven days before. Yet it didn't seem to be Fearing, and it certainly wasn't Smithback. Was it alive . . . or the reanimated dead? His skin crawled as he stared at the leering face; the pasty, withered skin; the painted curlicues and tendrils and crosses that showed through the grimy rags that passed as clothing. And yet, looking more closely, D'Agosta realized the man-thing wasn't wearing rags, after all, but the remnants of silk, or satin, or some other ancient finery, now tattered with age and stiff with dirt, blood, and grime.

The crowd murmured with something close to reverence as the man-thing skulked about hesitantly, looking up at the high priest as if for instruction, a thread of saliva dangling from thick gray lips, breath coming out like air squeezed from a wet bag. Its one good eye seemed dead—utterly.

Charrière reached into the folds of his robe, withdrew a small brass chalice. Dipping his fingers into it, he sprinkled what looked like oil over the head and shoulders of the form that stood swaying before him. Then, to D'Agosta's infinite surprise, the high priest sank to his knees before the creature, bowing low. The rest did likewise. D'Agosta felt a tug on his robe as Pendergast directed him to do the same. He went down on his knees, stretching forth his hands in the direction of the zombii—if that's indeed what it was—as he saw the others doing.

"We bow to the protector!" the high priest intoned. "Our sword, our rock, all hail!"

The rest chanted along.

Charrière continued in a foreign language, the others following suit.

D'Agosta glanced around. Bossong was no longer to be seen.

"As the gods above strengthen us," the high priest said, switching back into English, "may we now strengthen you!"

As if on cue, D'Agosta heard a crying sound. Turning, he spied, in the darkness, a small chestnut colt—no more than a week old—being led to the wooden post by a halter, its long wobbly legs stamping the floor as it moved back and forth, whinnying piteously, its large brown eyes round and frightened. The congregant tied it to the post and stepped back.

The priest rose. Moving in a sort of half-dancing, half-swaying motion, he raised a gleaming knife in the air, similar to the ones they had seized in the raid.

Oh dear God, no, thought D'Agosta.

The others stood, turning toward the high priest. The ceremony was clearly coming to a climax. Charrière worked himself into a frenzy, dancing now toward the colt; the congregation was swaying in rhythm; the glittering knife raised yet higher. The little colt stamped and whinnied in increasing terror, shaking its head, trying to get free.

The priest closed in.

D'Agosta turned away. He heard the shrill whinny, heard the sudden expelled breath of the crowd—and then a shriek of equine agony.

The crowd broke into a fast chant and D'Agosta turned back. The priest hoisted up the dying colt in his arms, its legs still twitching. He advanced down the nave, the crowd parting before him, as he once again approached the hideous man-thing. With a cry, the priest heaved the colt's body to the stone floor while the congregation abruptly knelt, all at once, D'Agosta and Pendergast hastening to keep up.

The zombii fell upon the dead colt with a hideous sound, tearing at it with his teeth, pulling out entrails with a bestial sound of gratification and stuffing them into his mouth.

The susurrus rose in volume: *Feed the protector! Envoie! Envoie!*

D'Agosta stared in horror at the crouching man. As he did so, a stab of atavistic fear plucked deep at his vitals. He glanced at Pendergast. A flick of the silver eyes from beneath the cowl directed D'Agosta's attention at a side door in the church—partially open, leading into a dark, empty corridor. A route of escape.

Envoie! Envoie!

The figure ate with furious speed. And then he was sated. He rose, face expressionless, as if awaiting orders. The crowd rose, too, as one.

With a gesture from the priest, the crowd parted, forming a human passageway. At the far end of the church came the creak and squeal of iron, and a congregant opened the door to the outside. A faint breath of twilight air entered, and over the top of the perimeter wall a single dull star could be seen shining in the darkness. Charrière placed one hand on the zombii's shoulder, raised the other, and pointed a long, bony finger at the open door.

"Envoie!" he whispered hoarsely, his finger trembling. *"Envoie!"*

Slowly, the figure began to shuffle toward the door. In a moment it had passed through and was gone. The door closed with a hollow boom.

At this, the crowd seemed to exhale, to relax, to shuffle and move about. The priest began loading the remains of the colt into a coffin-like box. The dreadful "service" was drawing to a conclusion.

Immediately, Pendergast began to drift toward the passageway, D'Agosta trailing, doing his best to convey a calm and purposeless manner. In a minute Pendergast had reached the open door and placed his hand on the knob.

"Just a moment!" One of the nearest congregants had turned from the appalling scene and taken notice of them. "No one can leave until the ceremony is complete—you know that!"

Pendergast gestured toward D'Agosta while keeping his head averted. "My friend is sick."

"No excuses are permitted." The man came forward and ducked to look at Pendergast's face under his cowl. "Who are you, friend?"

Pendergast bowed his head but the man had already glimpsed his face. "Outsiders!" he cried, yanking Pendergast's cowl away.

A sudden silence fell.

"Outsiders!"

Quickly Charrière threw open the outer door to the church. "Outsiders!" he cried into the darkness. *"Baka! Baka!"*

"Get him! Quickly!"

Suddenly, D'Agosta saw the man-thing framed in the doorway. For a minute, it stood there, swaying slightly. Then it began to move with a strange purpose—toward *them.*

"Envoie!" screeched the priest, pointing in their direction.

D'Agosta acted first, knocking their accuser to the ground; Pendergast leapt over his supine form, flung open the side door; D'Agosta charged through and Pendergast followed, slamming and locking it behind them.

64

They paused, finding themselves in a dim hallway, another door at the far end. A sudden pounding on the door they had just locked pushed them into action. They ran down the hall, but the door at the end was locked. D'Agosta backed up to kick it.

"Wait." A swift manipulation of Pendergast's lockpick and the lock gave way. Again they passed through and Pendergast relocked the door behind them.

They were at the top of a landing, with a wooden staircase leading down into a noisome darkness. Pendergast switched on a penlight, angling it down into the murk.

"That . . . that man . . . ," D'Agosta panted. "What the *hell* were they doing? Worshipping him?"

"Perhaps this is not the ideal time for speculation," Pendergast replied.

"I can tell you one thing: that's what attacked me outside the Ville." He could hear pounding on the door at the far end of the hall, the sound of breaking wood.

"After you," said Pendergast, indicating the stairs.

D'Agosta wrinkled his noise. "What other choice do we have?"

"Alas, none."

They descended the ancient staircase, the treads groaning loudly under their feet. The staircase ended at a half landing that led to a second staircase, this one of stone, spiraling down into blackness. When at last they reached the bottom, D'Agosta saw that a brick corridor stretched in front of them, damp, heavy with cobwebs and efflorescence. The air smelled of earth and mildew. From behind and above came muffled cries, the sound of fists pounding on wood.

D'Agosta pulled out his own flashlight.

"We need to find stonework matching that in the video," Pendergast said, shining the light along the damp walls. He moved swiftly through the dark, robe trailing behind him.

"Those bastards upstairs are going to be after us in a moment," said D'Agosta.

"They aren't what concerns me," murmured Pendergast. "*He* is."

They passed beneath several archways and a stone staircase leading upward. Beyond, the tunnel branched, and after brief consideration Pendergast chose the left-hand fork. A moment later they came to a large, circular room, with niches hewn at regular intervals into the walls. Within each niche, human bones were stacked like cordwood, the skulls hung on the long bones. Many still had wisps of hair clinging to the crania by bits of desiccated flesh.

"Charming," muttered D'Agosta.

Pendergast abruptly halted.

Then D'Agosta heard what stopped him: a disjointed shuffling, coming out of the darkness behind them. From beyond his light came a loud, phlegmy sniffing sound, as if of someone testing the air. A shambling tread, growing in speed, moving along an invisible passageway seemingly parallel to their chamber. D'Agosta caught the strong, gamy whiff of horseflesh drifting in the damp air.

"You smell that?"

"Only too well." Pendergast focused his light on a nearby archway, from which the smell seemed to flow on a draft of fresh air.

D'Agosta pulled his Glock, feeling a strong spike of fear despite himself. "That thing is in there. You take the left side, I'll take the right."

Pendergast drew his .45 from beneath his robe and they crept up to the doorway, one on either side.

"Now!" D'Agosta cried.

They spun into the doorway, D'Agosta with his own light held against his gun; within he saw nothing but blank walls of damp brick. Pendergast pointed to the floor, where a series of bloody footprints led off into blackness. D'Agosta knelt and touched one; the blood was so fresh it hadn't even congealed.

D'Agosta rose. "This is fucking weird," he muttered.

"It's also wasting time we don't have. Let us keep moving. Fast."

They backed out of the room and jogged across the open necropolis into a passageway at the far side. It soon opened into another cavern-like space, this one very crude, rough-hewn out of the living rock. They entered and shined their lights around.

"The walls are still unlike the stonework in the video," said Pendergast, sotto voce. "This is schist, not granite, and not cut the same way."

"It's like a maze down here."

Pendergast nodded toward a low archway. "Let's try that passage."

They ducked into the low tunnel. "Jesus, that *smell,*" said D'Agosta. It was a cloying stench of horse blood, thick, with an edge of iron to it, all the more horrible for its obvious freshness. It was accompanied by occasional eddies of cool air, coming from some invisible vent to the outside. In the distance, echoing through the tunnels, he could hear the cries and shouts of pursuing congregants, who also appeared to have gained the underground and were spreading out, searching for them.

They continued down the tunnel, Pendergast moving so swiftly

D'Agosta had to jog to keep up, splashing through standing pools of water and slime. Nitre and cobwebs coated the sweating walls, and as they moved D'Agosta could see white spiders scurrying into holes in the brickwork. At the edge of darkness, red rats' eyes gleamed and flickered at them as they passed.

They approached a junction in which three cross-tunnels met, forming a hexagonally shaped space. Pendergast slowed, putting his finger to his lips and gesturing for D'Agosta to creep along one wall of the tunnel while he took the other.

As they reached the junction, D'Agosta felt, rather than saw, a rapid movement above him. He dropped and rolled to one side just as something—the zombii-creature—dropped down, the tatters of ancient finery whipping and rustling over his knotted limbs like ruined sails in a strong breeze. D'Agosta squeezed off a shot, but the man-thing was ready, and it moved so unexpectedly that his shot went wide. It raced across his field of view, flashing through the beam of his flashlight, and as D'Agosta dropped to the ground to escape the charge a momentary, terrifying impression burned into his retinas: the single lolling eye; the whorls and curlicues of *vévé* painted or pasted on his skin; the wet lips quivering in a grin of desperate hilarity. And yet there was nothing vague or hilarious in its movements—it came after them with single-minded, horrifying purpose.

65

D'Agosta fired again, but it was a gratuitous shot: the thing had flitted back into the darkness and disappeared. He lay on the ground, shining the light around, this way and that, gun at the ready.

"Pendergast?"

The special agent stepped out of the darkness of a doorway, crouching, his Colt drawn and held in front of him with both hands.

Silence fell, broken only by the sound of dripping water.

"He's still out there," murmured D'Agosta, rising to a half crouch and making a three-hundred-sixty-degree turn with his gun. He strained to see into the darkness.

"Indeed. I don't think he will leave until we are dead—or *he* is."

The seconds dragged on into minutes.

Finally, D'Agosta straightened up, lowering the Glock. "There's no time for a waiting game, Pendergast. We've got to—"

The zombii came like a dull flash from the side, going straight for his light, slashing at it with a spidery hand and sending it spinning into the darkness with a crash. D'Agosta fired, but the thing had darted out of view and back into the relative protection of the darkness. He heard Pendergast's .45 go off almost simultaneously with his, a deafening double blast—and then darkness fell abruptly with the sound of Pendergast's own flashlight shattering against a wall.

The passageway was plunged into profound darkness—and almost immediately afterward, he heard the sounds of a desperate struggle.

He lunged toward the noise, holstering the Glock and pulling his knife, better for close-in work in the dark and less likely to hit Pendergast, who was now apparently locked in a life-or-death battle with the creature. He collided with the zombii's sinewed form and immediately slashed at it with the knife, but for all its shuffling movements it was dreadfully strong and quick, turning and clawing at D'Agosta like a panther, enveloping him in a suffocating stench. The knife was torn from his hands, and he went at the man-thing with his fists, pummeling it, seeking the soft gut, the head, all the while fending off the wiry hands that clawed and raked at him. In the dark, enveloped in a robe, he was at a disadvantage; the ragged creature, on the other hand, seemed to be in its element: no matter how D'Agosta twisted and struggled, it kept the advantage of position, aided by the slickness of its body, coated with sweat and blood and oil.

What the hell had happened to Pendergast?

An arm fastened around his neck, suddenly constricting like a steel cable. D'Agosta wrenched sideways, gasping and choking, trying to throw off his attacker while simultaneously feeling for his gun. But the slippery man-thing had muscles as hard as teak: no matter how D'Agosta struggled, one hand maintained its grip, constricting his airway, while the other pinned his gun hand. A cry of triumph went up from the creature, a banshee-like wail: *oaah-huuuoooooooo!*

Flashes of white sparkled in his field of vision. He knew he had only moments left. With a last explosive effort he wrenched his right arm free, pulling out the gun and firing, the flash-boom illuminating the sepulchral tunnel, deafening in the confined space.

Eeeeee! the zombii screamed, and D'Agosta immediately felt a sharp blow to the head. More stars exploded before his eyes. The thing had pinned his forearm again and was shaking and slamming it against the ground, trying to knock the weapon from his hand. *Eeeeee!* it cried again. Dazed as he was, D'Agosta nevertheless felt sure he had hit the creature—its agitation, its high-pitched keening, were obvious—and yet it seemed stronger than ever, fighting with an inhuman fury. It stomped his forearm and he heard bones snapping. Indescribable pain blossomed just above his wrist; the gun went flying and the thing fell on him once more, both hands now around his neck.

Twisting and turning, slamming at the zombii with his good arm, D'Agosta tried to break free—but he could feel the remains of his vitality ebbing fast.

"Pendergast!" he choked.

The steel fingers tightened further. D'Agosta heaved and bucked, but without oxygen it was a losing battle. A strange tingling stole over him, accompanied by a buzzing sound. His hand reached out, clawing the floor, looking for the knife. Instead, it closed around a large fragment of brick; he clutched it, swung it around with all his might, and slammed it into the zombii's head.

Eeeeaaaaaaahhh! it squealed in pain, tumbling back. He gasped, drawing in air, swinging the brick back, striking the creature again. Another shrill screech and it leapt off him.

Coughing, sucking in air, D'Agosta staggered to his feet and ran wildly in the dark. After a moment, he could hear the man-thing scurrying after him, bare feet slapping the slimy stone floor.

66

From his vantage point at a wide tear in the chain-link fence, Rich Plock scanned the crowd streaming through with a steely satisfaction. Ten initial groups, roughly two hundred per group—that meant two thousand in the crowd, less than he had expected but formidable in their determination. As New York City demonstrations went, it might still be a small one—but this was a demonstration with a difference. These people were dedicated. They were hard-core. The nervous and weak of heart, the day-trippers and sunshine friends—the Esteban types—had stayed home this time. So much the better. His was a purged group, a crowd with a purpose, unlikely to cave in the face of opposition, even violence. Although there couldn't be much violence—the inhabitants of the Ville had to be outnumbered ten to one by the protesters. They might resist at first, but they would quickly be overwhelmed.

It had come together like clockwork, a joy to witness. The police had been taken totally by surprise. The group of initial protesters, carefully outfitted to look as nonthreatening as possible, had lulled the cops into thinking it would be a small, ineffectual protest, all bark and no bite. And then within the space of mere minutes all the other groups had arrived, quietly, on foot, from multiple directions—and immediately, as planned, the crowd swung into motion as one, joining up and heading determinedly across the fields and down the road toward the Ville. The police had had no time to form a barricade, no time to arrest the leaders, no time to shift the positions of their forward units, no time to call in backup. All they could do was shout futilely into their bullhorns and plead for order, while a single police chopper circled overhead, broadcasting an unintelligible warning. He could hear the sirens and the bullhorns behind them as the police made a belated, rear-guard effort to stop the crowd from converging on the Ville.

No doubt reinforcements were already on their way. The NYPD were not a force to be trifled with. But by the time they arrived, Plock and his crowd would be inside the Ville and well on their way to accomplishing their objective—routing the murderers and, perhaps, finding the kidnapped woman, Nora Kelly.

The last of the crowd streamed through the gate and massed in the field facing the front entrance to the Ville, spreading out like shock troops. They parted as Plock stepped to the front for a few last words. The Ville itself stood silently in the evening twilight, brooding and monolithic, the only sign of life a few yellow windows high in the fabric of the church. The front door was shut and barred, but it would present no obstacle to the men with battering rams standing silent at the head of the crowd, ready to move.

Plock held up a hand and the crowd quieted.

"My dear friends." He pitched his voice low, which induced an even deeper silence among the people. "What are we here for?" He allowed a pause. "Let us be clear about that, of all things. What are we here for?"

He looked around. "We are here to break down that door and drive these animal torturers, these murderers, out. We will do it through our implacable moral condemnation, the weight of our numbers. We will press them from the field. We will liberate the animals in that hellhole."

The police helicopter circled overhead, still broadcasting its unintelligible message. He ignored it.

"One thing of the utmost importance I say to you: we are not killers. We will hold and maintain the moral high ground. But we are not pacifists, either, and if they choose to fight, we will fight. We *will* defend ourselves and we *will* defend the animals."

He took a deep breath. He knew that he wasn't an eloquent speaker, but he had the power of his convictions and he could see the crowd was stoked.

The police were coming up from the road now, but their numbers were ridiculously small compared with his own and Plock ignored them. He'd be inside the Ville before the police could even regroup. "Are we ready?" he cried.

There was an answering *READY!*

He pointed. *"Go!"*

With a single roar, the crowd surged forward toward the main doors of the Ville. They appeared to have been recently repaired and reinforced. The two men with battering rams were at the forefront, and they hit the doors at a run, wielding their rams, first one then the other, slamming them into the doors. The timbers shivered and split, and in less than a minute they were stove in, the crowd surging forward and pushing the remnants away. Plock joined the masses as they poured into a dark, narrow alleyway lined with listing wooden buildings. It was strangely deserted, no inhabitants to be seen. The roar from the crowd rose like an animal cry, amplified by the narrow confines of the Ville, and they broke into a trot, rounding the corner of the alley and coming face-to-face with the ancient church.

At this the crowd hesitated. The church was forbidding; it stood like a medieval structure of Boschean strangeness, crooked, half timbered with rude-looking buttresses projecting out into the air before stabbing into the ground, bristling and massive. The portal to the church stood in front—a second set of timbered doors, banded and riveted with iron.

The hesitation lasted only a moment. Then the roar went up

again, stronger than ever, and the men with battering rams advanced again and stood on either side of the banded doors, swinging the rams in an alternating, asynchronous rhythm: boom—*boom!* boom—*boom!* boom—*boom!* A massive cracking sound announced the yielding of the ancient oak as the relentless pounding continued. These doors were much tougher than the last set, but in the end they gave way with a splintering crash, to the ring of popping iron rivets and bars. They sagged inward, then collapsed under their own weight with a thunderous shudder . . .

And there in the dimness, blocking the way, stood two men. One was tall and striking, dressed in a long brown cloak, hood drawn back, heavy brows and massive cheekbones almost hiding a pair of black eyes, pale skin glowing in the light of a freshly rising moon, his nose like the blade of a knife, curved and honed. The other man, shorter and coarser looking, was gowned in a fantastically decorated ceremonial gown. He was clearly a holy man of some sort. He stared out at the invaders, his eyes glittering with malice.

The innate force of the taller man instantly subdued the crowd. He held out one hand and said: *"Do not proceed."* The voice was quiet, funereal, with a faint accent Plock didn't recognize—yet it conveyed great power.

Plock shoved forward and faced him. "Who are you?"

"My name is Bossong. And it is my community you are desecrating with your presence."

Plock drew himself up. He was fully aware that he was half his opponent's size and twice his width. Nevertheless, when he replied, his voice crackled with conviction: "*We* will proceed and *you* will step aside. You have no right to be here, *vivisector.*"

The men stood stock-still, and to his surprise Plock could see, standing in the red dimness behind him, at least a hundred people.

"We do no harm to anyone," Bossong went on. "We only want to be left alone."

"No harm? What do you call slitting innocent animals' throats?"

"Those are honored sacrifices, a central tenet of our religion—"

"Bull! And what about the woman you kidnapped? Where is she? And where are the animals? Where do you keep them? Tell me!"

"I know nothing of any woman."

"Liar!"

Now the priest abruptly held up a rattle in one hand and a strange-looking bundle of feathers in the other, and broke into a loud, quavering chant in some foreign language, as if casting a curse on the invading force.

Plock reached up and slapped the bundle out of his hand. "Get that mumbo-jumbo out of my face! Step aside, or we'll run you down!"

The man stared, saying nothing. Plock stepped forward as if to walk through him, and the crowd behind him responded with a roar and surged forward, propelling Plock against his will into the priest and driving him back, and in a moment the man was down, the crowd pouring around him into the dark church, Bossong pushed rudely to one side, the congregants inside grown hesitant at the sight of their fallen priest, crying out in fear and anger and outrage at the violation of their sanctuary.

"To the animals!" Plock cried. "Find the animals! Free the animals!"

67

Pendergast's clothes were torn and bloody and his ears still rang from the attack. He propped himself up and rose unsteadily to his feet. His encounter with the man-beast had knocked him senseless for a few minutes, and he'd come to in the dark. He reached into his suit coat, removed a tiny LED light he carried for emergencies such as this, and shined it around. Slowly, methodically, he searched the damp floor for his gun, but it was nowhere to be seen. He could make out faint signs of struggle, with what were evidently D'Agosta's fleeing footprints, the barefooted painted man in pursuit.

He flicked it off and remained in the dark, thinking. He made a quick calculation, a swift decision. This creature, this zombii, had been possessed by his minders of a terrible and murderous purpose. On the loose, he presented a grave threat to them both. And yet Pendergast had confidence in D'Agosta—a confidence almost amounting to faith. The lieutenant could take care of himself if anyone could.

But Nora—Nora still awaited rescue.

Pendergast flicked the light back on and examined the next room. It was a veritable necropolis of wooden coffins laid out on rows of elevated stone pedestals, some stacked two and three high, many collapsing and spilling their contents to the ground. It appeared as if many of the basement spaces of the Ville, originally built for other purposes, had been converted to storing the dead.

But as he turned away, preparing to renew his search for Nora, he caught a glimpse of something at the very head of the room—an unusual tomb. Something about it arrested his attention. He approached to examine it more closely, and then, making a decision, laid a hand on it.

It was a coffin, made of thick lead. Instead of being set on a bier like the others, it had been sunken into the stonework of the floor, only its top projecting above the ground. What caught his eye was that the lid was ajar and the vault within had clearly been looted—very recently looted.

He examined it more intently. In past centuries, lead had often been the material of choice for interring an important person because of its preservative qualities. Playing the light over it, he noted just how carefully the coffin had been sealed, the lead lid soldered firmly to the top. But someone had hacked open the lead cover with an ax, chopping violently through the seal and prying the lid off, leaving a ragged, gaping hole. This had been done not only recently, but in great haste. The marks in the soft metal were bright and shiny, showing no signs of dulling or oxidation.

Pendergast looked inside. The body—which had mummified in the sealed environment—had been roughly disturbed, something wrenched out of its crooked hands, the ossified fingers broken and scattered, one arm torn from its dusty socket.

He reached inside and felt the corpse dust, gauging its dryness. This had happened so recently that not even the damp air of the room had had time to settle inside the coffin. The looting must have occurred less than thirty minutes ago.

Coincidence? Certainly not.

Pendergast turned his attention to the dead body itself. It was a remarkably well-preserved corpse of an old man with a full white beard and long white hair. Two golden guineas were pressed on its eyes. The face was shriveled like an old apple, the lips drawn back from the teeth by desiccation, the skin darkened to the color of fine old ivory. The body was dressed in simple, Quaker-like clothes—a sober frock coat, shirt, brown waistcoat, and pale breeches—but the clothes around the chest had been ripped open and disarranged by the looting, buttons and bits scattered about in what appeared to have been a frenzied search of the corpse. On the man's disarranged chest, Pendergast could see pressure marks on the clothing of what had evidently been a small, square container—a box.

That, along with the broken fingers, told a story. The looter had wrenched a box from the corpse's dusty grasp.

On the floor behind the coffin, Pendergast spied the broken remains of what could only be the very box, the dry-rotted top wrenched off. He leaned over and examined it more closely, sniffing it, noting its dimensions. The faint smell of vellum confirmed his initial impression that the box had held a quarto-size document.

Slowly, deliberately, Pendergast walked around the coffin lid. At the top end, stamped into the lead, he could see an inscription, obscured by whitish blooms of oxide. He wiped the oxide away with his sleeve and read the inscription.

Elijah Esteban
who Departed this Life Novbr 22d 1745
In his 55th Year
How doleful is the Sound,
How vaſt the Stroke
which maketh the Mortall Wounde.
Ye living,
come View the Ground
Where ye muſt shortly lie.

Pendergast stared at the name on the tomb for a long time. And then, quite suddenly, everything fell into place and he understood. His face darkened as he thought of the catastrophic mistake he had made.

This looted coffin wasn't a coincidence, an irrelevant sideshow—it was the main event.

68

The creature was gone—somehow, D'Agosta had outrun it or it had given up the pursuit. Although the latter didn't seem likely: the thing might be a shambling zombii, but it had the tenacity of a pit bull. Maybe, he thought, its absence had something to do with a faint commotion he had heard from above, like a stampede. He sagged against the damp stone, half stunned, gasping for breath, the roar in his head gradually subsiding. He could still hear the faint hubbub coming from the church above.

He sat up. As he did, pain shot through his right forearm. He probed gingerly with his left hand, felt the bone grinding on bone. It was obviously fractured.

"Pendergast?" he spoke into the dark.

No sound.

He tried to orient himself, to place himself in the welter of tunnels, but it was pitch-dark and the flight had disoriented him. It was impossible to know how far he'd run, or where he'd gone. Wincing with pain, he tucked his broken arm into his shirt, buttoned it snug, and then crawled over the ground until the hand of his good arm found a brick wall. He pulled himself to his feet, feeling nausea wash over him. The voices continued above, overlaid now with another, much closer noise: cries and yells that echoed toward him from somewhere else in the basement, approaching rapidly.

So he was still being hunted, after all.

He called out as loudly as he dared. "Pendergast!"

No reply.

His flashlight was gone, but he remembered the old Zippo lighter he carried in his pocket, a habit from his cigar-smoking days. He took it out and flicked it on. He was in a small room, with an arched doorway opening into a brick tunnel. Moving slowly so as not to aggravate his pain and nausea, he staggered to the archway and looked around. More brick tunnels.

The heat from the lighter began to burn his finger and he let it go out. He had to make his way back, locate his gun and flashlight, find Pendergast. And, above all, they had to locate Nora.

He cursed out loud and flicked the lighter back on. Trying to ignore the stabbing pain in his arm, using the brick wall for support, he moved into the main tunnel. He didn't recognize it—it looked like all the others.

He staggered along slowly. Had they traveled down this tunnel? In the wavering glow of the lighter, he could see fresh marks on the wet, muddy floor, but were they his? Then he spied a large, splayed print of a bare foot. He shuddered.

The sounds from above were louder: yells, the squawk of a bull-horn, a crash. It didn't sound like a ceremony anymore. It sounded like the protesters had arrived.

Was that why the thing had vanished? Nothing else made sense.

"Pendergast!"

Suddenly, he saw lights in the darkness and a group of congregants appeared at a bend in the tunnel ahead of him. They were cowled and robed. Some held flashlights and torches in their hands, others an assortment of weapons, shovels, pitchforks. They numbered twenty, perhaps twenty-five.

D'Agosta swallowed, took a step back, wondering if they had spotted him in the dark.

Crying out with what seemed a single voice, the group charged toward him.

D'Agosta turned and ran, tucking his broken forearm against his chest, fleeing as best he could down the darkened tunnels, the lighter flickering and bluing in the draft. It went out and he paused to flick it on, took his bearings, began running again. He turned a corner and found himself in a dismal basement crowded with rotting stacks of lumber. At the far end was a door. He ran through the doorway and slammed the door behind him, then leaned against it, gasping. The pain in his forearm made him feel light-headed. The Zippo had guttered in his headlong run, and when he flicked it back on he found himself in what appeared to be another large storage room. He looked down at his feet—and his heart froze in his chest.

Not five feet before him was a pit, faced in stone. It was clearly an old well, with slick, rock-mortared walls. He approached it gingerly, held his lighter over its dark maw. It appeared bottomless. All around were stacked heaps of ancient furniture, broken ceramic tiles, moldy books, and other junk.

He cast about desperately for a hiding place. There were plenty, but none would last long if these freaks on his tail were to search every nook and cranny. He circled the ancient well, then ran on, knocking over an old cane chair in his flight, which broke and tangled around his foot. He shook it off violently, then ducked beneath an archway at the far end of the storage area. He now found himself in a vast, crypt-like space, with ancient stone columns and groined ceilings. He flashed the lighter around: it *was* another crypt, different from the first, its walls and floors laid with marble slabs carved with crosses, weeping willows, and skulls, birth and death dates crudely carved into them. There were also rows of crude wooden sarcophagi. It was a mess, everything covered in dust, the stone walls bulging and collapsing. This was beyond ancient: it had to predate the Ville's occupation by decades, maybe centuries. Overhead, the voices had swelled: it sounded like the beginnings of a confrontation, if not a riot.

He heard the door of the well-room roughly opened behind him, heard the running of many feet.

Spying an arched passageway at the far end of the crypt, he ran for it, dashed along its length, turned at an intersection, chose another tunnel at random, then another. This one was cruder but seemed to date to a later time, more like a catacomb dug out of the ground, with niches carved into the hard clay walls, the tunnel cribbed with old timbers. Here, voodoo imagery reigned, with moth-eaten bags, bundles of decaying feathers, strange constructions and graffiti, and the occasional oddly shaped shrines.

Crawling through a low archway, he found himself in a chamber whose walls sported floor-to-ceiling niches, each one of which held one or more skeletons. Without thinking, he forced his way into the biggest niche, favoring his broken arm, pushing the bones aside, wriggling as far to the back as he could, and then awkwardly scraping the bones back around with his feet to form an obscuring wall.

Then he waited.

The searchers were closer now: he could hear their voices echoing strangely through the underground spaces. This was no good: they were going to find him eventually. He examined the niche with his lighter and discovered it retreated still deeper into the earth. By squirming he could wedge his way farther in, all the while sweeping back with his legs the bones he'd pushed aside. Fortunately, dampness kept any telltale dust from rising from his efforts, although an unpleasant moldy, decaying stench now enveloped him. Some of the corpses still sported shreds of clothing, hair, belt buckles, buttons, and shriveled-up shoes. It seemed that the occupants of the Ville placed the corpses of their dead in these deep niches—and just kept shoving the old corpses back as new ones were placed inside.

The slickness of the walls allowed him to move farther back along the slight downslope as he pushed as deeply as he could into the niche.

And then he waited, listening, as the voices of the searchers waxed and waned, gradually growing closer. And then they grew all too clear: his pursuers were now in the chamber.

He was far back in darkness, too far for a flashlight to penetrate. He heard rattling sounds: they were jabbing a pole into the burial niches, trying to root him out. In a moment the pole came sliding into his own crawl space, knocking the bones aside, but he was too deep and the pole fell short. It prodded this way and that before finally withdrawing. He heard them probing in successive niches. Then, suddenly, their voices rose in both pitch and excitement. He heard the sound of retreating footsteps and then, quite quickly, their voices died away.

Silence.

Had they been called back to defend the Ville? It was the only possible explanation.

He waited a minute, then another, just to be safe. Then he moved to extricate himself from the niche. It was useless: he discovered that, in his panic, he had wedged himself in very tightly. Too tightly. A horrible sense of claustrophobia washed over him; he struggled to master it, to regulate his breathing. He wriggled again but he was firmly stuck. The panic threatened to surge back, stronger.

It couldn't be. He'd gotten in; surely he could get out.

He bent his leg, wedged it between the ceiling and the floor, and tried to leverage himself out while pushing with his good hand. No luck. The walls were slippery with damp and slime and the pitch was slightly uphill. He struggled, grunting, his good hand scrabbling on the wetness. In a fresh wave of panic, he dug his nails into the moist earth and tried to push his way forward, breaking several of them in the process.

My God, he thought. *I'm buried alive.*

It was all he could do to keep from screaming.

69

It took Special Agent Pendergast ten minutes of wrong turns and doubling-back to reach the dumbwaiter leading up to the pantry. He pulled out the groaning, semi-conscious man, climbed in, and—by reaching through a panel in the top and grasping the cables—was able to haul himself up and out of the basement. When the dumbwaiter bumped to a stop against the shaft ceiling, Pendergast slid open the door and jumped out. From the church came the sounds of a loud disturbance, one that seemed to have drawn off all members of the Ville within earshot. That left him an escape route. He sprinted through the darkened rooms of the old rectory, out the side door, and down the crooked back alley. In less than five minutes he was once again in the woods of Inwood Hill Park. He shrugged out of the cloak and hood and dropped them on the leafy ground, pulled out his cell phone and dialed.

"Hayward," came the clipped answer.

"Pendergast here."

"Now why does hearing your voice fill me with dread?"

"Are you in the vicinity of Inwood Hill Park?"

"I'm with Chislett and his men."

"Ah, yes. Chislett. A testament to the ultimate futility of higher education. Now listen: D'Agosta is in the basements of the Ville. He might be in a difficult situation."

A brief silence. "Vinnie? Inside the Ville? What the hell for?"

"I think you can guess—he's looking for Nora Kelly. But I've just now realized Nora isn't there. There's a confrontation brewing—"

"It's not just brewing. It's fully brewed, and—"

Pendergast cut her off. "I think Vincent might need your help—and need it rather badly."

A silence. "And what, exactly, are you up to?"

"No time for that, every minute counts now. Listen: there's something inside the Ville, something they themselves unleashed. It attacked us."

"Like a zombii?" came the sarcastic answer.

"A man—or, at least, a creature that was once a man, now transformed into something extremely dangerous. I repeat: Vincent needs help. His life might be in danger. Be careful."

Without waiting for a reply, Pendergast snapped the phone shut. In the distance, through the trees, he could see moonlight sparkling off the Harlem River. There was a sound of a motor, and then a searchlight probed through the darkness: a police boat, cruising back and forth, belatedly on the watch for protesters coming from the west or north. Quickly, Pendergast sprinted through the woods toward the river. As he reached the edge of the trees he slowed to a walk, adjusted his torn suit, then sauntered out onto the marsh grass and down to the pebbled beach. He waved to the police boat, pulling out his FBI shield and brandishing it with the aid of his penlight.

The boat slowed, turned, then nosed into the cove, idling just off the shingle shore. It was a jet-propelled patrol boat, the NYPD's latest model. Inside were a police sergeant and an officer of the marine unit.

"Who are you?" the sergeant asked, flicking the butt of a cigarette out into the water. He had a crew cut and a fleshy face with old acne scars, thick lips, a triple neck roll, and small triangular fingers. His partner, standing at the controls of the boat, looked like he spent most of his off-time in the gym. The muscles in his neck were as taut as the cables of the Brooklyn Bridge. "Man, you look like you've been through the wringer."

Pendergast returned his shield to his jacket pocket. "Special Agent Pendergast."

"Yeah? FBI? Happens every time, eh, Charlie?" He nudged his partner. "The FBI arrive, too late with too little. How do you guys manage it?"

"Sergeant—?" Pendergast waded into the water, coming up to the gunwale of the boat and laying a hand on it.

"Ruined your shoes, pal," said the sergeant, with another wry glance at his partner.

Pendergast glanced at the man's nameplate. "Sergeant Mulvaney, I'm afraid I require the use of this boat."

The sergeant stared at him, standing thigh-deep in the water, and cracked a smile. "You're *afraid* you *requiah* the use of this boat?" he drawled. "Well, I'm *afraid* I *requiah* authorization to that effect. Because I can't just give up police property to anyone, even J. Edgar *Hoovah.*"

The beefy partner rippled his muscles and snorted.

"Trust me, Sergeant, it's an emergency. I hereby invoke Section 302(b)2 of the Uniform Code—"

"Ah, we got a lawyer here too! An *emergency*. My, my, what kind of emergency?" Mulvaney hiked up his belt, setting his cuffs and keys ajangle, and waited, his head cocked to one side.

"A life. In danger. This has been a charming exchange, but I'm afraid I don't have any more time to bandy words with you, Sergeant. First and last warning."

"Look, I've got my orders. Keep an eye on the seaward approach to the Ville. And I'm not giving up this patrol boat just because you say so." The sergeant folded his hammy arms and smiled down at Pendergast.

"Mr. Mulvaney?" Pendergast leaned on the gunwale toward

Mulvaney, as if to speak confidentially in his ear. Mulvaney crouched to hear; there came a quick movement, Pendergast's fist arm shot upward into the cop's solar plexus, and with an abrupt sigh of expelled air Mulvaney bent over the gunwale. With a quick twist Pendergast flipped him in the water, where he landed with a huge splash.

"What the *fuck*—?" The partner straightened up, staring, reaching for his gun.

Pendergast hauled the dripping officer to his feet, having relieved him of his gun, and aimed it at the marine officer. "Toss your weapons out onto the beach."

"You can't—"

The report of the gun caused the officer to jump.

"All right! Jesus." The man removed his weapons and chucked them out on the shingle. "Is this FBI protocol?"

"Let me worry about protocol," Pendergast said, still gripping the gasping Mulvaney. "What you need to do is get out of the boat. Now."

The partner gingerly lowered himself into the water. In a flash Pendergast had vaulted into the cockpit. Pulling the shift into reverse, he backed the jet boat away from shore.

"So terribly sorry to discommode you gentlemen," he called out, spinning the wheel and slamming the shift into forward. He gunned the engine with a roar and vanished around the curve of shore.

70

Summoning all the presence of mind he could muster, D'Agosta slowed his breathing and focused on his mission. He had to free Nora. Somehow, shifting focus away from being trapped helped calm him down. The problem wasn't so much that he was stuck, but that the walls were so slippery; he simply couldn't get a purchase, especially with only one good arm. He'd ruined his nails in a futile effort, but what he really needed was something sharp and strong that would bite into the walls and help pull him out.

Bite . . .

There, not six inches from his hand, was a human jawbone, sporting all its teeth. He squirmed desperately, just managing to move his good arm sufficiently to grasp the mandible. Then he twisted his body sideways and jammed the teeth of the jawbone into a crack in the roof of the niche; by simultaneously pulling and wriggling at the same time, he eventually managed to work himself free.

With enormous relief he crawled back out of the niche and stood up in the chamber, breathing heavily. Everything was silent. Apparently, the zombii and the hunting party had both fallen back to deal with the protesters.

He returned to the central passageway and cautiously used his lighter to examine its length. It ended in a cul-de-sac. There were other crude burial chambers to either side, excavated from the same heavy clay and shored up with timbers, but they looked nothing like the mortared stone walls in the video. Nothing he had seen so far, in fact, resembled that kind of construction—the very stone was different. He had to look elsewhere.

Retracing his steps, skirting the well, he found himself back in the area of the vaulted necropolis. Along the walls were many small iron doors that led into what were, apparently, family crypts; he investigated each in turn, but there was no sign of Nora.

With mounting frustration, he painstakingly retraced his steps by trial and error, ultimately returning to the central cryptorium. There he stood, trying to build a map of the cellars in his head, to mentally fill in the sections through which he'd moved half senseless. There were doors in all four directions; one led to the catacombs, another—he realized—to the dead-end passageway from which he'd recently emerged. That left two more to try.

He picked one at random and took it.

Again it opened into a tunnel. Immediately this one appeared to be more promising: the walls were of crude mortared stone. Not precisely like the stone in the video, but closer.

A foul stench wafted down this corridor. D'Agosta paused, flicking his lighter on briefly, trying to conserve its fuel. The passageway was filthy, the stones splattered with mud and oozing with mold and fungus, the floor giving way unpleasantly at his touch.

As he played the light around, from the darkness ahead he heard a faint muffled cry—short, high-pitched, and full of terror . . .

. . . *Nora?*

Holding the lighter before him, he sprinted down the corridor toward the sound.

71

Plock led the protesters on a spree, tearing through the church, upending altars and fetish-festooned shrines. When their priest fell, the rest of the robed men fell back in confusion to the shadows, greatly outnumbered and temporarily at a loss. Plock realized that they had the initiative; the key was to seize it and keep it. With the crowd following, he swept toward the central altar. Here, there was a bloody, gore-flecked post where the animal sacrifices obviously took place—and a fresh pool of blood that awaited their outrage.

"Destroy this place of slaughter!" Plock cried as the crowd began swarming onto the elevated platform that held the altar and slaughtering pen, smashing down the post, breaking open boxes, and tossing relics.

"Blasphemers!" boomed the deep voice of Bossong. He was standing above the body of the fallen priest, who was out cold and had been badly trampled by the mob. Bossong was not unscathed, either—as he began walking down the central aisle, a trickle of blood was evident on his forehead.

The Ville leader's voice had a galvanizing effect on the robed crowds. They stopped retreating and paused in a kind of stasis. Knives appeared in some hands.

"Butcher!" screamed a protester at Bossong.

Plock realized that he had to keep the crowd moving, out of the church and into the rest of the Ville. A standoff here could quickly turn violent.

A robed congregant suddenly lunged forward with a shriek, slashing at a protester; there was a brief, violent struggle between the two that abruptly swelled into mob action, people from both groups rushing to the defense of their own. A ragged scream arose; someone had been knifed.

"Murderers!"

"Killers!"

The knot of people struggled and swirled, kicked and punched, all brown robes and khaki and pima cotton. It was an almost surreal sight. Within moments several were lying on the stone floor, bleeding.

"The animals!" cried Plock suddenly. He could hear and smell them, a muffled pandemonium behind a door at the head of the altar. "This way! Find and free the animals!" He dashed toward the door, pounded on it.

The leading edge of the crowd fell against the door, the battering rams once more appearing. It gave with a splintering crash and they poured beneath a stone archway, their way into the next room barred by a massive wrought-iron grate. On the other side was a scene from hell: dozens of baby animals, lambs, kids, calves—even puppies and kittens—locked in a huge stone chamber, the floor covered by a thin scattering of straw. The animals broke into a pathetic caterwauling, the lambs bleating, the puppies yipping.

For a moment Plock was speechless with horror. This was worse than anything he had imagined.

"Unbar these gates!" he cried. "Set free the animals!"

"No!" cried Bossong, as he struggled to approach, but he was shoved back and flung roughly to the floor.

The battering rams slammed into the iron grate, but it proved much sturdier than the wooden doors. Again and again they pounded the iron, the animals shrinking back and crying in terror.

"A key! Get a key!" cried Plock. "*He* must have one." He pointed at Bossong, who was on his feet again and now struggling with several of the protesters.

The mob rushed Bossong, and he disappeared in the swirl to the sound of tearing cloth.

"Here!" A man held up an iron ring with keys. It was quickly passed forward, and Plock inserted the heavy ancient keys into the lock, one after another. One worked. He flung the gate wide.

"Freedom!" he cried.

The vanguard of the crowd rushed in and herded out the animals, trying to keep them together, but as soon as the creatures were past the gate they scattered in terror, racing about, their cries rising to the massive wooden beams and echoing in the large space.

The dust had risen and the church had become a hellish scene of struggle and flight, with the protesters clearly gaining the upper hand. The animals stampeded down the nave, leaping as the congregants tried to grab them, rapidly disappearing through every doorway and opening they could find.

"Now's the moment!" screamed Plock. "Drive out these vivisectors! Drive them out! *Now!*"

72

The police speedboat, with Pendergast at the helm, tore down the Harlem River at fifty knots, curving around the northern tip of Manhattan Island and heading south. It flashed under a sequence of bridges: the West 207th Street Bridge; the George Washington Bridge; the Alexander Hamilton Bridge; the High Bridge; the Macombs Dam Bridge; the 145th Street Bridge; and finally the Willis Avenue Bridge. Here the Harlem River widened into a bay as it neared the junction with the East River. But instead of heading into the East River, Pendergast put the boat into a screaming turn and pointed it into the Bronx Kill, a narrow, foul creek separating the Bronx from Randall's Island.

Reducing speed to thirty knots, he headed down the Bronx Kill—more an open sewer and garbage dump than a navigable waterway—the boat throwing up a brown wake, the smell of marsh gas and sewage rising like a miasma. A dark railroad trestle rose up ahead and he passed underneath it, the diesel jet engine echoing weirdly as it went through the brief tunnel. Night had enveloped the bleak landscape and Pendergast grasped the handle of the boat's spotlight, directing the beam at various obstacles ahead as the boat slalomed among half-sunken hulks of old barges, rotting pilings of long-vanished bridges, and the submerged skeletons of ancient subway cars.

Quite suddenly the Bronx Kill widened again to a broad bay, opening into upper Hell Gate and the northern end of the East River. The vast prison complex of Rikers Island loomed directly ahead, the infamous X-shaped cement towers, bathed in pitiless sodium lights, rising up against a black sky.

Pendergast increased speed and the boat quickly left Manhattan behind; the Midtown skyline receded as he pounded up the East River toward the opening to Long Island Sound. Now, passing between Stepping Stones Light and City Island, Pendergast arced into the Sound and opened the boat up full throttle. The wind roared past, spray flying behind, the little vessel smacking the chop, swaying from side to side as it rocketed up the Sound, the full moon flashing off the water. It was a quiet evening, with only a few boats out and about. The channel buoys glowed softly in the moonlight.

Every minute counted. He might already be too late.

When Sands Point Light hove into view, he angled the boat near shore, crossed the broad mouth of Glen Cove, and headed straight for the mainland on the far side, keeping his eyes on the shorefront estates as they passed by, one after the other. A long pier came into view along a wooded shore and he aimed for it. Beyond the pier lay a dark expanse of lawn, rising to the turrets and shingled gables of a large Gold Coast mansion.

Pendergast brought the boat up to the pier at terrifying speed, reversing the engines at the last moment and spinning the boat so that it pointed back out into the Sound. Before the vessel had even stopped he jammed a boat fender between the edge of the wheel and the throttle, leapt from the bow onto the pier, and ran toward the dark, silent house. The uncaptained boat, throttle jammed in forward idle, chugged out from the pier and soon disappeared into the expanse of Long Island Sound, its red and green running lights gradually merging into darkness.

73

Captain Laura Hayward stared balefully at the shattered doors that led into the dark maw of the Ville, heard the din of chaos within. The protest action had been expertly planned. Her fears had come true. This was no ragged, piecemeal gathering: this was a group that had planned well and meant business. Chislett had been hopelessly overwhelmed and overmastered, clearly out of his depth. For five crucial minutes while the mob coalesced out of nowhere, he'd been stunned, doing nothing but standing in impotent surprise. Precious minutes had been lost; minutes in which the police could have at least slowed the progress or run a flying wedge into the leading edge of the protesters. When Chislett finally roused himself, he began shouting out a series of conflicting orders that had merely sown greater confusion among his officers. She could see several police from the forward field positions now taking matters into their own hands and running with tear gas and crowd control equipment toward the front doors of the Ville. But it was too late: the protesters were already inside and, as such, presented an extremely difficult and complex tactical situation.

Yet Hayward couldn't worry about that. Her thoughts were on the phone call she had received from Pendergast. *His life might be in danger,* he'd said. And Pendergast was not prone to exaggeration.

Her face darkened. This wasn't the first time Vinnie's association with Pendergast had ended in disaster—for Vinnie, of course. Pendergast always seemed to escape unscathed—as he had this time, leaving Vinnie to his own devices.

She shook away her anger. There would be time to confront Pendergast later. Right now, she had to act.

She approached the Ville, seeking to bypass the confrontation taking place in the church. The main doorway gaped wide, lambent light flickering from it. As she approached she could see riot police entering, ugly-sticks and tasers in their hands. Her own weapon at the ready, she followed quickly behind them. Beyond the shattered doors lay an ancient, narrow alley, lined on both sides with sagging wooden structures. She followed the uniformed officers past darkened doorways and shuttered windows. From ahead came the din of a thousand voices.

They rounded a bend and entered a stone plaza, beyond which lay the hulking fabric of the church itself. Here she was presented with a sight so bizarre it stopped her dead in her tracks. The plaza was a scene of desperate pandemonium, a Fellini-esque nightmare: men in brown robes were fleeing the church, some bleeding, others wailing or crying. Protesters, meanwhile, were trashing the place, racing about, breaking windows and smashing everything in sight. An indescribable din sounded from within the church walls. A profusion of animals—sheep, goats, chickens—raced about the square, tripping up the running figures and adding their own bleats and squeals to the general din. And among it all stood more riot police, milling around in disbelief, with no orders, no plan—uncertain and confused.

This was no good. She had to find access to the cellars below, where Vinnie had gone looking for Nora Kelly.

Turning away from the scene of bedlam, she left the plaza and ran down another dark cobbled alley, trying doors as she went. Many were locked, but one opened into a workshop of some kind, a tannery or primitive haberdashery. She looked around quickly but found no belowground access. Returning to the street, she continued on, trying doors as she went. Another heavy wooden door a few buildings farther yielded and she hurried in, closing it behind her. The yelling and caterwauling abruptly grew fainter.

This building, too, was deserted. It appeared to be a butcher shop. Walking past a row of glass cases into a back room, she spied a set of stairs leading down into a basement. Pulling a small flashlight from her jacket pocket and snapping it on, she descended. At the bottom was a chilly room lined with ancient panels of zinc: a larder. Hams, ribs, fat sausages, and half carcasses hung from the ceiling, curing. She moved carefully among them, sending one or two swinging gently, letting the beam of her light lick over the floor and the walls. At the back of the larder was a door leading to another staircase, lined with stone and apparently far older, descending into darkness. An unpleasant smell yawned up from the depths. Hayward hesitated, remembering the other thing Pendergast had said: *a creature that was once a man, now transformed into something extremely dangerous. I repeat: Vincent needs help. His life might be in danger.*

His life might be in danger . . .

Without further hesitation, Hayward probed the stairwell with her light and—gun in hand—began to descend farther into blackness.

74

Alexander Esteban turned from Pond Road, through the automatic gates, and onto the immaculate gravel driveway that wound among the thick-trunked oaks forming the approach to his estate. He drove slowly, savoring the feeling of returning home. Next to him, on the seat, lay a simple, two-page vellum document, signed, sealed, attested, and legally bulletproof.

A document that would, after a bit of a struggle no doubt, make him one of the richest men in the world.

It was late, almost nine o'clock, but there was no more rush. No more planning, directing, producing, executing. It had consumed practically his every waking moment for more months than he cared to count. But that was all behind him. The show had gone off perfectly to a standing ovation, and now there was just one little loose end to tie up. One last curtain call, as it were: a final bow.

As the car eased to a stop before the barn, Esteban felt his BlackBerry begin to vibrate. With a hiss of irritation he checked it: the rear kitchen door was registering an alarm. His spine stiffened. Surely it was a false alarm—they were a frequent occurrence on his large estate, one of the drawbacks of having such an extensive security system. Still, he had to be sure. He reached into the glove compartment and pulled out his favored handgun, a Browning Hi-Power 9mm parabellum with tangent sights. He checked the magazine and found it with its full complement of thirteen ball-point rounds. Slipping it into his pocket, he rose from the car and stepped out into the fragrant night. He checked the freshly raked gravel of the driveway—no sign of a car. Strolling across the broad expanse of lawn, he glanced down at the deserted pier, at the twinkling lights across the Sound, and found all in order. Gun in hand, he passed the greenhouse, entered a walled garden, and approached the back door of the kitchen, the one that had registered the alarm, moving noiselessly. He came to the door, tried the handle. It was closed and locked. The old brass keyhole showed no signs of being forced, no scratches in the old verdigris, no broken panes, nothing to indicate a disturbance.

False alarm.

He straightened up, checked his watch. He was almost looking forward to what was to come. A perverse pleasure, to be sure, but an ancient one. A pleasure encoded in the very genes: the pleasure of killing. He had done it before and found it a curiously cathartic experience. Perhaps, if he hadn't been a movie director, he might have made an excellent serial killer.

Chuckling to himself at this private little sally, he took out his key, opened the kitchen door, and punched in his code, turning off the alarm system in the house. But as he walked through the kitchen toward the door leading to the basement, he found himself hesitating. Why a false alarm now? They usually happened during thunderstorms or high winds. It was a calm, clear night, without the breath of wind. Was it a short circuit, a random static discharge? He felt uneasy, and that was a feeling he had learned never to ignore.

Instead of heading down to the basement, he turned and walked quietly through the darkened halls until he came to his study. He woke up his Mac, entered the password, and logged onto the Web site that handled his security cams. If someone had come in through the kitchen door, he would have had to cross the lawn behind the old greenhouse, where a cam would have picked him up. There was virtually no way to get into the house without being seen—coverage was more than one hundred percent—but if you were going to try, the kitchen side of the house, with its walled garden and ruined greenhouse, was perhaps the weakest point of the entire system. He tapped in the second password, and the live-cam image popped onto the screen. Checking his BlackBerry, he saw the alarm had registered at eight forty-one PM. He punched "8:36" into the digital time-stamp field, selected the camera to monitor, and began to watch.

It was well past sundown, and the image was dark—the night vision hadn't kicked in. He fiddled with the controls, enhancing the view as much as possible. He wondered at his own paranoia; he was, as usual, micromanaging. He thought, with a smile of irony, that it was both his worst, and his best, quality. And yet the uneasy feeling remained . . .

And that was when he saw a flash of black cross the corner of the screen.

Esteban stopped the action, backed it up, and moved it forward in slow motion. There it was again: a figure in black, flying through the very edge of the camera's field. He felt ice along his spine. Very, very clever; if he were to try to slip into the house, that's how he would have done it himself.

He stopped it and backed up again, frame by frame. The running man was only visible in six frames, less than a fifth of a second, but the high-def camera had caught him well; and in the middle frame he had a clear glimpse of the man's pale face and hands.

Esteban rose abruptly, knocking over his chair. It was that FBI agent, the one who had first visited him one week before. A momentary rush of panic threatened to overwhelm him, a suffocating tightness gripping his chest. Everything had gone perfectly so far—and now this. How did he know? *How did he know?*

With a great force of will, he exhaled the panic. Thinking under pressure was one of his strengths, something he had learned in the movie business. When things went wrong on the set, in the middle of a shoot, and everyone was standing around at a thousand dollars a minute waiting for him to figure things out, he had to make split-second, accurate decisions.

Pendergast. That was the FBI agent's name. He was alone. He'd left that beefy sidekick of his behind, the one with the Italian name. Why? It meant he was there on a hunch, freelancing as it were. If the man had hard evidence, he would have come in with a SWAT team, guns blazing. That was point one.

Point two was Pendergast didn't know he'd been smoked out. Perhaps he'd seen Esteban arrive by car or suspected he would come. But he didn't know Esteban *knew* he was there. That gave Esteban a distinct advantage.

Point three: Pendergast didn't know the layout of the estate, especially the extensive and confusing basements. Esteban knew them with his eyes closed.

He remained at his desk, thinking furiously. Pendergast would be headed for the basement—of that he was sure. He was looking for the woman. He'd have probably gone down via the back kitchen stairs, very close to the door through which he'd entered. And that's undoubtedly where he was right now: under the house, poking around among the old movie props, working his way through the south cellars. It would take him at least fifteen minutes to find his way through all that junk to the tunnel that ran to the barn.

Fortunately, the girl was in the barn cellar. Unfortunately, there was that tunnel connecting the house basements to the barn basements.

Abruptly, Esteban made a decision. He slid the gun into his waistband and rose, walking briskly out the front door and across the lawn to the barn. As he crossed the drive, a small smile broke out on his face as a plan took shape. The poor bastard had no idea what he was getting himself into. This little drama was going to have a charming finish—very charming. Not unlike his last movie, *Breakout Sing Sing.* Pity he couldn't film it.

75

Rich Plock stood in the chaotic dark, the cries and shouts of the congregants and protesters mingling with the screams of animals, the hiss of rattles and beating of drums. After the initial thrust into the church, the congregants had rallied for only a brief period and now they were falling back again, many fleeing through side doors into the narrow winding alleys and the maze of buildings that constituted the Ville.

For Plock, it was an unexpected turn and even a bit of an anticlimax. They had successfully liberated the animals—but now he realized there was no place to herd them, nowhere to keep them, and they were running wild, most already having disappeared out the shattered doors and into the courtyard. He hadn't thought ahead about that, and now he felt at a loss for what to do about the vanishing people. His plan had been to drive the residents out of the Ville, but he hadn't quite taken into account what a huge, confusing, rambling place it was; nor had he anticipated that the residents would break for cover so suddenly, fleeing into the depths of the Ville instead of putting up a longer fight during which they could be driven out. They were like Indians of old, melting away from direct confrontation.

He would have to rout them out.

And while routing them, they could also look for the kidnapped woman. Because Plock was beginning to realize that if they didn't save the woman as a way of justifying their foray into the Ville, they might—no, they *would*—find themselves in the deep end of the pool when it was all over. They would go through the Ville, purge it, sweep it clean, rout out the butchers, show them there was no place to run, no place to hide—and save the woman's life in the process. If they accomplished that, public opinion would be solidly on their side. And there would be a legal justification, of sorts. If not . . .

The protesters were still streaming in the shattered front doors of the church, filling up the space, while the last of the Ville residents disappeared. The only one remaining was the leader, Bossong, who stood like a statue, immovable, still bleeding from the forehead, watching the unfolding scene with baleful eyes.

As the last of the protesters packed into the church, Plock mounted the raised platform. "People!" he cried, raising his hands.

A hush fell on the multitude. He tried to ignore Bossong, standing in the corner, staring, projecting his malevolent presence throughout the room.

"We need to stay together!" Plock cried. "The torturers have gone to ground—we need to find them, flush them out! And above all, we must save the woman!"

Suddenly, from the corner, Bossong spoke. "This is our home."

Plock turned to him, his face contorting with fury. "Your home! This place of torture? You don't deserve a home!"

"This is our home," he repeated, his voice low. "And this is how we worship our gods."

Plock felt filled with rage. "How you worship your gods? By cutting the throats of helpless animals? By kidnapping and killing people?"

"Leave now. Leave while you can."

"Oooh, I'm scared now. So where's the woman? Where've you got her locked up?"

The crowd seethed with angry agreement.

"We honor the animals by sacrificing them for the nourishment of—our protector. With the blessings of our gods, we—"

"Spare us that crap!" Plock quivered with indignation as he shouted at the robed man. "You tell your people they're finished, that they'd better move on. Otherwise we're driving them out! You got that? Go somewhere else with your deviant religion!"

Bossong raised a finger and pointed it at Plock. "I fear it is already too late for you," he said quietly.

"I'm quaking in my boots!" Plock spread his arms in a welcoming gesture. "Strike me down, gods of the animal torturers! Go ahead!"

At that instant there was a sudden movement in one of the dark transepts of the church, a gasp from the protesters, a moment of hesitation. And then someone screamed and the crowd surged back like a rebounding wave, people pressing into the people behind them, shoving them into those farther behind—as a grotesque, misshapen figure lumbered into the wavering half-light. Plock gaped in horror and disbelief at the creature—but no, it was no creature. It was human. He stared at the scabby lips, rotten teeth, broad flat face; at the pale, slimy musculature draped in filthy rags. One hand held a bloody knife. Its stench filled the room, and it tilted its head back and bellowed like a wounded calf. A single, milky eye rolled in its head—then settled on Plock.

It took a step forward, then two, the thighs moving with a kind of slow, creeping deliberation. Plock was frozen, rooted, unable to move, to look away, even to speak.

In the sudden hush, there was a rustle of cloth and Bossong knelt, bowing his head and holding out his hands in supplication.

"Envoie," he said, quietly, almost sadly.

Instantly, the man-thing bounded straight at the platform with a crab-like shuffle, leapt onto it, opened his rotten mouth, and fell upon Plock.

Plock finally found his voice and tried to scream as the creature savaged him, but already it was too late for sound to emerge from his severed windpipe, and he expired in agonizing silence.

It was over very, very quickly.

76

Pendergast shined his penlight around the basement. The narrow beam revealed a chaos of bizarre objects, but he ignored them, focusing his attention on the basement wall—which consisted of flat, rough pieces of granite, stacked and carefully mortared.

His face tightened with recognition.

Now he turned his attention to the junk crowding the basement. Rising before him was an Egyptian obelisk of cracked plaster, weeping with damp and spiderwebbed with mildew. Beside it stood the truncated turret of a medieval castle, slapped together out of rotting plywood, complete with crenellations and machicolations, perhaps one-tenth actual size; next to that was a heap of broken plaster statues, stacked like cordwood, in which Pendergast could make out smaller-scale copies of the *David,* the *Winged Victory,* and the *Laocoön,* arms and legs and heads all tangled up, broken fingers lying about the cement floor beneath. The light revealed, in turn, a fiberglass shark, several plastic skeletons, a primitive tribal relic carved from Styrofoam, and a rubber human brain with a bite taken out of it.

The extensive clutter made for slow going, and it prevented him from grasping the full dimensions of the belowground areas. As he moved through the eerie piles of cast-off movie sets—for that was clearly what they were—he kept the penlight low, moving as swiftly and silently as he could manage. Though scattered and jumbled without hint of organization, the props and the concrete floor they lay on were unusually clean and dust free, attesting to an excessive interest on the part of Esteban.

The light flashed this way and that as Pendergast moved deeper into the clutter of Hollywoodiana. The claustrophobic spaces continued to branch out underground, room after room, stretching beyond the current footprint of the house, all manner of odd and unusual nooks and crannies, each stuffed with old props in various stages of decrepitude and decay, most from the grand historical epics for which Esteban was known. The basement was beginning to feel endless; it must have belonged to an earlier, even larger building occupying the site of Esteban's mansion.

Esteban. He would return home shortly, if he hadn't already. Time was passing—precious time that Pendergast could not afford to waste.

He moved to the next cellar—once apparently a smokehouse, now stacked with a witch-dunking chair, a gibbet, a set of stocks—and a spectacularly realistic guillotine from the French Revolution, blade poised to drop, the tumbrel below filled with severed wax heads, eyes open, mouths frozen in screams.

He moved on.

Reaching the end of the final cellar, he approached a rusty iron door, unlocked and standing ajar. He eased it open, surprised to find that the heavy door moved silently on oiled hinges. A long, narrow tunnel stretched ahead into darkness—a tunnel that at first glance appeared to have been dug out of the raw earth. Pendergast moved closer and touched a wall—and discovered it wasn't earth at all, but plaster painted to look like dirt. Another movie set, this one retrofitted into what had evidently been an older tunnel. From the direction, Pendergast guessed it led to the barn; such tunnels connecting house and barn were a common feature of nineteenth-century farms.

He shined the light down the murky passage. In places the fake plaster walls had peeled off, revealing the same stacked granite stones that had been used to build the house basement—and that were evident in the video of Nora.

He began moving cautiously down the tunnel, shading the penlight with his hand. If Nora was imprisoned on the grounds—and he was sure she was—she would have to be in the barn basement.

Esteban entered the barn through the side door and treaded softly in the vast space, fragrant with the smell of hay and old plaster. All around him loomed the props he had so assiduously collected and stored, at great expense, from his many films. He kept them for sentimental reasons he had never been able to explain. Like all movie props they had been built in haste, slapped together with spit and glue, designed to last only as long as the shooting. Now they were rapidly decaying. And yet he was deeply fond of them, could not in fact bear to part with them, see them broken up and hauled off. He had passed many a delicious evening strolling among them, brandy in hand, touching them, admiring them, fondly recalling the glory days of his career.

Now they were serving an unexpected purpose: slowing down that FBI agent, keeping him occupied and distracted, while at the same time helping to conceal Esteban and his movements.

Esteban threaded through the props to the back of the barn, where he unlocked and unbolted an iron door. A set of stairs descended into cool darkness, down into the barn's capacious underground rooms—once upon a time the fruit cellars, cheese aging rooms, root cellars, meat-curing vaults, and wine cellars of the grand hotel that had occupied the site. Even these spaces, the deepest on the estate, were chock-full of old props. Except for the old meat locker he had cleared out to imprison the girl.

Like a blind man in his own house, Esteban made his way through the mass of old props, not even bothering with a flashlight, moving surely and confidently in the dark. Soon he had reached the mouth of the tunnel that led from the barn to the house. Now he snapped on a small pocket LED; in the bluish glow he could make out the fake plaster walls and cribbing left over from shooting *Breakout Sing Sing,* in which he had used this very tunnel as a set—and saved a tidy sum. About twenty feet past the tunnel mouth, a plywood panel had been set into the wall, a small angle-iron lever protruding from it. Esteban gave it a quick inspection and found it to be in good condition. It had been a simple mechanism to begin with, requiring no electricity, only the force of gravity to operate—in the movie business, contraptions had to be reliable and easy to work, because it was well known that what *could* break, *would* break, inevitably when the cameras were rolling and the star was, finally, sober. Out of curiosity he had tested the device just the year before—a device he had designed himself—and found that it still functioned just as well as on the day he shot the immortal escape scene of the movie that had almost won him an Academy Award. *Almost.*

Flushing at the thought of the lost Oscar, he switched off his light and listened. *Yes:* he could hear the faint footsteps of the approaching agent. The man was about to make a gruesome discovery. And then, of course, there was no way the poor FBI agent—no matter how transcendentally clever—could possibly anticipate what would happen to him next.

77

Harry R. Chislett, deputy chief of the Washington Heights North district, stood at the central control point on Indian Road, a radio in each hand. Faced with an unprecedented and utterly unexpected development, he had nevertheless—so he considered—adapted with remarkable speed and economy. Who could have foreseen so many protesters, so quickly, all moving with the ruthless precision and purpose of a single mind? Yet Chislett had risen to the occasion. What a tragedy, then, that—for all his probity—he was surrounded by incompetence and ineptitude. His orders had been misinterpreted, improperly carried out, even ignored. Yes: there was no other word for it than tragedy.

Picking up his field glasses, he trained them on the entrance to the Ville. The protesters had managed to get inside, and his men had gone after them. The reports were chaotic and contradictory; God only knew what was really going on. He would go in himself except that a commander must not place his own person in danger. There might be violence; perhaps even murder. It was the fault of his men in the field, and that was how his report would most emphatically read.

He raised the radio in his right hand. "Forward position alpha," he rapped out. "Forward position alpha. Move up to defense position."

The radio cracked and sparked.

"Forward position alpha, do you read?"

"Position alpha, roger," came the voice. "Please verify that last order."

"I *said,* move up to defense position." It was outrageous. "In the future, I'll thank you to please *obey* my orders without asking me to *repeat* them."

"I just wanted to make sure, sir," came the voice again, "because two minutes ago you told us to fall back and—"

"Just do as you're told!"

From the gaggle of officers milling around confusedly on the baseball diamond, one figure in a dark suit separated itself and came trotting over. Inspector Minerva.

"Yes, Inspector," said Chislett, careful to let his voice radiate a dignified, McClellan-like tone of command.

"Reports are coming back, sir, from inside the Ville."

"You may proceed."

"There is significant conflict between the inhabitants and the protesters. There are reports of injuries, some serious. The interior of the church is being torn up. The streets of the Ville are filling with displaced residents."

"I'm not surprised."

Minerva hesitated.

"Yes, Inspector?"

"Sir, once again I'd recommend you take . . . well, firmer action."

Chislett looked at him. "Firmer action? What the devil are you talking about?"

"With all due respect, sir, when the protesters began their march on the Ville I recommended you immediately call for backup units. We've got to have more people."

"We have sufficient manpower," he said fussily.

"I also recommended that our officers move quickly to take up positions across the road to the Ville, to block the march."

"That is precisely what I ordered."

Minerva cleared his throat. "Sir . . . you ordered all units to maintain their positions."

"I gave no such command!"

"It's not too late for us to—"

"You have your orders," Chislett said. "Please carry them out." He glared at the man as he dropped his eyes and mumbled a "Yes sir," while walking slowly back to the gaggle of officers. Honestly, it was nothing but incompetence, incompetence, even from those he had hoped to rely on the most.

He raised his binoculars again. Now, this was interesting. He could see protesters—first just a few, but as he watched, more and more—running out of the Ville and back down the drive, faces contorted with fear. His officers were finally flushing them out. Sprinkled among them were robed and cowled figures, residents of the Ville itself. All were streaming out of the Ville, sprinting away from the ancient wooden structures, falling over one another in a panicked effort to get as far away as possible.

Excellent, excellent.

Lowering the binoculars, he raised his radio. "Forward position delta, come in."

After a moment, the radio squawked. "Forward position delta, Wegman speaking."

"Officer Wegman, the protesters are beginning to disperse," said Chislett primly. "Clearly, my tactics are having the intended effect. I want you and your men to shunt the protesters back toward the baseball diamond and the street, to effect an orderly dispersal."

"But, sir, we're all the way across the park at the moment, where you told us to—"

"Just do as you're told, Officer." And Chislett shut off the man's protests with the flick of the transmit button. Weak as water, the whole lot of them. Had ever a commander in the history of organized aggression ever been burdened with such monumental ineptitude?

He lowered the radio with a disheartened sigh and watched as the crowd of people streaming out of the Ville became a river, then a flood.

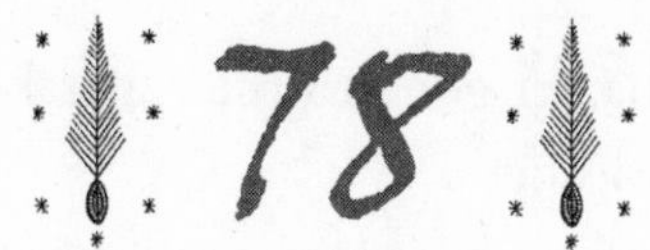

78

Pendergast moved through the tunnel, keeping close to the left-hand wall, the narrow beam of the penlight carefully shielded. As he came around a bend in the tunnel, he spied something in the dim glow—a long, whitish object lying on the tunnel floor.

He approached. It was a heavy plastic bag, zippered on one side, smeared with mud, dirt, and grass, as if it had been dragged. Printed on the side were the words MORGUE OF THE CITY OF NEW YORK and a number.

He knelt and reached out, grasping the zipper. Slowly he drew it back, keeping the sound as low as possible. An overpowering stench of formalin, alcohol, and decomposition assaulted his nostrils. Inch by inch, the corpse within was exposed. He pulled the zipper back until the bag was half open, grasped the edges of the plastic and spread them apart, exposing the face.

William Smithback, Jr.

For a long time, Pendergast stared. Then, with an almost reverent care, he fully opened the zipper, exposing the entire body. It was at the worst stage of decomposition. Smithback's cadaver had been autopsied and then, the day before it disappeared, reassembled for turning over to the family: the organs replaced, the Y-incision sewn up, the cranium reattached with the scalp pulled back over it and sutured closed, the face repaired, everything stuffed and packed and padded. It was a crude job—delicate work wasn't a pathologist's forte—but it was a package a good mortician could, at least, work with.

Only, the body hadn't gone to the funeral home. It had been stolen. And now it was here.

Suddenly, Pendergast peered more closely. Reaching into the pocket of his suit coat, he extracted a pair of tweezers and used them to pluck away a few bits of white latex rubber that were clinging to the corpse's face: one from a nostril, another from an earlobe. He examined them closely with the penlight, then placed them thoughtfully in his pocket.

He slowly played the light about—and saw, fifty feet away, another decaying corpse, neatened up and dressed for burial in a black suit. An unknown person, but tall and lanky, the same approximate height and build as Smithback and Fearing.

Looking at the two corpses, the final details of Esteban's plot crystallized in his mind. It was most elegant. Only one question now remained: what was in the document Esteban looted from the tomb? It would have to be something truly extraordinary, something of immense value, for a man to go to such risk. Cautiously and silently he closed the zipper. Pendergast was stunned, not only by the complexity of Esteban's plan, but by its audacity. Only a man of the rarest parts, of patience, strategic vision, and personal mettle, could have pulled it off. And pull it off he had; if Pendergast had not accidentally come across the looted tomb in the basement of the Ville, and combined that detail with the sanguineous wrappings of a crown roast of lamb found in the garbage, the man would have gotten away with it.

In the noisome dark, Pendergast thought intently. In his mad dash to get here as quickly as possible, to save Nora, he had neglected to consider in detail how he would deal with Esteban. He now realized he had underestimated the man—this was a formidable adversary. The distance by car from Inwood to Glen Cove was such that he had surely returned home by now. Such a man would know that Pendergast was here as well. Such a man would have a plan and would be waiting for him. He had to confound the man's expectations. He had to strike from—quite literally—an unexpected direction.

Carefully, noiselessly, he retreated down the passage the way he had come.

Esteban waited in the tunnel, standing beside the lever, listening intently. The FBI agent was damn quiet, but in these silent, underground spaces, even the smallest sounds traveled forever. Listening intently, he could reconstruct what was happening. First, the faint sound of a zipper; then the rustle of plastic; several minutes of silence—and the zipper again. Then he spied the faintest glow of light in the tunnel: Pendergast's flashlight. Still he waited.

It was amusing, really, the FBI agent finding the two bodies. What a shock that must be. He wondered just how much the man had figured out; with both corpses in front of him probably a great deal—this Pendergast fellow was clearly intelligent. Perhaps he knew everything but the crucial point: the nature of the document he had taken from his ancestor's tomb.

The important thing was that Pendergast was operating on a hunch, without proof—and that was why he was here alone, without backup or a SWAT team.

At the thought of the document, Esteban felt a sudden panic thread his spine. He didn't have it. Where had he left it? Inside his unlocked car, sitting in the driveway. That damn alarm coming in over his BlackBerry had distracted him just as he'd arrived home. What if it was stolen? What if Pendergast found it? But these were foolish thoughts: the gate into the estate was shut and locked, and Pendergast was down here, in the tunnel. He would retrieve the document at his earliest opportunity, but right now he had urgent business to attend to.

The silence from the tunnel was now absolute. Hardly breathing, he listened and waited.

And waited. The faint, indirect glow of the light remained steady, unmoving. As the minutes crawled by, Esteban began to realize something was awry.

"Mr. Esteban?" came the pleasant voice out of the darkness behind him. "Would you be so kind as to remain absolutely still, while slowly releasing your grip on the weapon and allowing it to fall to the ground? Let me warn you that the slightest movement, even an ill-timed twitch of an eyelash, will result in your immediate death."

79

Esteban released the gun. It fell to the ground with a thud.

"Now if you will slowly raise your hands and take two steps back, then lean against the wall."

Esteban took the two required steps and did as he was told. Pendergast reached down, picked up the Browning, and slipped it into his jacket pocket, then searched through Esteban's pockets and removed his flashlight. He stepped back and switched it on.

"Listen—" Esteban began.

"No talking, please, except to answer my questions. Now you will lead me to Nora Kelly. Nod if you understand."

Esteban nodded. All was not lost . . . It was always possible to be too intelligent. He moved slowly backward, in the direction of the house.

"She's not that way," said Pendergast. "I've already explored those areas. You've used up your only chit—next time you try to pull something off, I'll conclude you are unhelpful, kill you without further ado, and find Ms. Kelly myself. Nod if you understand."

Esteban nodded.

"She's in the basement of the barn?"

Esteban shook his head.

"Where is she? You may speak."

"She's in a room hidden in the tunnel, under the plaster. Not far from Smithback's body."

"There was no fresh plaster in the tunnel."

"The door is under a section of old wired-up plaster I can move and replace at will."

Pendergast seemed to ponder this. Then he waved his gun. "You first. Remember what will happen if you are unhelpful."

Once again, Esteban began walking back down the tunnel toward Smithback, keeping to the right wall. Pendergast followed about ten feet behind. Esteban stepped over a tiny penlight—clearly the agent's—lying on the floor of the tunnel. As he passed the lever, he pretended to stagger and fall, striking it on his way down.

The shot rang out but it was high, ruffling Esteban's hair. A grinding crash burst from the ceiling of the tunnel as the lever of his mechanism released a fake landslide. It wasn't a real cave-in, of course, but rather one consisting of Styrofoam boulders, pre-broken and stained plywood timbers, and sand and gravel mixed with painted popcorn filler. It wasn't as deadly as a true landslide, but it nevertheless dropped fast and furiously. Pendergast leapt aside, but as quick as he was, he wasn't able to escape the ton of material that had been unleashed directly on top of him. With a long, rumbling roar of timbers and popcorn and Styrofoam, he was knocked down and buried. Esteban scrambled forward, just escaping the leading edge of the avalanche himself.

All was pitch-dark—the lights had been buried with the agent. Esteban could hear the last bits and pieces of gravel rain down. Then he laughed out loud. This was the avalanche that had appeared to bury the pursuing prison guards in the climactic scene of *Breakout Sing Sing,* as the hero leapt from the tunnel mouth to safety. And here he had re-created it—for real!

Pendergast evidently was not a moviegoer. If he were, he might have recognized the tunnel and guessed what was coming. Too bad for him.

Esteban waded into the phony landslide, kicking the filler away, looking for Pendergast. After five minutes of forcing aside rubble, he spied the gleam of his flashlight, still lit, and next to it the agent's body, bloody and dust-covered, stunned by the sudden cascade. The Browning he had taken lay beside him. The agent's own gun was in his hand, cell phone lying nearby. He had been hit hard by the debris and might even be dead, but Esteban had to be sure. He first grabbed both of the guns. Next, he brought his foot down on the cell phone, smashing it. Then he raised the Browning, checked the magazine, aimed it at Pendergast's breastbone, and fired two rounds point-blank into the detective, a double tap to the heart, followed by a third to make sure, the body jumping with each impact, dust billowing upward from his chest and shoulders.

A spreading stain of blood appeared on the ground underneath.

Esteban stood there, amid the dust, and allowed himself a small smile. Pity that this little scene would never make the silver screen. Now it was time for the final act in his private epic: kill the girl and get rid of the bodies.

All four of them.

80

Laura Hayward made her way cautiously through the shadowy vaults deep beneath the alleys and cloisters of the Ville. The screams and cries overhead, which seemed to have reached a crescendo, had abruptly receded: either the confrontation had spilled out into Inwood Hill Park or she had descended too deep into the earth to hear it. The basement passages of the Ville spread across many levels and sported numerous architectural styles, from crude hand-carved grottoes to elaborate stone-lined vaults with groined ceilings. It was as if successive waves of occupants, with a variety of needs and levels of sophistication, had each extended the underground spaces for their own purposes.

A quick glance at her watch showed that she had been exploring the basements for fifteen minutes now—fifteen minutes of dead ends and circuitous windings each more confusing and macabre than the last. Just how far could this subterranean maze extend? And where was Vincent? More than once she had considered calling out his name, but each time some sixth sense had cautioned her against it. Her radio proved useless.

Now she paused at a crossroads from which four short passages led away to banded iron doors. She chose one passage at random, traversed it, stopped at the door to listen, then opened it and stepped through. Beyond lay a dirty and foul-smelling tunnel, the floor spongy with mold, the ceiling woven with cobwebs. A constant drip, drip, drip of condensate fell from the slimy stonework overhead. Greasy drops pattered Hayward's hair and shoulders as she walked, and she flicked them away in disgust.

After about twenty yards, the passage split in two directions. Hayward went right, in what she believed to be the direction of the central church. The air was slightly less noisome here, the walls constructed of primitively dressed stone. She peered closely at the stonework, examining it with her flashlight. This was clearly not the wall in the video of Nora Kelly.

Suddenly, she straightened up. Was that a cry?

She stood motionless in the dark, listening intently. But whatever she had heard—if indeed she'd heard anything at all—did not sound again.

She moved forward. The stone passage ended in a massive, vaulted archway. Ducking underneath, she found herself in a crudely constructed mausoleum, supported by rotting timbers, a set of a dozen burial niches carved into the clay walls, each one with a rotting coffin. Charms and fetishes were everywhere: bags of leather and sequins; grotesque dolls with leering, oversize heads; maddeningly complex designs of spirals and crosshatches, painted onto boards and stretched hides. It was a subterranean temple to the dead leaders of the Ville, it seemed—or, perhaps, the undead. The coffins themselves were strange, banded with iron and padlocked, as if to keep the dead inside, some with massive spikes driven through them and into the clay below. Hayward shuddered, recalling some of the more colorful stories of her old cohorts on the New Orleans PD.

. . . Now it came again, and this time there was no question: a female voice, sobbing quietly—and coming out of the darkness directly ahead.

Nora Kelly? She moved forward as silently as she could through the voodoo-laden chamber, gun ready, keeping her flashlight shielded. The voice was muffled but it sounded close, perhaps only two or three chambers away. The niche-filled room ended in a passage that forked again; the sounds were coming from the left, and Hayward headed toward them. If it was Nora, she would probably be guarded—the Ville would have sent somebody down at the first sign of trouble.

The passage doglegged, then suddenly gave onto a vast crypt, its vaulted ceiling supported by heavy columns. In the dust-fragrant darkness, Hayward could make out row after row of wooden sarcophagi stretching ahead to the rear wall. There in the distance she could make out three figures, backlit by the intermittent flicker of what appeared to be a cigarette lighter. Two were women, one of whom was weeping quietly. The other, a man, was speaking to them in a low voice. His back was to Hayward, but by his tone and gesture he seemed to be reassuring them about something.

She felt her heart quicken. She took a step closer, then another. And then she was certain: the man across the room was Vincent D'Agosta.

"Vinnie!"

He turned. For a moment, he looked confused. Then a relieved smile broke over his face. "Laura! What are you doing here?"

She came forward quickly, no longer bothering to conceal her light. The women looked toward her as she approached, their faces pinched with fear.

D'Agosta's right arm was in an improvised sling; his face was scratched and dirty; his suit was torn and badly rumpled. But she was so relieved to see him she barely noticed.

She gave him a hasty embrace, awkward because of the sling. Then she paused to look at him. "Vinnie, you look like you've been dragged behind a car."

"I feel like it. Got a couple of people here who need help. They were with the protesters, got set on by some of the residents of the

Ville and got lost trying to flee." He paused. "Are you down here looking for Nora, too?"

"No. I came for you."

"Me? What for?" He seemed almost offended.

"Pendergast told me you were down here, might be in danger."

"I was looking for Nora. You said Pendergast?"

"On his way out, he said he was going to get Nora. He told me she isn't here."

"*What?* Where is she?"

"He didn't say. But he said that something attacked you both. Something strange."

"That's right. Laura, if it's true Nora's not down here, we've got to get out of here. *Now.*"

Abruptly, he fell silent. A moment later Hayward heard it as well: a fleshy pattering out of the darkness, like broad hands drumming a tattoo against the cold stonework. It was distant, but coming closer. A moment later, the skittering sound was overlaid by a wet smacking and a low groan like the gasp of a punctured bellows: *aaaahuuuuuu . . .*

One of the women gasped, took an instinctive stumbling step back.

D'Agosta started. "Too late," he said. "It's back."

In the mildewed dark, Nora waited. Her head throbbed fiercely; just moving it sent a lance of pain searing from temple to temple. Her jailer had aggravated her concussion with that blow to the head. Despite the pain, she had to fight against a heavy torpor that threatened to overwhelm her. How many hours had passed? Twenty-four? Thirty-six? Strange how the dark preyed on one's perception of time.

She lay propped up against the wall, on one side of the door, awaiting her jailer's return, wondering if she would have the energy to attack him when he did. She had to admit to herself it was hopeless—the trick hadn't worked the first time and it would hardly work a second. But what other course was there? If she remained anywhere else in the room, he could shoot her through the window. She knew her jailer wasn't going to release her. He was keeping her alive for some obscure purpose, and when that purpose was complete, he would kill her.

In the black silence, her thoughts wandered. Into her mind came the image of a black limo at the marina in the tiny town of Page, Arizona, the red bluffs of Lake Powell rising in the background and the sky overhead a cloudless bowl of perfect blue. Heat rose from the parking lot in shimmering waves. The door of the limo opened and a lanky man climbed awkwardly out of it, dusted himself off, and straightened up. He looked silly in his Ray-Bans, his brown hair sticking out in multiple directions. He stooped slightly, as if embarrassed by his tallness; she recalled his aquiline nose, his long and lean face, and the squinting, perplexed, yet confident way he took in his surroundings. It was her first glimpse of the man who would become her husband, who had joined her archaeological expedition to the canyon country of Utah as the resident journalist. Right away she had thought him an ass. Only later did she learn he kept his better qualities, his wonderful qualities, deeply buried, as if mildly ashamed of them.

Other random memories drifted through her mind from those first days in Utah: Bill, calling her *Madam Chairman.* Bill, climbing on his horse, Hurricane Deck, cursing and swearing as the horse danced around. These recollections segued into memories of their early life together in New York: Bill, spilling brandy sauce on his new suit at Café des Artistes. Bill, decked out as a bum in order to sneak into a building site at night where thirty-six bodies had been found. Bill, lying in the hospital bed after being rescued from Leng . . . The images came unbidden, unwelcome and yet strangely comforting. No longer having the energy to resist, she let them pass through her memory as she drifted into a state midway between sleep and wakefulness. Now, at this extremity, her own life destined to end at any moment, she seemed somehow finally able to come to terms with her loss.

She was torn back to the present by a muffled rumble, a deep vibration both in the air and through the walls. She sat up, suddenly alert, headache temporarily forgotten. The rumble went on and on before dying away into silence. Minutes later, it was followed with the loud *boom! boom!* of two gunshots in rapid succession, followed by a pause, and then a third.

The shock of the sounds, so loud and sudden after such lengthy silence, galvanized her. Something was happening, and this might be her only chance to act. She tensed, listening intently. At first faintly, and then more pronounced, came the sounds of something heavy being dragged over the cellar floor. A grunt, a pause, more dragging. Silence. And then the sound of the grate in her door being opened.

The voice of her jailer rang out. "Got a visitor!"

Nora did not move.

A light shined in through the opening, the black bars of the grate thrown into relief against the far wall.

Still Nora waited. To force him to enter and then make her attack—it was her only chance.

She heard a key in the lock, saw the door swing partway open. But instead of stepping in, her jailer flopped something on the floor—a body—and immediately backed out, slamming the door behind him. In the retreating light she stared at the body's face, silhouetted in the light from the grate: the chiseled features, high cheekbones, marble skin and fine hair; the eyes like slits showing only the whites; dust and blood caked in the hair; the once black suit now a powdery gray, rumpled and torn; a pool of dark blood still spreading across his shirt.

Pendergast. Dead.

She cried out in surprise and dismay.

"Friend of yours?" the voice jeered through the grate. The lock turned, the padlock rattled, and darkness returned once again.

82

Alexander Esteban hurried back through the basements he knew so well and took the stairs up to ground level, two at a time. In a moment he was out of the barn and outside. It was a fresh, cold fall night, the stars sprinkled hard across a velvet sky. Breaking into a run, he headed to his car, flung open the door, and—thank God, thank *God*—grabbed the manila envelope that lay on the passenger's seat. He opened it, slid out the old vellum sheets within, checked them, and—more slowly now—slid them back in.

He leaned against the car, breathing hard. It was silly, this panic. Of course the document was safe. It wasn't worth anything to anyone else but him, anyway. Few would even understand it. Even so, it had tormented him dreadfully, thinking of it sitting there in the car unprotected. He had planned so carefully, cultivated relationships, spent several fortunes, misled and suborned and intimidated and murdered—all for that double sheet of vellum. The thought that it had lain unguarded in his car, open to some opportunistic sneak thief or even the caprice of the Long Island weather, had been a torture. But all had ended well. It was safe. And now, with it once again in his hand, he could afford to laugh at his own paranoia.

Smiling a little ruefully to himself, he went back into the house, walked through the darkened halls to his office, and opened his safe. He put the envelope inside the steel confines and gazed at it fondly for a moment. Now his mind was fully at ease. Now he could go back to the basement and finish things off. Pendergast was dead; he only had to do the girl. Their bodies would go deep beneath the basement floor—he had already worked out the spot—and nobody would ever see them again.

He pushed the massive steel door shut and punched in the electronic code. As the locking mechanism whispered and clicked when the tumblers eased into place, Esteban thought about the coming weeks, months, years . . . and he smiled. It would be a struggle, but he would emerge from it a very, very rich man.

Leaving the house, he strolled back across the lawn, breathing easily, his hand on the grips of the gun he'd taken from the FBI agent's body. It was clearly a police-issue firearm, perfect for the anonymous job he had in mind. He'd get rid of it, of course—after he had used it on the girl.

The girl. She'd already surprised him with her resourcefulness and physical resilience. One should never underestimate human ingenuity in the face of death. Despite her being injured and locked up, he'd have to be careful—no sense slipping up at the last minute, with everything he desired now in his possession.

Inside the barn, he flicked on his flashlight and descended to the basement. He wondered if the girl was going to make it hard on him, crouching behind the damn door like she'd done before. He didn't think so—tossing Pendergast's body into the cell had clearly freaked her out. She'd probably be hysterical, pleading, trying to talk her way out of it. Good luck—he wouldn't even give her the chance.

He reached the door to her cellar room and opened the barred window, shining his light inside. There she was, once again in the center of the room, lying on the straw, sobbing, all fight gone, head bent forward, covered by her hands. Her broad back made a perfect target. Off to her right, still visible, was the FBI agent's corpse, clothes in disarray, as if she'd been searching him for his gun. Perhaps the lack of a weapon was what had made her ultimately give up hope.

He felt a pang of remorse. This was a cold thing to do. It wasn't like killing Fearing or Kidd—they were opportunistic scum, low-life criminals who would do anything for a buck. And yet killing the woman was a necessary evil, unavoidable. Squinting through the sights, he took careful aim at her upper back, directly above her heart, and squeezed off a round from the Colt. The force of the bullet knocked her sideways and she screamed—a short, sharp scream. The second shot caught her lower down, just above her kidneys, knocking her sideways again. There was no scream this time.

That took care of that.

But he had to be sure. A bullet to the brain for each was in order—and then a quick burial in the place of his choice. He would get rid of Smithback's and the researcher's bodies at the same time. Husband and wife together—wouldn't that be appropriate?

Gun at the ready, he inserted the key in the lock and eased open the door.

83

D'Agosta turned to the two protesters, their faces tight with anxiety, cashmere sweaters and deck shoes shockingly out of place in this gothic hall of the dead. "Get behind that crypt," he said, pointing to a nearby slab of marble. "Duck down, out of sight. Hurry."

He wheeled back toward Hayward, his broken forearm protesting at the sudden movement. "Give me your flashlight."

She passed it to him and he quickly shielded it against his palm, muting the beam. "Laura, I've got no weapon. We can't hide from it, and we can't outrun it. When it comes in, shoot."

"When what comes in?"

"You'll know. It doesn't seem to feel pain, fear, anything. It looks like a man, at first . . . but it's not fully human. It's fast and determined as hell. I'll spotlight it for you. If you hesitate, we're dead."

She swallowed, nodded, checked her handgun.

Tucking the flashlight into his pocket, he took up position behind a large marble tomb and motioned Hayward to take up a position behind the adjacent one. Then they waited. For a minute, all he heard was Hayward's rapid breathing; a faint whimpering from one of the protesters; the hammering of his heart in his chest. Then it came again: the pattering of bare feet against wet stone. It seemed farther away now. A low groan echoed through the cavernous space, long and drawn out, yet freighted with a hungry urgency: *aaaaaahhhhuuuuu . . .*

From the darkness behind them, D'Agosta heard the whimpering of the protester rise, grow panicky.

"Quiet!" he whispered.

The pattering of feet stopped. D'Agosta felt his heart quicken. He reached into his pocket for the flashlight. As he did so, his hand closed over the medallion of Saint Michael, patron saint of policemen. His mother had given it to him when he first joined the force. Every morning he slipped it into his pocket almost without thought. Even though he hadn't prayed in probably half a dozen years and hadn't been to church for even longer, he heard himself begin to pray now: *God, Who knows us to be set in the midst of great perils . . .*

Aaaaaiiihhuuuuuuuuuuuuuu came the groan, nearer now.

. . . We beg you, Lord, banish the deadly power of the evil one. Saint Michael the Archangel, defend us in battle . . .

At the far end of the vaulted space something moved in the fetid dark. A low, creeping form—shadow against shadow—slunk between the farthest set of tombs. D'Agosta pulled the flashlight from his pocket. "Ready?" he whispered.

Hayward trained her weapon ahead in a two-handed combat grip.

D'Agosta aimed the flashlight toward the distant archway and switched it on.

There it was, caught in the beam: pale, crouching, the palm of one hand splayed flat on the stone floor before it, the other gripping its side, where the rags were stained by a growing spread of crimson. Its one good eye rolled wildly toward the light; the other was ruined and black with hemorrhaged blood, leaking fluid. Its lower jaw sagged loosely, swinging with each movement, and a heavy rope of saliva hung from its dark and swollen tongue. It was scratched and filthy and bleeding. But its injuries did nothing to slow it down or decrease its sense of terrible purpose. With another hungry groan it leapt toward the light.

Whang! went Hayward's gun. *Whang! Whang!*

D'Agosta switched off the light to reduce their chances of being targeted. His ears rang from the explosions and the ragged scream of the protesters behind them.

The sounds of the gunshots rolled away in the underground passageways, and silence resumed.

"My God," Hayward breathed. "My God."

"Did you get it?"

"I think so."

D'Agosta crouched down, listening intently, waiting for the ringing in his ears to die away. Over his shoulder, the screams subsided into racking sobs. Then there was no other noise save Hayward's gasps of breath.

Had she killed it?

He waited another minute, then another. Then he turned on the light and shined it around the spaces ahead. Nothing.

Dead or alive, this was enemy territory and they had to keep moving. "Come on," he said. "Let's get the hell out of here."

D'Agosta scooped up the two protesters, got them on their feet. Moving rapidly, they traversed the forest of tombs and reached the archway in the far wall. He cast the hooded light around the nearby floor. A few drops of fresh blood and nothing else. Stepping beneath the archway, he beckoned them to follow him into the large storeroom beyond.

"Careful," he whispered. "There's a deep pit in the center of the room. Keep to the walls."

As they began to make their way through the heaps of moldering leather-bound books and ancient decomposing furniture, there was a sharp hiss from one side. D'Agosta turned, raising the light, just as the thing shot out of the darkness, leaping toward them, muddy mouth wide, broken black nails raised to rend and tear. Hayward brought up her gun but it was on her in a flash, sending her crashing to the floor and the gun spinning across the room. Heedless of the pain in his shattered forearm, D'Agosta leapt onto the creature, slugging it repeatedly. It ignored his blows and tightened its grip around the neck of the struggling Hayward, all the while barking with bloodthirsty pleasure: *Aihu! Aihu! Aihu!*

Suddenly the storeroom filled with a violent orange light. D'Agosta turned toward it; Bossong stood in the opposite doorway, a huge burning torch held high in one hand. His face was bloodied but he had lost none of his forbidding, almost regal bearing.

"Arrêt!" he cried, his deep voice reverberating through the subterranean chamber.

The creature paused to look up, cringing, jaundiced eye lolling.

D'Agosta noticed that Hayward's gun was lying mere inches from the community leader's feet. He made a move toward it but Bossong immediately swept it up and pointed it at them.

"Bossong!" D'Agosta cried. "Call it off!"

The leader of the Ville said nothing, aiming the gun at them.

"Is this what your religion is about? This monster?"

"That *monster*"—Bossong spat out the word—"is our protector."

"And this is how he *protects*? By trying to kill a police officer acting in the line of duty?"

Bossong looked from D'Agosta, to the zombii, to Hayward, and back to D'Agosta.

"She did nothing! Call it off!"

"She invaded our community, defiled our church."

"She came here to rescue me, rescue these others." D'Agosta stared at the leader. "I've always thought you were just a bloodthirsty cultist, killing animals for some perverse, fucked-up pleasure. Come on, Bossong—prove me wrong. Now's your chance. Show me you're something more. That your *religion* is something more."

For a moment, Bossong remained motionless. Then he drew himself up to his full height. He turned toward the zombii. *"C'est suffice!"* he cried. *"N'est-ce envoi pas!"*

The thing made an inarticulate slurping groan. Saliva boiled in its throat as it stared upward at the priest. Its hold on Hayward's throat loosened and she wriggled free, coughing and gasping. D'Agosta pulled her to her feet and together they backed away.

"This must stop!" Bossong said. "The violence must end."

The man-thing jerked and twitched in an agony of indecision. It looked from Hayward to Bossong and back again. As D'Agosta watched, he saw a mad hunger flood over it again. It crouched, leapt at Hayward.

The gunshot was deafening in the enclosed space. The creature, caught midair, spun around, then dropped to the floor. With a howl of pain and bestial rage it rose to its hands and knees, blood pouring from a second wound in its side, and began shambling—faster and faster, with a horrible new purpose—toward Bossong. The next bullet hit it in the gut and it buckled forward, gurgling horribly. Unbelievably it tried to rise once again, blood spurting from its wounds and from its yawning mouth, but the third bullet caught it in the chest and it fell again to the ground, rolling, shaking, and jerking uncontrollably. D'Agosta tried to catch it, but it was too late: writhing and groaning hideously, the thing half toppled, half spasmed over the edge of the well. It let out a wet gargling shriek that—after a dreadfully long second—ended in a faint splash.

Slowly, Bossong lowered the smoking gun. "So it ends as it began," he said. "In darkness."

Esteban stepped inside the cell and paused. Which one first? But he was not one to agonize over a decision, and he stepped over the girl's body and strode up to the bloody form of the FBI agent. He in particular deserved to die. *But of course,* Esteban thought, smiling wryly, *he's already dead, or mostly so.* It was going to be a mess, and the sound of the pistol in the confined space would leave his ears ringing. He ran through the steps he'd have to follow as he reloaded the magazine. He'd have to bury his own clothes with the bodies and guns—no problems there. Blood was impossible to eradicate these days, what with the powerful chemical tools now at the disposal of crime-scene investigators; but the cellar room itself could be walled up with nothing to show it had ever existed. All the bodies could go in here. Perhaps in the coming days there would be people snooping around here, looking for the FBI agent. He may have even told someone where he was going. But there was no clue he had ever arrived: no car, no boat, nothing.

He slapped the magazine in, racked a round into the chamber, and raised the gun with one hand, the other training the flashlight carefully on the still form.

The blow came from behind, a stunning crack to the back of his head, and then something was on top of him like a monkey, two claw-like hands tearing into his face, one finger snagging the rim of the orbit and then digging into the eye socket, prying at the eyeball itself. He screamed at the explosion of pain, whirling about, trying to fling off his attacker, grappling at it with one hand, the gun in the other hand firing wildly with a tremendous series of booms. The flashlight fell to the ground with a crash and blackness swallowed them.

For a moment his mind, reeling with surprise and pain, staggered in incomprehension. Then he realized: it was the girl. He yelled, bucking and shaking, his free hand flailing blindly at her, but the girl's tight, digging grip didn't slacken and he felt his eyeball pop out of its socket with a wet, sucking sound, the horror and pain such that for a moment he lost all capability for rational thought.

He fell to the ground with a roar, the heavy blow finally loosening her grasp, but as he rolled and tried to bring the gun around he realized there was a second person fighting him now—surely the FBI agent—and the gun was roughly kicked from his grasp. He punched wildly, broke free, and scrambled to his feet and ran, slamming hard against the wall, then feeling desperately along it while the gasps of his assailants seemed to come from everywhere around him.

. . . *The door!* He stumbled through it and ran out into the blackness, dazed and disoriented, careening off props and walls and doorways like a pinball, losing his bearings in his pain and panic, crashing and scrambling among the forest of junk in an effort to get away. The girl and the FBI agent—how had they both survived? But as soon as the question occurred to him he knew the answer—and cursed his monumental, colossal stupidity. As he ran, he felt his eyeball—free, hanging by the optical nerve—bouncing with every movement in a swinging arc of pain.

The Browning! He'd forgotten about the second gun. Digging into his waistband, he pulled it out, turned, and fired back in the direction of his pursuers. A moment later his shot was answered by the boom of the Colt and the smack of a heavy-caliber bullet ripping through a prop next to his ear, spraying him with splinters.

Jesus, that was close. He turned and ran, scrambling frantically among the old sets, trying to reorient himself. He could hear their fumbling pursuit. To fire on them again in the dark was only to make himself a target.

He crashed into something and realized he had gotten turned around, somehow, in his desperate attempt to escape. Where the hell was he? What prop was this? A massive plaster wall—the outline of blocks . . . was it the castle turret? Yes, it had to be! He shoved the gun back into his waistband and scrambled up to the battlements, feeling his way along. A little farther, just a little . . . The battlement ended and he jumped down to the other side, landing on what felt like a ramp. What was this? He'd expected to find himself by the faux-stone sarcophagus of the Egyptian pharaoh Raneb, but this was something else entirely. Had he gone the other way? His mind reeled as yet again he tried to orient himself amid the endless props, his mind reeling from the pain. He crawled up the ramp, stumbled and fell, and lay on a wooden platform, heaving. Maybe if he just lay there, absolutely silently, they wouldn't find him. But no, that was stupid. They would find him, find him and . . . He *had* to get out, get to where he could fight them. Or run.

He could hear them in the blackness, moving along the battlements, searching for him.

The sudden reversal of his hopes left him stunned with grief and pain. He had to face it: running was now the only option left to him. Mexico, perhaps; or Indonesia, maybe Somalia. But first he had to get out of this black prison, get his eye attended to. He sat up, feeling a hanging rope brush against his face, grasped it and began to hoist himself up—but then the rope suddenly gave way and he heard a strange rushing sound from above, and then a split second later he realized what he had done, what rope he had pulled, but it was too late and his world abruptly ended with a short sharp *shock.*

Nora heard a scratching sound, followed by a hiss, and then a wavering yellow light appeared. Pendergast was holding a twisted piece of newspaper, one end afire. The open casing of a bullet lay on the cement floor, from which he had extracted the cordite to start the fire.

"Come and look," he said weakly.

Pendergast held out his hand and Nora took it. She was a mass of pain; all the ribs in her back seemed broken from the force of the gunshots; her concussed head throbbed. Pendergast's bulletproof vest, which the agent had passed her in the darkness of the cell, was an unfamiliar weight beneath her hospital gown. She came around an old section of a medieval castle wall and there, in front of her, was a guillotine, blade down, a body sprawled on the platform; and in the tumbrel below, a fresh head. The head of her captor, one eye wide open in surprise, the other horribly mangled, dangling by a ropy nerve.

"Oh my *God* . . ." She put a hand over her mouth.

"Look well," said Pendergast. "That's the man who was responsible for the murder of your husband and Caitlyn Kidd. The man who killed Colin Fearing and Martin Wartek, and who tried to kill you and me."

She gasped. "Why?"

"An almost perfectly choreographed—or should I say storyboarded—drama. We will know the final reason why when we locate a certain document." His voice was so low, so whispery, she could barely make it out. "Right now, we need to call an ambulance. When . . . when you are done here."

Staring at the scene of horror, she realized that she did, in fact, feel a certain grim catharsis through the curtain of pain. She turned away.

"Seen enough?"

She nodded. "We have to get out of here. You're bleeding—badly."

"Esteban's third bullet missed my vest. I believe it has punctured my left lung." He coughed; flecks of blood came from his mouth.

Using the taper as a light, they slowly, painfully, made their way through the basement, up the stairs, across the shadowy lawn, and to the mansion. There, in the darkened living room, Pendergast helped Nora onto a sofa, then picked up the phone and dialed 911.

And then he collapsed unconscious to the floor, where he lay motionless in a spreading pool of his own blood.

85

With the coming of night, the seventh floor of North Shore University Hospital had grown quiet. The squeaking of wheelchairs and gurneys, the chimes and announcements from the speakers at the nurses' station, had almost ceased. Yet still there were the sounds that never stopped: the hiss of respirators, the faint snores and murmurs, the bleating and beeping of vital-sign monitors.

D'Agosta heard none of it. He sat where he had remained for the last eighteen hours: beside the lone bed in the private room. His eyes were on the floor, and he alternately clenched and unclenched his good hand.

Out of the corner of his eye he noticed movement. Nora Kelly stood framed in the doorway. Her head was bandaged, and beneath her hospital gown her ribs were taped and padded. She walked up to the foot of the bed.

"How is he?" she asked.

"Same." He sighed. "And you?"

"Much better." She hesitated. "And what about you? How are you doing?"

D'Agosta shook his bowed head.

"Lieutenant, I want to thank you. For your support through it all. For believing me. For everything."

D'Agosta felt his face burn. "I did nothing."

"You did everything. Really." He felt her hand on his shoulder, and then she was gone.

When next he looked up, another two hours had passed. And this time it was Laura Hayward who was standing in the doorway. Seeing him, she came over quickly, kissed him lightly, took the chair beside him.

"You need to eat something," she said. "You can't just sit here forever."

"Not hungry," he replied.

She bent closer. "Vinnie, I don't like seeing you like this. When Pendergast called me, told me you'd gone into the basement of the Ville, I . . ." She paused, took his hand. "I suddenly realized I simply couldn't face losing you for good. Listen. You just can't keep blaming yourself."

"I was too pissed off. If I'd kept my anger under control, he wouldn't have been shot. That's the truth and you know it."

"No, I don't know it. Who knows what might have happened if things went a different way? It's the uncertainty of law enforcement—we all live with it. And anyway, you heard the doctors: the crisis has passed. Pendergast lost a lot of blood, but he's going to pull through."

There was a faint movement from the bed. Both D'Agosta and Hayward looked over. Agent Pendergast was regarding them through half-closed eyes. He was paler than D'Agosta had ever seen him—as pale as death—and his limbs, always slender, had assumed an almost spectral gauntness.

The FBI agent simply looked back at them for a moment, the heavy-lidded silver eyes unblinking. For a dreadful moment, D'Agosta feared he was dead. But then Pendergast's lips moved. The two bent closer in order to hear.

"I'm glad to see you both looking well," he said.

"You, too," D'Agosta replied, trying to smile. "How are you?"

"I've been lying here thinking a great deal, as well as enjoying your solicitude. What happened to your arm, Vincent?"

"Broken ulna. No big deal."

Pendergast's eyes fluttered closed. After a moment, they opened once again.

"What was in it?" he asked.

"In what?" D'Agosta said.

"Esteban's safe."

"An old will and a deed."

"Ah," Pendergast whispered. "The last will and testament of Elijah Esteban?"

D'Agosta started. "How'd you know?"

"I found Elijah Esteban's tomb in the basement of the Ville. It had been broken into just minutes earlier and looted—no doubt of that very will and deed. A property deed, I expect?"

"Right. To a twenty-acre farm," said D'Agosta.

A slow nod. "A farm that, I assume, is a farm no longer."

"You got it. Now twenty acres of prime Manhattan real estate, stretching between Times Square and Madison Avenue, taking in much of the midforties. The will was written in such a way that Esteban would have had clear title as the only heir."

"Naturally, he wouldn't have tried to actually take over the land. He would have used the document as the basis of an extremely lucrative lawsuit—ending in a multibillion-dollar settlement, I have no doubt. Worth killing for, Vincent?"

"Maybe for some people."

Pendergast eased his arms above the covers, arranged them with minute care, his white fingers touching what D'Agosta noticed was unusually fine linen. No doubt Proctor was to thank for that. "Where the Ville is now, there was an earlier religious community—of a very different kind," he said. "Wren told me its original founder became a gentleman farmer in southern Manhattan after the community failed. That farmer and Elijah Esteban must be one and the same. On his death, he was buried in the basement of the settlement he founded—along, it seems, with the fateful documents: the deed and will."

"Makes sense," said D'Agosta. "So how did Alexander Esteban learn about it?"

"After he retired from Hollywood, it seems he acquired a passion for studying his family tree. He employed a researcher to paw through old records for him. It was the researcher who made the discovery—and who was murdered for his pains. His is the second, unidentified body in the tunnel, by the way."

"We found it," said Hayward.

"A very handy corpse, too. It was tossed off the bridge into the Harlem River and misidentified as Fearing by our very busy friend, Wayne Heffler, with the help of the so-called sister."

"So Colin Fearing *was* alive," said D'Agosta. "When he killed Smithback, I mean."

A nod. "Remarkable what one can do with theatrical makeup. Esteban was a film director *par excellence*."

"Perhaps we should let Agent Pendergast rest," Hayward said.

Pendergast waved one hand feebly. "Nonsense, Captain. Talking helps clear my mind."

"I still don't get it," said D'Agosta.

"Straightforward, once you've grasped the thread." Pendergast closed his eyes, folded his pale hands on the coverlet. "Esteban had learned of the existence, and location, of a document that would make him fabulously rich. Unfortunately, it was sealed in a tomb and locked in the basement of what was now the Ville des Zirondelles: a secretive cult deeply suspicious of outsiders. So secretive that only one hundred forty-four could ever be members; only when one died was a new one recruited. Impossible for Esteban to penetrate. So he tried to whip up public sentiment against the Ville, get the city to condemn the property, evict the squatters.

That's why he joined Humans for Other Animals and enlisted Smithback to write stories about it for the *Times*."

"I'm seeing it now," said D'Agosta. "By itself that wasn't enough. So Esteban escalated—by murdering Smithback and pinning it on the Ville—and cooking up all that voodoo and zombii stuff."

Pendergast gave the barest nod. "He didn't get the Vôdou quite right—for example, the tiny coffin in Fearing's empty crypt—which is why my friend Bertin was so stymied by it. A clue I regrettably missed. Ironic, since what the Ville practiced was not Vôdou anyway, so much as their own strange and bizarre cult, transformed and twisted over decades of insularity." He paused. "He hired two accomplices. Colin Fearing—and Caitlyn Kidd."

"Caitlyn Kidd?" D'Agosta repeated in disbelief. "The reporter?"

"Correct. She was part of the plan. Esteban would have made a list of precise qualifications, then gone out to find the people who matched them exactly. I expect it happened something like this: Fearing was an out-of-work actor of disreputable background, badly in need of money. He lived in Smithback's building and was roughly his weight and height. A perfect choice for Esteban. Caitlyn Kidd was a rather unscrupulous reporter, eager to get ahead." He glanced over at Hayward. "You don't look surprised by this."

Hayward hesitated just a moment before replying. "I requested deep background checks on everyone involved with the case. Kidd's came back just a few hours ago. She's got a prison record—quite well hidden, it turns out—for fraud. She ran a confidence scam in which she extorted money from older men."

D'Agosta looked at her in shock.

Pendergast merely nodded. "The criminal record is how Esteban found her, I imagine. In any case, he would pay her a great deal for her starring role. Esteban wrote a script for this little drama, in which Fearing faked his own death, using the researcher's corpse as a body. Caitlyn Kidd played the role of the sister who identified him, and the overly busy Dr. Heffler completed the picture. Once everybody thought Fearing was dead, Esteban simply heightened the illusion with makeup—he was a film producer, after all. And he had Fearing—playing himself, only now risen from the dead as a zombii—kill Smithback and attack Nora Kelly."

D'Agosta shook his head ruefully. "Seems almost obvious now that you point it out."

"Recall how Fearing looked so deliberately into the security camera when he left Smithback's apartment building? How he made sure the neighbors got a good look at him? At the time it struck me as odd, but now it makes perfect sense. Having Fearing seen, and identified, was a critical element—perhaps *the* critical element—of Esteban's plan."

There was a longer silence. Pendergast at last opened his eyes. "Then Esteban launched the next act in his screenplay. Caitlyn Kidd approached the grieving Nora, enlisting her into the effort to pin the murder on the Ville. Her first assignment was to get close to Nora, trick her into thinking that going after the Ville was *Nora's* own idea. They maintained the pressure on Nora by having Fearing stalk her in the museum and elsewhere. Next, Esteban stole Smithback's body from the morgue—to give the illusion that he, too, had risen from the dead as a zombii. But he needed Smithback's body for another, even more critical reason: to make a mask of his face for Fearing's use. I found traces of latex rubber on Smithback's face, the remains of the mold. Fearing wore the mask—suitably made up for horrific effect—to murder Kidd before a gathering guaranteed to know Smithback by sight."

"But why kill Kidd?" D'Agosta asked.

"She had played her role to perfection—she'd outlived her usefulness. Time to give her the hook. Easier to kill her than pay her, and it's always prudent to get rid of one's accomplices. A lesson Fearing should have taken to heart. Do you recall how Kidd shouted out Smithback's name before she was killed? I would surmise Esteban had told her that Fearing, disguised as the dead Smithback, was going to kill someone else at that ceremony. Her role—her last scene—was to cry out Smithback's name in mock terror—to immediately establish in everyone's minds who he was, to help drive home the illusion. Only she got more than she bargained for."

"And then Esteban had Fearing kill Wartek as soon as the man started eviction proceedings against the Ville," said D'Agosta.

Pendergast nodded.

"And he kidnapped Nora, once again framing the Ville for the crime."

"Yes. The pressure against the Ville had to be ratcheted up to the breaking point. Esteban wasn't going to wait for a lengthy eviction proceeding. His pacing was perfect, just like the great director he was. When he released the video of Nora that everyone assumed was shot in the basement of the Ville, the third act was almost upon us. That's when he knew it was time to strike."

"So Esteban himself murdered Fearing?" asked Hayward.

"I believe so. Esteban no doubt wanted to remove his second accomplice the same way he'd removed the first. Dumping his body near the Ville had the added advantage of framing them for the murder."

"One thing I don't get," said D'Agosta. "That first march on the Ville—Esteban whipped up the crowd, then defused them again. Why? Why didn't he simply go in?"

Pendergast didn't answer for a moment. "I found that puzzling at first. Then I considered that there weren't enough of them to succeed. It was premature. He had one shot at getting into the Ville and robbing the tomb. He needed a riot—a big one, not a brief disturbance, to get in unseen, seize his prize, and retreat. The first was merely a rehearsal. That's why Esteban didn't lead the second, major demonstration. He egged it on and then pretended to bow out. He was down there, Vincent, even while we were. It was only chance that we didn't cross paths. By the time that creature attacked us, he was already gone."

Hayward frowned. "What was that creature, anyway?"

"A man. At least, it had once been a man. The ritual transformed it into something else."

"What ritual?" D'Agosta asked.

"Do you recall those strange implements we saw on the Ville's altar? The tools with the bone handles and a long, twisting metal point with a tiny blade at one end? They served the same function as an old medical instrument known as a leucotome."

"A leucotome?" D'Agosta repeated.

"The device used in performing a lobotomy—in this case, a transorbital lobotomy, done by entering the brain from the eye socket. The members of the Ville learned long ago that destroying a specific portion of the brain, in a region called Broca's area, rendered the unfortunate victim impervious to pain, free of moral or ethical constraints, extremely violent, and yet submissive to its minders. Something less than human but more than animal."

"And you're saying the Ville did this to someone *intentionally*?"

"Absolutely. The victim was chosen by the cult to be a sacrifice for the community, but he was also revered and worshipped for making that sacrifice. It may even have been an honor, vied for by many. That man-thing was, in fact, a central part of their religious ritual: his creation, his nurturing, his training, his feeding, and his release were all part of the ritual cycle. He served to protect the community from a hostile world, and they in turn fed him, kept him, revered him. In some societies, certain individuals are given leave to perform actions that are normally considered wrong. Perhaps the Ville lobotomized the man as a way of protecting his soul, allowing him to murder, to kill, to defend the Ville without incurring the stain of sin on his soul."

"But how could an operation turn a person into that kind of monster?" Hayward asked.

"The operation isn't difficult. Many years ago, a physician named Walter Freeman could perform what became known as ice-pick lobotomies in just a few minutes. Stick it in, a quick back-and-forth motion, and the offending part of the brain is destroyed. Along with half the person's personality, his soul, his sense of self. The Ville just took it a step farther."

"Those old murders Wren uncovered?" D'Agosta said. "Perhaps they were caused by similar zombiis."

"Exactly: the creation of a living zombii that, through murder and fear, convinced Isidor Straus not to proceed with clear-cutting Inwood Hill Park. It seems that the Straus groundskeeper himself became a convert to the Ville cult—and then was honored by elevation to sacred status, and became that zombii."

Hayward shuddered. "How horrible."

"Indeed. The irony is almost palpable: Esteban had Fearing act like a zombii to convince the public he was a creation of the Ville. Yet the Ville *was,* in a manner of speaking, creating zombiis—though for rather different purposes than Esteban apprehended. By the way, what's happened to the Ville?"

"It seems they'll stay where they are, for the time being. They promised no more animal sacrifices."

"And, let us hope, no more zombiis. I wouldn't be surprised to learn that, in the future, rather than being the malevolent presence we assumed, Bossong becomes something of a rehabilitating influence on the Ville. I sensed a tension between him and the high priest."

"It was Bossong who killed the zombii," D'Agosta said. "At the end, when it was at the point of killing us."

"Indeed? That is reassuring: such a heroic action is not, shall we say, the sort of thing a true believer would do—kill the vessel of one's own gods." Pendergast glanced at Hayward. "By the way, Captain, I've been meaning to tell you how sorry I was to hear you'd been passed over for the mayor's task force."

"Don't be." Hayward brushed back her black hair. "I think I'm actually better off for losing the opportunity—the latest word is that task force is going to become just the bureaucratic nightmare everyone swore it would never be. And that reminds me: remember our friend Kline, the software developer? Looks like he's going to be sorry he strong-armed the commissioner. I just heard the FBI was wiretapping Rocker's phone in a sting operation and got the whole blackmail conversation on tape. Both are going down—hard. Kline is finished."

"A pity. Rocker wasn't a bad man."

Hayward nodded. "He did it for good motives—the Dyson Fund. A tragedy, in a way. But one side effect is I'm leaving the commissioner's office, getting my job as homicide captain back."

A silence settled in the room.

D'Agosta spoke all in a rush. "Listen, Pendergast, I just wanted to apologize for my goddamn stupidity back there—for dragging you into the Ville, for getting you shot, for almost losing Nora. I've done some idiotic things, but this took the cake."

"My dear Vincent," murmured Pendergast, "if we hadn't gone into the Ville, I never would have found the looted tomb, I never would have seen the name Esteban . . . and where would we be now? Nora would be dead and Esteban the new Donald Trump. So you see, your 'stupidity' was crucial in solving this case."

D'Agosta didn't quite know how to respond to this.

"And now, if you don't mind, Vincent, I shall rest."

As they exited the hospital room, D'Agosta turned to Hayward. "What's this about deep background checks on everyone involved with the case?"

Hayward looked uncharacteristically embarrassed. "I couldn't just stand there and watch Pendergast pull you in over your head. So . . . I started looking into the case myself. Just a little."

D'Agosta felt a strange mixture of emotions: mild annoyance at the thought he might need bailing out, great satisfaction knowing she cared enough about him to do it at all. "You're forever looking after me," he said.

In response, she slipped her hand through his arm. "Got any dinner plans?"

"Yes. I'm taking you out."

"Where to?"

"How about Le Cirque?"

She looked at him in surprise. "Wow. Twice in one year. What's the occasion?"

"No occasion. Just a very special lady."

At that moment, an elderly man in the corridor stopped them. D'Agosta looked at him, astonished. He was short and stocky and dressed as if he had just stepped out of Edwardian London: a black cutaway jacket, a white carnation in his boutonniere, a spotless bowler hat.

"Pardon me," he said. "Is the room you just exited where Aloysius Pendergast is staying?"

"Yes," D'Agosta said. "Why?"

"I have a letter I must deliver to him." And in fact the man was holding a letter: fancy, cream-laid paper, hand-pressed by the look of it. Pendergast's name was written on its front in a broad hand.

"You'll have to come back with your letter," D'Agosta said. "Pendergast is resting."

"I assure you, he'll want to see *this* particular letter right away." And the man began to step past them toward the door.

D'Agosta put a restraining hand on the man's shoulder. "Just who are you?" he demanded.

"The name is Ogilby, and I'm the solicitor for the Pendergast family. Now, if you'll excuse me?" And—freeing himself from D'Agosta's grasp with one fawn-gloved hand—he bowed, raised his hat to Hayward, and stepped past into Pendergast's room.

Epilogue

The small powerboat cut easily through the glassy waters of Lake Powell. It was a cold, clear day in early April, the Arizona air as crisp and clean as fresh laundry. The late-morning sun glowed orange against the great sandstone walls of the Grand Bench, and as the boat came around the bend, the prow of Kaiparowits Plateau rose far behind it, purple in the rising sun, wild and inaccessible.

Nora Kelly stood at the helm, the wind stirring her short hair. The rumble of the engine echoed softly against the cliffs, and the water hissed along the hull as the boat moved through the mystical world of stone. The air was fragrant with the smell of cedar and warm sandstone, and as the boat moved through the cathedral-like stillness, a golden eagle soared above the canyon rims, issuing a thin cry.

She eased down on the throttle and the boat slowed to a trolling pace. As the lake took another turn, the mouth of a narrow, flooded canyon came into view—Serpentine Canyon, two smooth walls of red sandstone with a lane of green water between.

Nora turned the boat into the canyon. The engine sound grew louder, more confined. True to its name, the canyon twisted and turned like a country road. It was cooler in the canyon, even cold, and Nora could see her breath in the frosty air. A mile in, the boat reached a particularly beautiful spot, where a tiny waterfall threaded and tumbled its way down a channel of stone, creating in its fall a microcosm of hanging ferns and mosses, with a stand of miniature twisted piñons growing sideways out of a cleft in the rock. She cut the engine and drifted, listening to the splash of the waterfall, inhaling the perfume of sweet fern and water.

She remembered this magical place like yesterday. Here, on the expedition to Quivira almost five years earlier, their boat had passed this same waterfall. Bill Smithback, whom she had met only the day before, had stood at the boat railing and waved her over.

"See that, Nora?" he had said, nudging her and smiling. "That's where the fairies wash their gossamer wings. It's the fairy shower."

It was the first time he had surprised her with his poetry, his insight, his humor and love of beauty. It caused her to look at him more closely, not to trust her original impression. It might also have marked the moment when she began to fall in love with him.

Two weeks ago she had returned to New Mexico, after having been offered a job as curator at the Santa Fe Archaeological Institute. Staying with her brother Skip, she had spent the last week learning more about the job and discussing the position with the museum's president and board. If she took the job, it would be contingent on working out details for funding her already planned expedition to Utah the upcoming summer. Skip had been a tremendous help and support, glad to return the favor from the time, years before, when she had helped him pick up the pieces of his own life.

But there had been another, more private, reason for the journey. She was, for the most part, coming to terms with the horror of Bill's death. New York City—their favorite restaurants and parks, even the apartment itself—held no more terrors for her. And yet the past was a different story. She had no idea how the canyon country of the Southwest would affect her. Places like Page, Arizona, where they first met, or Lake Powell itself, or the wild country beyond where they had searched for the half-mythical city of Quivira. She felt a need to explore these places again, perhaps as part of laying the ghosts to rest. As the boat drifted down the canyon, memories—shrouded in a wistful veil of time that made them bittersweet rather than painful—began to surface. Bill, complaining loudly after being bitten by his horse, Hurricane Deck. Bill, shielding her from a flash flood with his own body. Bill, his form outlined in brilliant starlight, reaching for her hand. This magical land had brought such memories back to her, and for that she was grateful.

The boat came to rest, drifting ever so slightly in the mirror-like water. Nora reached down and picked up a small bronze urn, pulled away the paper seal on its rim, and removed the lid. She held it over the side of the boat and shook a few handfuls of ashes out into the water. They splashed down, sinking slowly into the jade-colored depths. She watched them dissolve in a turbulent plume that dimmed as it sank. And then they were gone.

"Good-bye, dear friend," she said softly.

A Word from the Authors

THE PRESTON-CHILD NOVELS

We are very frequently asked in what order, if any, our books should be read.

The question is most applicable to the novels that feature Special Agent Pendergast. Although most of our novels are written to be stand-alone stories, very few have turned out to be set in discrete worlds. Quite the opposite: it seems the more novels we write together, the more "bleed-through" occurs between the characters and events that comprise them all. Characters from one book will appear in a later one, for example, or events in one novel could spill into a subsequent one. In short, we have slowly been building up a universe in which all the characters in our novels, and the experiences they have, take place and overlap.

Reading the novels in a particular order, however, is rarely necessary. We have worked hard to make almost all of our books into stories that can be enjoyed without reading any of the others, with a few exceptions.

Here, then, is our own breakdown of our books.

THE PENDERGAST NOVELS

Relic was our first novel, and the first to feature Agent Pendergast, and as such has no antecedents.

Reliquary is the sequel to *Relic*.

The Cabinet of Curiosities is our next Pendergast novel, and it stands completely on its own.

Still Life with Crows is next. It is also a self-contained story (although people curious about Constance Greene will find a little more information here, as well as in *The Cabinet of Curiosities*).

Brimstone is next, and it is the first novel in what we informally call the Diogenes trilogy. Although it is also self-contained, it does pick up some threads begun in *The Cabinet of Curiosities.*

Dance of Death is the middle novel of the Diogenes trilogy. While it can be read as a stand-alone book, readers may wish to read *Brimstone* before *Dance of Death.*

The Book of the Dead is the culminating novel in the Diogenes trilogy. For greatest enjoyment, the reader should read at least *Dance of Death* first.

The Wheel of Darkness follows next. It is a stand-alone novel that takes place after the events in *The Book of the Dead.*

Cemetery Dance, which you presently hold in your hands, is our most recent Pendergast novel. It is self-contained but, as is our custom, does at times reference or build upon what has come before.

THE NON-PENDERGAST NOVELS

We have also written a number of self-contained tales of adventure that do not feature Special Agent Pendergast. They are, by date of publication, *Mount Dragon, Riptide, Thunderhead,* and *The Ice Limit.*

Thunderhead introduces the archaeologist Nora Kelly, who appears in most of the later Pendergast novels. *The Ice Limit* introduces Eli Glinn, who appears in *Dance of Death* and *The Book of the Dead.*

In closing, we want to assure our readers that this note is not intended as some kind of onerous syllabus, but rather as an answer to the question *In what order should I read your novels?* We feel extraordinarily fortunate that there are people like you who enjoy reading our novels as much as we enjoy writing them.

With our best wishes,